THE TRUTH

He is fluent in four languages. Yet he devours grubs, insects, and palpitating flesh.

He communes with wild beasts and proffers them his love. Men he butchers.

He is feared as a ghost. Yet those who have suffered most crave his sexual revenge.

He is *Ras Tyger,* Philip José Farmer's monumental incarnation of a modern-day Jungle Lord. Savage and innocent, he is master of the world—until the day when the incredible truth of his existence begins to unfold . . .

D1348093

More Science Fiction from SIGNET

LORD TYGER

Philip José Farmer

A SIGNET BOOK from
NEW AMERICAN LIBRARY
TIMES MIRROR

This story is dedicated to Edgar Rice Burroughs, without whom my childhood and youth would have been inestimably deprived and colorless, and to Vernell Coriell, a Lord Tyger in his own right.

CHAPTER 1

THE PYTHON THAT RAPED

A VILLAGE

"My mother is an ape. My father is God."

Ras Tyger sat on a branch, his shoulder against the trunk. He wore only a leopardskin belt that held a crocodile-leather sheath from which stuck the ivory handle of a big knife. A wooden flute was in his left hand.

"I am the only white man in the world.

"I come from the Land of the Ghosts."

He sang in the language of the Wantso. Throughout his singing, he kept turning his head to watch for anybody who might be sneaking up on him. The tree was twenty-five feet from the bank of the river and only two trees away from the village.. He could see everything; the village, the fields to the east of the village, and the islet, separated from the peninsula by a narrow channel.

As he sang, he grinned. The panic racing through the Wantso was his own music fluted back to him.

"O brown-skinned beauties, I love you. I love you as the lightning its tall tree, the fish its water, the snake its hole in the ground.

"Most of all, I love you, Wilida, because you are the most beautiful and because you are guarded from me.

"I, Lord Tyger, beautiful and fierce, leopard-beautiful, leopard-angry, Tyger, Tyger, from the Land of the Ghosts, ghost with the long, long python between the thighs and the great beehives that fountain forth honey on honey.

"O brown-skinned beauties, I love you, I love you as

7

the stone its fall, the eagle its wind, the civet its egg.

"Most of all, I love you, Wilida, because you are the most beautiful and because you are guarded from me."

He stopped singing to play on his flute the music that a Wantso man plays on his wedding night for his bride, who sits in her prison on the islet. The flute was loud and shrill.

The river, flowing west, began to make a great sweep to the south at the point where the village stood. The river ran south for about a mile and then abruptly cut back to the east. For three quarters of a mile it continued straight east, swerved north, and then arced back to the south. At the point where it turned southward, a man could run north from that part of the river across the neck of land to the river again in a minute. Here the Wantso had built a wall of twenty-foot-high sharpened logs to defend the peninsula.

To the west of the wall were the fields, where the women grew yams, teff, millet, barley, cabbage, and bush banana. Between the fields and the riverbank was the village. It was ringed with a double row of poles cut from tree trunks and sharpened at the upper end. Thorns crowned the poles.

Within the walls were fourteen buildings. The Great House, the communal council-house, worship-house, chief's-house occupied the exact center of the circle formed by the double palisades. The Great House was round and had a diameter of about seventy feet. The main structure was of bamboo. The triple-coned roof was thatched with long grasses and elephant's-ear leaves. It was raised, on many thick logs, about four feet from the ground. There was one broad entranceway, before which a folding bamboo staircase was placed.

Eight huts formed a circle around the Great House, and four more an outer circle. All were small and round, and each had one high, conical roof, and was based on a single tree stump that raised it three feet above the ground. Folding bamboo steps led to the single doorway.

The fourteenth house broke the symmetry. It was near the north gate of the palisades. It was the spirit-talker's house. The tip of the roof was only four feet below the thick branch that projected over the wall from the huge tree just outside the wall. Leopards sometimes used this branch to drop in for a meal, and Ras had used it several times.

Ras thought it was stupid to build a wall and then leave the branch as a bridge for invaders. When he was

a child, he had asked his Wantso playmates why the
branch was not chopped off. The children replied that
the tree was sacred. A very powerful spirit lived in it.
Shabagu, the great chief who had led the Wantso into
this world, lived there.

When a Wantso died, and the mourning over the corpse
in the Great House was over, the body was carried into
the spirit-talker's house. Here, after the ceremony of release was over, Shabagu lifted the dead person's ghost
up by the hair and took him into the tree. Ras's playmates had been vague about what happened after that.

This, however, explained why Wantsos grew their kinky
hair long and then plastered it into an upright double
cone with goat's butter mingled with red clay. Shabagu
could get a good grip with both hands when he lifted
the ghost from his perch on the branch.

This interested Ras. On six occasions, when a Wantso
had died, he had spent a night high on a branch of the
sacred tree. Once, he thought he saw Shabagu flitting
across the branch on his errand. Ras had been so excited, and scared, he had almost fallen out of the tree.
But the ghost of Shabagu was only his imagination, plus
his wish to see it, plus the mingling of moonlight and
fluttering leaves.

Now he played on his flute and quivered with delight as
he watched the panic. Men were running into houses to
get their war dress, spears, bows and arrows, and clubs.
The women in the fields had dropped their hoes and
diggers, picked up their babies, and were shooing the
older children ahead of them as fast as the children could
go.

The red-and-black, long-tailed chickens, the blue-and-
white, long-horned goats, and the orange hogs were adding to the racket. The chickens squawked and ran this
way and that. The goats baaed and dodged away from
the running men and women. The hogs grunted and
squealed. Men shouted; women screamed; children
squalled.

Tibaso, the chief, and Wuwufa, the spirit-talker, stood
in front of the Great House. Nose to nose, they yelled at
each other while their hands flew in all directions, like
a flock of rock pigeons attacked by a hawk.

Presently, twelve men had gathered before Tibaso and
Wuwufa. Two men stood guard on the platform above
the wall across the neck of the peninsula. Three old men,
too feeble to count as warriors, sat in the shade of their

houses. After counting, Ras knew that there were six out hunting.

Four boys, not quite old enough for the initiation into manhood, sat in a group behind the warriors and gestured with their slender spears.

Sewatu and Giinado, middle-aged men, put down their spears and went into the Great House. They staggered out, with the Chief's chair between them. They set it on the big, round stone before the House, where it glistened redly in the late-afternoon sun. It was mahogany smeared with palm oil and carved all over with the snarling faces of tall spirits.

Tibaso covered his graying hair with a feathered headdress shaped to fit over the double cone of his hair. He took the eight-foot-high wand from Wuwufa and sat down in the chair. The others had put on their feathered headdresses, their only clothing besides the square, barkcloth fore-and-aft aprons. They squatted down before the chief and painted each other's faces. Two old women, Muzutha and Gimibi, stumped out of the Great House, carrying between them a large earthenware pot painted with geometric symbols. They placed it near Tibaso and then ran back into the House as fast as their creaking bones and stiff muscles could take them.

The men rose and lined up, according to their rank, before the chief. Sewatu dipped a gourd of beer for the chief and Wuwufa and then for the others. The men returned to their places to squat down and drink the beer. They looked up at the tree in which Ras sat, but looked away quickly.

Ras, knowing he was visible, grinned and played more loudly. He would be in no danger for a while because they would have to hold a long conference before taking action—if any. Meanwhile, they would be drinking much beer to keep their throats moist during the furious disputes and long speeches and to prime their courage. To attack what they believed to be a ghost would take much courage.

Ras stopped playing the flute and began singing loudly in the direction of the islet. Bigagi stood on the islet end of the bridge from the mainland. He was the tallest man of the Wantso, though a head shorter than Ras. A very handsome man, too, although his face was hidden at the moment with the great spray of pink flamingo feathers that fell down past his face. It was, Ras thought, peculiar to half blind a man who was guarding his bride. But Wantso custom demanded it. Bigagi also wore a leopardskin cape. He was naked elsewhere, although his penis was painted red and a long cord with a feathered tassel hung from it to his knees.

Bigagi, understanding the song even at his distance from Ras, pushed aside the feathers, shook his spear, and shouted angrily. The copper spearhead flashed dull red in the sun.

There was one tree on the islet. It had one branch, the rest having been chopped away. A crocodile-hide rope was tied at one end to the middle of the branch. From its other end a bamboo structure hung about ten feet above the grass and mud of the islet. The rope was attached to the middle of the center pole of the platform, and other ropes, one at each end of the platform, ran up to the central rope to provide an unsteady balance for the structure.

Wilida sat by the central rope, one hand clinging to it. She could not move around much without tipping the structure to one side. She was hidden from the view of anyone standing below her by a bamboo railing plaited with vines and leaves and interspersed with carved wooden images of spirits. She sat on a little stool. A huge, conical hat of plaited straw with a broad, floppy brim shaded her whole body, and she also wore a straw mask. Her breasts were full and cone-shaped, with a slight upward tilt of the nipples, each as large as the end of her thumb. The nipples were painted white, and her breasts were painted with three concentric circles of red, white, and black. Her buttocks were painted crimson, and her shaven pubes was also painted scarlet. This was, however, covered with a white bark-cloth triangle.

Wilida lifted the mask, and her teeth flashed whitely at Ras before she quickly replaced it.

The loglike snouts and knot-eyes of crocodiles patrolled the channel between the peninsula and the islet. The long jaws of one lay half-sunk in the mud at the south end of the islet. Usually, the Wantso kept this part of the river cleared of crocodiles by monthly hunts. During a bride-guarding, however, the crocodiles were enticed back. A goat or hog, throat spurting blood, was hung upside down, and the crocodiles were drawn in by the blood floating from upstream. Thereafter, the villagers threw their food scraps into the river, or, if a baby was born dead, or one of the many miscarriages occurred, these were thrown to the crocodiles.

"But you have thrown your spears at me, at me, the white ghost, Lord Tyger, who would be your friend. So,

Wantso men, I return snarl for snarl, I throw the spear
back at you. And I come to your women at night, O
men; I send the great white snake whose tail grows from
between my legs. It crawls through your village at night,
and it sniffs at doorways, and it smells your women, O
men with scarred and limping dongs. It smells your wom-
en, and it follows their odor with blind, bulging head
and it takes root in them as they lie by your side, O
men.

"And two great beehives that dangle below the branch,
from the branch of the tree of my body, they fountain
forth honey on honey, O men whose gourds rattle dry in
the night of the python and the honey.

"I am lightning that burns the flesh of your women, O
Wantso men, and you are as sparks that fall on leaves
after a rainstorm. I, Lord Tyger, have taken vengeance
on you. And tonight, despite your crocodiles and spears,
I will fly to beautiful Wilida as the bat to its cave, and
she shall know me."

Bigagi screamed and threw his spear, though he knew
it had no chance of coming near Ras. The men in the
village shouted. But some women were laughing.

Tibaso, the chief, jumped up from his chair, shook his
wand, and yelled at Ras. Wuwufa, the spirit-talker, flopped
on the ground like a fish just hauled out of the water.

They would not come running out of the northern gate
at him. They wanted more beer, and they had to discuss
the matter fully. Ras knew them well. Though the chief
had the final decision on any important matter, he had
to hear every man's opinion. And when a man stood
to talk, the speaker had to argue his points afterward
with every man who disagreed.

Nevertheless he watched the bushes and trees along the
riverbank. A hunter returning home might try to sneak
up on him. If the hunter were an older man, one who
had not known Ras as a playmate, he would avoid him.
But if the hunter were in Ras's age group, he might not
sincerely believe that Ras was a ghost.

"O Wantso youths, truly I loved you, and most of all,
I loved you, Bigagi. You were beautiful; you loved me
then, I know you did, and you know it. We were closer
than the rosettes to the leopard, and we were as beautiful together. But now, the leopard and his rosettes have
flown apart, and the rosettes are nothing and the leopard
is ugly. The leopard is ugly and he mourns. The rosettes
are sad, and they mourn. But they, leopard and rosettes,
now hate, hate, hate, hate! And I weep, I weep! But I

also laugh, I laugh. Because this world is made for tears, but Ras is not made for tears. He will not dissolve himself in tears. This world is made for tears and hate, but this world is made also for laughter, and Ras laughs, and Ras mocks you and will return hate for hate.

"O men and women, you share the secret and the guilt, and yet you open not your mouths, because you would all be thrown to the crocodiles if every man and every woman confessed the guilt. And that is why Wuwufa dares not hunt out the witches among you. Crazed old man, he himself would feed the crocodiles.

"I, Ras Tyger, know this. I, the outsider, the demon, the pale ghost, know this. I have come as stealthily as the leopard, as silently as a ghost, into your village of nights, and I have crouched in the shadows, a shadow myself, and watched and listened. And I could name names, and the crocodiles would grow fat and happy, they would belch Wantso and pass Wantso, and your children would weep and have no one to feed them nor defend them against the leopard, nor give them love.

"O Wantso men, your women feared me as a ghost, but they swallowed their fear with desire for the python and the honey that Ras brings them from the jungle, from the Land of the Ghosts. They have desired and known me, O men; even your aged crones have desired me and have wept that they were no longer beautiful. And I, Ras Tyger, have crept into the shadows where your wives and daughters have sneaked away into the bushes, and there they know that Ras Tyger is no pale ghost, Ras Tyger is the flesh of flesh, blood of blood, flesh unscarred, uncrippled, unblocked. And . . ."

This time, he had gone too far. Bigagi, screaming, forgetting that he was not to leave his post under any circumstances, ran across the bridge, another spear in his hand. Sewatu fitted an arrow to the string and loosed it at Ras. It went wide and fell into the river, where a crocodile dived after it. Tibaso led the roaring men through the northern gate and toward the tree in which Ras sat.

An arrow thunked into the bark of the trunk near Ras. He stood up and went around the trunk to shield himself. Not wanting to be encumbered by the flute, he put it in a shallow depression where a branch and trunk met. He put his knife between his teeth and ran out along the branch. It was a very large one and extended out over the river far enough for him to get at least forty feet from the bank before it bent so much he could no longer keep from sliding off it.

A spear sailed by him. An arrow whistled so close he decided he had better make haste. He dived out and fell thirty feet and struck the water cleanly. He swam up as quickly as possible but did not break the surface. The river was still clear enough so that the Wantso could see him under water; it had not gotten dark with mud. He would have to stay under until he could come up at an unexpected point, and the Wantso would have to shoot or throw quickly.

Below and to his left was a large form shooting toward him, too indistinct to be identifiable, though he knew it was a crocodile. Ras fought back the panic and swam under water until the blur became clearly distinguishable. Another form appeared behind it.

Ras rose to the surface then, breathed in, saw the men aiming their arrows and bringing up their spears before casting them. The nearest crocodile shot toward him. Ras dived again, swam a few strokes, and then cleared the surface once more. His timing had been exact. Although most of the arrows and spears had glanced off the beast, it had taken a spear just behind the jaw. It was turning over and over, legs working, tail thrashing, and dark blood pouring around it.

The second crocodile was now heading toward the source of blood. Ras swam away, dived again, swam, came up for air, dived, swam, came up for air, and then stayed on the surface. He could still be hit by an arrow, but it would be by chance, and he did not really believe that death could touch him.

He climbed up the bank and then jumped into the cover of the bush. An arrow buried itself in the dirt near him, leaving a ragged hole in an elephant's-ear plant behind it. Laughing, Ras crawled swiftly behind a tree. There was a little sun inside him, warming him and tickling his nerves. This was delicious; this was living.

CHAPTER 2

ON THE EDGE OF HUMANITY

By the time Ras was nine, Mariyam and Yusufu had given up trying to restrain him. Until then, at least one of the two had insisted that he never get out of their sight. Ras used to get away from them anyway, although he knew he would be whipped when he returned. He chafed at their supervision, and he believed that he knew enough about leopards and poisonous snakes to take care of himself. It he was on the ground, he just ran away until Yusufu's short, bowed legs and wind gave out. If he was in the trees, he could not outdistance Yusufu as swiftly, because Yusufu was every bit as agile as he.

However, since Yusufu would not take the chances Ras would, he soon gave up. He would scream out oaths and threats in Amharic, Arabic, and Swahili, which Ras ignored. Ras would feel a little guilty, because he loved his parents and did not want to distress them. But he wanted more to be free. Yusufu was always telling him not to do this or that, don't go near there, be careful of this or that. Ras felt that the whippings when he returned canceled any guilt he felt. Certainly, the joy from his solo quests was greater than the pain of the whip.

Ras wandered all over the country between the cliffs and lake to the north, the cliffs east and west, and the edge of the plateau. At that time, however, he never climbed down from the plateau. The jungle down below looked as sinister as Mariyam and Yusufu said it was. Moreover, the one time he had given in to his curiosity and had started down the cliffs, the Bird of God had stopped him.

The Bird had been around ever since Ras could remember. This was the first time, however, that it had shown any close interest in him. It had always either flown high over him on some mysterious errand or had hovered high up above him for a while.

The Bird of Igziyabher, or, in English, God, was like no other bird, although the other birds had also been created by Igziyabher. This Bird was especially created, long after the world was created, if Ras was to believe his mother, Mariyam. It watched over the world, and especially over Ras, for Igziyabher. Indeed, it contained in its belly an angel, or so Ras had been told.

It was larger than fifty fish-eagles put together, and its body was shaped something like a deformed fish. Part of the body reflected sunshine; the rays bounced off it as they did off Ras's mirror. Its legs were rigid, hanging below the belly and held out a little to both sides. Its claws were very strange; they were round and never opened.

Its wings were attached to a bone that projected above the Bird, and the wings went around and around so fast, with a chop-chop-chop, that Ras could see them only as a blur.

It appeared high in the sky that day when Ras was about a quarter of the way down from the edge of the plateau. Ras glanced at it and then ignored it, but presently the Bird was hovering below him and then rising toward him. Its noise deafened him, and the wind from its wings was strong. Ras clung in terror to the face of the cliff while the Bird hung about forty feet out from the cliff.

The body of the Bird was hollow—it seemed to lack a heart and lungs and guts—and two angels were inside the body. Both had scarlet faces which looked like masks. Their bodies were covered with some kind of brown material, but their hands and necks were pinkish. One sat in the front of the belly, and the other, standing up farther back, was pointing a black box with a blind eye at him.

Then the angel with the box put it down and gestured at Ras to go back up the cliff. Ras was too scared to defy him. He went back up so fast he almost slipped once. The Bird followed him, staying high up, until Ras had run all the way home.

He had intended to say nothing about the Bird to his parents. But they knew all about it, and it was then that

Ras wondered if Igziyabher did not truly speak to them, as they claimed.

On his ninth birthday, he was told that he could go down below the plateau. He must not, however, go so far away that he could not return home before nightfall.

"Why am I now permitted to do this?" Ras said.

"Because it is written."

Yusufu was always saying this. Because it is written. Because it is not written.

"Written where?"

"In The Book."

Yusufu would never say any more than that.

The morning he left on his first trip, Mariyam wept and hugged him and pleaded with him not to go. He was her beautiful baby; if he died, she would die. He should stay home and be with her always, where he was safe.

Yusufu growled that the boy must become a man. Besides, It Was Written. Yusufu had tears in his eyes, however, and he insisted on accompanying him as far as the edge of the forest. When they got to the plain, which ran for several miles before losing itself in the thick growth of trees, Yusufu checked out Ras's weapons. These were the big knife Ras had found in the cabin on the lake, a rope, a quiver with ten arrows, and a bow. Ras also carried on his belt an antelopeskin bag that held a small mirror, a whetstone for sharpening the knife, and a tortoise-shell comb.

"Now I could have allowed you to find the Wantsos yourself, and I should have," Yusufu said, scowling. "But you have encountered no other human beings—you are the only human you know and you do not know yourself—and so I have to warn you: The Wantso are dangerous; they will try to kill you. So do not go openly to them, expecting them to love you as your mother and I love you.

"Go through the jungle softly as if it were full of leopards, which it is, by the way. You will hear the Wantso from far off, and you will hide yourself and sneak up on them. Observe them as much as you wish, but do not ever let them know of your presence. They would kill you or worse if they should capture you alive.

"You have one advantage. The Wantso may believe you to be a ghost, since they have never seen a white person. They think that ghosts are pale, and indeed they may be right, since I have never seen a ghost myself. But you are no ghost. They do not know this, so if they run away if they see you, do not follow them."

Yusufu embraced him. Ras was touched, though he could not help noting that his father was no longer as tall as he. How small he would be when his son was full grown!

Ras kissed him and then ran away, feeling the tears choke him. He went through the jungle and then climbed down the cliffs. This time, there was no Bird of Igziyabher. The river split into two cataracts here, and then merged again at the foot of the cliffs. Ras followed the river in its meanderings until night fell. He slept in a nest he made in a tree, shot a small monkey, and ate it after cooking it over a small fire. He went on and, several hours later, heard voices.

This was a thrill he always remembered, his first hearing of strange voices. He went cautiously until he saw the walls of the village across the river. He climbed a tree and observed the Wantso for a while, then came down and swam across the river, where the slope of bank and heavy bush growth would keep him hidden. He climbed another tree and watched the women working in the fields, and their children.

His amazement and curiosity, threaded with a little fear, made him shake. Although he had been told by his parents that the Wantso were black and had kinky hair and were horrible monsters, only half human, he had visualized them otherwise. They were not "as black as a vulture's asshole"—his father's expression—but were a deep brown. Mariyam, Ras's mother, was as dark as they, though she had straight hair and a nose like a fish-eagle's and lips as thin as a leopard's. The Wantso hair was fascinatingly twisted in on itself—as crooked and intertwined as their sinister character as described by Yusufu. Their noses were broad and pushed-in, with nostrils flaring as if they were gasping for their last breath. Their lips were fat.

Yusufu looked something like them. But he was much shorter than any Wantso, except the children, of course. And the Wantso did not have the relatively huge heads of Yusufu and Mariyam, nor their short arms and tiny, bowed legs. Moreover, Yusufu had a black, very wavy beard that reached to his knees, but the Wantso had no hair on their faces.

Ras had a slightly brown skin, which was as pale as a fish on the neck, under his shoulder-length hair. He had seen his face in the mirror his mother had given him a year before, and so he knew he did not look at all like his parents. In fact, he had been frightened and disgusted the first time he had seen himself in the mirror. He had always thought of himself as looking like Yusufu, except for his skin, and beard, of course. But those large, gray eyes and thin nose and thin lips!

Later, he reconciled himself to some of his features, because, thinking about it, he knew that his nose was something like his mother's—although straight, not curved—and his lips were like hers, although not as thin.

This day—the mirror day, as he called it later—was the day that he had begun to doubt seriously that he was the child of Yusufu and Mariyam. At the same time, he had begun to doubt that they were apes. If they were, they were not apes like the chimpanzees and gorillas. He had begun to question Yusufu and Mariyam; he would not shut up despite their evasions and threats, and, after six months, Mariyam had given in and answered some of the questions. She had told him that Yusufu was not his real father. Yusufu had become her mate after Ras was born.

She never admitted that Ras was not her son. Despite all the verbal hammering she took from Ras, she maintained that she had conceived, carried, and borne him. But, one night, while Yusufu was out fishing, she confessed that Igziyabher was Ras's father.

Ras had never understood how God could be his father. Mariyam had told him so many contradictory stories of how she became pregnant that Ras had given up trying to get a logical, consistent, believable story. For the time being, anyway.

As for Yusufu, he would only say that he was not the begetter of Ras. But he loved Ras more than he would have loved his own son, because Ras was tall and had a head the proper size and arms and legs the proper length and was beautiful. But he wished that Igziyabher had taken Mariyam home with Him and not wished her on Yusufu.

"Even God could not stand that woman's never-quiet tongue. And her temper! Like that of a constipated she-camel fenced off from bulls during mating season!"

Much of the effect of this simile was lost on Ras. He had never seen a camel in the flesh, though he remembered a picture of it in a book in the cabin by the lake. Yusufu said that there had been camels in this world, but they were all dead now.

"And lucky for you, my son, because you will never have to smell one."

Ras, hiding in the grass, watching the Wantso, had

thought of all this while he quivered with curiosity and fear. One part, the larger, was concentrated on the Wantso; a small part was listening and sniffing and watching the jungle behind and on both sides for dangers; the third was with his parents, and he could see them and hear their voices just as if they were with him now. And a fourth speculated briefly on this three-part Ras, on how his world folded in on itself so that what had happened was happening at the same time as several other happenings were moving outside and within him.

And then the four parts, the five parts, of him faded to become one, and this one, down to the darkest, deepest part of him, flesh and ghost, was wholly part of that before his eyes.

He had made no attempt during the first day of spying to approach the Wantso. During his next ten visits, he had stayed hidden. A week had separated successive visits, because Ras had not wanted to upset his parents. Even so, the Wantso were far away for him to travel from his home to their village, observe them for several hours, and then travel as swiftly as he dared and reach home before dusk. He always found Yusufu and Mariyam looking out the windows or over the veranda of the tree house. He was always scolded, and he always tried to put off the whipping with a story of being treed by a leopard or delayed because he was stalking game which, unfortunately, got away. He always got whipped, and if he flinched or yelled when the whip struck, he was given extra lashes.

Then, suddenly, on his eleventh birthday, Yusufu and Mariyam had said that he could stay out all night or as long as he wished. He had not understood why they had changed their minds. Mariyam had finally told him that Igziyabher had allowed this.

Mariyam seemed to talk directly to God. Ras spent much time spying on her, because he hoped to see her and God talking face to face. He was always disappointed. She talked only to Yusufu or to herself, when Ras was not around.

Thereafter, when he felt like it, which was frequently, he would be gone several days, sometimes a week. He explored all the country south of the plateau as far as the point where the river became the Many-Legged Swamp. He built a raft to carry him through the swamp, but, just before he launched it, he was bitten on the ankle by a viper.

He almost died there. He lay on the raft, onto which

he had jumped, and suffered pain as if ants were crawling through his veins and arteries and stinging him with every other step forward and they had crawled into his head and were eating his brain. After a while, his heart beat out agony as a drummer beats out a message of horror. Paralyzed, he could think only of the pain, of what might come to eat him while he was defenseless, and of how his parents would suffer if he never came back.

The sun and the stars shone on him four times. Various insects took great liberties with him, but the ants did not find him, the crocodiles missed him, the vultures and ravens did not see him, and finally he was able to drag himself off the raft and under a tree on the islet. After two more days, during which he managed to eat enough to give him some strength—his turn to eat the insects, after they had covered his body with bites and stings— he made his way slowly homeward. It took him three days and half a night to do this.

For some time thereafter, he contented himself with staying close to home or going up into the hills to play with the gorilla young. After he got his full strength back, he became footloose again, but decided to put off trying the Many-Legged Swamp for a while.

Besides, the Wantso so intrigued him that he forgot about the swamp.

Just by eavesdropping and observing, he was able to understand some of the Wantso language. It was a curious speech. It used four levels of pitch to distinguish the meanings of words that had the same sounds. It also used pitch to indicate whether something had happened, was happening, would happen, or took place in the Land of the Ghosts.

The Land, he came to understand, was the plateau where he lived. This explained why the Wantso never went any farther north than the foot of the cliffs on top of which was the plateau.

Making the first direct contact with a Wantso was not easy, because he wanted to speak to one his own age. The men carried spears and clubs and looked as if they would use them without hesitation. The women seldom left the village except to dip water from or wash in the river or to work in the fields. The fields were walled off at one end and were always guarded. The children would sometimes go with the women when they went into the jungle to dig for roots or to pick fruit and berries.

Then the children were watched too closely by the mothers or by the men who accompanied them as guards.

However, the children did play along the banks of the peninsula. There were many trees and thick bushes on the banks, and it was in the bush that Ras hid to spy.

Here Ras surprised Wilida. She was an attractive and happy little girl who was very active in the games that the children played in the bushes. Ras, having made up his mind to make friends with them, waited until they were playing hide-and-seek and Wilida had run off toward a bush near which he was hiding. Grinning so that she would know he was friendly, he rose and stepped out to bar her path. She stopped suddenly. Her hands went up and out before her, as if she would push, not him, but the vision of him, away. She turned gray under the brown, her eyes rolled, and she fell to the ground.

Ras was distressed. He had not known that anyone could be so frightened of anything, and especially of him.

He squatted by her, and when he saw her eyelids flutter open, he raised his finger to his lips. Her mouth worked silently. He was forced to clamp his hand over her mouth to kill the scream churning to get out. She rolled her eyes but did not struggle. She listened to him say the few phrases of Wantso he knew. The gray faded away. Presently, she nodded when he asked her if she would keep quiet if he removed his hand, although she could not move her head much because his hand was pressing it into the dirt.

He took his hand off, and she screamed loudly. Ras fled, and in his panic he plunged into the river and swam to the other side. Luckily, no crocodiles were around at that time. As soon as he was hidden by a bush from those on the other bank, he watched. Men were running up and poking in the bushes with their spears. They talked loudly to each other and did not seem eager to uncover anything.

At home, Ras was so silent and inactive that Mariyam asked what was troubling him. He answered that he was thinking, that was all. And so he was, but his thoughts hurt him. Why would Wilida, or any of the Wantso, be so frightened of him? Was he truly ugly or monstrous? He did not think so. If he were, would he be loved by Yusufu and Mariyam so much?

When he came back six days later, he saw that the children were again playing in the bushes. Ras crossed the river and waited until he could catch Wilida alone again. This time, he held his hand close to her mouth after her promise to keep quiet. Wilida did not scream.

They talked, or tried to talk, for some time. She stopped shivering like a monkey trying to pass a big seed. Before they parted, she even managed to smile. But once she was out of his reach, she ran off swiftly. However, she did not cry out or tell anybody of him, as far as he could determine. And she did meet him behind a bush at the promised time. First, he scouted around carefully to make sure that she was not setting an ambush. They talked with less difficulty this time, and during the next five times they met, he progressed rapidly in Wantso.

The sixth meeting, Wilida brought a friend, a girl named Fuwitha. Fuwitha would not come close the first meeting, or even speak to him. But, the second time, she lost her fear and joined in helping him learn the language.

It was three weeks before Ras met some of the other children. They came silently, except for Wilida and Fuwitha, who were very proud of their friendship with the white ghost-child. By then, Ras understood that he was supposed to be the spirit of a dead boy. This was why Wilida had fainted when she first saw him and why the others had been so apprehensive. But their curiosity, plus the assurances of the two girls, had brought them.

They squatted down to talk to him, to giggle nervously at his strange mouthings of their speech, and to reach out after many hesitations to touch him. He smiled and talked softly, saying that he would not harm them and that he was a good ghost.

This was the day he met Bigagi, who was supposed to be Wilida's husband when they came of age.

Later, he began to play their games with them, although he was hampered because he had to keep out of sight of the adults and older children in the fields. He became more proficient in Wantso. He wrestled with the boys, all of whom he bested easily. They did not seem humiliated. A living person could not expect to outwrestle a ghost.

He entertained them with his stories of the Ghost-Country and of his ape mother and ape foster father. His insistence that he was the son of Igziyabher, or Mutsungo, as the Wantso called the chief spirit, the Creater-Spider, awed them. At first.

Bigagi asked him why he wasn't dark-skinned and woolly-haired. Mutsungo had made the First People, from whom the Wantso were descended, out of spider webs and mud, and they had all been brown-skinned, thick-lipped, and kinky-haired. The Shaliku, who lived on the other side of the Swamp, were the offspring of Wantso and crocodiles. But if Mutsungo was indeed the father of Ras, why wasn't he like the Wantso? Or at least half spider?

Ras was a match for his mother when it came to making up stories on the spot. He replied that he wasn't the son of Mutsungo but of Igziyabher, who had kicked Mutsungo from the chair of godhood and seated himself thereon. And Ras was white because Igziyabher had washed the brown out of his skin as a sign that he was, indeed, Igziyabher's only son.

This upset the children, not so much that Ras was the son of God as his statement that Mutsungo had been kicked out as chief spirit. Ras added that Mutsungo now dwelt in the Many-Legged Swamp, where he was king of the spiders.

But when he saw that they were disturbed and that they might question their parents about it and so might reveal where they got this idea, he laughed and said that he had told all this merely to entertain them. He was the son of Mutsungo, but he did not look like a spider because Mutsungo had wanted him to look like his mother. She was an ape, and that was why his lips were thin and his hair was straight. And he was white because his mother had conceived by a lightning stroke sent by Mutsungo, and everything in her womb had turned white. The thin nose resulted from Mutsungo grabbing him too hard when he had pulled him out of the mother's womb by his nose.

The story of the lightning stroke was Mariyam's; the other details, Ras's.

Bigagi said that this could all be true, but Ras, whom he called Lazazi, to fit the sounds and structure of Wantso, was still a ghost-child.

Ras bristled and had to control himself to keep from violently arguing with Bigagi. Wilida smoothed out their tempers then by saying that perhaps this spirit-father of Ras's was chief spirit in the land to the north (she tactfully avoided saying Ghost-Land) while Mutsungo was chief spirit in this land. Just as Basama, the Crocodile-Spirit, was chief spirit of the Shaliku, and so on. The whole question could be settled when they grew up, and then they would be able, if they had the courage, to go south on the river, through the Swamp, through the land of Shaliku, and to the end of the river and the world, where the river plunged into the land beneath the earth.

Here, on an islet just before the entrance to the land beneath the earth, lived Wizozu.

Wizozu was a very very very ancient man who knew everything and who would answer a question—for a price. He had lived forever and would live forever, and he was a terrible old man.

Ras was to hear more of Wizozu, and eventually he decided that when he became a man he would journey to the end of the river and the world and ask Wizozu several questions that no one seemed to be able to answer.

He was going to question his parents about him, but since neither had ever mentioned anything like Wizozu, he thought he would keep silent. They would suspect that he had been talking to the Wantso, and he did not want that. Although they no longer tried to keep him from wandering, they still warned him against the wicked and dangerous Wantso. Igziyabher would not like it if He knew that Ras went near them. When Ras became older, then he could approach them.

Sometimes, Ras would pack six of his rubber balls in his antelope-hide bag and take them to the meeting-place. The children were amazed. They knew nothing of rubber, and asked him where the balls came from. He said that they had appeared mysteriously in the tree house one morning. His foster father had said they were a gift from Igziyabher. Allah, rather, since that was the day scheduled for Arabic to be spoken.

Ras showed the children the juggling tricks with the balls that he had learned from Yusufu. He also performed backflips and somersaults. He showed them how he could hit a small target at forty feet with a knife.

Sometimes, Ras performed tricks on the tightrope three feet above the ground between two trees. He wanted to put the rope much higher to impress them, but he did not want to be exposed to the view of the women in the fields or the guards on the wall across the neck of the peninsula. He chose a place where the ground sloped down to the river. There, while the children squatted to watch, he walked back and forth from tree to tree and then stopped in the middle and backflipped, turning over once and landing on his feet on the rope.

The wide-eyed children would clap their hands over their mouths to keep from making so much noise they would attract the women or older children.

Ras would cap all his tricks by walking on his hands across the rope while he bounced a ball between his feet. The Wantso children wanted to try ropewalking, of course.

Some were eventually able to get from one tree to the other. Many fell, and some hurt themselves, and then Ras was worried that they would run screaming to their parents.

No one ever told. Ras was their secret. Though they must have swelled almost to rupture with the desire to talk, they managed to keep silent for several years. Ras, not their own self-control, was mainly responsible for this. He told them that he would take any betrayer to Ghost-Land with him. Moreover, Igziyabher, his Father, would destroy the village and kill everyone in it with lightning.

The children turned gray and speechless at this threat. Wilida, however, managed to say, "But if we're all killed, we'll be ghosts anyway, and we'll all be with you in Ghost-Land."

"No, you won't," Ras said quickly. "I'll send the one who talks to the underworld, in the big cave into which the river empties, and he'll be tortured forever by demons and monsters and won't ever get to see his friends or parents again."

The children shrieked, but they must have half-enjoyed their terror, because they insisted that he describe what would happen to the betrayer. He enjoyed telling them, because he got very excited and exercised his imagination as if it were a muscle, making it grow and grow. He also told them about Wizozu, the All-Wise, All-Horrible Old Man on the islet at the gateway to the underworld. He knew less than they did about Wizozu, but this did not stop him, and after many descriptions and stories of Wizozu, punctuated by rollings of eyes and little shrieks from his audience, he had convinced them, and himself, that he was an authority on Wizozu.

He was vague on what Wizozu demanded in return for answering your questions. He hinted at things too terrible to even think about; even then he knew that hints were sometimes far more effective than the most grisly descriptions.

The children said that Wuwufa, the spirit-talker of the Wantso, had traveled through the Many-Legged Swamp, slipping by the Great Spider, and through the land of the terrible Shaliku and their even more terrible crocodile god, and had gone on down the river to the island of Wizozu. Nobody knew what Wizozu's price had been, although some said that it was Wuwufa's liver. According to the Wantso, the liver was the seat of thought. Whether this was true or not, all agreed it could be true.

Wuwufa acted as if he had lost his mind, sometimes, and he often went into convulsions.

Ras told himself that he, too, would some day visit Wizozu. At the age of nine, he had had many questions to which he could get no answers that satisfied him. Three years later, he still wanted to visit Wizozu, but some of the questions had changed.

The group numbered five. There were two boys, Bigagi and Sutino, and three girls, Wilida, Fuwitha, and Golabi. After six months, they introduced him to some other games besides hide-and-seek, guess-which-finger, and puzzle stories. One afternoon, as they all squatted under a bush only four feet from the river, Wilida, giggling, referred to the whiteness and largeness of Ras's penis. Bigagi resented this. He said that his was every bit as big as Ras's and that the whiteness made Ras's look like a worm under a rock. A dead worm, at that. Wilida, still giggling, said that she did not think it was as dead as it looked at this moment. She had seen it become very much alive when Ras was wrestling with the boys or the girls. And she was certain that it was bigger than Bigagi's.

Bigagi stood up and began to play with his penis. He dared Ras to do the same. Ras stood up by Bigagi's side and began to slide his foreskin back and forth. He was no stranger to his genitals. Despite Yusufu and Mariyam's harsh warnings of idiocy and impotency if he played with himself, he had done so many times when he was out of their sight. And he had had a monkey pet which had loved to suck on his penis, although Ras had never been able to top the erection with orgasm.

Now he was determined to prove his superiority over his playmates in this as in all other things. Besides, he got a high excitement out of doing this before others.

Sutino, stimulated by watching them and urged by the girls' jibes, stood up alongside the two boys. The three girls, laughing, compared the results and then decided that Sutino was eliminated. Sutino was angry but he kept on masturbating. Bigagi and Ras seemed to be neck and neck in length, but Ras was undoubtedly winner in thickness. Bigagi said that he could be even thicker than Ras if he got some help. Golabi understood him. She got down on her knees and started to suck. Ras motioned to Wilida, who giggled as she let herself down on her knees in the mud before him. She looked down at the big white root disappearing and reappearing between her fat lips and then she looked up at Ras. He grabbed her kinky hair and then her ears and jabbed his hips back and forth.

The feeling was exquisite, but it always ended in a sharp ache in his testicles. He could not ejaculate. His only consolation was that the two boys were also unable.

Ras was declared the winner. Thereafter, in addition to other games, the boys and girls experimented with each other, and sometimes one boy sucked on another and a girl licked at another's clitoris. Wilida told them of her experiences with Tuguba, an older boy. Every once in a while, when he was able to get her away from the adults and other children, he tried to stick his penis in her vagina. She had tried it several times and then had refused because it hurt her too much. So he had stuck his penis in her mouth and had ejaculated in it. During this, she had felt a very warm rush of something deep inside her—she felt it difficult to describe it exactly—but she was sure that the feeling was similar, but not as ecstatic, as that described by the older women when they were comparing experiences. And, judging from the groans, sighs, moans, shrieks, and calls from her mother during intercourse, Wilida had not yet experienced orgasm. But she liked the excitement of sex and the sometimes "warm rush."

The sex games were delightful, although Ras balked, at first, at inserting his penis in an anus. His parents' never-ceasing admonitions to be clean, and their disgust of anything connected with feces, had affected him. But he could not turn down a dare, so he, too, buggered the girls and, later, the boys. He always washed off afterward and insisted that they do the same.

Then there were the pissing contests, which Ras usually won. He could send his arc higher and farther than Bigagi by several inches.

CHAPTER 3

THE WOMEN AT NIGHT

As time went on, Ras came close to being caught by the older children. He always managed to run out of sight and behind a bush. After the twelfth near escape, he decided that it would be safer if he stayed on the other side of the river—at least during the daytime.

There was one place where the children could swim across without being observed from the fields or from the sentinel post above the fence across the peninsula neck. They began to meet Ras in the bushes on the opposite bank, where they then retreated far enough into the jungle so that their voices would not be heard. Venturing into forbidden territory was thrilling, but they were never quite at ease. Besides the leopards to worry about, they were not quite sure that Ras was not trying to entice them to the Land of the Ghosts.

Ras did not spend as much time with them as he wished. Five days a week, his daylight hours were taken up with schooling. He was put through weight-lifting, running, acrobatics, juggling, spearwork, knife-throwing, and archery. He was taught all the tricks Yusufu knew about offense and defense with only the weapons of the body, and Yusufu seemed to know a hundred. Then there was learning to read and write English, Arabic, Swahili, and Amharic, with emphasis on English.

The books in the old cabin by the lake had been English books. They were mostly picture books with words underneath the illustrations, such as A IS FOR ARCHER and B IS FOR BOY. Some of the picture books had stories with simple sentences under each, such as "Jim and Jane see the dog run." Perhaps Jim and Jane saw a dog, but Ras had never seen one. The dog looked like a jackal.

Yusufu had been forced to help him learn to connect the words beneath the pictures with the pictures themselves. Yusufu had been exasperated when he had asked Ras if he had learned to read yet. Ras had replied by asking what reading was. Yusufu said that Ras was supposed to learn by himself.

"Why?" Ras said.

"Because it is written."

Finally, Yusufu had told Ras that he would give him some lessons to get him started. However, he would not do it in the cabin, where the books were. Ras must bring the picture book to him in the forest for his lessons. He must promise never to say a word about this while he was in the cabin or in the tree house.

"Why?"

"Because it is written."

So Ras had learned the rudiments of English writing and speech while sitting by a big baobab a half mile inland from the tree house. The time came when he and Yusufu could carry on a conversation in English, although Yusufu continued to insist that under no circumstances was he to talk it, except when Yusufu said he could.

As Ras and his playmates got older, they had less time to get together. The girls were working more in the fields or at home, and the boys were being taught to hunt by their fathers. Ras was glad it was not the other way around, because he enjoyed the games with the girls more, and especially with Wilida. She was more daring than the other two in slipping off from work or often creeping out at night to meet him.

They talked and laughed, she telling him interesting events of the village or asking him to figure out the latest puzzle story, and he would tell her what he had been doing. They loved to caress and finger and kiss each other and do all the things they knew to stimulate each other. It was while Ras was showing her, one night, how the gorillas mated, the female on all fours, the male inserting from behind, that Wilida had her first orgasm. Ras was glad for her but disappointed because he did not have one. In fact, he was beginning to wonder if the pleasure was worth the painful aching in his testicles afterward.

Then he was not able to meet Wilida or any of the

girls for weeks. Wilida had told him that soon she would be kept inside the village stockade and allowed out into the fields only when closely watched. The time for initiation into womanhood was near. After that, she would not be permitted sexual play. She would not be allowed to touch an adult male, not even her father. This would last for a year, after which she would be married. To Bigagi, of course. Nor would she have much opportunity after that to meet Ras. Adultery was forbidden. For the first offense, a woman had to run the gauntlet of whips and thornsticks wielded by every man and woman in the village. A second-time offender was thrown to the crocodiles.

The guilty man paid for his first offense with a beating from his wife and the husband he had cuckolded. The second time, the guilty man went to the crocodiles, too.

Ras was distressed. He did not see any sense to the punishments.

"It's the custom," Wilida said.

"And what happens to the children of parents who are thrown to the crocodiles?"

"They go into the uncle's house."

Ras did not argue with her. He had heard the phrase "It's the custom" too many times. What was, was. It was as unarguable as Yusufu's "It is written."

"I don't want to be left alone," he said. "I want to be with you, to play with you, talk with you, make love to you."

"I can't. It is the custom," Wilida said. She was very sad.

"But you'll see me when you get the chance?"

Wilida was silent for a while. Then she said, "Would you want me to be eaten by crocodiles?"

"No! But I'll be hiding, watching you, waiting for the chance to meet you. If I'm caught, I might be killed. So if I'll take a chance, why won't you?"

She did not answer.

Then he said, "Come with me to my home. Now!"

She shrank back, eyes wide, and said, "Not to the Land of the Ghosts! I'd be afraid!"

"Am I a ghost?" Ras said. "Am I not flesh! When I am in you, do I feel to you like a ghost?"

Wilida shook her head and then rose to go.

She leaned over and kissed him briefly on the lips

"My grandmother told me stories of girls who were

seduced by ghosts and went away to their land and were never seen again."

Ras permitted her to leave, although he thought for a moment of forcing her to go with him. After that, he skulked around the village at night and at day. He often saw Wilida and the others, and he also saw why it would be difficult for the girls to get away, even if they wanted to. Two old women were always with them.

As for the two boys, Bigagi and Sutino, they had become suddenly hostile. One day, as Ras stepped out from behind a tree to greet Bigagi, he had to throw himself to the ground to dodge a spear. He was so shocked that he ran off crying. Later, he became angry and wanted to kill Bigagi and probably would have if he could have gotten close enough to attack. Now, he could not approach the village as easily or as frequently. The Wantso seemed to be on the watch for him. While eavesdropping on two women working in the fields near the bush, he learned that Bigagi and Sutino had told the elders about him. Everybody was close to panic. Wuwufa, the old spirit-talker, put the children through a cleansing ceremony. They had to wear amulets thereafter to ward off the Ghost-Boy. And the girls were watched closely for several months to make sure that they had not conceived by the ghost.

Ras longed for Wilida. He ached for her in his dreams. He sat for long hours on the branch of a tree across the river from the village and waited for her to come into view. He pretended to talk to her and made up her replies to him while, unaware of him, she bent over the cooking fire in front of her house. She was now wearing a bark-fiber belt and a white, triangular bark-fiber apron. A band of mousehide, turned out to expose the white inner side, encircled her head. From it hung many tassels and tiny wooden fetishes. Her buttocks were painted white every morning.

Ras knew now what Yusufu had meant when he had said a man could eat his heart out for something he could not get. There was a pain in his chest and an ache that started from the root of his penis and spread through his belly. It was like a poisoned arrow sticking in him. The poison was sweet-paining, not fire-deadly, and there were times when he knew that he was enjoying his suffering. No, he did not really enjoy it. It was just that it was better to be feeling this denial than to know that she was dead, forever lost to him. Ras had no intention of skulking around the village for long. He meant to do something about getting her back. And that he could not have done if she were dead.

One moonless night he climbed the big sacred tree and swiftly let himself down on the roof of Wuwufa's house. It was impossible to keep from making noise, because the branches and leaves rustled under his feet and the ribs of the roof bent and creaked under his weight. A rat on the beam under the roof squeaked and ran across the beam. Ras stood still for a while until he was sure that Wuwufa was not disturbed. The spirit-talker had been drinking much beer with the other men all evening. His wife, however, might be a light sleeper.

A nearby hog grunted. A bat fluttered above him, as black and swift and chilling as the thought of death. He waited, and presently eased himself down on the roof and thence onto the ground. His feet hit the earth with a noise he regretted making but could not help. The hog grunted again, and the bat winged above his head by three feet, then returned, like a piece of night fallen off, to flutter past his shoulder and close to the ground before it rose again. Another bat joined it in its zigs and zags. Ras was happy to see them. According to the Wantso, demons and ghosts sometimes took the form of bats. They would fly out of the shadows and reach down with tiny hands and seize a Wantso by the two cones of his hair. This made the Wantso more than reluctant to leave their houses at night unless there were many torches blazing and many people around.

Despite which, some did come out at night and quietly so that very few others would know they were out. There were forces stronger than the fear of demons and ghosts. Ras knew this because he had observed the breakers of the night from his perch on the branch of the big sacred tree.

He drew his knife, and crouching, ran to the Great House. He squatted in the shadows underneath the floor, his back against one of the tree-trunk supports, and waited. Somebody inside the Great House was snoring. Somebody else groaned and muttered. He grinned and was just about to crawl out from under the house when he saw a woman letting herself down from a hut directly across from him. The collapsible stairs had been taken in. The hut was Tobato and Seliza's, and, while he could not see the woman's features, he could recognize the silhouette of body and her manner of walking.

Seliza was a good-looking woman who had begun to get fat. She was still attractive enough so that Ras had speculated on what she would be like in the bush, as he had speculated about every woman, attractive or not, in the village. If she were out in the demon-ridden air, she was herself driven by a demon. Certainly, she was not climbing out of the house just to relieve herself of excrement. Wilida had told him that every hut had several pots for evacuation. These were emptied into a large hole outside the village, and the contents of the hole were later taken out for fertilizer when needed. Nobody except Ras seemed to mind the odor that enveloped the village when the wind blew north, and his opinions did not count.

Seliza circled behind her hut, where she stopped. Presently, a form identifiable as a man's walked out from behind a hut on the outer circle. The man went on out of Ras's sight to meet Seliza behind her house. A minute passed. The two, hand in hand, walked swiftly toward the Great House. Ras retreated to hide behind the thick central post. Evidently, they were going to crawl under the Great House, though why they should choose this place he could not guess. They would not be able to sneak out the north or the south gate without making too much noise, and there were guards at the east and west gates. They were, as usual, asleep, but the creak of wood might awaken them.

Perhaps they were coming here because the old chief and his wife had a reputation as heavy sleepers. Chufija, their son, had been a simpleton after becoming very sick when he was a young boy. He was good for nothing except to keep the birds and monkeys off the crops, drink beer, and grin at the insults and jibes of all.

Seliza whispered something and giggled. The man growled at her to be quiet. By then Ras had recognized his walk; the voice confirmed the identification. He was Jabubi, Wilida's father. Wilida had spoken of how he could not keep his hands off women when he thought no one was looking. Although he had never been caught in adultery, he had several times been accused. So far, Wuwufa's guilt-search had not made Jabubi confess, and Jabubi apparently had not been scared enough.

Ras was delighted. If Jabubi was here, he would make one less to guard his daughter. The only trouble was, the two were crawling toward the post behind which he was hiding. He would have to get away, and quickly, before they arrived. His white skin made him easier to see, so he would have to retreat without noise to attract their gaze to him. He got on his hands and knees and, keeping the central post between him and them, crawled backward.

When his feet touched another post, he turned to go around it. At that moment, Seliza and Jabubi came around the central post. Ras did not try to keep moving; he froze for a second. He then let himself down slowly until he was flat on the ground.

Seliza and Jabubi, in each other's arms, were breathing so loudly and making such smackings and gigglings and groanings that Ras wondered if they had lost all sense, and then knew that they had, of course.

Suddenly, Seliza grunted and said something. Jabubi whispered to her; she whispered back. They got up on all fours and began to crawl directly toward him. Ras knew that they had not noticed him as yet. If they had thought there was somebody else under the house, they would have fled at once and with much noise, thinking that he was a ghost. They must have left the first place because Seliza had complained of unevenness of the ground or a stone pushing into her back. Whatever the reason, they had gone only a few feet before they stopped. And then Ras pulled in his first breath since they had rolled apart and lurched on hands and knees toward him.

Ras had nobody in his way then; he did not think that they would be observant enough to see him if he circled through the huts the long way to Wilida's. The two-in-one lump that Seliza and Jabubi formed in the shadows, the raspings of breath torn through arched nostrils, the smacks and gulps and sucking noises, the giggles, the groans that came up from the tip of the spine and half escaped from the lips, these had excited Ras so that his penis stood up and throbbed. However, instead of flying him toward Wilida, it seemed to turn him, as the nose of a hungry leopard turns it toward a deer, to Seliza. Once oriented, he was pulled along, or, so intense and forceful was his sudden feeling, he was not so much pulled as borne.

Barely able to cram back a sob of ecstasy, he crawled up behind Jabubi, who was just getting onto his knees before letting himself down on Seliza. She had raised her legs to hook them over Jabubi's shoulders.

Ras hit him hard in the back of the neck with the hilt of the reversed knife. Jabubi grunted and began to fall forward; Ras shoved him to one side and was on Seliza, a hand over her mouth, before she could scream. She trembled like a flow of mud just before it went over a cliff, and her eyes were so wide that he could see the whites even in this dark place. But she did not try to fight or to escape. Suddenly, the whites disappeared. Her eyelids had closed. Her body seemed to draw in on itself and became a lump. She had fainted.

Ras was able to control himself long enough to make sure that Jabubi was still unconscious. Jabubi lay on his right side, his mouth open, breathing deeply. Then Ras was on Seliza, and, after a few strokes, he had an orgasm.

It was the first in his life, the final culmination of so many almost-jettings, and he became, for a few seconds, unable to care about enemies or anything. At that moment, anyone could have attacked him without fear of retaliation.

Just as control returned, Seliza began to come out of her faint. Ras spoke to her softly, telling her that if she kept quiet, she would not be carried off to the Land of the Ghosts.

Some of the shock and fright may have been pared off because he was not entirely unknown or unexpected. For at least a year the Wantso had talked about the ghost-child that their children had played with, and he had been glimpsed a few times in daylight and once at night. The adults knew that the ghost-child had not harmed the children and had never made any threats against anybody. He had become somewhat familiar.

So, although her heart now thudded like the feet of a rabbit being chased across hard earth by a serval cat, it was not so shocked that it stopped. She groaned and began shaking again. Ras, who had not withdrawn, began to move back and forth, and presently Seliza, her terror pushed out a little farther with every thrust, also began to move. Perhaps she thought that, if she made the Ghost-Boy happy, she would not be harmed. Whatever her reasoning, her actions seemed to be sincere, and after his second orgasm had shaken him as a dog shakes a rat to death, he became aware that she had scratched his back deeply during her own ecstasy.

Jabubi added his groans and moved a little. Ras hit him again, this time on the side of the head, and turned back to Seliza. He had expected her to try to escape when he was busy with Jabubi. Instead, she had lain quietly and then had reached out for him when he turned back to her from Jabubi.

Later, she told him why. She was so eager to get a man who could have a complete erection that she had momentarily forgotten—or had been able to push aside—her terror of ghosts. She did not know what he meant to do with her afterward, but, for the moment, especially since she could do nothing else anyway, she was happy to take him in. His repeated assurances that he would not harm her helped to quiet her fears.

Ras did not get to Wilida that night. He was afraid to leave Seliza and stay inside the walls, because she might arouse the village. Or, if she kept silence, Jabubi might make an uproar when he became conscious. So he stayed with Seliza several hours more. He had to pause for a while to tie Jabubi's hands and feet with his rope and to threaten to cut his tongue out if he cried out. Jabubi, teeth chattering with fear of the Ghost-Boy, promised that he would say nothing. Ras reminded him that he would have a difficult time explaining what he was doing under the Great House.

Seliza did not like to have Jabubi watch, so they crawled over behind a post, where he could not see them. And when Ras decided that he must leave before it got too light to escape the guards' watch, he knocked out Jabubi again and untied him. He felt sorry for him; he hoped he would not be hurt too much. But tonight he would have killed him to get Seliza.

Jabubi did raise an uproar that day, but he was forced to do so. His wife and others noticed the lumps on his neck and head when he complained of being sick. Old Wuwufa came to shake administering rattles at him and sprinkle powders and incantations over him. After hearing Jabubi's story of being beaten in a dream by demons, he put him through an exorcism. This hurt Jabubi more than Ras's blows; he had to drink a cathartic to expel any residue of evil left by the denizens of night.

This was the beginning of Ras's affair with almost the entire adult female population. He met Seliza in the bush many times thereafter. If she still thought that he was a ghost, she had told herself that he meant her no evil. On the contrary, he was doing her more good than anyone she had ever known. He had not been crippled by the savage flint knife during the circumcision rites of the Wantso.

It was inevitable that Seliza, who had a big and busy mouth, should confide to a friend. Seliza did not fear that Pamathi would betray her and so send her to the gauntlet.

Pamathi was as guilty as she of adultery, although not with the same men. Pamathi was horrified—but intrigued—and she talked Seliza into letting her watch the two from behind a tree.

Seliza had said nothing to Ras about this arrangement. However, he was aware that Pamathi was a hidden witness. Before meeting Seliza, he always scouted the area carefully from several trees, and so he had known that Seliza was with Pamathi. The second time they met, he suddenly disappeared and, before Pamathi realized what was happening, she was seized from behind.

Thereafter, the two met him together and took turns.

In the meantime, Ras was frustrated in his attempt to get to Wilida. During the day, she was too closely watched. At night, his efforts to sneak into her house were blocked by the adult women. They were lying in wait for him— seemingly under every house—and would not let him by. Nor was he able—at first—to say no to them. One night, when he did manage to bypass the wives, he was almost killed. Jabubi, Wilida's father, may have been awake by accident or he may have been waiting every night since Ras had interrupted him with Seliza. This moonless night, as Ras, heart lurching with anticipation of his beloved Wilida, his skin cold, began to crawl past the door-curtain, he heard a gasp inside the hut. At the same time he saw—or seemed to see—a darker mass within the blackness, and he threw himself back out by placing both hands on the floor and lifting himself up and back and out. Something thudded into the bamboo wall near the entrance—probably a spear—and then Jabubi yelled. Ras fled while the village woke on every side. He went up the wall of Wuwufa's house and onto the roof and onto the branch of the tree and down it to the ground outside the wall.

Ras was balked this time and many times. Yet it was when Wilida was most watched and most encaged that he was able to be with her.

Between his twelfth and fourteenth year, he spied on many circumcision ceremonies of the boys at thirteen and the clitoris-cutting rites for the girls of twelve. Both rituals were supposed to be secret; they were enacted in the jungle near the foot of the eastern hills. No women were allowed near the place for the boys and no men near that for the girls. Any unauthorized person caught spying would have been torn to pieces by the nails and teeth of the outraged men or women.

But Ras had no trouble observing either ceremony from positions high in trees or in bushes very close to the participants and behind the guards' backs. He became familiar with the words of incantation and song, with the ritualized gestures, the sawing off of the foreskin and the cutting of the skin on the shaft to cause great scars and with the severing of the clitoris tip.

He saw no sense in either rite; he hurt with the victims; he became enraged when Sutino, his playmate, was infected as a result of the circumcision and died in agonies two weeks later.

And he could not imagine why any boy would submit willingly to a practice that would make him only a half man for the rest of his life, a half man before he became a man. The children explained to him that it was the custom. Bigagi, who survived the cutting, ripping, and sawing, never told Ras how he felt about the custom. Unless the spear thrown at Ras was comment enough.

A year after Wilida and two of her friends had been initiated into womanhood, they were placed in bamboo cages hung from the branches of trees about a mile from the village. Here each in her own cage, within sound but not sight of the other, they lived for six months. Old women stood guard and fed and bathed them once a day when they lowered the cages and allowed the girls to step out for a few minutes. The old women gave them counsel day and night—enough to last them for the rest of their lives.

Ras, listening, learned more about the Wantsos than he dreamed could exist.

Once every four days, the girls' mothers visited them and, squatting under the cages, shouted news and gossip. At other times, other women also visited them. The girls were, however, mostly lonely, miserable, and scared. The leopards prowled beneath the cages or sometimes came up onto the branches and dropped down on the cages and tried to reach through the bars. The girls screamed then, and the old women guards—safe in their huts on the ground—screamed at the leopards.

Ras felt sorry—and also furious at times—because Wilida was being treated so cruelly. But he lost much of his fury when he found that the situation, though bad for the girls, was good for him. And in some ways it was also good for the girls. When he was sure that the old women were barricaded in for the night, he would climb the tree and go on all fours out along the branch. And after calling softly to Wilida so that she would not think he was a leopard, he would slide down one of the thick grass ropes from which the cage hung. He would untie the door and swing into the cage.

Wilida was very happy to see him because she had someone to talk to, to make love to, to keep her warm, to protect her from the leopards. She lost some of his company, however, when she mentioned how lonely the other girls were. Thereafter, he spent a night now and then with Fuwitha and Kamasa. At the same time, he was also meeting some of the women in the bushes or even sneaking into the village for meetings under the floors of the houses.

His parents were worried at this time about him because he was so pale, seemed to be losing some weight, and had dark bags under his eyes—"like little bats of weariness sleeping upside down, hanging onto his lower eyelids," as Yusufu said.

And so Ras found the six months of encagement for the girls a happy time for him. But when he was told by Wilida that this would soon be over, he became unhappy again. Moreover, Wilida would be married to Bigagi at the end of the year. Between now and then she would remain in her mother's house, continuing the work necessary for the household. Then she would be placed in the bridal cage on the islet just west of the village, and Bigagi would take up his vigil outside her cage. After two nights and a day, the wedding would be held.

Ras begged her to go off with him to his country. She would be happy there—he swore it.

She refused to go. Yes, she loved him, but she also loved her parents, her people, her village. She would die if she had to leave them.

But Ras could still see her and talk to her and now and then make love to her. That is, if he had time and energy to spare for her, she added sarcastically.

Ras replied that he did not want to see her under such conditions. He wanted to live freely with her. And if she would leave with him, he would promise never to visit any of the Wantso women.

Wilida continued to say no. The time came when he quit pleading. He also gave up his fantasies of carrying her off. She meant it when she said that she would die if she were cut off from the tribe.

Nevertheless, he was angry, and he could not quite surrender her. When Wilida had been put in the bridal cage and Bigagi had taken his post before her, Ras had been driven to come out into the open—although at a distance—to taunt the Wantso men. He had to do it; he was hoping that something would happen to cause him and Bigagi to tangle, so that he could kill Bigagi. At the same time, he did not want this.

He also wanted to kill Wilida, and he did not want to kill her.

Now he had been driven off and was hiding behind a bush and thinking about swimming to the islet when night came, subduing Bigagi, and making love to Wilida, whom he would kill afterward, he was so angry with her.

Nightfall came. . . . The noise was a far-off, fluttering sound, like a bat's wings in the night. It quickly became louder and then became a chuttering, as of a spear being whirled around and around until the cutting of the head through the air chopped off the air in chunks. Chut-chut-chut. And beneath the chuttering was a deeper, roaring sound that presently became so loud that it almost smothered the chuttering.

It was the Bird of God, and the Bird would soon be above him.

CHAPTER 4

BIRDS THAT BURN

The Bird of God had always been around. It nested on top of the black stone pillar soaring from the middle of the lake and reaching almost to the sky. Days would pass, sometimes months, and Ras would wonder if perhaps it would never come back. Then he would hear the faint chop-chop-chop of its rotating wings, and it would appear out of the sky. It would become larger, stop to hover above the pillar, and would sink out of sight to its hidden nest.

Days and sometimes months would pass. One day Ras would hear the chop-chop-chop. He would run down to the shore of the lake unless he happened to be swimming or in his dugout. Up the Bird of God would rise, high, higher, and it would fly over the cliffs, the edge of the world, and disappear into the sky.

Ras sometimes saw the Bird of God fly inland. If he were out in the open, he would see the Bird approach him. At first he used to run away into the forest to hide. Later, he would stand up, holding his spear, and wait for it to come nearer. He never did this, though, unless he had a good chance to run for shelter if he were to be forced to run.

Sometimes, the Bird of God hovered over him so close that he could see a man in its belly. Twice, he saw two men in its belly.

"Those are not men but angels," Mariyam, his mother, would reply to his questions. "Igziyabher sends his angels to ride in the belly of the Bird to observe you. They are

42

to report on whether or not you have been a good boy."

Igziyabher was God, Allah, Dio, or Mungu, depending upon which language his parents were speaking at the time. Ras usually thought of God as Igziyabher, because that was the name his mother had first spoken and most often used.

"Mother, if Igziyabher wants to find out if I am good, why does He have to send angels to look for Him? I thought you said that He can see everything from where He sits on the Seat of Glory?"

Mariyam always had an answer, even when she contradicted herself, which was frequently.

"He sends angels to give them something to do, O son. They don't work but sit at God's feet and sing all day and night in praise of Him. But angels like to take a vacation now and then, and they are very happy to ride around in the belly of the Bird and watch over the creatures."

Once Mariyam had said that the angel inside the Bird was being punished for sassing God. The Bird had swallowed him up and was slowly digesting him with the acids of its belly. The angel was being eaten alive by the acids and would suffer until he dissolved. Then Igziyabher would take the pieces of meat and bone of the angel and put them back together. The angel would be a new angel then and would no longer sass God.

This had been told shortly after Ras had snarled at his mother. She had beaten him with a whip made of hippo hide. Ras had stood silently, trying to keep from smiling at her. The whip had hurt somewhat, but she was tiny, with little strength. Besides, she had not been snapping it as hard as she could. Afterward, she had wept because she had drawn blood twice from his back.

She had smeared ointment over his back and then had wept some more.

"You have such a golden skin, son, it hurts me to mar it. When I first held you in my arms, you were a pink baby, beautiful, beautiful, with large, dark gray eyes, and with the smile of a newly born angel. Now, your skin is darker, kissed with the sun, smooth as the polished tusk of an elephant."

"Maybe so, maybe so, here and there," Ras had said. "But I would not worry about several more scars, especially such tiny ones. I have a hundred scars. This shoulder is puckered up because of the leopard that almost killed me before I killed him. The tip of this ear bears the tooth-mark of Wilida, who loves me so much she wants to eat me up."

Mariyam had screamed and grabbed the whip and begun laying it on him. Ras had run away, laughing, though she had threatened to stake him out on an ant hill if he did not come back and take his rightful punishment.

"I have told you and your father has told you, too, a thousand, thousand times, stay away from those Wantso girls! Igziyabher will catch you with them some day, and then He will plunge you forever into the fires of hell!"

Hell, according to one of her stories, was the cavern at the other end of the world. There was an opening to it where the river ran into it.

"But I thought you said that Igziyabher was at the end of the world?"

"And so I did, empty-head. But He sits on high beyond the cavern of hell, and a soul must go through hell first before he can get to heaven."

"And when is Igziyabher coming to see me, His favorite child, if I am to believe you? Is He afraid of me?"

"He is afraid of nothing! Why should He be afraid? Do you think He is stupid enough to create beings who would harm Him?"

"There are many stupid things in this world," Ras had said. "I think that he should have given more thought before He made this world."

"Do not blaspheme, O son! He may hear you and come down to face you, and the glory of His being would make you curl up and smoke away, like fat left too long on the pan."

"I would tell Him a few things and perhaps pull that long white beard of His."

Mariyam had put her hands to her ears and moaned and rocked back and forth. "Blasphemy! Blasphemy! Surely you will suffer the pains of hell!"

"The boy has great spirit," Yusufu said. "He is afraid of nothing."

Now, this morning, as Ras started to walk across the plain toward home, he saw the Bird of God for the first time in so many weeks he could not count them. The sun had risen above the mountains by the breadth of his hand. The bird was so far away that he could not hear its wings. Nor would he have seen it if it had not reflected the sun. Thereafter, by straining his eyes, he could catch it now and then, especially since it flashed three more times.

Suddenly, another great bird appeared. It was closer to him, so he could hear its roar and see its outline. It flew from the sky as if the sky were a blue skin with a blue pimple that had burst and shot out a black knot of corruption. It startled him and even sickened him. For a moment, he thought that Igziyabher had sent another bird out to finally punish him for his deeds and his loud, boastful words.

He murmured, "But why should He wait so long? I have done nothing that I have not been doing for a long time."

He hefted his spear. If this bird carried an angel, or Igziyabher Himself, the bird would have to settle down on the ground to let the passenger out. When the angel, or Igziyabher, stepped out to confront Ras, he had better be prepared to dodge quickly. If he didn't, he was going to get the iron point of the spear in his belly.

Mariyam had said that angels and their Maker were invulnerable to the weapons of men. Maybe so. But they had better have hides thicker than a hippo's. Ras had driven his spear into more than one hippo. And if the being in the bird truly had a hide of iron, he would still know he had been in a fight before he conquered Ras.

The second bird became larger and noisier. It was high above Ras and going past him. Ras sighed with relief. Evidently it had no designs on him.

Standing beneath it, he could see that it was different from the Bird that nested on the pillar. The wings extended stiffly out to both sides, as a fish-eagle's when it rides the currents of air. But these were not attached to the shoulders, but to the underside of the body, which in shape reminded him of the body of a fish.

Like a fish's also was the color: silvery gray. It bore markings, letters much like the letters in the books he had found in the old cabin by the lake when he was a boy.

This bird did not have the peculiar round claws that hung at the ends of the skinny legs beneath the Bird of God. It did not have any legs or claws. Perhaps these were folded up and held close to the body, hidden in the feathers, as they were with many of the small birds when they flew.

It shot above him at a height even above that of the pillar, which must rear a thousand feet. The Bird of God had changed its course now and was heading straight for the intruder. The two were on a level with each other and closing in swiftly. They were about to meet over the low hills just south of the lake when the stiff-winged bird lifted its left wing and veered to the right. It completed a half turn while climbing, continued to go up, and then turned back toward Ras. The Bird of God flew upward at a slant on the trail of the stiff-wings.

Sunlight flashed off the front of the intruder and off the front of the Bird of God. For a second, Ras saw two flashes of red from something dark sticking out of the side of the pursuer.

Then they were overhead, and the chop-chop-chop and the growl of the second bird mingled. Abruptly, flame gouted from the rear of the stiff-wings and smoke bannered out. The stiff-wings turned again and headed straight for the Bird of God. This whirled and went back to the north. Then it turned again as if pivoting on an invisible pin.

The flames leaped out from the stiff-wings. Its roar rose and fell as it climbed up above the Bird of God. It rose almost straight up and dived down away. The black things were sticking out of the other side now, but Ras could not see any red spurting from it. It dropped swiftly, then shot off at an angle. The flaming bird twisted with it, still coming fast. Something black fell from its side, turned over and over, then shot out a small black object. The small object unfolded as a flower unfolds and became a great white bloom. Below it hung the figure of a human being—or of an angel. The white flower and the body drifted southward, falling slowly, carried with the wind.

Ras had wanted to see where the angel hit the ground. At that moment, however, the change in sounds from the two birds made him turn to look at them. The stiff-wings, a bloom of fire with petals of dark smoke, had caught up with the Bird of God. It flashed by on its side, wings perpendicular to the ground, and one wing struck the whirling wings of the Bird of God. The stiff-wings flew into pieces; the Bird of God staggered and began to fall.

Immediately thereafter, the stiff-wings exploded. A ball of scarlet, it swelled and enveloped the Bird of God. Then the ball had gone by and was falling. The Bird of God was falling also, but more slowly. A black figure hurtled from it, and presently it also bloomed and a human figure was swaying beneath the flower, which was a bright yellow.

Ras could see that there was still a man in the belly of the Bird of God. He rose from his seat and leaped through the opening in the side and out into the air. He flamed as he fell.

There were many small white objects floating from the

wounded side of the bird. They streamed out like loose feathers and began to dance back and forth, coming down slowly. They floated out behind the Bird of God; they were rectangular beads strung on blue threads of air. The threads disintegrated and the beads were everywhere. And when the lowest came close enough to Ras for him to see them, he knew that they were sheets of paper, like the pages of the books in the old cabin.

The Bird of God gave birth to flame with a bellow of anguish. It passed overhead, still streaming paper now, but burning paper. The last man to jump from it struck the ground beyond a tree a hundred yards away from Ras.

The first to jump was about four hundred yards away to the southeast and near the jungle. Ras watched the figure and then shouted with surprise when long, yellow hair floated out from her.

Yellow hair?!

"Your wife will be white and perhaps she will have yellow hair," Mariyam had said.

Ras had thought this strange. He was not sure he would like yellow hair.

"It is written that you will have a wife," Yusufu had said. "But there is no promise that she will have yellow hair."

The Bird of God brushed against the tops of the trees to the southeast and blocked off his view of the yellow-haired person. It crashed with a great noise, and flames shot up, and screaming birds flew up, so numerous they were like specks of pepper. Pepper in the eyes they were, because if the yellow hair was still falling, she was curtained off by the birds. Smoke poured out from the trees then and obscured the birds also.

By now, the being beneath the yellow flower was also out of sight. Ras started toward the flames but stopped, his spear held before him. A leopard had burst out of the jungle and was bounding toward him. Its ears were laid back flat, and it was snarling.

"O beautiful with Death, you will have a mate today!" he shouted. "My spear!"

The leopard bounded past with not a glance at him. Behind it came three tiny, twist-horned antelope, a long-necked serval cat, and a mongoose, all running shoulder to shoulder and paying no attention to anything but the terror that had also driven the leopard. Ras laughed and ran on, though he still held his spear ready. The beasts were not going to heed him except as an obstacle to their flight.

He passed through the thick brush and under the branches of the vine-strangled trees. No more animals rushed out of the jungle. He smelled smoke and presently was crouched behind a bush near the bank of the river. The Bird of God had struck a dozen branches and broken them off and then had smashed into the soft mud. It burned not three yards from the water. The bushes near it blackened, and their leaves curled up. Some caught on fire, which would have made Ras very uneasy if this were the dry season. There was little chance that the bushes beyond would also catch fire.

The Bird certainly was not flesh and blood and feathers. It was made of unknown material and of iron. It would be too hot for a long time for him to investigate, so he decided to search for the yellow-haired person. She —he was thinking of the person as she because of what Yusufu had told him—must have fallen on the other side of the river. At this point, the river was two hundred yards wide. It was also so close to its origin in the lake that the waters would be too cold for the crocodiles. Besides, he doubted that any would have stayed in the neighborhood after the noise the Bird had made. A crocodile would have scooted on down the river like a fish, propelled by panic-shot excrement.

Ras walked down the sloping banks, noting in the mud the webbed imprints of a giant water shrew. The sun had not reached this side of the river yet, so the mud was cool as it squished between his toes. The water was cold when he dived into it; he swam on his side, kicking his feet and stroking with one hand while he held his spear, bow, and quiver up above the surface with his right hand.

On the other side, he walked straight westward but looked intently on both sides. The underbrush was not thick here because of the pale darkness cast down by the many vine-matted branches. A bush here seldom or almost never felt the kiss of the sun, lord of life; the growths that survived had to inch painfully and weakly up the trunks of the trees that were killing them until they reached the thin area, where the sun blessed. He could see about a hundred yards on either side of him, although the yellow-hair could be behind one of the huge trunks.

It would not be so easy for the great white bloom to be hidden.

He had gone several hundred yards from the river when he gave a low cry and leaped into the air. He slapped at his legs and feet to knock off the black ants biting into him. They were everywhere, merging with the shadows, swarming, intent on their drive toward an unknown goal. They formed a column that spread out between him and the interior. He retreated and then tried to walk parallel with the living blanket on the soil. He would get ahead of them and cut across them and try to come around the other side. But after he had covered a mile, he realized that the army might stretch for several more miles. Meantime, the yellow-haired angel must have been forced by the same ants to go westward.

"Angels have wings," his mother had said.

"Why doesn't the angel in the Bird's belly have wings?" Ras had said.

"Because angels often go down among men to find out what's going on or to deliver a message from Igziyabher. When they do that, they take off their wings and hang them on a hook."

"Yes, but the angel in the Bird's belly isn't pretending to be a man. Why doesn't he wear his wings?"

"How do you know he isn't? Have you been close enough to see if he has wings?"

What would an angel do when stranded on earth without wings? Would Igziyabher come after her Himself, or would He send some winged angels, or another bird, to lift her up and take her back to Heaven?

He prowled on, unwilling to give up and hoping to come to the head of the army. Another thing about angels occurred to him. Sometimes, his mother and father spoke of them as if they had no sex.

"They are as smooth between the legs as your forehead," Yusufu had said. "When Igziyabher wants more angels, He creates them."

"Out of the fire of the stars," Mariyam had said, eager to explain the workings of the world and of God. "He keeps making new angels from starfire, and so, some day, He'll use up all the stars and then the skies will be black, and the End of the World will be near. Pray then, son, pray, because the God of Wrath . . ."

"Shut up, Mariyam! You know better than that!" Yusufu had said. "There are ears that hear and hands that take vengeance because of what some liars say."

Ras had had many questions that day, one of which was about Mariyam's earlier story of the angels coming down and mating with the daughters of men. If the angels had no sex, then . . .

He stopped walking. A sound like the snapping off of a large branch had come from his right. It was not quite like a branch breaking, so he had no way of knowing how far away the origin of the sound was. There was something sinister in it.

The cracking was repeated, though this time it was not so loud. It did come from the same direction.

A woman screamed. Another cracking, followed by a man screaming. Then there was silence.

Ras hesitated, shrugged, and ran as swiftly as he could through the ants. He traveled a hundred yards before the first of the ants closed their pincers on his feet. He gritted his teeth and ran on. If he stopped to scrape them off, he would just be attacked by a greater number. Now that he had made his decision, he could not change his mind. Rather, he would not. He would keep running, no matter what the agony, until he reached whoever was screaming. He was not fool enough to run directly up to the people who were making the noise; for all he knew, they might not be the angels but Wantso. He doubted that the Wantso would dare come this close to their Land of the Ghosts, but he also knew that their actions could not be predicted. The Wantso, like his parents, were always doing unexpected things, some of them stupid.

Moreover, the angels might be dangerous in some unknown manner. There were the cracking sounds, which for some reason prickled him.

When he thought he could no longer endure the little fires on his feet and legs, he saw the first angel. He lay on his back, arms outstretched, his jaw dropped. He was black with ants, but when Ras, hopping around him, brushed some ants off his face, his face was red. The skin was eaten away, and the red muscles stared at Ras. The hair, however, knocked free of ants, was brown and straight. A peculiar object of metal lay beside the right hand of the corpse.

Ras could not tarry to investigate. If he did not get going, and swiftly, he would be as dead as the angel—if it was an angel. The corpse looked too human. Also, could angels die? If they could, who could kill one besides another angel, a fallen angel, Satan's legionnaire?

There was no more thinking about that then. The agony of the stings burned away all thoughts. There was only the frantic desire to get away.

He ran for two hundred yards, dodging around the

bushes, leaping over fallen trunks, until he decided that he could no longer withstand the urge to scream. He was already making so much noise that he could be heard half a mile away. Moreover, he doubted that anybody would be hidden in ambush with the ants swarming over him.

He screamed, and then he saw the creek ahead of him, and he spurted forward and dived headlong into the waters. He rolled over and over in the mud of the bottom while he scraped away at his feet and legs. Mud rose to dirty the water, mingled with the tiny crushed bodies. He lay still for a while after that, watching the stream clear itself, and grateful for the relief given by the cold waters.

When he left the creek, he picked up his spear and bow, which he had thrown on the opposite bank just before dropping into the creek. His quiver had to be taken off and upended to dump the water out. The feathers were soaked and muddied.

There were no army ants on this side of the creek. He cast back and forth, looking for tracks in the damp soil, but found none. After two hours' search, he decided that the other angel had run off in a different direction or perhaps was also dead and being stripped of flesh.

Which of the two was the angel? Igziyabher's angels did not fight each other, so one must be a devil. Was the dead one the devil? Mariyam had said that Good always triumphs over Evil, at which Yusufu had snorted and replied, "Would we be here, living this life, if that were true? The devil rules this world, and you know it, Grandmother of Lies."

Yusufu was always making remarks that he would not explain when Ras asked for light. "I open my mouth and the words fly out before I can catch them, my son. But a man has to say something once in a while; otherwise he goes mad."

Ras searched for another hour or more before deciding that he would find the angel—if she were one—only by accident. By then he was beginning to think that neither of the two might be devils or angels. The corpse had looked so human and was so dead that there seemed to be nothing of divinity about it. The only thing that caused him doubt was that he had seen no wound on the corpse. If he had had a chance to investigate, he might have found one. But what kind of a weapon was it that left no evidence of its passage?

On the other hand, if the yellow-haired being were an angel, why had it allowed its bird to be killed?

It was all very puzzling, as so many things were. There were answers to all his questions, but there were so many different answers. Mariyam never stuck to the same story: Yusufu's did not vary; the Wantso girls all had the same story but theirs differed from his parents'.

And then there was Gilluk, king of the Sharrikt, whom he had sneaked out of the Wantso village where he had been held prisoner. Ras had kept Gilluk in a cage in the jungle for six months while he learned the Sharrikt language, and then questioned him. Gilluk's answers had little resemblance to anybody else's.

CHAPTER 5

A LETTER FROM GOD

TO THE MOON

While the inward eyes were concentrated upon the past, the outward missed nothing of the present. As he walked to the north, he saw something white far off to the northeast, and he approached it cautiously. Now and then he stood motionless behind a tree and listened. Monkeys chattered or screamed; a tiny bird with a huge head and long, straight beak rawked as it flew over him. He became more careful the closer he got, but finally satisfied himself that the yellow-haired angel was not around. The white object was the flower below which she had descended from the bird. It had lost its shape and hung drooping, as if drained of juice, from a branch. He climbed up to touch it, and found that it was of some smooth material. There were cords of another unknown stuff hanging from it and straps attached to these.

Ras worked the dead flower—or whatever it was— for a while before he got it untangled and folded into a bundle. He located a huge hole in a dead tree and cached the bundle in it. Though he was eager to take it home and look it over more carefully, he did not want to be burdened with it at present.

The tracks leading from beneath the tree were small and made with coverings such as he had seen on the dead being's feet. They led to one of the many streams in this area; there were none on the other bank. Ras crisscrossed the stream for several miles southeastward, then returned to the place where the tracks entered the stream and zigzagged from bank to bank northwestward.

His belly rumbled with hunger, but he did not want to stop for a long time to hunt. He could have shot a monkey at any time now that the feathers of his arrows were dried.

There was no time to skin and cook a monkey. Although he preferred cooked food, he could have carried the monkey along while he ate it raw. There was a time when his parents had encouraged him to eat raw meat, although they would not eat anything unless it was cooked; and when he asked why, they replied that he was to learn to enjoy raw meat. It was written that he should.

Then he had become very sick after eating uncooked guinea fowl. He rolled and sweated in a fever and had many wild and terrifying dreams. His parents stayed with him every minute then, except when Yusufu had to hunt. Mariyam wept and cradled him in her arms, though he was bigger than she then, and she crooned to him and called him her beautiful baby. Yusufu muttered oaths and swore vengeance against somebody, but would not answer when Ras asked him of whom he was speaking.

When Ras recovered, he found that his parents now demanded that he never eat raw flesh again. There were many deadly poisons and little deadly creatures in uncooked flesh. He must never touch it again. It was too late then. He had a taste for it. Although he did prefer meat cooked a little bit, he sometimes had no time to prepare it when he was out alone. So he would tear away at flesh still warm with departed life. Or, as now, he would pause briefly to lift a rock and munch on the blind, white, legless creatures under it.

The sun was dropping toward the mountains when he decided that the angel had left the stream without leaving tracks. By then he was far to the northwest and in the steep, rugged hills and dense undergrowth. He came across an abandoned gorilla site and once heard the muffled beat of hands against a huge chest.

He did not try to find the band. The gorillas here would have nothing to do with him; they either fled when he made an appearance or sometimes a male would stand his ground and try to outbluff him. Only the band in the hills to the east of Ras's home knew him and accepted his presence. And even then he had to approach slowly if he had been away a long time. That group had known him from his infanthood, when Yusufu had carried him up and introduced him.

Later, when Ras could talk, he was told that Yusufu had spent two years in the slow and cautious integration with them.

Why had he done this? Because it was written that he should, so Ras could play with the gorillas and become one of them. Why was he suppposed to do this? Because it was written.

At that time Ras did not know what writing was. Later, when Yusufu permitted him to enter the old log cabin on the lake shore, Ras found the books. He looked through the books and was especially interested in the pictures. There was writing—printing, rather—under the pictures. When Ras became older, he was to try to learn what the printing said. Yusufu insisted on that.

Then Yusufu had taken him out of the cabin and locked it up, saying that when Ras got older, he could look through the books again. Ras had asked him if the books contained the "It is written." Yusufu had said no. That book was elsewhere. He made a vague gesture and then said, "It is in Igziyabher's hands. I myself have never seen The Book."

Ras decided to spend the night in the jungle instead of going the six circuitous miles home. He would resume the search in the morning and spend all day looking. If he did not find the yellow-haired angel by the following sunset, he would quit. No one could escape him in this area; of that he was sure. The only thing to be said if he did not find her was that she had somehow grown wings and flown away.

He looked for a place where a nest could be built. It would have to be high enough so that a leopard coming up after him would make enough noise to wake him. It had to be a meeting-place of trunk and branch broad enough to lay a platform of broken limbs, twigs, and leaves. He would get rained on and be cold, but he could endure that.

He found the place and built the nest and, just before dusk, shot a monkey. After taking it about a half mile from his nest, he skinned it, cut the head and hands, feet and tail off. He disemboweled the monkey, making sure he did not cut the entrails open. Then he built a small fire quickly and stuck the body out over the fire on a green stick. It was very rare meat, still bloody. The leopards were prowling now, and while they were not likely to attack him under ordinary circumstances, the odor of monkey blood might be too much for them. Moreover, there were man-eating leopards in the area of the Wantso village. It was possible they were hunting this area, although again it was not likely. The big cats had their own territories, their own circuits, and the man-eaters usually did not come up this way.

They were creatures of habit, like human beings, but, also like human beings, they could not always be relied upon to follow their habits.

He ate quickly, tearing off big chunks, chewing them a few times, and swallowing them with loud gulps. He returned to the nest, stopping every few steps to listen and look intently. Once something moved in the shadows, causing him to freeze with his spear ready. Then the bulk grunted, after which something squealed. It was a river hog with some young.

He fell asleep quickly and dreamed of a leopard pacing back and forth beneath the tree and rearing up now and then to sharpen its claws on the bark. It glared up at him with yellow-green eyes so fierce and bright they looked as if they had once seen God and now carried some memory of the glory. The leopard, fluid rosettes and a long thick tail, prowled back and forth, and looked up at him and pulled its lips back to show sharp, yellow teeth.

He shivered with excitement and the beauty of the animal.

Smooth, tawny beast with black rosettes and furry, white belly. Dressed to kill. Glory come to rip you apart, to lick your flesh and blood with that red, rasping tongue.

Suddenly, the leopard was on a branch above him and crouching before it leaped. He raised his spear and thrust at the fang-filled yawn. The flint tip went through the spotted head without harming it, and then the beast drew in on itself, like shadows before light, the flesh disappearing. The skull of the leopard, hanging in the air, became a human skull. It grinned at him. Its sockets were not empty; pale blue eyes glared from them at him. Where had he seen those eyes before?

He did not know, but they angered him. He raised a fist—the spear was gone—and he struck out. The skull faded. And Ras saw on the ground the carcass of a goat. It was the same goat he had seen several days before. It had been half-hidden in a bush, where a large male leopard hunched over it and ate the entrails he had ripped out from the belly.

Now, as Ras watched the goat, it swelled with the gas of putrefaction. Worms crawled out of it, and then little things, hopping things. These were tiny black men with four crocodile legs and with heads as big as their bodies. The heads were hideous; the mouths ran all the way to the back of the neck and were filled with many rows of sharp, white teeth.

The heads were those of Guluba, the spirit who brings death to the Wantso.

The blue-eyed skull had returned. "Out of death, more life," it chanted in Wantso.

The heads of the tiny hopping things also chanted. "And out of life, more death."

They swarmed over Ras; their little paws were cold. Ras knew they were going to eat him. He sprang upward to shake them off.

Now he was awake, the dream flowing off him as if it were water draining away as he walked out of the lake after swimming. But the many tiny cold paws were no dream. On every side of him, above and below—and on him—were hundreds of tree frogs. A river of flesh, they poured over the tree, over his nest, over him.

Ras was neither frightened nor repulsed. He endured their passage until the last of the horde had hopped onto and then off him. The night sky was cloudless and moonful. Light seemed to fall like a cataract through the leaves or like a cloud of shiny, gray-yellow butterflies. The light bounced off the minute creatures, soundless in their intent progress on a goal only they—and perhaps not they —knew. The only noise they made was the rustling of the leaves disturbed by their hopping. In the daylight, Ras knew, the tree frogs would have been a pale green except for their suckered paws, which were bark brown.

Finally the rustling was gone. He was alone. He lay back down and tried to sleep but could not. He sat up and fished around in the antelope-hide bag and brought out flint chisels, gougers, and a block of fine-textured, light-pink wood of a medium hardness. He worked on the block until it brought forth what he had conceived. When the *wolf's-tail*, the false dawn, grayed the night, he was done. The block had become his compression of the nightmare. It was a leopard's skull with flowers growing out of the eye sockets.

He turned it over and over and back and forth and finally said, "Not bad, but not good." He rose, stretched, and looked out, and there, caught in the branches of a bush about fifty yards away, almost hidden by the trunk of a tree, was a piece of paper. It had not been there when he had first climbed the tree; it must have blown

there during the night. No, there had been no wind; he
had just not seen it, because it had been too dark.

After scrutinizing the area to make sure that nothing
dangerous was close—nothing large and dangerous, anyway; the small dangers would have to be chanced—he
climbed down and cautiously approached the paper. He
had seen paper before, and this seemed harmless, but the
fact that it came from the Bird of God gave it a possibility of something dreadful.

Slowly, he extended his hand to it, touched it, withdrew the hand, and then, after looking quickly upward
to make sure that God had not been summoned by this
touching of His possession and was about to catch him
off guard, he pulled the paper loose from the barky em-
brace.

It was torn around the sides and three places elsewhere, but he could read most of it. The top printing
was –24–, which he supposed was the number of the page
of the book in which the sheet had been.

The first died of pneumonia! The second became
an idiot! Or as good as an idiot! What a waste,
what a tragedy! All my money, time, thought, hope-
fulness, and tremendous effort had been lost, spent
to no avail. But no! I had not totally wasted my time,
for I had learned much. After being plunged into
the blackest of despairs for a long time, almost, but
not quite, on the point of giving up, I finally recovered my spirits. The same courage and persever-
ance that had enabled me to come up as a penniless
immigrant from America during the depths of the
depression to attain one of the largest fortunes in
South Africa now kept me from abandoning my
project, so dear to me for so many years, so important not only to me but to the world, the world
which would have been horrified if it had known
but will some day honor me for this.

Fortunately, the second failure had a younger
brother, born six years later, and only three months
old when I began to plan again. This time I made
the arrangements for securing him through entirely
different channels, since the previous agents had tried
to blackmail me. They paid for their mistakes. I
made sure they would not try such treachery on me
or on anyone ever again. Word went through the
grapevine about them, and I was sure that nobody
would try that dastardly trick again. The name of

Ras did not understand much of the printing. There were a number of words he had not encountered. Pneumonia, tragedy, money, avail, penniless immigrant, America, South Africa, and many others. Yusufu might be able to explain their meanings.

He folded the sheet and put it in his antelope-hide bag. After finishing the monkey, he threw the bones down onto the ground, and then climbed down and resumed his search. By noon he had found nothing. There was no sign of the yellow-haired angel or of the stiff-winged bird, which should have fallen close to the burning Bird of God.

He returned to the dead Bird. The flames were burned out now, and the ashes and the bones had cooled off. He touched various parts of it and was surprised. So the Bird had bones made of the same stuff as his knife. Some thought about this convinced him that a bird made by Igziyabher was just as likely to have metal bones as bone bones. After all, Igziyabher had made his knife. According to Mariyam, a knife was what was left after a lightning stroke hit the ground. Igziyabher dealt with metal, and He had fashioned this Bird, so why wouldn't He give the Bird metal bones? Or make it entirely out of metal, since it was evident that the Bird had no flesh, was, in fact, all bones?

It was then that Ras began to wonder if Igziyabher had not been experimenting when He made the first creatures and, after some thought, had decided that all-bone creatures were superior to those of flesh and bone. Perhaps. But from the viewpoint of the creature itself, flesh was superior. How much could an all-bone being *feel?*

As he examined the remnants of the Bird, he heard the faint chuttering. For a few seconds he crouched in bewilderment and fear. There was another Bird coming!

Then he disappeared into the jungle, where he hid beneath a bush. Presently another Bird, just like the first, rode into the sky and hovered about fifty feet above the dead one. He could see that there were two angels—or men—in the belly of this one, and they wore masks. He hoped that they would land to investigate, but the Bird began to cast back and forth above the jungle, as if the angels in it were searching for those who had been in the dead Bird. And, of course, they must be looking for the yellow-haired angel.

After a while the Bird went northward, presumably

back to its nest on top of the pillar of black stone in the middle of the lake.

Ras spent some more time going over the area that had been covered by the ants. He found the mud-prints of the angel and followed them, but they curved around until they came to the bank of the creek. Here they disappeared. There were none on the other side. She could have waded up- or downstream for some distance, and so he went upstream for several miles, looking on both sides, and then downstream for the same distance from the point where the prints ceased. He had no luck.

Her apparent soaring into the sky, combined with his desire to have Yusufu interpret the full meaning of the sheet, finally decided him to return home. He waded back up the stream for many miles, because it was the easiest way to travel for a while. Then he cut across the land toward the river, which would lead him to the foot of the cataracts. Near them was a trail up the cliffs to the plateau. It was not recognizable to anybody besides him as a trail. Its identity as a path consisted in his knowing exactly where to go and when to go, what toeholds and handholds existed, what slivers of ledges, what slight projections and recesses. Where a stranger would have taken hours finding the correct places on which to get up, he could scale the five hundred or so feet within ten minutes, if he felt like doing it.

Today he felt like it, and so he was soon on the lip of the plateau. The ground from here sloped generally upward, ending nine miles to the north against the glossy black wall. The black wall rose straight up for many thousands of feet, as if the angry hand of God was held out, black, wrathful palms vertical, and saying, "Not one step more!"

Mariyam had said, many times, that the black cliffs were the limits of the world. The sky, which was actually a blue extension of the cliffs, formed a ceiling over the world. The sun climbed up the ceiling every day, just as a fly or lizard could climb up the walls and across the ceiling of their hut, and the sun went into a tunnel in the west and traveled underground through the hole in the stone of the world, and he got to the end of the tunnel just at daybreak.

The sun, Sehay in Amharic, was, in some as yet undefined way, also Igziyabher. Battered by Ras's questions, Mariyam said that it was a flaming bird on which Igziyabher sometimes rode. Ras had managed to see the sun when it was low on the horizon of the cliff tops and other times through fog, and he thought that the sun looked more like a flaming egg than a bird. This was when Mariyam had further confused him by saying that the bird had not hatched yet, but when it did, there was no telling what horrors might result. Perhaps the world might burn up.

Ras might have been more scared by her story if Yusufu had not yelled at her to quit telling the boy such lies.

Where the plateau ended in the drop-off, the distance from west wall to east wall was about ten miles. That same length was maintained as the walls marched northward until near the end, where the walls moved in closer to each other and thus made the north wall about seven miles across.

The jungle started up again close to the edge of the plateau and continued for three miles through hilly and sometimes rough country. Then a plain with many scattered trees ran for three miles. The land became suddenly higher here, and the trees more numerous but not enough to earn the name of jungle. The vegetation in the hills near the cliffs was jungly, however, and it was here that the gorilla bands were usually found.

From the place where black stone met blue sky, three broad cataracts fell. These were along the northwest side, and they fell into the lake, which was three miles broad along the foot of the cliff but narrowed to two miles of breadth along its southern shore. Three creeks flowed out from the south border of the lake and came close to each other after many windings to the edge of the plateau. They fell side by side to form the headwaters of the river at the bottom of the plateau.

Ras followed a deer trail through the jungle and then was on the plain. Here, at various distances, were small groups of elephants, a family of buffalo, antelope, and some wart hogs. In the distance, a jackal yapped. There was not much game on the plains, which were about five miles across and three miles deep. But it was increasing, because most of the leopards had been killed by Ras. He and Yusufu hunted the plains for meat, but they did not kill as much as the leopards had, who had been getting too numerous. Janhoy, the lion, hunted here, too, but he did not catch much. He needed fellow hunters to run the prey toward him, and it was only occasionally that Ras went with him.

Once out of the jungle, Ras saw the top of the stone pillar that thrust up from the middle of the lake. As Ras passed across the plain and then climbed up the steepness leading to the forest land, he saw the pillar rising up. When he got through the trees of the forest and came out upon the comparatively clear land by the shore of the lake, he saw it in its fullness.

It was glossy and black and twisted. It was roughly four-cornered and did not rise straight but leaned out a little this way and then curved back in and began to lean out a little the other way and so on up to the top, which was at least a thousand feet from the surface of the lake.

Even when Ras had been a very little child, he had thought that this torque of stone was strange, if not sinister. Why was it alone? Why were there no other structures of rock to break the otherwise smooth lake? What had made the stone spurt up from the water and then freeze? It seemed to him that something had given way to a tremendous pressure against the crust of the world at the bottom of the lake. The stone had been so hot it was liquid, and it had spurted upward to reach so high, and then the stone had cooled and so stopped—soaring forever.

And at some time in the dawn of life, the Bird of God had come to build a nest on its top.

Ras walked from the southeast corner of the lake northward along the eastern beach until he came to the still-blackened stones that marked where the cabin had once stood. From here he turned to the east, went up the easily sloping hill covered with tall grass, and so into the forest. The trees here were mainly tall and thick-trunked with few, but broad and flat-topped, branches that extended far out. The leaves were no larger than his hand, almost square, curving in slightly at the ends, which formed a double tip. The smaller leaf-bearing branches were numerous, however, so that the upper part of the trees were fat with green. Once a year, the *thimato* trees grew white, stiff, seven-petaled flowers and large, triangular, flattened-out nuts with shiny black cases.

The trees also grew thousands of many-shaped and many-colored birds and monkeys and other creatures the year around. The chattering, squeaking, squawking, whistling, clacking, chirping, hooting, whinnying, cawing, grunting, yaayaaing, drumming, bugling, and so forth went on loudly during the day and somewhat less noisily at night. Ras's earliest memories were of this somehow tuneful and pleasing racket.

He looked upward and grinned at familiar figures. Some of the monkeys came down and ran up to him

but did not stay with him long, since he had no food
for them. The brush beneath the trees was moderately
heavy, far from being a jungle, because the closeness of
the trees, their binding together with many parasitical
python-thick vines, and the meeting of branches of neigh-
boring trees, darkened the earth beneath and killed all
but the lucky and the hardiest. Except for several hours
during noon, the space beneath the trees was gloomy.

But in the upper parts, the sun penetrated more easily,
and here the birds and animals thronged. And here, at
least seventy-five feet up, was set a house for Mariyam,
Yusufu, and Ras. It was on a platform of split logs on
two great branches that grew outward at just the right
angle for placement of a platform. The house, of bamboo brought down from the hills, was round, with a conical roof of elephant's-ear leaves and bamboo understruc-
ture, and had three doors, two windows, and three rooms.
There was enough space between the walls of the house
and the edge of the platform to form a wide veranda
that completely circled the house. The veranda had a
bamboo fence along its outer edge, and Ras remembered
when he was first held by Mariyam and allowed to peer
over the fence into what seemed then an interestingly
vast distance to the ground.

There were three ways to get up to the house. One
was to climb up the wooden rungs nailed into the trunk.
The second was to use the lift, which could be let down
or hauled up by ropes and complicated tackle. The third
was to climb hand over hand up a ladder of rope. The
last two required so much muscle work (not to mention
the balkiness of the lift), that they were seldom used to
get up, although they were handy in getting down.

When Ras had been young, only this house had existed.
But five years ago, the aging Yusufu and Mariyam had
decided that it was too inconvenient and demanding to
go up and down the ladder or the lift a dozen times a
day. So they had built another house, almost a duplicate,
directly below. The tree house was used mainly during
the night.

Several monkeys sat on the roof or the veranda. A
female chimpanzee slept on top of a table on the veranda.
A pangolin, a scaly-armored anteater, prowled around
the base of the house. The shrill voices of Mariyam and
Yusufu reached him even at this distance. He frowned
and felt a roiling in the pit of his stomach. There were
times when he was amused by their quarreling and bick-

ering, but usually he felt disturbed, ill at ease, and often angry with them.

They had been always gentle and loving and happy-voiced when he was young, or so it seemed to him. But as the years went by, as their companions, the other adults, died, and they were left alone with each other, they seemed to find it more difficult to endure each other. Ras could understand this somewhat. But when they had a third person to talk to, they lessened their arguments only slightly. Often, they both turned on him when he entered. It seemed that they were, somehow, blaming him for their being in this predicament, but what the predicament was, they would not, or could not, explain.

There were other things he did not understand about them.

"You think you're not an ape?" Yusufu would say. Yusufu, tiny man with the big head, long body, and short, bowed legs, legs not much longer than Ras's arm from elbow to wrist, would reach up to Ras. His woolly, white hair and frizzly, white beard, brown-skinned, smudged face with pushed-in nose and nostrils like a gorilla's, his thick lips (not as thick as the Wantsos) would rise as high as tiptoes would carry them.

"Bend down, son of a camel," he would growl. "Bend over, djinn, so that I, your father, begetter of a gorilla, to my everlasting shame, may switch you properly and painfully and so teach you better manners."

Ras would remain upright. He would grin down at him. Yusufu, dark face twisted, beard flying, would jump up and down. He would curse in Swahili, Arabic, English, and Amharic.

"Must I punish you, O *Lord* Tyger, whip you into the trees you love so much, like the true monkey you are? Bend down; do as I, your father and disposer of your body, command you. O droppings of a camel, accidentally formed as a man, bend down!"

"What is a camel?" Ras would say, although Yusufu had described the beast to him many times.

"It is your true father, that son of Shaitan, that stinking, spitting, humped thinker of evil thoughts! And you, your father was a camel and your mother was an ape!"

"But you once told me you were my father and that you were an ape!" Ras would say.

"And he is an ape!" Mariyam would scream. "But he is not your true father! He is your stepfather, and he would do well to remember that! That monster hatched from a raven's egg!"

The two seemed lately to act as if they blamed him for being in this world. What was wrong with this world? Where else could they be?

Looking past the hut, through the openings between the branches of the trees of the forest, he could see the black cliffs that walled the world.

"Black as the tongue of the devil," Mariyam had said of them.

"Black as a vulture's anus," Yusufu had said. And in saying this, both revealed the cast of their minds and the course of their speech.

"Six thousand feet straight up," Yusufu had said in answer to Ras's question.

"Feet?"

How long was a foot? Yusufu said it was as long as one of Ras's feet. But Ras remembered that his feet had been shorter at one time.

"A child's foot?" he had said.

"O my beloved, banana of my eye," Yusufu had said. "You are teasing me, an old man with white hairs and many wrinkles, gotten from worrying over you. Do not mock me or I will strip the skin off you and make from the skin a whip to whip you to death."

"What is a foot?" Ras had said. "I know how long my feet are now. But I am growing. What if I keep on growing, and the walls of the world, now six thousand feet, become only half as much? What if I grow, the world shrink, and I become as tall as the pillar in the middle of the lake?"

Yusufu would laugh at this picture, and he would be happy for a while.

Ras stopped when he was fifty feet from the house and hallooed, since it would be dangerous to burst into the house on Yusufu, who was nervous and might throw his knife before he realized at whom he was throwing it.

The quarreling voices stopped, and then the door swung open and Mariyam ran out. Yusufu followed her. Mariyam's head was no higher than Ras's hip. Her head was huge in proportion to her body, and her legs were short and bandy. She wore a white robe that came to her calves. She was smiling and weeping at the same time. He took her in his arms and lifted her up and cuddled her while she kissed him and her tears were smeared over his face.

"Ah, son, I thought that truly I would never see you again!"

Mariyam always said this if he were gone for more

than a day, and while she did not fully mean it, yet her words did mean that she had missed him. He had never tired of receiving this greeting.

Finally, he put her down and patted her white, black-speckled head and waited for the scolding that always came because he had grieved her by staying away so long.

Yusufu, who was perhaps an inch taller than his wife, whose head-hair was all white and whose long beard was gray with black threads, waddled on stubby, curved legs to Ras and said, "Bend down, you taller-than-an-ostrich, that you may kiss me as a respectful son does his father."

Ras did so, and the old man kissed him on the lips in return.

Ras waited until they had entered the house, where a fire burned in a mortared-stone fireplace in the middle of the room. The room had many odors: monkeys, monkey excrement not yet removed, birds and bird excrement, a sweat-soaked shirt of Yusufu's overdue for washing, and, most powerful, the odor of smoke. The chimney of the fireplace was faulty, and any adverse breeze was likely to blow down the chimney and spread smoke around the room. One of Ras's earliest memories was of Mariyam nagging at Yusufu to repair the chimney and Yusufu replying that he would certainly do so when the weather permitted. When Ras was older, he had offered many times to repair or completely rebuild the fireplace and chimney. Yusufu had resented the implication that he would never do the job. No, by Allah, he would get the work done at the first chance. But he never did.

Ras coughed and then said, "Look!" and pulled the letter from the antelope-hide bag. Mariyam and Yusufu grayed under their dark skins, but their faces expressed only puzzlement. Mariyam said that she could not read the writing. Yusufu took a long time going over the letter and then said that most of the words were unknown to him.

Ras felt that Yusufu was acting. His comments and his facial expressions had something controlled about them. And Mariyam's reactions had also been more restrained than they should have been. Both were too silent.

Ras became angry and said that they knew much more than they were telling him. They became indignant and began to shout abuse. They were overacting. But nothing he could say could get them to admit anything. Mariyam said that she was of the opinion that the paper was a letter from Igziyabher, that is, a message, to the Virgin of the Moon, or perhaps Igziyabher was writing the story of the history of the world from creation to the present.

"Why don't you ask me where I got the letter?" Ras shouted. "Isn't it strange that that was not the first thing you asked me about it?"

Neither of the two would admit that this was strange. Nor did they then ask him where it came from. Nevertheless, Ras told them about the stiff-winged bird, its fiery encounter with the Bird of God, the yellow-haired creature, and the dead brown man.

Mariyam cried, "Of course, the yellow-haired thing was a demon! She was flying in a demonic bird, one of Satan's, and so attacked the Bird of God! The dead man must be one of her fellow demons, struck down by Igziyabher!"

"You have said many times that Igziyabher is all-powerful," Ras said. "How, then, could the bird of Satan take the Bird of God along with it in its fall? And why did not Igziyabher kill the yellow-haired demon, too, if He killed the brown one?"

"Who knows why Igziyabher does this or does that?" Mariyam said. "His ways are many and devious and ones that we, his creatures, cannot understand. But truly I am happy that you did not come across the yellow-haired demon, because she would have destroyed you or, worse, taken you back to hell with her!"

"How do you know that the demon is a she?" Ras said.

Mariyam stuttered for a minute and then said, "Because it is likely that Satan would have sent a female demon to entice you the more easily to hell."

Ras had always been more curious than frightened by her stories of devils and Satan and hell in the cave at the river's end. Besides, he now had heard the stories of the evil spirits of the Wantso and of the Sharrikt, and no one of the three versions agreed with any other, yet the Wantso and Gilluk, the Sharrikt king, had been as convinced as Mariyam that their stories were the truth.

That Yusufu and Mariyam did not press him for details was proof that they were concealing knowledge from him. Raging, repressing the desire to shake the truth out of them, he left the house with a mighty slam of the door behind him. He strode through the forest and then along the lake shore for hours. Finally, he realized that he had wasted his time by coming home. He would have to return to the area into which the yellow-haired being had fallen and search for her.

That, however, would be done later. In three days, Wilida would be let out of her cage by Bigagi, who would conduct her over the bridge to the village, where the all-day wedding ceremony would start. Ras would sneak onto the islet late tomorrow night and take Wilida away. When he had her safely hidden away, he would take up the search for the angel or demon or whatever she was.

It was an hour before dark when he came back to the house. Mariyam was baking bread in the brick oven on the veranda. Yusufu walked in a few minutes later with a hare he had killed with an arrow. Both his parents greeted him, but they were unusually quiet. Ras wanted to talk, but forced himself to be silent. After a while, Mariyam and Yusufu became nervous and started talking about this and that, quarreling over trifles but saying nothing about the letter or the two birds or the yellow-haired creature.

CHAPTER 6

LIGHTNING TURNS TO STONE

—AND A KNIFE

He watched Mariyam bring a few glowing coals of wood from the hut. She started a fire in the brazier on the veranda and stuck the hare on a rod of iron and set it over the fire.

Iron, Ras thought. Where had she gotten iron? As far back as he could remember, the brazier and other articles of iron had been here. But not until recently had he questioned their origin.

"What did you eat?" Mariyam said.

"Some pig that I killed several days ago. And a tree rat I caught yesterday."

Mariyam and Yusufu looked disgusted. Mariyam, he knew, did not care about the pig, but she was upset about the rat. Yusufu was sickened by the thought of eating either animal.

And that was strange, strange. When he was a child, he had been encouraged to eat anything that could be eaten: worms, spiders, bamboo shoots, mice, everything except carrion. Yet his parents had refused to eat much of what he ate. They had managed to conceal their disgust then, or else he had not noticed it. But he was seeing much now that he had taken for granted then.

"I am going swimming," he said suddenly. "Maybe I'll go fishing. I'll be back in time to eat."

They did not object. He walked away but turned once to look back. They were squatting on the veranda, face to face, their noses almost touching, their mouths working, their hands flying. So, they were even more upset than he; yet, for some reason, they had not wanted him to know. His story and the letter had disturbed them.

Ras shrugged and walked on through the gloom of the great trees and the shriek of monkeys and birds. At the lake, he swam for a few minutes. When he came out of the water, he saw Kebbede, a chimpanzee, running off with his leopardskin belt with the sheathed knife. He gave chase, but the chimpanzee, hooting madly, scampered up a tree and became lost in the higher levels of the forest. All Ras could do was to howl curses and promise vengeance in many languages but mostly in Arabic. This had a vast and beautiful range of oaths, obscenities, exquisitely described tortures, and insults.

When he returned to the house, he told his parents what had happened. Mariyam said that, doubtless, Igziyabher would furnish His son with another just like the one stolen. Perhaps very soon, since clouds were forming. Igziyabher was wrathful about something, and when He became angry, He sweated clouds and, after a while, cursed thunder and then threw down His knives, which looked like lightning while descending.

Before sundown, the clouds, big-browed, black, and swirling, sped over the western edge of the mountains, bringing with them the chill of the cold stone sky. Ras, his parents, and the animals huddled around the central brick fireplace. They coughed when the wind blew down the chimney and spread the smoke through the hut. Yusufu hacked and swore; he spat in the fire, and the odor of burning saliva mingled with that of the smoke.

Ras was not as cold as the two old ones, since he had been used to sleeping outdoors even in winter with little covering. But he was shaking inwardly; the ice of the unknown and the threatening future was a lump in his belly.

"Where do the knives come from?" he said suddenly.

Yusufu growled and said, "We have told that tale a thousand of a thousand times, O witless."

"A thousand of a thousand lies," Ras said. He looked through the smoke at the old man's reddened and weeping eyes. "If the Devil is the Father of Lies, you are the Devil."

"And you are an impertinent, ungrateful son. If you were not such an elephant, and I so enfeebled by my years and by the sickness brought about by worrying over you,

I would thrash you until you howled louder than the storm."

The wind increased until it was a shrilling. Thunder boomed as if great pieces of the cliffs were falling off. Lightning smashed deafeningly nearby, and the smoky air was whitened. All three jumped.

Ras said with unconcealed sarcasm, "O mother, tell me again the story of how Igziyabher hurls knives to the earth, and every knife is a lightning stroke."

Mariyam looked up at him through the smoke with misery on her face. "O son, it is true. Would I, your mother, lie to you? When it storms, it is because Igziyabher is wrathful. He rages because His creations have been sinful, and He wishes to frighten them back into a state of grace. And sometimes He kills the especially sinful as an example to the others.

"You, my son, and it grieves me to say it, have been lying with the black women of the Wantso. Igziyabher does not like this."

Ras, panting with repressed rage, stood up, looked around, and then kicked the door with the flat of his foot so hard that the bamboo bar securing it broke. The door banged open outward. The wind and rain rushed in. Lightning exploded and whitened the air. Yusufu and Mariyam yelled in terror.

"I haven't been evil!" Ras shouted. "What have I done that nobody else does? Why should I suffer when Yusufu and the Wantso men and every male beast in the world have a female? Why?"

He shook his fist at the howling blackness outside. Mariyam screamed and ran to him and wrapped her tiny arms around his thigh.

"Igziyabher is saving a white woman for you! He wants you to take to wife a woman of your own kind. That is why He forbids you to whore around with those blacks!"

"And how do you know that Igziyabher has a white woman for me?" he bellowed. "Does He whisper His secrets to you?"

Mariyam, her brown, eaglish face upturned, clung fiercely to his leg.

"Trust me, my son! I know!"

"How do you know? When have you talked to Him?"

Tears ran down her cheeks, and she said, "Believe me, my son, I know!"

"Let loose of me, mother! I am going out there where He can see me, and I will dare Him to strike me! I haven't been evil! He is evil, because He wants to kill me for doing what He made me do."

Mariyam shrieked, released her hold, stepped back, and held her ears.

"I won't listen to such talk! He will kill you!"

Yusufu took a long drink from a goatskin bag. He wiped his lips and growled, "Let the simpleton go out and get struck down, Mariyam. It won't be your fault."

He took another drink of the wine, wiped his lips with the back of his hand, belched, and said, "It won't be Igziyabher's doing, either, if Ras gets killed. It'll be nothing but an accident caused by his foolishness."

"Shut your mouth, you . . . !" Mariyam yelled, but Ras did not hear the rest. He ran out into the rain and wind. He ran and ran toward the hills, slipping many times on the wet grass or mud and almost falling. By the frequent flashes of lightning, he could see where he was going and so avoid most of the obstacles, the bushes, fallen trees, and the creek. Up the hill he charged, up the slope into the jungle, where the gorillas lived.

"Strike me, you big hyena up there!" he screamed as he shook his fist. "Hurl your knives of fire; see if you can stab me with hot white death!"

On and up he ran, slowed down now by the steepness and the slipperiness of the hill. Several times he went down to his knees or fell on his chest, but, each time, he leaped up and charged on.

"I'm not afraid of you! Mariyam, my mother, has tried to make me scared of you! But I don't scare! Mother, did I say? That brown, misshapen, little thing is not my mother! She lied when she told me she was an ape, and she lied when she told me she was my mother!

"How could I, I, come out of a thing like her! I am not her son!"

He stopped to raise both hands, more in question than in defiance.

"Whose son, then, am I?"

It was a strange thing that followed. He should have been knocked unconscious instantly. He should have had no idea of what struck him.

But, afterward, he swore that all did not become black and empty. Not for a part of a second, anyway.

The world became luminous. He was in the heart of fire. Moreover, the arms held upward became full of light. He could see through their skin and to the bones. He was a skeleton fleshed in flame.

Lightning enveloped him, danced down the tree trunk

on his right, undulated along the ground, slithered down a hole in the ground as if it were a snake.

A small globe of fire—ember of the lightning—was somewhere inside him. The globe expanded, and he could see that part of the world he remembered best inside its glow. But it was very tiny. As if the world had been re-created inside his head. There, three threads: the cataracts. A blue smudge: the lake. Rearing out of the lake, like the outstretched arm of a black giant going down for the last time; the pillar. By the lake shore, the old cabin. Dancing around it, seven minute and naked black figures.

These would be Mariyam, Yusufu, Abdul, Ibrahimu, Sara, Yohannis, and Kokeb. He remembered Kokeb well, but the others, except for his parents, of course, he remembered dimly. Now many things about them came back.

Abdul had died of pneumonia. Sara had been murdered by Ibrahimu, who had cut his own throat afterward. Yohannis had drowned in the lake. Kokeb had disappeared when Ras was nine. Supposedly, a leopard had carried him off.

Now they danced around the glare inside Ras, leaped, cavorted, ran on all fours sometimes like the apes they had said they were. Dance, little black apes, dance!

He saw himself, a tiny boy, the sun flashing whitely off him. He was throwing knives, hour after hour. He was shooting arrows; he was flipping into the air backward, walking on a tightrope, swallowing fire, doing all the tricks the little men and women knew so well and insisted that he know also. The globe of fire grew even more swiftly. Now he saw the band of gorillas with whom he and his parents and Kokeb had sometimes lived. Now he was climbing the trees, speeding along branches, leaping like a young gorilla, he was better at this than the hairy, long-armed teachers, agile, sure, unafraid. And he was happy because of his superiority at this.

For a long time, he had been convinced that he was a gorilla freak, hairless and funny-faced and weak and inferior except in racing through the trees. And, of course, so much more intelligent!

The fiery ball rushed up from him at him. It was a big heart of white pushing through flesh of black. It drove back the shadows within him and outside him.

From the top of the pillar rose the big Bird, screaming and squawking. God, Igziyabher, sat on its back. God was a white man. Hence, he looked much like Ras himself. But his face, when it got closer, was vague and kept changing shape.

Then two faces floated by Igziyabher's. One was a young white man who had Ras's face. The other was a young white woman who had Ras's face.

Seeing them, he remembered that he had dreamed of these faces when he had been much younger.

When he awoke, he could move only his eyelids. It was dawn; the sky was blue above and yellow-red on the lower sides. He was lying on his back on the hillside and must have spun around before falling, because he was now looking down the hill. Water dripped from the branch above and fell a few inches from his head. A small, yellow bird with scarlet tail feathers passed overhead. Something grunted nearby.

He was cold, yet he could feel nothing outside his skin. The cold moved from within. The ball of fire had become cold, heavy stone and was rolling through the rut of his body.

He tried to struggle, to break loose from the chains of himself, but he could not move. He grew afraid, but after a while he became angry. The cold within became heat. Who had done this to him? Igziyabher?

"You have no right to do this to me!" he shouted silently. "What have I done to you? Nothing! Oh, if only I could get my hands on you! I'd kill you!"

The fury closed to a small, hot fist for a while. Feeding on its warmth, he studied his situation as best he could. By moving his eyes he could see the top of the pillar above the trees. Also, he could see part of the hillside and the country beyond that was not hidden by the trees and the bamboo.

Nothing moved except the leaves. He hoped he would see nothing else move. Unless it would be his parents looking for him. But why should they? He went away whenever he felt like it and returned when he felt like it. They would think that he was off on an adventure or perhaps punishing them by staying away.

However, they could be worried because of the lightning and might come looking for him.

Something grunted near him, and he was startled inwardly, but outwardly was as calm as a rock. Had he heard a pig? He hoped not, although it would not make much difference if he stayed out here long. Soon enough a jackal, a leopard, or ants would come along.

A shadow fell on him. It was followed immediately by a long-legged bird, five feet high at the shoulder, with blackish wings and a white lower tail. The neck was long; the head, naked; the bill, long and sharp. It stank of excrement and long-dead flesh; it strutted as if it were all-important.

Its bearing was not incongruous. Eaters of carrion were important.

"Oh, marabou," Ras said soundlessly. "I am not yet carrion! But if someone who loves me does not come soon, I will be carrion."

Oh, God! he thought. I am buried in my own flesh!

He wanted to scream. If only he could, he might frighten it off for a while. Only a little while. Then it would come back. Those dead eyes, dead from having seen so much death, would soon be looking down that long, sharp beak at his own eyes. The beak would stab down, and one of his eyes would be plucked out.

With the other eye, he would be able to see the big head on the long neck rise, the bill tip upward so that the marabou could swallow. Then the dead eyes looking at him, then looking around quickly, because the marabou had enemies, too. Then, a flashing stab, and the knifelike beak would be the last thing he would see in this world. But it would not be the last thing he would feel.

The marabou gave a harsh sound and lurched away, its wings half spread. Another shadow fell on his face. The caster of blackness had a black face. Its nose was two enormous nostrils, like two blind eyes. The jaws thrust out, and the open lips revealed large, yellow canines. Below the bulge of bone covered by coarse hair were two large, russet eyes.

"Nigus!" Ras tried to say. "Nigus! Help me!"

Nigus, Amharic for emperor, was Ras's name for the gorilla. The five-hundred-pound monster was chief of the little band now, but he had been Ras's playmate eight years before. He had been a good-tempered little fellow. Ras had used to wrestle with him all day long and chase him around or be chased. But one day, Ras, leaping upon Nigus from ambush and roaring like a leopard, had been astonished when Nigus, instead of screaming and running away, had turned on him. A big scar on Ras's shoulder would always show how deep a startled gorilla could bite.

Nigus grunted and bent over to look into Ras's eyes. His breath was pleasant with bamboo shoots. He passed a huge, wrinkled, black thumb over Ras's eyes, pushing them in a little, and then rocked Ras back and forth as if Ras were a log.

"Do something!" Ras tried to shout. "Go after Yusufu and Mariyam!"

But he knew that even if he could voice his desperation, he could not make Nigus understand. And even if he could understand, he probably would not have gone for help. He tolerated Ras now, and that was all.

"You ungrateful mass of brainless hair!" Ras thought. "I saved you from a leopard only two years ago. I scared it off. If it weren't for me, you'd be scattered bones under a tree. Help me!"

Nigus moaned, and Ras wondered if he was mourning his death or just puzzling over the mystery of death. If so, he was not much disturbed. Presently, his head moved out of sight and the sound of his jaws vigorously chewing, of his lips smacking, came to Ras.

Other sounds told Ras that there was more than one gorilla nearby. There were muffled grunts, chomp-chomps, a belch. Once, slapping of open palms on a great chest.

Then, he heard a yap-yapping that thrust cold through him.

He waited, because there was nothing else he could do. The jackals would be on him in a minute. They would not be scared off by the presence of the gorillas. He had seen jackals run in behind a leopard over his kill, tear off a strip of meat, and run away just out of reach of slashing claws. They were not cowards; they went after what they wanted.

Suddenly, another face was above his, and he felt the pressure of two paws. A brownish, sharp-snouted head was grinning down at him, the tongue hanging out of one side of the mouth. Two bright, black eyes looked into his, and he smelled the sharp stink emanated by the gland at the base of the jackal's tail.

Ras wished he could scream. He would feel better, if only briefly so, if he could utter some of his desperation.

At this moment, and the thought seemed irrelevant, he became aware that he could feel the paws of the jackal. Some of his senses were returning to him.

There was a roar. The ground under him trembled. The sharp face disappeared with a yelp and a bark; a bushy tail flicked over his face as the jackal whirled and ran.

A leopard? No, the roar had been too deep, unless it had been an unusually large cat. Whatever it was, it had frightened not only the jackals but the gorillas. They screamed, and the bamboos broke under their stampede. Nigus' huge, reddish body soared over Ras.

Janhoy! he thought. Another face appeared. It was topped by a tangled, thorn-studded mass of brown-yellow hair. Below the mane were two large ears, a pair of large, golden eyes, and a bulbous nose. And the biggest, sharpest teeth in the world.

"Janhoy!" Ras tried to say. Tears ran down his cheek, and even in the ecstasy of relief he noted that he could feel them. Immediately after, the lion put both paws on Ras's chest, and the great weight pressed him.

His throat was full of stopped-up words. "Janhoy! Go home! Get my parents!"

The beast moaned and licked his face, and Ras was almost sorry that he could feel. The tongue rasped him; if Janhoy kept up the licking, the tongue would soon wear the skin off his face.

A tremendous purr vibrated Janhoy and was transmitted through Ras.

"Don't be so happy, you bumbling idiot!" Ras thought. "Do something! Oh, you brainless cat, you big-nosed lack-of-wits!"

But he was happy in his anger. At least, nothing was going to eat him while Janhoy stayed with him. But how long would he remain here?

The lion rubbed his big head against Ras. He quit purring and stood up and whined and extended one paw to shake Ras. Getting no response, he licked Ras on the chest.

"He's trying to dig me up out of my own body," Ras thought. "Keep it up, Janhoy, and soon I'll be able to spring free of my flesh and bones. I'll go to that place on the other side of the sky that Mariyam talks about so much. And you, my big, lovely, brainless lion, will be down here without anyone to take care of you because you tried to lick me back to life but licked off my skin and flesh instead!"

Janhoy began to roar. He glared down between roars as if angry because Ras would not awaken. The skin around the black ball of his nose wrinkled back.

"Roar!" Ras said to himself. "Roar until the whole world shakes with fear of you!"

And he visualized the great voice of Janhoy flying out over the world. A shadow-lion, it was palely golden, it had big teeth and claws, and it spread out and out. It darkened the world between the cliffs, and every living thing shivered with dread. Except for Mariyam and Yusufu, of course, who would come running.

Presently, he heard shouts. Janhoy roared back, but he stopped when the two human beings were near. Mariyam's wizened, brown face was over Ras, and her tears fell to mingle with his.

"Oh, son, we thought you were dead!"

It was three days before Ras could fully move his legs and arms and bend his fingers to hold anything. After staggering out of the house to breathe the clean, sweet air and see the blue sky again, he said, "How weak I am, coming back from the land of the dead. There is no strength in the Land of the Ghosts, mother."

"Have you truly been to Heaven?" she said. Her eyes were wide.

He laughed and said, "If that was the Heaven you talk about, mother, give me the Hell you talk about."

"Truly, it was Hell you saw, not Heaven. Otherwise, you'd not be so blasphemous and mocking."

Yusufu growled, "The lad was scared shitless. Or would have been if his bowels had not also been paralyzed."

Ras was not listening. He was feeling the burn of the lightning stroke. About the width of his little finger's tip, it started just below the hairline above his right temple, followed the hairline as the beach followed the lake's edge, shot straight down his left cheek and the side of his neck, angled across his chest, cut back to zigzag down his left ribs, wriggled across his belly and dived into the pubic hairs, reappeared below the hollow inside the thigh, coursed down the inside of his thigh, turned right to come out below his knee, fell straight above his shinbone, swerved to circle under the anklebone, and ended on the back of his left heel.

Yusufu also examined the red streak. "It's not so bad. It should heal within a week, maybe sooner, you're so healthy. You have all the luck of the young and the stupid. I knew a man once got hit by lightning and lived. But he was always a little silly afterward. With you, how can one tell the difference?"

"Keep your insults to yourself, dirty little bighead," Mariyam said. "I thank Igziyabher that He spared my son."

"Where's the knife?" Ras said.

"What?"

"The knife. I saw no knife."

Yusufu went into the house and returned with a shiny knife just like the one that the chimpanzee had stolen.

He handed it to Ras and said, "Here. We found this near you."

"You did?" Ras said. "It's strange that you can always find a knife after a storm, and I can't."

CHAPTER 7

THE ARROW

Not until the next day did Ras think about Wilida. Her face awoke him just before dawn. She had been married yesterday!

He could do nothing about it. Although he was able to move his arms and legs and turn his head and sit up for a while, he was too weak and unco-ordinated to stand without support by Mariyam and Yusufu.

He raged. If only he had not gone out into the storm to challenge Igziyabher! And Igziyabher had met his challenge. No doubt, if He had wished, He could have killed him instead of burning him a little and paralyzing him.

Ras hoped that the weakness was temporary. What if it lasted for the rest of his life?

He became angrier instead of frightened. Igziyabher was punishing him unjustly and was cruelly depriving him of the chance to steal Wilida away from Bigagi. When he regained his strength, he would take her away from Bigagi and the Wantso. He would love her so much that she would not be sad to leave her people and would be happy for as long as they lived. Together, they would look for the yellow-haired creature, because that was a mystery he just could not ignore. Whether or not they found her, they would then go on down the river to river's end to confront Igziyabher. There Ras would receive the answers to his questions, and then he and Wilida would return to this forest, and he would build a house near this house. And everybody would be happy.

First, he had to become as strong as he was before

the lightning stroke. This took longer than he had expected. Two weeks passed before he was able to run swiftly again, to swarm up a tree like a chimpanzee, to throw a knife accurately, to swim to the pillar in the middle of the lake and back again at top speed without stopping, to lift Janhoy above his head to the full extent of his arms.

"And now I am going again," Ras said the morning of the fourteenth day after the lightning. "I am going to the end of the river to the home of Igziyabher. And there we will have it out."

He did not think he should say anything about Wilida at this time.

Mariyam screamed and said that he was insane. The lightning had cooked his brains. He would be killed when Igziyabher realized how truly disrespectful and impertinent —even blasphemous—he was. Had Ras forgotten what happened to the people who built the tower to storm Heaven?

"Igziyabher will punish you!" Mariyam cried behind him. Then her dark, fish-eagle's face shot out over the railing. "You cannot disobey Him! Remember the lightning! He has struck you with his fiery knife and marked you! Next time, you will die! My beautiful, beloved baby, do not die!"

He looked up at her wail and almost stopped climbing down the rope. He felt anguished, as he always did when she was truly sorrowing and not acting.

The black, pushed-in face of Yusufu appeared beside her, and his long, black-and-gray beard hung over the railing like the moss on the branches of the swamp trees.

"O son, your mother usually chatters like a brainless monkey. But now she speaks wisely! Do not leave this place and go in search of Igziyabher!"

"Why shouldn't I go?" Ras shouted. "You are not father of me, nor is your wife my mother! I am not the child of apes!"

He reached the ground and let loose of the rope, but he could not walk away. They seemed so frightened for him. And he loved them, even if they were greater liars than the Wantso hunters.

Yusufu shouted down, "You should not go, because you will die! Moreover, it is not yet time!"

Ras was silent for a moment. Then he spoke quietly but loudly enough to be heard.

"Time for what? Answer me this!"

Mariyam screamed, "It is not time! Not time, I tell you! Igziyabher has said so!"

"Oh! Igziyabher!" Ras yelled. "May He thrust His head up His anus and sneeze!"

He laughed loudly and then said, "Igziyabher! I will find Him and talk to Him myself! I will get answers to my questions!"

Mariyam screamed as Ras walked away between the tree trunks, each of which was thicker than the distance he could make in a running broad jump. Her wails became weaker, as if they were getting tired as they darted from trunk to trunk, and soon they were shouldered off by the trees. Their massive branches met each other, and vines grew from branch to branch, and there also grew flowers scarlet as the wrath of a leopard and black as a gorilla under a tree in a rainstorm and as warm, soft, pale red as the insides of the lips of the vagina of a Wantso virgin. Monkeys, large and black, with silver side whiskers and stormcloud-blue-gray eyes, raced over the vines. They called to him, but he did not answer. A stick hit the ground near him, and he did not look up. He knew it had been thrown by the chief pest, the young male with leopard-claw scars on his face and back. Ras had been hit too many times by sticks and rotten fruit and sometimes globs of stinking, sticky, watery, yellow-green monkey shit. He quickened his pace while his tormentor howled his disappointment at him.

It was a mile from the house to the edge of the forest. Beyond this, the ground sloped at a gentle angle for two hundred yards and then met the lake. Ankle-high grass, toothed and rasping, covered the downsloping earth from the forest until close to the lake. Something or somebody—Mariyam said it was Igziyabher—had piled up round stones ranging in size from his fist to boulders large enough for Ras to take two steps from one edge of the top to the other edge.

He leaped onto one and stood for a while, looking out across the waters. He had learned to swim here at so early an age that he could not remember learning. The waters were so cold that he could not stay in long without turning blue and chattering like a frightened monkey. Then how wonderful the blanket of the sun and the delicious warmth as the cold-pimples smoothed out.

North of the lake the cliffs reared abruptly from the water. They were black and whorled, contrasting with the white of the three cataracts. The closest cataract was a mile and a half away. Ras had often paddled in his dugout as close as he could get to the roaring, misty waters and had found that the cliff receded at the base. He could get behind the falls and scoot the boat over the whirling waters and through the almost-rain mist. And that was one of his favorite secret places.

Now he looked down from the boulder at the shallow water near the edge. A fish whipped back and forth through the weeds. Old Kimba was about four feet long and had huge, staring eyes with a horn over each eye and one sticking straight up from the top of his head.

"Don't tease me today, Kimba!" Ras said. "I have fished for you for many years, and some day I may catch you. But not today. I have more important matters, though I do not say this to hurt your feelings!"

To his left, flamingos were a throbbing pink cloud, half on the beach, half in the lake. Ducks and pelicans swam a few hundred yards away. Ras wondered if he would ever see the lake again. How many times he had run down here, Mariyam or Yusufu following. It seemed to him that he was closer to the breast of the world then.

"I pecked my way out of night's shell each morning," he murmured. "There was a feeling then that I can't now shape with words. It all seemed so glorious, so pulsing with beauty and the unknown. Now, it's still beautiful and the unknown cries to me with a voice that . . . that what? It calls to me, and I must find it. But it is not quite the same as when I was naked to the glory, and the world was a living thing.

"Yet, if I'd stayed that way, I'd never have known what it feels like to be in a woman."

He remembered the day that Yusufu and Mariyam greeted him at the shore as he swam out.

"O son, you are no longer an innocent child. You must clothe your nakedness," Mariyam had said. She had held out a leopardskin loin-covering.

"He has not been so innocent for a long time," Yusufu had growled. "I have seen him thrusting into a gorilla female—that one he calls Keyy—from behind, as a beast."

Mariyam had given a little scream.

"O wicked one! Sodomy! Surely you were hidden from the eyes of Igziyabher when you committed this hideous deed! Otherwise, He would have burned you like that roast duckling your foster father ruined the other day when he was sleeping drunkenly instead of watching the little bird!"

Yusufu had been trying to maintain his scowl. Now, grinning slightly, he said, "Moreover, I saw him and his chimpanzee friend—that mocking son of Satan—jacking each other off."

Mariyam's scream was louder, and she shook the leopardskin at Ras. "You are evil, a perverted child of a clapridden buggerer! At least the gorilla was female, but this chimpanzee is a male! O Igziyabher!"

"I am getting sick of hearing that name," Ras had said. "Must I wait until the old liar sends me the beautiful white woman you say He has promised me? I can't wait. Does the leopard wait for permission from Igziyabher before he mounts his female?"

"Put on the loin-covering," Yusufu had said sharply. "Your dong is enormous, truly like a bull elephant's. Your hairs are sprouting like grass after a rain. You are a man now and must clothe your nakedness. Otherwise, you will offend and anger Igziyabher."

Ras had not felt like taking a beating or arguing, so he had put the leopardskin on. Though he had not admitted it to his parents, he had felt a thrill in doing so. This marked an important day in his life.

Later, he wore the loincloth only when he felt like it, which was not often.

But he had not been able to resist asking them why he had to wear clothing and they went as naked as apes, more naked, because they had no hair to cover their sex.

"Because we are apes," Yusufu had said.

It had been then that Ras had had a thought that shocked him. His parents were *not* apes. They did not look like apes, and they *talked*. No ape could talk. Only he and his parents, and the Wantsos, who also were not apes, could talk.

His parents were lying to him. Why? Or did they really believe they were apes? The Wantso children believed they were descended from two creatures made from mud and spider webs by Mutsungo. Maybe they were the children of two mud people. Ras did not think so. Then he had looked at the black stone that pillared from the center of the lake. It was about a quarter mile wide and thrust up to at least a thousand feet. It was smooth at the base but not so smooth that he could not, somehow, if he were determined enough, climb up it. This pillar was the only unhappy, dreaded thing about the lake. Since he had first understood words, he had been warned by his parents to stay away from it. It was horrible and dangerous. It meant certain death for anyone to try to climb it.

"The original people, those whom Igziyabher first created in this world, built that," Mariyam had said. "They built a tower to reach the skies. At that time, there was no lake there; the land was as dry as that which you now stand on. The people built a tower to reach to the skies. And when Igziyabher saw this, he said, 'If they can do this, what next? They will be climbing from the top of the tower to Heaven, and we will be thrown out of our palace in Heaven.' "

"We?" Ras said. "Igziyabher is *we?*"

"That's the way the story—a true one—is told. Don't interrupt, child," Mariyam had said. "So Igziyabher became angry, and He sent down a flood, and it drowned all the builders of the tower.

"That is why the lake is there. Once the land was dry, but now it is a valley filled up with water. And the skulls of the proud builders look up from the mud and see you as you swim above them."

Ras had shivered and said, "But the pillar. How can people build a solid pillar of rock? A tower, you say?"

"Igziyabher turned the tower to solid rock so that it would stand forever as a reminder to people, and especially to mocking, big-mouthed, empty-headed boys, to bear themselves humbly and fearfully before Him."

Now Ras was thinking about this story, told so many years ago but now sounding in his ears as if just told and seen inside his eyes, as if it had just taken place. He heard the chop-chop-chop of the Bird of God's wings, and looked up. It was rising from its hidden nest on top of the pillar of rock, the one-time tower built by the men who would storm Heaven.

Then it was flying across the lake toward him. Presently it was high above him, then past him, and its shadow flitted across the water a few yards from him. Squinting against the sun, Ras turned to watch it. It continued at the same height until it disappeared behind the trees. He estimated that it had descended to a place about three miles from where he stood.

For a moment, he thought of paddling back to shore and running through the forest to find it. What was it doing so near? Why had it come down so close? Or had it? Perhaps it was just hovering near the ground, as it sometimes did, apparently so that the angel in its belly could observe more closely whatever it was interested in.

Probably it would be as futile now to try to get close to the Bird as it had always been. Every time he had sneaked through the brush to spy on it, the Bird had risen high before he could get near to it. So why make another attempt?

Besides, now that the Bird was off on its mysterious errand, its nest was unguarded.

Ras paddled to the base of the pillar and circled it. The rock was black and shiny and smooth when seen from a distance, but when he was close, he could see many little holes in the blackness. Its surface was like the armor of a giant black beetle when seen through the magnifying glass Mariyam had given him on his tenth birthday.

Ras went around and around the base. On the east side, the leeward, about seven feet above the water, the rock bulged. The bulge was slight, but its upper part did form a slanting ledge. There was enough extension for Ras to pull himself up onto it if he gripped the stone edge very tightly, and he could then stand on the ledge if he pressed closely against the rock. He had tried it many times; most of his attempts to get on it had resulted in his slipping and a fall backward into the lake. If he did not get onto the ledge at the first try, he had an even more difficult time thereafter, because his hands were wet. After every fall, he had to get into the dugout without tipping it over. Then he had to wait until his hands were dry before leaping up from the pitching boat again. But once he was on the ledge and upright, he could find other minute gripping-places. Once, he had gotten forty feet before he had slipped and fallen off. That time, though he had twisted to enter the water vertically, his hands before him, he had just missed hitting the edge of the dugout.

Yusufu and Mariyam had known about his fall. He had never found out how they knew. They had not left the house beneath the tree house, and they could not see him from it. But they lectured him savagely about his climb, and Yusufu had whipped him. Apparently, Igziyabher had notified them in His mysterious way.

Now he considered trying again at the same place. He was stronger than when he had tried a year before, although he was also heavier. But he felt more confident, and the Bird was not around. Why not try again?

The only trouble was that the Bird might come back while he was part way up. He would wait until it went westward, and then take a chance that it had gone to report to Igziyabher and so would not return for some time.

There was one drawback to the plan. He had made up his mind to find Igziyabher, Who was God and also his Father. Igziyabher alone could answer his questions.

There was no reason why His son should wait until Igzi-yabher decided to come down from the skies to talk to him. Ras was tired of waiting for answers. Why eat darkness when a banquet of light was on Igziyabher's table?

If only he could build a trap for the Bird and catch it! Then he would force it to answer his questions. He would force the angel in its belly to talk to him, as he had forced Gilluk, the Sharrikt king, when he had imprisoned him for six months after rescuing him from the Wantsos. Perhaps, instead of wandering westward through the world, he could ride in the Bird's belly to the house of Igziyabher.

Deciding that the climb of the pillar would have to come later, he paddled the dugout back to the eastern shore. He had just beached the boat when he heard the chopping of wings and the muted roaring again, and the Bird appeared above him. It was at least five hundred feet high and rising swiftly toward the top of the pillar. He was glad that he had decided not to climb that day.

Ras walked slowly homeward. He dreaded the pleas and threats when he told Yusufu and Mariyam that he was really leaving. This time, he would not argue. He would inform them of his determination, pick them up and kiss them good-by, and then walk out. They must understand that he was a man now. He could no longer tolerate being treated as a child.

Then there was Wilida. If it had not been for the appearance of the strange, stiff-winged bird, he would have stolen her from the cage on the islet. She would have gone with him to live in the house he would have built for her on the plateau. And, in time, he would have introduced her to Mariyam and Yusufu. They would have screamed and cursed, but they would have had to accept her. If they loved him, and they did, they would have to love her, too.

He tried not to think about the possibility of her refusing to go with him. She did love him; he knew that. But meeting him secretly in the bush was not the same as leaving her village. Although she could take delight in him, love him, would she go to the Land of the Ghosts with him?

She had said that she would die if she were separated from her people. She would close her eyes, and she would close her heart, too, and she would stop living. Any Wantso would die. Exile was a punishment worse than being thrown to the crocodiles or burned to death.

The other women had said the same thing when he

had half-jokingly asked them if they would come to live
with him. They desired his love-making, but they did not
want anything to do with him beyond that.

He had even considered trying to get accepted as a
Wantso. If he could live in the village, be a Wantso, then
Wilida could have both him and her people. But that was
before he understood how deeply the men hated him.
Even if he had not offended them with his uncrippled
virility and his seduction of their women, they would
not have accepted him. He was forever a stranger. And
though he could have erased some of their fear of him as
a ghost, he still would always make them uneasy. He
would always be a ghost.

No matter, he thought. If Wilida loves me as much as
I love her, she will come with me.

Together, we'll go look for Igziyabher.

At least, I'll ask her if she will.

He walked past a big tree into the clearing where the
two houses were. He stopped. A little bird with a green
body, black wings, white neck, and red head seemed to
be frozen in its flight across the clearing.

There was a thump as his heart began to beat again,
slowly, slowly.

The little brown body on the ground at the foot of the
steps to the veranda, the body on its back, arms outflung,
jaw dropped, eyes open, an arrow sticking from its heart—
that body was Mariyam's.

For a long time thereafter, Ras seemed to move slowly
and with difficulty, as if he were an insect caught in sap
flowing from a wound in a tree. He held Mariyam, still
warm, the blood around the wound not yet dried, and
rocked her back and forth. Her head lolled with each
movement. He hurt, but the hurt was as cold as the water
far below the surface of the lake. It was there but had
not thawed yet.

Then, when he quit trying to wake her up, he left her
to look for Yusufu. He called for him and searched the
house on the ground and the house in the tree and then
wandered through the forest while loudly speaking Yusufu's name.

Finally, he lurched back to Mariyam and sat down with
her in his arms again and rocked back and forth.

The sun began to climb down from the zenith before
he quit holding her. He examined the arrow. It was
Wantso, made of lemonwood painted black and red and
with four feathers from a green-tailed bird, and the cop-

per head bound with a yellow strip of skin from a golden mouse.

The numbness went away. Guilt filled its place. He yelled and wept with grief and remorse. The Wantso had come here and killed his mother because he had angered them with his seductions and his mocking songs. They had been so furious that they had conquered their fear of the Land of the Ghosts and had come after him into it. They had not found him, but they had found Mariyam. And they must have taken Yusufu with them. They would save him for torture.

Perhaps the Wantso had not yet left. Perhaps they were out in the forest now, hoping to ambush him. Or they might be creeping up on him.

He rose with the arrow in his hand, and he howled, "Come on out, Wantso men! I will kill you all!"

There was no answer. Monkeys chattered. A bird clut-clut-clutted. Far away, a fish-eagle screamed.

He looked for tracks in the hard-packed earth under the tree. There were none except his freshly made prints. The Wantso had used branches to wipe away the imprints in the light dust. The ground around the clearing had been similarly treated. Evidently, the Wantso did not want him to be able to catch up with them while they were in his territory.

The sun was sliding toward the tops of the cliffs now. Ras carried Mariyam into the forest until he found a place where the earth was soft. It was near the foot of a hill where rain had been collected in a pool for a long time but had almost dried away. He dug with his knife and scooped out dirt with his hands until he had a hole two feet deep. Weeping, he placed Mariyam in it, but kissed her cheek before lowering her. He put her on her side, her knees drawn up against her stomach. Then he threw dirt until she was covered. He held the last handful of dirt for a long time. A small patch of skin was still visible, and it seemed that when that was gone, she would also be gone with no hope of her ever coming back.

Then he dropped the dirt, and she was gone.

The rest of the day he looked for large stones and did not finish piling them on the grave until after dusk. Satisfied that no scavengers could dig down to her, he left.

In the tree house, he cleaned off the point of the Wantso arrow and put it in his quiver. The arrow would return to the Wantso.

He was not able to get to sleep until shortly before dawn. He wept and moaned and called for Mariyam many times. The sun rose, and Ras with it. He shaved, as he did every morning. The mirror showed him a red-eyed, haggard face. He ate some dried meat and fruit. He put the comb and the mirror in the antelope-hide bag. After he had sharpened his knife on the whetstone, he put the stone into the bag. Before descending, he scanned the forest. Even in his grief, he had not forgotten that the Wantso might still be hoping to ambush him, although he doubted that they would dare to stay overnight in the Land of the Ghosts.

It was logical for them to take Yusufu with them and expect Ras to come after them. They would lie in wait for him somewhere below the plateau. Or they might have taken Yusufu back to the village, where they would feel safer, and where Yusufu could be tortured.

Ras had gone only a mile when he saw Janhoy sneaking through the bushes toward him. He did not feel like playing the stalking game with the lion, so he called out to him. Janhoy was very disappointed; his eyes looked hurt. Ras petted him and roughed him up a bit. He told Janhoy, "You cannot go with me today. You would be a hindrance; also, you could get hurt. I could not bear to lose you, too, Janhoy. You are too dear to me."

The lion insisted on going with him. Even when they reached the steep cliffs at the edge of the plateau, the lion tried to follow him down. Ras shouted at him and threw stones and presently Janhoy scrambled back up from a ledge to the top of the cliff.

At the bottom of the cliffs, Ras looked back up. Janhoy's big nose and hurt eyes were still visible.

"I will be back!" Ras shouted.

He was worried about Janhoy. Although the lion had been taught how to hunt by Ras and Yusufu, he had a difficult time getting enough to eat by his own efforts. Aside from leopards, antelopes, hogs, and gorillas, no large game existed on the plateau. There had been a few zebras when Ras was younger, but these had been eaten out by the leopards. Janhoy did kill a hog now and then. Antelopes were not easy for a single lion to catch, and leopards were too fast and agile for Janhoy. He was so accustomed to gorillas, having been taken as a cub to them by Ras, that he classed them with Yusufu, Mariyam, and Ras. They were not-meat.

If Ras and Yusufu had not occasionally hunted antelope for him, or with him, he would have starved to death. Now, what would he do with his only support gone?

He would have to get by, somehow.

CHAPTER 8

THE BURNING OF EVIL

A half mile into the jungle, Ras stopped. The thought of Janhoy starving was almost too painful to bear. Yet, he could not climb back up the cliffs and take time to hunt an antelope or hog to hold the lion until he returned. Yusufu needed him. He might be tortured at this moment. Ras shook his head and went on.

From the foot of the plateau-cliffs, where the river cataracted, it was five miles straight to the Wantso village. The river curved back and forth so much that its length from falls to village was ten miles. Ras took the straight line, trotting where the bush was not too thick, going from branch to branch where the trees were close enough—a slow method of progress because of his weight—and swimming across the river whenever it blocked his path. It was fifteen straight miles from the tree house to the Wantso village, but he traveled twenty-two because of unavoidable detours. The sun was settling down like a big, golden-red bird in its nest. He decided that he would kill a monkey and eat before going on. Hunger would be draining his strength so swiftly that he would not be very effective when he got to the village.

At this time, he came across a path much used by the Wantso. About to step out onto it, he heard footsteps. He withdrew into the bush just in time to avoid being seen. Gubado, the old harpist, was trotting along with a little bow and quiver, used for small game, on his back. He held a dead spotted rat in one hand and a spear in the other and two square white things between his teeth. They fluttered in the wind made by Gubado's passage.

The old man had found two Letters from God.

Ras stepped out from behind a bush a few feet before the old man. Gubado stopped. His jaw fell open; his eyes widened. The papers curved toward the ground. Ras gestured with his knife and started to ask him about Yusufu. Gubado dropped the rat and the spear and clutched at his chest. His head was thrown back and his face was twisted. He staggered backward, his mouth working soundlessly. Then he said, "Uh-uh-uh!" and fell backward and lay still.

Ras knelt by the corpse. "Old man, I had not meant to harm you. I know that you were too old and weak to go with the warriors that killed my mother. And I loved to hear your harp when I listened to you out in the bush. In fact, I made my own harp and learned to play it, remembering how you plucked the strings."

He began to cut away at Gubado's neck.

"But then, if you had been young enough, you would have been with the killers, perhaps the killer himself. And, remembering this, I would have killed you if your fear had not stopped your heart."

The flesh gave way easily enough to the knife. The neckbones were not so easy. After he had hacked and sawed through the spinal cord, Ras cleaned his knife and sharpened it on the whetstone. Gubado's dull eyes stared up at him.

Ras said, "Do not reproach me, old man. You would have done the same to me if you had been able."

He put the knife in its scabbard and picked up the papers. By now, it was too dark to read, the moon had not yet come up, so he folded the papers and put them in his bag. He picked the head up by the right cone of hair and walked swiftly along the path. Before he had gone ten yards, he heard a roar behind him.

"Janhoy!"

He turned back and traveled a hundred yards. There was the great beast, still roaring.

"Hush!" Ras said. "You will notify the Wantso."

He patted the mane of Janhoy, who rubbed against him, and purred loudly. Janhoy followed him as far as the corpse of Gubado, where the lion stopped. Saliva ran from his jaws.

"So you managed to get down the cliffs? You must be half goat, you clumsy monster. Now, what will I do with you? You are the ghost, not I, haunting me and encumbering me."

It was too late and too dark to hunt. Janhoy would have to go hungry until dawn and perhaps after that. Yusufu had to be rescued, if possible. If not, he must be revenged.

Janhoy was now creeping toward Gubado's headless body. Ras hesitated, then said, "Eat, Janhoy. There is nothing else for you, and it will keep you occupied while I am gone."

He did not like the idea of encouraging the lion to eat human flesh. However, there seemed nothing else for Janhoy to do.

But Janhoy, though hungry, seemed doubtful. He wanted to eat Gubado, but he also did not think he should. He sniffed at the body and then, swiftly, licked some blood off the neck. After a glance at Ras, as if to see his reaction, Janhoy settled down on the body and began to tear away at it.

Ras swung into the bush so he would not come near Janhoy, because he did not want him to think he had designs on Gubado. The lion was so hungry that, now he was in the first stages of eating, he might violently resent even Ras's approach to his food. Ras walked rapidly down the path, and soon the windings of the trail cut off the sound of ripping flesh.

Ras crossed the river above the village, where the water rose no higher than his chest. There were no crocodiles here, because the water was too chilly. Nevertheless, he thought his heart would stop when a fish brushed against his leg. When he came to the wall across the neck of the peninsula, he put Gubado's head down and went back into the bush. There were two torches on the platform behind the wall. In their light, Thikawa, a middle-aged man, and Sazangu, his juvenile nephew, were visible from the waist up. Their faces gleamed as if smeared with oil. Thikawa wore a white-feathered headdress, and his face was streaked with white paint. He leaned on a huge spear while he murmured to his nephew.

Ras strung his bow, fitted an arrow to the string, and took careful aim. The twang of the string made both guards jump, and Sazangu gave a little yell. Thikawa straightened up and then fell backward with the arrow sticking out of his breastbone. Sazangu yelled louder and ducked behind the wall before Ras could draw another arrow from his quiver. Ras placed the bow over his shoulder and climbed a tall tree. It was awkward work with the bow, but he took his time and presently was above the platform.

Sazangu was crouching down against the wall and still

yelling. He was paying no attention to the big drum, which he was supposed to beat to sound the alarm. Thikawa was not in sight; he must have fallen off the platform. Ras fitted an arrow to the bow and called out Sazangu's name. Sazangu stopped yelling, jumped up, and then launched himself out from the platform. The arrow hit him in the lower back just as he cleared the railing.

The torches above the east gate of the village across the fields were bright enough to reveal that the gates were opening. Other torches appeared within the gateway, danced around, and then started across the fields toward the peninsula wall. Ras came down from the tree, went back to Gubado's head, and then into the river by the wall. He managed to hold the head, spear, bow, and quiver above the surface with one hand while he swam on his side. It was only a few yards of semicircle from the bank on one side of the wall to the bank on the other side. Back on the land, he went through the trees and brush until he came to a large tree. Here he retrieved a rope from its cache in a hollow and slung its coil over his left shoulder.

Now there were torches burning above each of the four gates of the village, with a man or boy on guard at each. Torches were fixed to the posts just below the branch from the sacred tree, and there was probably a guard below it. The eastern gate, however, had been left open while the noise at the peninsula wall was being investigated.

Ras walked close to the village wall along its eastern front until he was almost to the gate. He called, "Chufiya! Chufiya!"

The chief's son leaned out over the wall to look into the darkness.

"Who is it?"

"Lalazi Taigaidi!"

The arrow hit Chufiya between the shoulder and neck. He was spun around by the impact and then fell down behind the wall onto the platform floor. Ras ran forward with a cone of hair of Gubado's head clutched in his left hand. He placed the head at the gateway and ran away. A woman screamed, and men shouted. Ras stopped outside the northern gate. Kufuna, the guard, was looking toward the commotion. Ras called his name and, when Kufuna turned, he received the arrow in his solar plexus. Without a sound, he fell back off the platform.

There were more shouts, near where Kufuna must have struck the earth. Ras went along the wall to the western gate. Bigagi was no longer standing on the bridge, and the cage was gone. Shewego, an elderly man, was the guard above the western gate. Always nervous, he was even more jittery now. Like a bird, he looked everywhere. He saw Ras's white skin in the blaze of the torches, yelled, and dived across the platform railing without thought of the twenty-foot drop to the earth. The arrow missed him.

Ras cursed in Amharic and ran on around the wall to the western gate. Pathapi, one of his childhood playmates, was the guard here. Somebody must have warned him, or he had deduced what was happening from the sequence of events. He turned and threw his spear at Ras and then deserted his post.

Ras whirled around and ran back into the shadows of the walls on the west side. He stopped at the bridge to hack away with the knife at the cables on the land end of the bridge. Then he ran to the islet across the bridge and cut into the ropes there until a few threads held it. He gave a long, wavering scream. There was silence inside the village except for some children crying, hogs squealing, and chickens squawking. A minute passed. Wuwufa's voice, a high-pitched gabble, suddenly arose. Soon, bars creaked and the western gates swung slowly open. Six men, holding torches, peered into the darkness.

"Here I am!" Ras cried, and he stood up at the end of the bridge. "Here I am! I, Lord Tyger!"

Wuwufa danced behind the six warriors and screamed at them to kill the ghost. None of them moved. Tibaso waddled up and shouted at them. They shifted from one foot to the other and glanced at each other. Tibaso tore a spear from a man. He advanced onto the bridge and threw it at Ras.

Ras ducked to one side, jumped back, and slashed at the half-severed rope. It parted with a twang, its end slashing into his cheek. He ran to the opposite side and slashed the rope holding it. Tibaso yelled with consternation. The bridge fell at the islet end; Tibaso slid headlong down the bridge and into the water.

By then, Ras had seen the three heads of crocodiles stuck on poles in the banks. This meant that the crocodiles had been cleared out of the area as part of Wilida's wedding ceremony. The bodies of the animals had probably been the main course during the wedding banquet.

Tibaso was safe from being eaten alive. He had swum back to the bank and was heaving himself up its steep incline like a hippo. The six men had fitted arrows to their bows and were about to deliver a covering fire for the chief. Ras had to take refuge behind a tree while the shafts thunked near him or whistled by.

Immediately afterward, he stepped out from behind the tree and shot at Tibaso. The dim light and his haste marred the shot; the arrow went through Tibaso's left thigh instead of the center of his back. Tibaso screamed and reared up from all fours to his feet. He staggered up the bank and limped through the gates while six men sent another volley at Ras, who had jumped back behind the tree. Then they ran back through the gateway and shut the gates.

Ras threw his spear across the channel to the bank and swam across to the bank. He climbed the tree in which he had sung that afternoon two weeks before. The entire population was milling about in front of the Great House. Tibaso was face down on the chair on the earth platform. His hands were gripping the arms, and his two wives were holding him down or trying to, while Wuwufa was drawing the arrow out. The shaft had gone all the way through the fleshy part of the thigh and come out in front. Wuwufa had removed the arrowhead and now was slowly pulling the shaft out. Tibaso was uttering no sound; a wounded man, if he was to be thought a great warrior, must not cry out when being treated for wounds.

The bodies of the men that Ras had killed were laid out side by side near the chief. The crowd kept a respectful distance from the corpses; even the loudly mourning women did not go near them. Children were crying; the goats, pigs, and chickens, disturbed by the commotion, were adding baas, squeals, and clucks to the racket. The light from the many torches shone on glistening black skins, and reddish two-coned hair, on reddish copper spearheads, and on the white, zigzag warpaint on the men's faces.

There were corpses and Gubado's head on the ground. Ras counted them and was puzzled. There should only have been four, but there were five. At this distance and in the shifting torchlights, the identity of the extra body was uncertain. Ras knew intimately the features, body form, walk, gestures, and voice of every Wantso, but the body had the flatness and lumpishness of a dead man. Ras had to name the living and then the dead before he could identify the extra corpse. It had to be Wiviki, husband of Shuthuna and father of Fibida, a six-year-old girl. Wiviki must have died earlier in the day. He should, therefore, be lying in the Great House now. Why was he out on display with the others?

Now Bigagi was standing in front of the chief. He was

waving his spear and shouting something. The other men had quit talking, and the women and children had become subdued in their grief and terror. Bigagi was evidently urging them to some kind of action. At the end of a long speech, the men clashed spears and yelled something in which Ras thought he could hear his own name.

Bigagi had taken control; he seemed to have become larger and heavier and more powerful. He was the man who could be the most danger to Ras. He knew Ras well, and he did not have the horror of Ras that possessed the others. He also was ambitious. Ras had often heard him say that he would like to be chief, although Ras had interpreted Bigagi's desires as childish dreams of greatness, just as Ras had dreamed of being Igziyabher. But Tibaso, the chief, had lost control. Tibaso could think of nothing but the agony of the wound in his thigh.

Bigagi turned away from the crowd and walked to the chief's chair and seized the wand of the chief, which was leaning against the side of the chair. Tibaso half rose and then fell back into the chair, his head lolling to one side. Bigagi shouted something, and Tibaso's two wives lifted him up and supported him between them as they staggered into the Great House. Wuwufa, the old spirit-talker, and Bigagi talked loudly at each other, and presently Wuwufa fell to the ground and began to roll back and forth.

Ras waited for a while to watch developments before leaving. He wanted to find out where Yusufu was being kept, but it looked as if he was going to be disappointed. He had no chance of sneaking into the village now. Yusufu was not going to be tortured, because the Wantso had more urgent business. Bigagi would be organizing a party to search in the area around the village.

He decided to retreat across the river and get some sleep before dawn. The Wantso could tire themselves out beating up and down in the bush of the peninsula and perhaps on the banks across the river, though he doubted that they would dare that. He climbed down from the tree, swam the river, and walked a mile and a half to a tree that offered him a nest for the rest of the night. He slept uneasily, awakening several times, once thinking that he had heard Janhoy roaring in the distance.

By the light of dawn, he took from the bag the papers that Gubado had found, and read them. They were still wet; the print had run, and many letters were blurred. He could, however, distinguish most of the words.

—139—

only place where Africa is as it was before the
white man. And unlike most of pre-Caucasian Africa,
it's a healthy place. There are no mosquitoes, because there are no stagnant pools. Even the water in
the great swamp is continually moving. Hence, there
is no malaria. There are also no tsetse flies, no bilharziasis, no smallpox, no venereal diseases. Colds
don't exist among the Wantso and Sharrikt. The main
causes of death are warfare, accidents, man-eating
leopards, snake bites, crocodiles (among the Sharrikt), and infection from cuts or wounds. The circumcision rites of the Wantso, besides rendering the men
half-impotent, also result quite often in infection and
death. The Wantso are well aware of this; they, like
people everywhere, persist in continuing a custom
even if it's non-survival. The custom has, however,
in a broader sense, a survival value, since it keeps the
population at a certain level (50 ± 5), although the
Wantso knowledge of birth control really doesn't
make the high death rate among males necessary
for population balance.

I may as well admit right here that I loathe the
Wantso—with good reason, as my readers will see.
They're a depraved people, and they've pulled Ras
into their circle of wickedness. Somehow, he's become fond of these nauseatingly base Yahoos. He's
subscribed to their evil sexual play, which I won't describe here because of the sensibilities of my readers,
who won't read this, of course, until after I'm dead
and I really shouldn't care, but to me morality is for
the dead as well as for the living and

The second sheet was numbered —230—.

my sons, the ungrateful swine, take after their mother, wretched shrew, who left me long ago. But she
knew better than they. She didn't try to get much of
my money; she knew what would happen to her if she
did try. My sons have permitted their greediness to
overcome their sense of what's good for them. They
tried to oust me from my own business, the great
industry that I built up from a thousand dollars
(loaned to me) to its present thirty million gross.
My business, for which I worked like a slave, suf-

fered privation and lack of sleep, which I made into a vast enterprise for one end only: this valley, this Ras Tyger, so that I could make The Book real, and could some day show the scoffers what ignorant, brainless, shallow-souled hyenas they are! If I have spent more than three million on this project, that is my business and mine only! They (my sons) demanded that I tell them where the money had gone; they hired detectives to find out where I went when I disappeared from Johannesburg. But I thank God I had some loyal servants to look after my interests and to warn me—very well-paid servants, of course, servants who knew what would happen to them if they betrayed me. And so the detectives dropped out of men's sight forever when they tried to follow me, and serve them right, too. They met the same fate as others who've tried to balk me or, not knowing of me or my prior claim, tried to get into this valley.

The existence of this place has been known for a long time, of course, but nobody except me—and my helpers—know its nature, what it contains, what is being done here. Nor will

Ras did not understand much of what he read. There were many words the meanings of which he did not know: Africa, malaria, bilharziasis, depraved, venereal, Johannesburg, detectives, and so forth. If the dictionary in the cabin by the lake had not been burned along with the cabin, he could have tracked down the meanings of the words. Yusufu might know them—if Yusufu were still living and could be found.

Ras folded the papers up and put them back in the bag with the other one. He stuffed the bag into a hole in the trunk just above the butt of the branch and jammed the hole with leaves and twigs. He returned to the river at a point close to the southern end of the peninsular wall. There were no guards on the platform above the gates in the wall. Drums were beating in the village, the bull-roarer was throoming, and gourds were rattling. Ras took a station in a tree near the bank to the south of the village. From there, he could see all taking place inside the stockade.

The corpses and Gubado's head were still arranged side by side on the ground in the center of the village. There was a body at one end that had not been there the night before. Its enormity made it easily identifiable as Tibaso.

The wound in the thigh must have been his death, unless, perhaps, Bigagi had killed him, although this did not seem likely. The entire population was massed before the chief's chair, in which Bigagi sat. Tibaso's two wives, and Wilida, stood behind him. Wuwufa, his face and shoulders hidden inside a conical tower of wood and straw, was dancing before the crowd. He held a fly swatter made of the tail from a river buffalo. He waved it up and down, shook it at the crowd, and now and then stopped to crouch and lean to one side as if he were listening.

It was some time before Ras understood what was happening. The silence of the crowd, their squatting stance, and their wide eyes, intent on Wuwufa, their obvious dread, and the fly swatter, gave him his clue. Though he had never witnessed this event, he had heard descriptions of it from Wilida. Wuwufa was smelling out a doer of evil.

The Wantso had suffered a catastrophe. Half the adult males had been killed; great evil had been done to them. Someone was responsible, and that someone would be sniffed out before more evil was worked among them. All were evil, men, women, and children, but one was more evil than the others, one had so much evil that it had leaked out of him and caused death among the Wantso. Someone must be caught before more evil could bite like a snake.

Wuwufa stomped up and down before the crowd and shook the buffalo's tail. He danced before the first row of men and women and waved the tail in their faces, and they cowered and shrank back. Wuwufa went up and down the rows, bringing horror with him and leaving relief behind him. He passed through the rows without touching anyone with the swatter, and then he stomped and ducked and leaned this way and that as he worked toward Bigagi, Thiliza, Favina, and Wilida.

Bigagi was the only one not to show fear. He glared at Wuwufa as if daring him to touch him with the buffalo's tail. The three women shrank back and tried to keep the chair between them and the approaching spirit-talker.

Ras wondered if Bigagi and Wuwufa had opposed each other last night. Had Wuwufa protested at Bigagi's seizing of the chief's chair? Did Wuwufa think to get rid of Bigagi by sniffing him out as the secreter of evil? Or did he have one of the women in mind?

Wuwufa paused before the chair, waved the swatter before Bigagi, who clenched his wand but would not stop glaring at Wuwufa. The spirit-talker stomped back and

forth and leaned the conical structure to one side. Then
he went by Bigagi and waved the swatter in front of the
women. They turned to face him, as if they feared to be
touched upon the back if they did not look at him. Their
heads jerked back as the buffalo tail whipped at their
faces. They held their hands before them, and Thiliza
went to her knees with terror.

Wuwufa passed her by and went back to Wilida. He
approached her from her right and then from her left.
He cocked his body this way and that, posing for a long
time. He shook the swatter above and around her and
once between her legs. He held the swatter close to his
mask as if smelling it.

Ras gripped the branch. He knew now whom the witch
would be. Logically, she would be the causer of evil.
She was the first to meet him; she had been the best
friend, and, later, the greatest lover of the Ghost-Boy.
The Ghost-Boy had gotten access to the people of the
village because she had not run away from him. The
Ghost-Boy had bragged before the entire village that he
loved her most of all. The Ghost-Boy, Ras Tyger, had
caused the deaths of half the men. So, Wilida must be
the guilty of the guilty.

It seemed to Ras that there must be another element
influencing Wuwufa's decision. By naming her as the
witch, he showed the new chief that his power was not
as great as Wuwufa's. Wuwufa controlled the world of
spirits, and that was always stronger than the world of
flesh. So Yusufu had told Ras, and now Ras could see the
truth of his words.

The crowd groaned as the buffalo tail flicked Wilida's
face again and again. Wilida slumped, her head down, her
arms hanging by her sides, her knees slowly giving way.
Bigagi had jumped up from his chair and was shouting
and banging the end of his wand against the earth. Wuwufa paid no attention to him. He called to Tuguba and
Sewatu, who took Wilida away between them into the
Great House. The women scattered to gather wood to
build the hut for burning the witch.

The men were busy with their allotted work. They were
setting the corpses up on little stools, propping them up
with long sticks behind them. Most of them were as stiff as
felled trees. Gubado's head was placed on a stool so that
he, too, could watch the burning.

Ras was close to vomiting because of what was going
to happen to Wilida. But he got down off the tree immediately, because a woman, Seliza, was coming through

the bush toward him. Several yards behind her was Thifavi, Wuwufa's son, armed with a spear. He called to Seliza to hurry with the wood-collecting. His jerky glances around him made it evident that he dreaded being in the bush, even if it was bright daylight.

Ras slipped up behind Thifavi while Seliza was bending over, her back to them, hacking away with a copper axe at a bush. Thifavi must have heard Ras, or else he was turning to look behind him. His eyes widened, his mouth fell open, and he started to complete his turn and to bring up his spear. Ras stepped inside the range of the spearhead and drove in his knife just below Thifavi's jaw. He let Thifavi down easily to avoid attracting Seliza with the noise of his falling body. He pulled the knife loose with some effort because its point was wedged in the windpipe. Then he came upon Seliza from behind and bore her, face down, to the earth. His left hand was on her mouth, and the edge of the bloody knife was against her jugular vein.

"You will lie here with Death, Seliza," he said. "Not I but the knife will be in your body if you tell me lies."

Seliza shook violently. Ras took his hand off her lips and allowed her to sit up.

"Tell me the truth," he said. "Who shot the arrow that killed my mother?"

Her teeth chattered so much that she could barely get the words out.

"I . . . I . . . truly . . . I . . . don't . . . know!"

"Your men must have boasted of going into the Land of Ghosts and of killing the ape mother of Ras Tyger, the ghost, though she was no ape and I am no ghost, as you well know. Who did it? Bigagi? He is the only one with enough courage."

Seliza nodded her head and then could not stop nodding.

"Bigagi did it! I thought so! Bigagi shall die slowly. All your men shall die, but they shall go swiftly, except for Bigagi. Now tell me, where is Yusufu, my father?"

Seliza, still shivering, said, "Yusufu? Your father? Truly there is no Yusufu, your father, in the village, and I do not know of him!"

"The little black man with the long gray hairs on his face?" Ras said. "My beloved foster father. You know! Where is he? In the Great House?"

Seliza nodded again and could not stop.

"And when do they plan to burn Wilida?"

"Today, of course! As soon as the hut is built!"

Ras stood up and away from her, though he still held the knife threateningly. He said, "Go now and tell Bigagi that Wilida and Yusufu must be released at once. They are to be let out of the western gate so that they may cross the river on a dugout. And they are not to be followed.

"If they are not released, if they are harmed in any way, I will kill every man in the village, and I will burn down every hut and the walls so that the women and children will be homeless and defenseless against the leopards.

"And also tell Bigagi that even though he let Wilida and Yusufu . . ."

Ras stopped. It would not be wise to push Bigagi too far. He could find out later that Ras still meant to kill him.

He raised his knife but stopped and said, "Wiviki? What killed him?"

"A yellow-haired ghost killed him!" Seliza said. "He and Sazangu were hunting when they heard something in the bushes. They crept toward the noise, and they suddenly saw the ghost, smaller than you, paler, with long yellow hair and covered with strange, brown stuff. It had something like a blunt axe in its hand, and it pointed the end of the haft at Wiviki when Wiviki jumped up and started to throw a spear at it. There was a noise, like a branch splitting, and Wiviki fell dead. The ghost ran off then. Wiviki had no wound except for a small hole in his chest. He . . ."

"That's enough!" Ras said. He slashed Seliza across the arm with the edge of his knife, and he said, "Go!"

Seliza, screaming, ran as swiftly as her fat legs would permit her through the bush toward the village. Ras ran to the bank, swam across the river and went west and then north until he was opposite the village. From the top of a tree, he watched the scene inside the walls. Seliza was still screaming as she was led off to her hut by some women. Bigagi was pacing back and forth before the warriors, who now included all males big enough to hold a spear upright. Bigagi was shouting at them and now and then brandishing his wand in the direction of the bushes where Thifavi lay.

Ras, after counting those present and then scanning the area outside the village, saw one of the missing men —Zibedi—in the bushes on the bank opposite the tree from which Ras had leaped into the river two weeks before. And near the tree, also hiding behind a bush, was a twelve-year-old boy, Fatsaku. Bigagi was not to be scorned. He had set Fatsaku to call others if Ras should climb the tree again. And Zibedi, armed with two spears and a bow and arrows, was to kill Ras if he tried the same escape route.

Ras again counted the men within the walls to make sure there were no others hiding in ambush. He left the tree and crawled to Zibedi, and presently Zibedi was jetting his life out through a severed jugular vein while Ras shoved his face into the dirt to keep him from crying out.

After Zibedi had quit bleeding, Ras circled north and east and crossed the river again. He got behind Fatsaku, but the boy was as nervous as a monkey that smells leopard. During one of his frequent glances behind him, he saw a patch of white skin. Yelling, he leaped up, his spear abandoned, and ran to the village. Ras threw his knife but missed him. After retrieving the knife, he sped back across the river to resume his post in the tree.

By then the hut had been finished. It was a hastily built construction, tied together with long grasses and threatening to fall over. But it was built well enough for its purpose.

Wilida was brought out of the Great House to the center of the village, where Wuwufa harangued her from behind his mask. Bigagi, leaning forward, sat on his chair. He said nothing. Wilida's head sagged forward, and she was silent. Even from his distance, Ras could see the grayness of her skin. She did not struggle when she was pushed forward and then shoved into the hut. Her hands were tied behind her, and she fell so that her feet stuck out through the doorway. The women kicked the feet until they were withdrawn into the hut.

The women then piled tree branches and bushes at the doorway until it was completely blocked. Wuwufa took a torch from his wife and applied it to the piles at the north, east, south, and west. Bigagi, as if he knew that Ras must be watching from somewhere, rose from the chair and made a complete circle, stopping four times to shake his wand at the world outside the village and yell something.

There was no wind, but the hut caught fire quickly enough. The flames spurted upward; smoke rose straight up. Wilida began screaming and did not stop until the hut collapsed inward and the blazing roof fell down.

CHAPTER 9

PAYMENT

Ras vomited. Afterward, he lay for a long time on the branch, face down, and stared at the bushes and the elephant's-ear plants. Then he climbed down, noting on the way that some insects were already eating the vomit sprayed on the trunk. He went to the river to wash the taste from his mouth and cleanse his throat and his soiled body.

There was nothing he could do for Wilida except to grieve for her and to kill her killers. But Yusufu was not dead yet—if he could believe Seliza. He was not sure now that she had not told him what she thought he wanted to hear. Certainly, he had seen nothing of Yusufu. Perhaps the Wantso had killed him while on their way back to the village. Or perhaps Yusufu had escaped them at the tree house and fled far away into the hills.

It was too much for him now. The two he loved most, except for Yusufu, were dead.

"Everything happens in threes," Mariyam had often said.

"Not this time!" Ras said aloud.

He returned to Gubado's body to find Janhoy. There was not much left of the old man. His bones were spread around, and two jackals were gnawing on them, while six ravens waited in a semicircle a few feet from the jackals. Nearby, behind a bush, Janhoy was sleeping on his back, his belly distended, his forepaws folded on his chest and his back legs up in the air.

"If I were a Wantso, I could drive a spear through your

fat stomach, and you would never wake up from the dreams of whatever a lion dreams of," Ras said. "Sleep well and long, Janhoy, because I do not have time for you now nor for some time to come."

He removed from the quiver the Wantso arrow that had killed Mariyam, and said, "And you, you will fly back to the man who sent you into Mariyam's heart. You will return to his heart. Bigagi will die tonight."

He slept uneasily in the tree the rest of the day. The cries of monkeys and birds jarred him loose from his precarious hold on sleep. Several times he dreamed of Mariyam and Wilida as still alive, and woke up weeping. The last dream was of Yusufu imprisoned in a hut by the Wantso. Then he knew that he could not allow himself to sleep again until he was certain that Yusufu was safe. He returned to the big tree across the river from the village shortly before dusk.

The twilight sifted down purplishly. The day animals ceased their noise. The night animals took over. Far off, a leopard screamed. Presently, Ras heard a slight sound and guessed that a leopard had found Zebedi's body. There were some more noises. The leopard was dragging the corpse away to a place more suited for the cat to eat. Most of Zebedi, who was known as the Laugher, would soon be in the leopard's belly. The bones would be stripped clean by jackals and ravens. The grass would cover the bones. And that would be all of Zebedi. Just as the old harpist, Gubado, would be lion dung and grass-ridden bones.

"Yet I well remember Zebedi's laugh and the jokes he told, which Wilida told me. And I remember Gubado's harp and its music, and I will play his songs on my harp. And Mariyam and Wilida . . ."

He tried to make himself quit thinking of Mariyam and Wilida. Their memory cut him to the bone of his soul.

Torches lit the inside of the walls now, and he saw that the corpses were being taken down from their stools and were being carried off into the Great House. Some women were cooking the evening meals on the stones and in the pots before their houses. The rest were mourning loudly over the dead. Bigagi was on the chief's chair and eating from a wooden platter held by Seliza. He was talking with a full mouth to Wuwufa and the warriors squatting before him. Torches were blazing over each of the gates, lighting up a little boy on each platform. Only the upper parts of the children's heads stuck up above the notch of the V formed by two sharp-pointed poles. They were making as small a target as possible.

And Yusufu, where was he?

Ras changed trees to get a different angle of view. As he had expected, he saw a man, Pathapi, by the wall under the branch of the sacred tree. He had been set there to watch if Ras should try to enter the village by the tree.

The darkness deepened. The moon had not yet risen. The women and children went to their huts, except for the women who were sitting with the dead in the Great House. The warriors gathered around Bigagi to hear his instructions. The children were called down from the platforms and sent to their houses. All but one torch were extinguished. By its light, Ras could perceive the men scattering to the shadows under the hut. Pathapi went under Wuwufa's hut. Bigagi had walked into the Great House, but Ras supposed that he was sitting on a stool just inside the doorway.

The single torch was doused in a pot of water. Darkness and quiet settled. Even the moans and cries of the women in the Great House stopped.

Ras climbed down from the tree and crossed the river. He took some fire sticks from a hollow in a tree and set to work to make a fire. After touching off the end of a long, dry stick from the blaze, he walked to the sacred tree. Though it was awkward holding the brand in one hand, he climbed the tree and threw the brand onto the roof of Wuwufa's hut.

Somebody—probably Wuwufa—yelled, and there was the slap-slap of bare feet on the hard earth. Ras jumped down from the tree and circled the stockade to the west gate. He cast his rope to secure the noose around the pointed top of a pole. When he had hauled himself up, he looked through the thorn barricade between the pole-ends. By the blaze of the rooftop, he could see Wuwufa and his wife jittering outside the hut, other men yelling advice to two men on the roof trying to beat the fire out with dugout paddles. They were, however, succeeding only in knocking burning parts over the rest of the roof. Several women were bringing up pots of water. Bigagi was not in sight.

Suddenly, Bigagi stepped out from behind the house nearest to Ras. He gave a cry and threw his spear at Ras, who released his hold on the rope to drop down below the top of the poles before he clutched the rope again. Then, hanging on with one hand to the V between two poles, despite the pain from long thorns, he loosened the noose and then dropped to the ground. The butt of the spear had rattled against the top of the pole as it shot over him. Ras picked it up and ran around the wall until he was near the north gate. He had expected the Wantso to come out the south gate or perhaps to send one party through it and the other through the west gate to catch him between them. However, as he drew near the north gate, he saw it beginning to swing open. He changed his course to make for the trees and the bush away from the village. Then, changing his mind, he turned to wait until the gate was almost open, and he threw the spear.

It caught Gifavu, the first man out, in the belly. Gifavu fell backward, knocking down the man behind him. Ras saw that the south gate was also being opened and that Bigagi and three men were coming through it. They whirled as they heard the cries of those at the north gate and ran toward it.

Now Ras knew that Bigagi would not let up until he had killed Ras or Ras had killed him. Ras could pick off the men one by one and retreat each time into the jungle to come back later to kill again. He could keep this up as long as he wished, and the Wantso could not just stay within the village. They had to get out so they could get food and water. Besides, Ras could burn them out if he was determined to do so. Bigagi must have explained this to his people and given them the courage to come out into the night after him. Even Gifavu's death was not stopping them.

Ras fled to the river and swam across. Arrows hissed into the water so near him that he was forced to dive. His bowstring and arrows were wet, so he abandoned them and the rope, but kept the arrow that had killed Mariyam. He stuck this through his belt, the only thing he was wearing.

He rose just long enough to catch a breath of air and to see that three men were swimming after him. Six figures, darker than the night, were on the shore, waiting for him to come up. They did not see him, however, before he let himself sink back under. He swam in the lightlessness toward the three in the river, pausing briefly now and then to listen for their thrashings. When he was sure that one was directly above him, he came up under him. It was difficult to drive a knife against the water with any force, but he grabbed a leg to give him leverage and shoved the blade with all his strength. Its point went into the swimmer's belly. After pulling it out, he emerged to find himself between the other two. The stabbed man was floating face down, arms out.

Bigagi shouted at the two, who closed in on Ras, but very slowly. Ras dived deep, felt fingers touch his foot, and kept on going down. His ears began to hurt. Then, his hand plunged into cold mud. Above him were faint sounds, like hands and feet beating a long way off. Had the men on shore also come in after him? If most of them had, Bigagi would make sure that at least one archer was still on the bank. Yet it was so dark that accuracy would be difficult. So far, no one had thought to fetch torches.

He did not know his direction. He swam along the bottom until it abruptly curved upward. He was heading toward the wrong bank. Very well, let it be the wrong bank. They would not be expecting him to come up by the bank he had just left. Or, if they did, there was little he could do about it. He was almost out of air; the panic to open his mouth and breathe was a fist squeezing him.

The surface was a band of lesser darkness just above him. Slowly, fighting the urge to lunge up and suck in air, he rolled over and allowed himself to drift up. The waters broke on his face and rolled off, and he breathed out slowly and breathed in. Splashes and shouts were muffled because his ears were under water. Then, slowly, he sank back down and groped along the mud, the surface only a few inches above him. His hands felt roots, a piece of broken pottery, a bone that had the shape of a hog's lower back legbone. He groped on until the current suddenly became swifter, and he knew he was in the channel between the bank and the islet. He kept on going until he felt as if the last of air had burned away in him and he was a dying emptiness. Only then he rose up and, struggling to fight off panic, lifted his head into the air. Throttling his gasps to long, well-controlled indrafts, he crawled across the bank to the wall and leaned against the poles for a while. There was much noise on the bank where he had first dived in, and there were now many torches. There were also voices of women and children. It sounded as if the entire village were on the bank or in the river.

Perhaps this was true. Bigagi may have summoned everybody to join in the search. Strength was in numbers, and courage also.

Ras stood up, somewhat shakily, and walked along the wall until he came to the south gate, which was still open. He peeked around its corner. Wuwufa's hut was completely on fire; its flames enfolded the branch above it. No one was in sight except Wuwufa, who sat on the ground and stared at the blaze. Even the babies were at the river.

Ras came up behind the old man and tapped him on the shoulder. Wuwufa jerked and gasped and then looked up. His eyes became huge; his jaw dropped.

"You caused Wilida to be burned," Ras said.

Wuwufa quivered and tried to get off his haunches. Ras struck him on the jaw with his foot, the sole of which was so deeply callused that it was like iron. Unconscious, Wuwufa fell backward. His jaw was askew, and blood ran from his mouth. Ras put his knife back in its sheath and picked the old man up. He raised him above his head, walked as close to the doorway of the hut as the heat would permit, and hurled Wuwufa through the flaming entrance. A few seconds later, the roof fell in and then the walls.

Ras looked into the Great House first. The only occupants were the corpses and Gubado's head. There was no sign of Yusufu nor any indication that he had ever been in the Great House. Ras took a torch from a pile against the wall and touched it off against the low fire in a large, shallow, stone bowl. He upset the bowl against the wall and then set fire to the wall and hanging mats at several places.

Thereafter, as he searched each house, he kicked over the fire-bowls and applied the torch. He worked swiftly, because the Wantso would soon see the fires. If Bigagi was as intelligent as he thought, Bigagi would send men around to the other gates before entering the north gate.

The chickens and goats and hogs were terrified. The chickens were running and squawking every which way except that which would have led them to safety, out through the gates. After huddling together near a hut that was as yet unburning, the goats followed an old billy out the south gate. The hogs hurled themselves against the sides of the pens. Ras considered for a second releasing them, then decided that it would take too long. He did not have much time left. Even above the bedlam of the animals, he could hear a change in the voices of the Wantso by the river. They had suddenly found out that their village was burning down. He did not have much time left.

Three houses were still not touched off. He ran into one and, seeing a bow and quiver of arrows, remembered that he had ditched his in the river. He strung the bow, and slid the quiver over one shoulder and the bow over the other. He held the torch with his left hand and the knife in his right. And, as he started to leave the hut, he just had time to get into a knife-throwing position. A man, screaming with insane fury, burst into the hut and launched his spear at Ras.

There was not much room to dodge inside the hut. Ras threw the knife and at the same time began his forward fall. The knife hurtled into the solar plexus of Pathapi, and the spear struck Ras on the top of his head. Its point slid along his scalp; its butt came down and rapped him sharply. Ras jumped up, jerked the knife out of Pathapi, and then wiped the blood away from his eyes. It was streaming down blindingly.

Pathapi must have been so eager because he was trying to show his fellows that he was not a coward, even if he had deserted his post earlier in the evening. Also, this was Pathapi's hut, and almost any man will become a lion when he defends his home. Or so it seemed to Ras. But Pathapi had worked his courage into a frenzy and so had attacked Ras stupidly, when he should have waited outside and speared Ras as he stepped through the doorway. Ras wiped some more blood away, fitted an arrow to his bow, and ran out. The fire by this time was so hot that he could not have stayed in a second longer, even if he had wished to. Outside, the smoke had filled the space between the walls, and he could see nothing except the flames of the huts. His eyes burned, and he began coughing. He got down on all fours to crawl under the cloud, and as he did so, he saw the legs of men coming through the south gateway.

The blood blinded him again, and he scooped up mud where an overturned pot had fallen on the dirt and plastered this on his head to stop the flow of blood. Then he refitted the bow with an arrow and, though his eyes watered, aimed at a point above the nearest of the approaching legs. There was a screech, the legs moved backward, and the body of a man, the arrow sticking from his chest, was on the ground. The other legs turned and ran through the gateway. The gate swung shut. Although the smoke was too thick for him to see the other gates, he supposed that they, too, would be closed. He was trapped inside the village, the heat increasing, the smoke sinking toward the ground.

He crawled to the wall and pressed his face against the earth and lay there the rest of the night, waiting. The smoke never quite entirely encoiled him, nor did the heat become unendurable. The huts burned swiftly, and the walls did not catch fire. The top of his head felt as if it had caught fire under the mud, but he ground his teeth together and did not cry out. He became very thirsty; his mouth felt as if a river of ants was drinking every particle of moisture within his pores.

The sun rose. The smoke was gone, except for pale phantoms rising from the mounds of ashes that had been the huts and the Great House. His body was gray-black with smoke; his eyes felt as hot as the ashes looked. He rubbed off some of the dried mud on top of his head. It was reddish-black with blood under the gray ash covering.

The sun rose higher. His thirst increased. The odor of smoke and of burned flesh hung like the breath of Death over the charred walls. The man he had shot had been unrecognizable because of the smoke, but the sun did not enlighten Ras. The face was a gray mask.

Ras barred the gates, one by one. If the Wantso wished to come in after him, they would have to scale the walls now. There were shouts outside, and then the sound of wood being piled against the walls, and the crack of axes. At first, he thought that they meant to burn down the walls, but presently he saw Bigagi's head thrust above the south gate, and he knew that they had piled wood to climb up on.

Ras, standing in the exact center of the village, the blackened chief's chair behind him, pointed an arrow at Bigagi. Bigagi withdrew his head. There were more shouts. Ras sat down in the chair and waited. Soon enough, they would attack from four points. He would kill a few, and then they would kill him.

How many men survived? He counted the dead again in his mind, and then he grinned. They had five left. These five would come over the wall after him, and, unless they were quick, they would not live to mutilate his corpse. Perhaps the women would come after him then.

The sun rose higher. He became thirstier. Noon came. The Wantso talked loudly outside the walls but no one called to him. He thought of the river and became even thirstier. Bigagi and two men climbed into trees to watch him. He yelled taunts at them until his throat closed up in dryness. He showed them the two spears, the axe, and the extra bow and arrows that he had taken from the man he had killed.

Presently, the three left the trees. Women, armed with bows, appeared in trees and shot at him. He did not move from his chair. The women were unused to bows; their

arrows went wide. And for every arrow shot now, he
had one more and they one less.

Then Bigagi's head arose above the south gate. Thaigulo's appeared at the west; Jabubi, Wilida's father, was
at the north gate. Wakuba, a white-haired old man, was at
the east. Ziipagu was climbing a tree, a bow and arrow
strapped to his back, and cursing the women because
they were useless.

Ras stood up and shot at Ziipagu. Because his hand
shook from weariness and thirst, the arrow struck a foot
above Ziipagu's head. Ziipagu yelled and dropped out of
sight. Kanathi, the woman in the tree, dropped her bow
and hid on the other side of the trunk.

Bigagi and the other men stood up, each with a bow
ready to launch an arrow.

Ras shot first and then dropped onto the ground by the
chair as soon as the arrow was well sent. His target had
been Wakuba, the old man, because he thought that the
old man would not be as swift as the others to duck. He
thought correctly. Wakuba's arrow, like the others, missed,
though two plunged into the ground a few feet from
his legs and one struck the chair a glancing blow and slid
off elsewhere. Wakuba was hit in the shoulder, and he
spun around and fell back. The others fitted arrows again,
but this time they did not shoot in unison. Ras dropped
his bow and rolled across the ground away from the chair,
then leaped up and dived back at the bow. The second
volley had missed him, and now it was his turn by a few
seconds.

Ziipagu's head appeared just in time to draw Ras's aim
from Thaigulo. He spun and released the arrow with the
unthinking smoothness and accuracy born of many, many
long days of practice under Yusufu's unrelenting disci-
pline. The arrow went through Ziipagu's throat to the
feathers, and Ziipagu dropped.

The arrows missed Ras, although one buried its head
into the ground so close that the shaft quivered against
the inside of his calf. The men yelled with dismay; some
of the women screamed. Bigagi raved, when he should
have been shooting. Ras shook the arrow that he had
saved for Bigagi and managed, despite his dry throat, to
tell him that it was intended for him and him alone.

Suddenly, Ras dropped the bow, bent down, scooped up
a spear, and ran at Jabubi. Jabubi stared at him for a while;
his eyes were so wide that Ras could see the whites. Then
Jabubi seemed to come out of his amazement, and he
aimed an arrow. Ras ran straight at him until Jabubi re-

leased the shaft, and then he leaped to one side. Jabubi's arrow went wide, but two shot by others missed Ras by an inch and by two feet. Ras resumed his charge at Jabubi, who had time to draw another arrow and fit it to his bow. But he seemed clumsy. Perhaps the thought that the Ghost-Boy was intent on him, that the Ghost-Boy had so far managed to live and to burn down the village and kill most of the men made him shake. He dropped the arrow and stooped to pick it up, disappearing for a moment. When he straightened up, he saw the spear rushing along the downward leg of the arc at him.

He yelled and dropped the bow and arrow down along the wall into the village. He turned as if to run back down the pile of wood when he should have let his knees loose and slumped back down behind the wall. Thus, the spearhead entered through the muscle above the collarbone, and he slid on down the wood.

Ras picked up the bow and the arrow dropped by Jabubi, and he shot at Thaigulo. Thaigulo ducked. The arrow drove into the top of the pole, and its shaft broke off. Ras was breathing so heavily and his legs were so tired that he could only walk back to the chair and the weapons by its side. Bigagi shot twice at him; Ras continued to walk straight ahead. Both arrows whispered near him, but by this time he felt that he could not be stopped. Not, at least, by the Wantso. Perhaps by his own hunger, thirst, and exhaustion.

Thaigulo reappeared and shot twice also, and did not even come near Ras. Perhaps he felt as Ras did, that Ras was going to win. There was only himself and Bigagi left to fight the Ghost-Boy, and he may suddenly have felt deserted.

At that moment, the chop-chop-chop of the wings of the Bird of God came from the distance. Bigagi, Thaigulo, and Ras looked up into the sky. Then Ras looked away and took the arrow that had killed Mariyam and placed its nock on the string. He took careful aim at Bigagi, but Bigagi must have seen him out of the corner of his eye. He suddenly ceased to be a still target against the sky framed between two trees. He was gone behind the wall. Ras growled with disappointment, but waited for him to reappear.

Then the Bird was there. It flew just above the treetops and came over the river. It rose higher, stopped, and hovered. The Wantso screamed. Bigagi rose from behind the wall and shot quickly at Ras and dodged behind the wall. His arrow, too hastily launched, angled upward several feet above Ras's head.

There was a strange noise, a chatter-chatter. Chips flew from the tops of the poles behind which Bigagi had been standing. The Bird sank down, and Ras could see one of the masked angels clutching the end of two cylindrical contrivances. Fire spurted out of the end of each.

The Bird swung past the walls and then circled above the village. The chatter-chatter continued; the twin cylinders blew flame.

The Wantso women and children screamed and screamed.

Presently, there was silence. The Bird of God rose, and, flying only a few feet above the trees, which whipped in the air driven by its wings, disappeared. The chop-chop and the roar became fainter and then were gone.

Ras waited a while before opening the west gate. He swung the gates out slowly and looked out. The bodies of three women were outside the gate. They had great holes in their flesh. Blood was over them and the ground around them. The head of one woman was a shatter of bone and of flesh splashed with blood.

He stepped over and through the bodies to get to the river for a drink. By then, several large bodies of blood, like misshapen rafts, were drifting down the stream. A child, face down, floated by him as he scooped up water in his palm. His thirst washed away, he rose and painfully circled the village, starting along the south wall. Some of the Wantso lay on the ground where the invisible stones hurled from the cylindrical weapon of the Bird had caught them as they ran for the trees; the rest floated away down the river.

While he was going by the east gate, he saw a man slip from the bushes by the river about two hundred yards away. The man was Bigagi. He shoved a dugout from the bank, jumped in, and began paddling furiously down-river, his body bent forward against the winds of terror.

Ras watched him until he was out of sight. He felt nothing at this moment except a numbed wonder that Bigagi, who was responsible for all this, should escape. And after he had searched all around the village, he was sure that Bigagi was the only Wantso not dead.

Two ravens floated down from a high branch and hopped cautiously toward a baby. Its ribs were torn away on one side, and it was half-covered by ants. The first raven began to tear at the edges of the wound; the second pecked at an open eye. Soon enough the vultures

would see and would settle down out of the skies, and
jackals and hyenas would come loping toward the scent.
These would have a feast until the leopards arrived with
night, and even then the lesser carrion eaters might continue, since surely there was enough for all, for once.

Ras sat down in the mud of the bank. Except for the
croaking of ravens and occasional flapping of wings and
the cries of far-off birds, it was silent. He felt as empty as
the silence. The mouths of the Wantso would never speak
again. The only sound in them would be the buzz of flies,
and then after a while even the flies would be gone.

He remembered that he had listened to the Wantso with
such delight, as he hid in the bushes. He remembered
exciting and interesting and funny conversations with
Wilida, Fuwitha, Bigagi, and others. What a noise the
villagers had made, the voices of men, women, children,
and babies spiraling up like smoke from the jungle to the
sky! Surely, Igziyabher must have sniffed the smoke of
human voices; surely, He must have savored it, just as
His son, hidden in the bushes, savored it.

Now, he had no one to talk to except Bigagi, no one
anywhere in the world. And he could not talk with Bigagi.
He must kill Bigagi. His hatred was gone. He did not even
hate Bigagi any more. But he would have to kill Bigagi.
If the desire for vengeance seemed gone, duty still remained.

He thought of Igziyabher. He was protecting His son.
He had seen the fire in the village and He had sent angels
in the Bird to rescue His son. For this, Ras was not grateful. He could have taken care of the men by himself,
even if he was wounded and surrounded. Moreover, Bigagi would not then have escaped. Nor would the women
and children have been killed. He could have become
chief of the Wantso, and, after he had explained to the
women why he had had to kill their men, he would have
taken the women as wives. They would have had to accept
him as a man, not a ghost, because he would have been the
only man left to protect them, hunt for them, and bed
them.

Or was that a dream that would have quickly died
when a woman stabbed him as he slept? Perhaps the
women would never have forgiven him for what he did,
even if he could have done nothing else and it was the
fault of the men that he had had to kill them. Perhaps he
dreamed falsely. He would never know.

He rose and drank again from the river. Now, as if the
river water had given him fluid for tears, he wept. He

wept for Mariyam and Yusufu, for Wilida, for the dead women and children, and, even, though he did not understand why, for the dead men and for Bigagi.

Most of all, it seemed to him, he was weeping for himself.

The others, except Bigagi, were past grief and pain. Ras was the unlucky one, because only he could grieve, and he had nothing left but grief.

After a while, his sorrow-twisted body could squeeze out no more tears, and the gash in his head reminded him that he was alive. He wanted to get rid of the pain, but he did not wish to do it by dying. Not even in the bottommost pain of sorrow had he really wanted to join the dead.

He washed the wound in his head and then, seeing that the blood had started again, repacked the wound with mud. He picked up some arrows the Wantso had dropped and swam the river, holding the quiver and bow above the water. His goal was a tree nest, where he would sleep tonight, or try to sleep, and tomorrow he would hunt for food.

Halfway to the nest, he had to sit down to rest with his back against a tree trunk. His muscles were quivering, and he felt dizzy and weak. It was then that he heard a rustle in the bushes, and he saw a white face looking at him through leaves. Hair shone yellow in the sunlight.

CHAPTER 10

THE YELLOW-HAIRED

ANGEL—OR DEMON

The angel—or demon—from the stiff-winged bird had come out with empty hands from the bushes. She was smiling; her teeth were even and white. She looked eerie, she was so pale, and her nose was so thin and high-bridged and her lips were so thin! Her eyes were as gray as the blade of his knife. Her body was clothed much as the body of the angel that had fallen from the burning Bird of God. The soft, brown material was so loose that he would not have known she was a woman, except that it was tight enough around the chest to hint at large, well-rounded breasts. Her feet and legs from the calf down were covered with cured hide of an animal. She wore a belt with two sheaths. One held a knife and the other contained a device of iron.

She helped him to the tree that held the nest and followed him after he had painfully and weakly climbed up the tree. She inspected his wound, cluck-clucked, and then took a bag out of a bulging pocket. She poured a whitish powder over the gash in his scalp.

Her speech was gibberish. Ras shook his head at her and closed his eyes. If she meant harm, she could have captured or killed him. Moreover, the iron device seemed to him to be responsible for the death of the man who had floated down out of the flaming Bird. He was sure that it carried the same kind of death that the twin cylinders in the Bird had spat at the Wantso. Undoubtedly, she had killed Wiviki.

He woke sometime during the night to find her sitting by his side. The moon was just coming up, so he could see her smile at him. He could also see that she was very tired, and, judging from the gurgling and rumbling of her stomach, very hungry. She spoke softly, and, though he did not understand her this time either, it seemed to him that she was using a different language. In Amharic, he asked her for her name. She said something in what he was certain was yet another language. Then he went back to sleep.

Ras recovered rapidly. Within six days, he was able to run with all his usual vigor. By then he had become accustomed to her white skin and squeezed-in features and yellow hair. He was even beginning to think that he might some day find them attractive. Moreover, when he watched her take a bath in the river on the seventh day, he got an erection. She was thinner than Wilida and longer-legged, but her breasts were almost as large and quite as firm—to the eye, anyway. Her pubic hair was reddish-brown, a color he found stimulating.

He left his cover behind a bush and joined her. She was startled and backed away until the water was up to her neck. He wondered about that, but if she wanted to do it in the water and standing up, for some peculiar reason, he would co-operate. He started to wade toward her, while checking again to make sure that no crocodiles were near. But she left the water and hurriedly put on her clothes.

When he came out of the water, he was confronted with the iron device. She spoke harshly while she pointed its open end at him. Ras, remembering what had happened to Wiviki, came no closer. Grinning, he stood before her and made thrusting motions with his hips.

Her reply was a disgusted face and a disgusted sound in her throat.

He was both puzzled and hurt. The only woman to refuse him had been Mariyam. That was painful to remember, because he had gotten the worst whipping of his life when he had asked Mariyam if she would lie with him. During the whipping, both Yusufu and Mariyam had screamed at him that he was wicked, vile, degenerate, and perverted. "You do not lie with your own mother!

Surely, this is unheard of since the days of the evil men of Noah! If Igziyabher finds this unholy desire in you, He will strike you dead!"

Ras still did not think that it was wrong to offer affection in its most intense form to his beloved mother, but if she was so convinced that his desire was wicked, she was not going to change her mind. And later on, when he saw that the Wantso also thought of this as monstrous, he began to wonder if perhaps there might not be something wrong with him.

But this woman was not his mother. Was it possible that angels—or demons—were also forbidden this highest of pleasures? Or was she Igziyabher's woman and so did not want to bring his jealous wrath down upon her? Certainly, she was not as smooth between the legs as his forehead, as Yusufu had described angels.

Whatever her reason, she made it plain that she did not want him. Moreover, she insisted he cover his genitals, which she seemed to think repugnant, although he could not understand why such beauties would offend anyone except the Wantso men, who were so jealous of them and with good reason.

At her urging, he went to another tree, where he had cached the leopardskin loin-covering a long time ago, and he put it on. She seemed pleased at this although the skin was badly chewed by insects and rodents.

By then, Ras knew that one of the languages she was trying on him was English. This knowledge did not help him much. Except for a mangled word here and there, it was still gibberish. Nor did she comprehend his English, although she must have recognized some words. Immediately after his first attempt with it, she pulled two half-burnt papers from a pocket. These were also Letters from God.

He read them as best he could. The first went thus.

suspect that they are—that they have been for a long time—disobeying my injunctions. From the very beginning, and many times since, I have instructed them in exactly what they should tell him, given them minutest details of how they should behave when in his presence, and, indeed, when he is not around, in case he should be spying on them. But they are
       they hate me, even though I saved them
from
        out working or having to worry about

The second read:

become acquainted with the Wantso   an early age. He must have been visiting them for   years before I found out. Otherwise, he would not have known their language so well. This is an example of what I meant when I said things seem to go their own way, no matter how I tried to keep the situation as the Master described it. Of course, I am a hard-headed realist—ask anybody in South Africa who's dealt with me!—and I knew that

Ras read the two half-papers several times before he took his collection from his antelope bag and handed them to her. She exclaimed several times while reading and then returned them with a shrug. Very lovely shoulders, he thought.

That night he reached for her again, and she pulled the weapon—which she called a thirty-two—and pointed it at him. He grinned and lay back but pulled his leopardskin off so that she could see what she was denying herself. She spat at him and spoke rapidly in an un-English tongue. She did not, however, turn her back on him, which Ras thought showed intelligence and foresight.

Later that night, he left the tree to scout the Wantso village. The noise from there had lessened considerably. For several days and nights the leopards had roared, jackals barked, hyenas laughed. The second night, Janhoy's roars had reached Ras. There were sounds that could be nothing other than Janhoy fighting leopards. Ras had been too weary to investigate. Besides, Janhoy had never lost a battle with a leopard yet, although there was no telling what might happen if he were ganged up on.

The moon was up when he swam across the river. A rat slithered away into the shadows as he passed an armbone. Bones glinted grayly; a skull with some shreds of meat still on it stared at the moon. Ras made sure there were no leopards in the branches before he climbed a tree. He called Janhoy, and almost immediately a rumble answered him. The lion padded out into the clearing and glared about him. Ras came down out of the tree to greet him.

When morning came, he returned with Janhoy to the nest in which the woman still slept. Ras made the introductions carefully. Janhoy behaved as if he were thinking of her as a potential meal. The woman objected when Ras pulled her to him and started to hug and caress her, but she quickly caught on to what he was doing, and submitted. She did not even try to push his hand away when he fondled her right breast, although she stiffened. Janhoy sniffed her to make sure that she was acceptable and that Ras wasn't making a mistake—at least, it seemed to Ras that this was what the lion was doing. When the woman was sure that Janhoy had decided she was classifiable and not dangerous, she pushed Ras's hand away and walked off, though slowly. Ras grinned. He had felt her nipple swell and harden and so knew that her repulsion was not genuine.

But why was she pretending?

A few minutes later, he heard the chop-chop of the Bird. He glimpsed it through the branches of a tree as it went east. After a while, it returned and circled around. It seemed to him that it was searching, and that its object was he. Then it disappeared southward.

Why was the Bird—or the angels in it—looking for him? Had Igziyabher instructed them to make sure he was safe? Whatever the reason, the angels—if they were angels—had limitations, just as Igziyabher had limitations. They could not see through the trees, and Igziyabher did not have the all-seeing eyes that Mariyam had claimed for him. Nevertheless, the angels did possess the shooters of invisible death, and Ras respected these.

Shortly after the Bird was out of hearing, the woman spoke to him in a very slow English.

"My nim iss Eeva Rantanen."

Ras was delighted. He spoke as slowly and carefully.

"I am Ras Tyger. Ras means *Lord* in Amharic."

Eeva smiled and said, "You tell me, vhy you sepeak—speak—English so peculiar?"

"You talk funny, not me," Ras said. "Anyway, we can talk now, if we go slow. Why didn't you do this before?"

She shrugged and said, "I tought you could not sepeak English vell or maype not at all. Vhen I saw you looking at the paperss, I tought you vere yust curious and did not know vhat te vordss mint. Put—but I tought I vould tery—try—again. You unterstant me?"

"Yes. You were right in one thing. There are some words in the letters I don't understand. Could you explain them to me?"

She asked him to repeat his question. He did so. They squatted side by side then while Ras pointed out the words in doubt. When they had gone through all the pages, she said, "You cawt-cawed dem letterss. Vhat you mean py —by—dat?"

Ras told her what he thought they were. She looked flabbergasted and said, "You muss tell me all about yourself."

Ras stood up. "Later. I can tell you while we're on our way, in the dugout."

They walked to the river and swam across it. Janhoy followed them. Ras led them to the bank just outside the west gate, where the Wantso kept the dugouts. He had not examined them the night before and was disappointed to find all four unwaterworthy. The weapons of the Bird had blown even through the thick wood. All were riddled with holes and unrepairable.

Not wishing to labor for four or five days to make a new dugout, Ras decided to build a raft. Even this, however, took two days. He had to poke through the ashes until he had recovered enough iron and copper axheads, adzes, shovels, and hoes. These he fitted with new handles he had fashioned with his knife from branches. The blade became dulled many times, and he had to take time out to rewhet its edges with the stone from his antelope-hide bag. Then he set to work digging up some wall-poles. Eeva helped him. Janhoy disappeared, presumably to hunt.

At dusk of the next day, Ras had a raft. It was twelve feet long, four feet wide, and held together by vines. The forepart was shaped into a broad, water-cutting head. There were two poles for pushing against the river-bottom or banks, and three paddles that had escaped destruction.

By now, he knew what the deadly things were that the twin cylinders had spat. While going through the bones of the Wantso, he had discovered several rough discs of soft, gray metal. He had connected these with the conical gray metal in the dull yellow cylinders Eeva put into the revolving barrel of her thirty-two. He asked her to explain; she did as best she could. The angels' weapons shot a bigger "caliber" and the ends of their "calibers" were notched to become *dum-dums.*

Ras was startled. This word made him remember his childhood, when all seven of the "apes" had been alive. At full moons, they would go naked into the woods where a drum of hard-packed earth stood in the middle of a clearing. And there they would dance the *dum-dum* while Mariyam and Sara beat a rhythm on the drum with sticks and the five men would caper wildly around it and give long, ululating screams. Ras would dance with them and thought it was great fun. But after the first three of the "apes" died, the *dum-dums* ceased. Yusufu said that there was not much point in it any more. Ras tried to organize a *dum-dum* among the gorillas, but had gotten nowhere. A few of the young ones had danced with him for a while, but they could not keep an interest in it long enough for Ras to feel that they were really enacting the dance properly.

Ras did not tell Eeva of this. The memory made him sad. He still grieved when he thought of his parents.

Ras and Eeva launched the raft on the third morning. They ate monkey meat and fruit for breakfast as soon as the raft was moving well in the middle of the stream. Eeva asked him about Janhoy. He said, "I hate to leave him behind, because he may go hungry. But I can't take him along. He'd get in the way, and I'd have to spend too much time hunting for him. He'll get along."

At that moment, Janhoy roared nearby. He was on the south bank opposite them. Ras shouted at him to go away, but the lion swam out to them and almost tipped the raft over getting up onto it. Ras cursed him in Arabic and Amharic, although he was glad that Janhoy had insisted on coming along. He had felt guilty about deserting him. However, Janhoy's weight made the raft sink so that there was a continual wash over its deck. It was some time before Ras could get him to lie down in the middle of the raft and not move. And the extra weight made propulsion more difficult.

Eeva asked him why they were going down-river. He opened his mouth to explain, but she said, "Iss it pecausse you vant to ket out off de valley? If so, it von't pe—be —eassy. Maype it's not possiple."

Ras said, "What valley? We won't be in any valley."

She stared at him for a while, and then she opened her mouth to say something. At that moment, just as the raft cleared a bend, the first crocodile appeared. It rowed its length down the bank with its short legs, oozed into the water, and slanted against the grain of the current to intercept them.

Farther down the bank, at least twenty others launched themselves down the mud bank. A few, some distance away from the river, lifted their bodies up and ran to the bank, where they slid down. Their voices were like far-off thunder.

Janhoy stood up and answered their thunder with one stored deep in his chest.

Ras said, "I don't think they'll come up on the raft, but you never know about them. And if they get under the raft, and Janhoy gets excited and moves around, the raft'll tip over."

He wished that his guilt and his affection for the lion had not induced him to take him along.

"We'd better push in to the bank," he said, "so we can jump for it if we have to. I've never seen them so unafraid."

Eeva started to lean her weight on her pole, but she suddenly laid it down. A ridged back had cracked open the water near her. Ras yelled at her to push. She pulled the thirty-two from the holster and pointed it at the beast. The unexpected loudness of the explosion made Ras and Janhoy jump. The crocodile whirled around and around like a carcass on a spit. The waters around it reddened, and the other crocodiles closed in on it. Eeva resumed poling, and presently they were going around another bend. There was only one crocodile in sight, and it was heading toward the bellowing around the bend.

"They must have been holding a meeting," Ras said. "Or a mating."

He laughed. It was not often he got a chance to pun in English. Eeva looked as if she wondered what his laughter was about. He did not bother to explain. And for a moment the thought that Yusufu would have understood and would have laughed saddened him.

He told Eeva why he was going down the river.

She said, "Who iss Iksiyapher—Igziyabher?"

"He is God."

"Your fater?"

"So my mother, Mariyam, said," Ras replied. "She was an ape. Or so she said, but I do not think so. And if she lied about that, then perhaps she lied about Igziyabher."

Eeva was confused by more than his pronunciation of English. She asked him to start at the beginning of his story. He said he did not know where to begin. She should keep silent while he finished answering the first question.

"You can't keep quiet any more than Mariyam could."

He was silent for a moment as he thought of that dear little brown face.

"Vhat iss te . . . de . . . the . . . matter?"

"There are ghosts, but not the kind the Wantso believe—believed—in."

"What?"

"Also, Bigagi, who killed my mother and father . . ."

"Your fater? You sait . . . said . . . dat he vass God."

"My foster father, Mariyam's husband."

"Husspant?"

"Bigagi killed them. He led the Wantso men; otherwise they'd never have been brave enough. They think . . . thought . . . I was a ghost."

A good thing for me, he thought. If they had not been so afraid of me, and so afraid of the night, I would never have been able to kill so many. It was their . . . what was the word? Superstition! That had killed them, or helped me kill them, anyway. Of course, I am easily a match for any three of them at once, far stronger, far swifter, deadly as a leopard. Nevertheless, if they had thought with their brains instead of their entrails, I would not have dared to attack the whole village. And if they had not had that senseless circumcision, maybe their women would not have been so eager to betray their men.

Eeva was irritated. "Vhy don't you answer me?"

"Bigagi must die," he said. "I think he knows I won't stop until I've found him and killed him. Of course, he was terrified by the Bird of God and wanted to get away from it. I think he's gone south; he'll go to the land of the Sharrikt. He can't reveal himself to them, because they'll kill him or enslave him. But he'll hang around the Sharrikt, just as I did around the Wantso. He'll have to, even if he might get caught. Just seeing other human beings or hearing their voices, even if they're his enemies, will be better than silence, the mouths of the dead. He might even surrender to them and become a slave. The Sharrikt have slaves, descended from the Wantso. Bigagi might think it's better to be a slave than a man with nobody to talk to or care about him."

He was silent for a minute. He pushed the raft away from the south bank, toward which it had been drifting. Then he said, "If it wasn't for you, I'd have nobody to talk to. Except the Sharrikt. But I wouldn't be a slave. I'd go into the Many-Legged Swamp—Gilluk will be there now—and I'd kill him and so become the king of the Sharrikt. Only . . . I liked Gilluk, even if he was . . . arrogant? I wouldn't want to kill him. But how else could I be king? You know, Eeva, things are sometimes hard to figure out. Anything you do, you have to give up something or do something you don't like to do."

"I ton't . . . don't . . . understand all you're saying," Eeva replied.

Abruptly, he asked her a question that left her puzzled. She said, "Vhat? Vhy von't I let you do vhat to me?"

"You don't know the word? All right then. Why won't you let me make love to you?"

Tears ran from her eyes. She said, "My husspant . . . husband . . . died only tree veeks ago. Anyvay, I don't love you."

That seemed to explain everything to her satisfaction. It certainly did not satisfy or explain anything to Ras. He could understand her grief and how it might rob her of desire. But that had been three weeks ago, and surely she must be feeling a return of some desire. She was alive, and what better way to celebrate being alive? What better way to drive away the ghosts? He loved Mariyam and Yusufu and Wilida, and he would be feeling sorrow at various times for a long time to come. He was sure of that. But, in between times, he would remember that he was alive. Had she stopped eating because her husband had been killed?

Not that making love was the same as eating. But both were things that must be done if you wanted to live.

He and Eeva were silent for a long time and only talked of matters that seemed safely remote from his question. When the sun was two hands broad above the cliffs, she said, "A pygmy hippo!"

The beast came waddling and snuffling and snorting out of the bush river and onto the bank. Ras knew it was a hippo. Yusufu had never told him that it was a *pygmy* hippo.

Janhoy, growling, got to his feet.

"You are hungry," Ras said in Amharic. He spoke in English to Eeva. "Kill the hippo with your thirty-two."

"No. I vant to save my pullets for emerchencies," she said.

He looked puzzled. She continued, "Emergencies. Dangers vhich vill apsolutely require I use the . . . bullets."

"Emergencies? Like me?" he said.

"Yes. And like the Syarrikt."

They nudged the raft onto the soft mud. Ras tied one end of his rope to an upright adz-head he had wedged between two poles of the raft, and the other end to a bush. The three then followed the hippo tracks until, hearing gruntings and snortings, they crept slowly toward the source of the noise. There were four adults and a baby, all feeding.

Janhoy stalked them while Ras circled widely to the north, stopping before he was upwind of them. Eeva remained behind a bush. Ras fitted the nock of an arrow to the bowstring, and, crouching, inched forward. Presently, Janhoy raced from behind a bush.

The hippos fled. Ras put an arrow into the leg of a bull and then another into its belly as it floundered on the ground. Janhoy caught the baby, but shortly afterward wished that he had not. Its mother charged the lion, opened her mouth, and clomped down on him. Janhoy tore loose at the price of two deep gashes. Abruptly, one of the fleeing males, no longer fleeing or else on the leg of a panicky zigzag, burst out of the bushes and thundered toward Janhoy. The lion dodged him and then had to run to get away from the female. Squealing, the two adults and the baby trotted off toward the river. Janhoy followed them but retreated whenever one of them turned and made a short charge at him.

"He'll be back in a moment," Ras said. He began hacking at the dead hippo's left rear leg. "We'll have steaks tonight, and Janhoy will fill his belly. Enough here for him for a week—if he can keep the leopards, jackals, hyenas, and vultures off. And while he's stuffing himself, we'll be going on. I don't intend to put up with him any longer."

That night, as they ate meat by a small fire, Eeva said, "Is it true you have never been out of this valley?"

Ras's ear was quick to shape itself to the shapes of her words, so quick that he now heard them as if they were "correctly" pronounced.

"If you mean, have I ever been beyond the cliffs—that is what you mean, isn't it?—no. I've tried to climb them—although my parents said that Igziyabher would kill me if he saw me. I couldn't get more than halfway up anywhere. And I can climb like a baboon. Mariyam said there wasn't anything beyond, anyway. The sky is a ceiling of blue stone. It is all stone, the rest of the world. But where does Igziyabher live? Where does the Bird go? Where did you come from? What are you? Woman, angel, demon, animal of some kind? Ghost?"

"Being a woman, I am all of them, except the ghost," she said.

They talked some more, with the result that Ras was more confused than before. He put the fire out and they walked until he thought they were far enough away from the hippo carcass. He built a small platform on two branches, and they tried to sleep. The racket from the area of the dead hippo seemed to go on all night. Several times, Eeva said, "Aren't you afraid that Janhoy will be killed by the leopards?"

"He can take care of himself," Ras said. "At least, he had better do it. I can't stay up all night shooting leopards."

"Don't you worry about him?"

"Yusufu said Janhoy was king of the beasts. Of course, if enough leopards ganged up on him . . ."

He started down the tree. She said, "Where are you going?"

"To shoot some leopards," he said. "That'll drive the rest off, or keep them so busy eating the dead ones they won't bother Janhoy."

"But you might get killed!"

"That's true."

"Please don't go."

He climbed back up onto the platform and lay down. He said, "You want me, but you only want part of me."

"You didn't intend to leave!" she said. "You were threatening just so I . . ."

She was silent. He said, "Think about how you will feel if I leave you."

She still did not answer. He waited for a while and then, suddenly feeling tired, he fell asleep.

In the morning, they left while Janhoy was still sleeping. Ras gave him a silent farewell and walked off, leaving the lion behind a bush, on his back, his legs half up in the air, his belly a solidly packed hump. Ras felt guilty again, although he assured himself that Janhoy would not starve. There was enough hippo, river buffalo, river hog, for Janhoy, and, if he had to, he could catch and kill the crocodiles or even the leopards.

He untied the rope from the bush and pushed the raft down the bank from the slight mound onto which he had shoved it before cooking the hippo. He sat down in the middle of the raft and let Eeva do all the poling. She looked quizzically at him but said nothing. The rising sun warmed the air and greened the trees. The water was a soft brown from the mud it was beginning to pick up.

Ras hunched down and looked up only when a raven shot over his head like a black thought. He brought the flute out of the bag and played a gentle but melancholy piece that he had composed during his adolescence, when occasional moods of sadness fell on him like the passing shadow of a cloud. The riverbanks flowed by with Eeva thrusting the pole now and then to keep the raft from grounding. After a while, Ras quit the flute.

Eeva said, "The river winds back and forth across the valley as if it's crazy. The valley must not be more than thirty-five miles long, but the river must be sixty miles long, at least."

"It's like a snake looking for a female in mating season," Ras said. He did not seem to have fully heard her. More minutes of silence passed. He began to beat on the raft with the palm of his right hand. Two light beats and then a heavy. Two more light beats and a heavy. A pause, and then the pattern was repeated.

Still pounding on the wood, he said, "Sometimes, I feel good. Sometimes, bad. Then I take wood and carve a figure to show how I feel. Now, I have no wood. But the flute can carve a figure of music for me. And sometimes I can carve a figure of words."

He wet his lips, and, beating on the raft, chanted,

> "White is the skull in the green,
> Green is the grass in the white.
> White is her ghost in the light,
> Light as her voice in the blue,
> Blue of the grief in the black,
> Black of the pain in the night,
> Night of the worms in the red,
> Red of the scraps on the white.
> White is the skull in the green,
> Green of the grass in the white."

His palm beat: DOOM! do do DOOM! do do DOOM! For a while, after he had stopped, both were silent. The banks of the river wriggled by and curved in and out. A brilliant green and red and white kingfisher shot by like the exclamation of a god who speaks birds.

Finally, Eeva said, "That is your poem? You made it up?"

"Just now," he said. "I prefer to make up my poems in Amharic, which I know best, but if I had done so this time, you wouldn't have understood it. I need someone to listen who can listen with the heart."

Tears trickled down his cheeks. He looked up at her and saw that she was weeping, too. He said, "You cry for your husband."

"And for me, too," she said. "I don't know how to get out of this trap. From what I could see when we flew in, the river goes into the mountains at its end, and it must go for many, many miles before it comes out on the other side."

Ras said, "I don't understand you. Explain."

He listened, and now and then had to interrupt her to ask that something be clarified. Even then, he could not believe some things.

She said, "If I had been raised in this valley and I had always thought this was the entire world, the sky was a dome of blue stone, and God lived down at the end of the river, on the edge of the world, and all those other things you've told me—well, I wouldn't understand, either. As for you, I don't know how you came here or why you're here. I can tell you, though, that I am amazed. And I was shocked when we were attacked by the copter."

"The Bird of God is only a . . . a machine? A canoe that flies? And you're not an angel or devil?"

"You don't believe me," she said. "You feel as I would feel if somebody told me that this universe was an illusion, a papier-mâché stage-prop."

"Universe? Illusion? Papier-mâché? Stage-prop?"

Eeva had trouble defining these.

"The Birds . . . the copters . . . You saw them? I would like to get up there and see their nest. But Mariyam told me that Igziyabher lived at the end of the river."

He stopped. If even a small part of what Eeva said was true, then Mariyam had lied even more than he had suspected.

Eeva asked him about Igziyabher. He explained, and then said, "When you came over the mountains, did you see Igziyabher?"

She shook her head and said, "No. No one has ever seen God."

"He is my father," Ras said.

Eeva said, "Who told you that?"

"My mother. She should know."

"I really don't know where to begin with your education," she said. "You're a unique. I think you've been victimized—horribly. I think that those papers—the ones you call Letters from God—were from a book this . . . person . . . was writing. He was describing his . . . what would be the correct word? . . . experiment? Project?"

"Prayect?"

"Project," she said slowly and carefully.

He did not understand the word in either pronunciation. Again, she entered a seemingly endless labyrinth of explanations, of explanations that had to be explained.

He learned something of her, too. She was a Suomailinen, or, in English, a Finn. She was born in the city of Helsinki, where she had spent most of her life. Her mother was of Swedish descent and a Lutheran. Her father came from a Jewish family that had emigrated from Germany two hundred years before. Her father's father had been converted to Swedenborgianism, but her father was an atheist and so was she. She had gotten a doctor's degree in anthropology at the University of Stockholm, in Sweden.

It took an hour to clarify these few statements. Ras had to know the definition of every unfamiliar word, and the definitions led both of them into labyrinths. The sun burned through the last of the blue and let darkness in. They put into shore and found a place where they had an overhanging cliff to their back and a fire in front. Ras shot a monkey and roasted it as well as he could for Eeva, who was disgusted by the raw arm he first offered her. At the same time, she asked if they had to have a fire. Couldn't Bigagi be in the neighborhood?

Ras said that he doubted it very much. He would be as far away as possible from the death dealt out by the Bird, not to mention, although he would do so, that Bigagi would be afraid of Ras also and would want to put as much distance as he could between Ras and himself. Moreover, the Wantso did not leave their shelters at night except in extreme emergencies.

Ras said, "An anthropologist, then, is one who studies people? I must be an anthropologist. I studied my parents, and the Wantso, and Gilluk, king of the Sharrikt."

"Not scientifically," she said. "Although, with the methods you used, you could probably describe the Wantso far more deeply than any anthropologist."

She resumed her story. She had lived in Sweden during the war because the Germans had come to Finland to help fight the Russians. Although the Finns did not subscribe to anti-Semitism and did not allow the Germans to impose this practice while they were in Finland, her father had sent her mother and herself to Sweden. He was killed while fighting side by side with the Germans.

She said this was ironic (a term she had to explain), but he had loved his country, and he hated the Russians as much as the Germans, since he knew that the Russians, despite their official policy, were actively anti-Semitic.

CHAPTER 11

A SHORT ACQUAINTANCE

Ras, hearing all the new words and the explanations, felt as if his head were the inside of a termite colony attacked by an anteater. Thoughts ran against each other, fell over, kicking all six legs, banged against his skull, and bit into him.

"You are angry," she said. "Why?"

"I don't know. But what you tell me makes me angry. I feel as if . . . as if someone was about to attack me with a knife. Or was trying to take something away from me."

"So that's it! You don't like to hear this! It threatens you! It makes all you've believed a lie! Shall I stop talking?"

"Talk," he said grimly.

Her husband had also been an anthropologist. She had met him at the university, where he was a student. After they returned to Helsinki, they were married. They taught at the University of Helsinki and also at Munich. They had made one field trip into the Amazon basin and several to Africa and were on this expedition on an American grant.

The existence of this valley had been known for a long time. A previous expedition, an American one, had intended to fly into the valley in an amphibian plane. But the plane had crashed shortly after take-off and killed everybody aboard.

"There was no explanation of the cause of the crash. I doubt that it was an accident. We had a terrible time

133

getting a permit to come here from the authorities. It was so difficult that we knew somebody was trying to stop us. Mika suspected that the authorities were being bribed, but he couldn't prove it. When he began a determined investigation, we suddenly got a permit. But our troubles didn't stop. My husband had to run off a native who was trying to set our plane on fire the night before we were to fly up here. And then, the attack by the helicopter . . . someone didn't want us to be here. I think it was the writer of what you call the Letters from God. Someone who is playing God."

Ras said slowly, "If you're telling me the truth . . . you said this . . . valley? . . . had been known for some time. What do you mean?"

"Oh, some airliners forced off course from time to time had reported it, and a military plane went over it once."

"Why didn't I see them?"

"Because they were flying so high. Have you ever seen several long, thin clouds, streamers, suddenly appear high in the sky, last for a few minutes, and then die out?"

Ras shook his head.

"Then you missed them. But if you ever see any, they'll be the frozen exhaust trails of a jet."

This led to more clarifications. Finally, Ras sighed and said, "I think we ought to go to sleep."

He was so disturbed that he abandoned the earlier idea of asking her to lie with him. She looked sleepy, but she did not want to stop talking.

"The copters come from the top of that pillar in the lake. You say that it can't be climbed?"

"I said I hadn't been able to do it yet."

"Do you intend to try again, perhaps at night, when you can't be seen?"

"It would be much harder to do at night. But I will do it. Later. First, I want to kill Bigagi. And then I want to find Igziyabher. He can answer my questions."

"There is no Igziyabher. Not at the end of this valley, or in the big world outside here. Nowhere."

"I'll see for myself."

He stood up. "I think I'll pile up some more brush. I'm not worried about Bigagi, but there are leopards around here."

He had just finished the construction and thrown some big, heavy branches on the fire when Eeva fell asleep. Again, he felt desire for her. The upset caused by her story and the sorrow for his parents and Wilida had deflated him. But the upset had drained away and the ghosts of Wilida, Mariyam, and Yusufu were thinning, and he could—at this time, at least—think of them without feeling as if a sharp knife were in his chest.

Eeva, as if she were reading his mind, came awake with a snort. She looked with eyes from which the dullness was swiftly polished away. She said, "Don't think about me, Ras. I don't want to shoot you."

"Why won't you lie with me?"

"Because my husband hasn't been dead very long and I still grieve for him. It's true that we weren't getting along well; we'd been on the edge of a divorce for a long time. Part of the reason for this was . . . he was infertile. He felt as if he weren't a complete man. I told him we could adopt children, God knew there were enough who needed parents, but he said no. We either had his children or none at all. And . . . there were other things.

"But even if this weren't so, even if I had no one to sorrow for, I wouldn't have anything to do with you in that way. I don't want to get pregnant and have to bear a child in this wilderness.

"That still isn't all of it. Mostly, I don't love you."

Ras was astonished. "You don't hate me, do you?"

"No."

"I didn't love the female gorillas or any of the Wantso women, except Wilida. But I lay with them. Why can't I lie with you? Don't you like to lie with a man?"

She said, "How can I explain to you what I mean? You're completely the innocent, not in the deed but in the knowledge of certain things. You're Rousseau's Noble Savage; in some respects, anyway."

"Rousseau?"

There were more explanations. Ras, half listening, thought of crawling over upon her. It would be easy to take the gun away as she slept. She must know that. Yet she slept. Did she want him to take the gun?

Force. She had said something about evil men forcing unwilling women. That had been one of the many puzzlers. He had never forced a woman or even known of the idea. Perhaps, though, that was not quite true. When he had surprised the Wantso women at night, he had used their fear of him as a ghost to get his way. At the time, he had not, however, expected a refusal or even thought of refusal on any ground except that he was a ghost.

"I don't understand why you don't want me," Ras said. "It has been weeks since you have had a man, and you have not been sick. Am I ugly? My parents and the Wantso women told me I was beautiful. And I am not

like the Wantso men. No stone knife has made me unable
to get more than a half erection. My temper is not that
of a half-starved leopard; I laugh and joke, and I like
to talk and to listen. I love to caress, to love. I love
laughter and fun and the feel of flesh. If you don't love
me, you don't hate me, either, and you haven't said you
didn't like me or told me I'm repulsive. So I don't understand."

"You're hurt," she said. "I suppose you think you have
reason to be. But don't be hurt. My background is alien
to yours. I am from a different society, so different that
you can't imagine. So don't be hurt. Just take my word
for it that I have good reasons for saying no."

Ras sighed and said, *"No* is a short word but a wide
one. There can be a whole world behind it."

"A world you'd be better off never to know," Eeva
said. "Unfortunately, the world isn't going to let you alone.
It's growing smaller every day, and its humans have less
and less room, and they're going to spill over into this
valley. There will be others to follow my husband and
me. Then . . . I don't know. I hate to think of it. What
will they make of you; what will they do to you?"

Her words made him uneasy. Something enormous and
black and deadly was over on the other side of the mountains. She spoke so convincingly. Perhaps the sky was not
blue stone.

"Just go to sleep and forget about it while you can,"
she said.

He said, "What am I supposed to do? Jack off?"

Eeva said something in what he presumed was Finnish.
It sounded as if it were a curse.

"I don't care what you do! Just don't try to force me!
Now—go to sleep!"

The moon was up when she awoke again. She sat up,
the gun in her hand, and said shrilly, "What is it? Ras!
What's shaking the branches? Ras! A leopard!"

Ras did not stop. The shadows of branches and leaves
dappled most of him, but a shaft of moonlight struck him
in the center of the body so that she could see what he
was doing. Silver spurted.

"Jumala!" she said disgustedly. And then in English,
"You filthy beast!"

Ras said, panting, "It's better than suffering."

She was silent for a while and then spoke, "Who were
you thinking of?"

He groaned and said, "Wilida!"

Eeva made a sound of disgust. She said, "And you

want me to make love to you, so you can pretend that I am your black woman. Ugh! I can smell that foul stuff. Go down to the river and wash."

"Does it excite you?" Ras said.

"I ought to shoot you!"

"Does it excite you?"

There was no answer. Ras closed his eyes and presently was asleep. In the morning, Eeva said nothing for a long while. Her eyes were red and had bluish bags under them. She moved stiffly, as if she had been in a cramped position all night. Ras grinned at her and said that she looked as if she were a hundred years old. He had expected her to snarl or strike out at him, as his parents had sometimes done when he had teased them too much before they had had breakfast.

Instead, she wept. He put his hand on her shoulder to tell her he felt sorry for her, but she jerked away.

Then, on seeing him send a high arc of urine over the top of the branchy wall, she screamed at him.

"Don't you have any shame at all? I hate you! Are you a man or a baby? You make me want to vomit, the way you act, think, eat! Especially your eating manners! You grunt and gobble and dribble and slobber like a pig! That's what you are, a pig!"

She began to weep again. Ras said, "I think I'll go on alone. You make me angry all the time. Anyway, I can go much faster without you. And, also, when I'm not angry with you, then I want to lie with you, and that is hard on me. I don't like that."

Eeva cried even more loudly. Between sobs, she said, "I am so scared. And I'm lonely!"

"Why should you be? You're with me. You're safe. And you have me to talk to, to make love to, if you weren't so crazy."

"*I'm* the one that's crazy?" she yelled. After a while, she stopped snuffling, and she dried her eyes. "I always thought I was so strong. I *am* very capable. I've never been in a situation I couldn't handle. You should see me on a field trip. I'm as capable as any man. I'm not a coward, either. Only . . . this . . . it's all so sudden, so savage, so utterly strange. And so hard. I don't think I can get out of this valley, and it may be a long time before anybody comes looking for me. And somebody wants to kill me; why, I don't know."

"You be my woman, and you'll be safe."

"I can take care of myself," she said.

Ras laughed.

"I just had a moment of weakness," she said. "I'll be all right. I feel much better now."

"You look like a red-eyed hyena."

"*Jumala!* What do you expect? I don't have any make-up, I've been half-starved and never sleeping for more than a half hour at a time, I'm dirty, my clothes are torn and almost rotted off, my hair is a mess, and . . ."

Ras said, "Yusufu told me once that Igziyabher had promised that the white woman who would be my woman would have golden hair. She would be a blond jane. You have golden hair. Are you a jane? You don't act like my woman, you act more like the demon that Mariyam said you must be. Certainly, you don't act like any woman Igziyabher would send me, unless He hated me."

Eeva stared a long time before speaking. "I think *jane* is an English slang word for a woman. It's out of date now, I think. What do you mean, you were promised her?"

Ras explained. But she did not fully understand what he was saying. And now that he considered his explanation, neither did he fully understand. Talking seemed to help her, however. She even smiled at something he said, and then she disappeared into the bushes for a while. He went in the opposite direction and finally flushed out a golden rat and pinned it to the earth with an arrow. She was waiting somewhat apprehensively when he returned. She had bathed and washed her hair as best she could in the muddy water. She looked doubtfully at the rat, but helped him build the fire, and after the rat was cooked enough so that it could not be called raw, she ate hungrily enough.

After he put the fire out, he asked her to look at the gash in his head.

She said, "It doesn't seem to be infected. In fact, it's healing amazingly fast. You must have tremendous recuperative powers." Then she explained what *recuperative* meant.

Ras shaved at the river. She watched him sharpen his razor with the whetstone, soften the bristle with water and the sliver of soap remaining, and scrape off the hairs while he squatted before the fallen tree on which the mirror was set.

"Who taught you to shave?" she said.

"Yusufu. He said that I should shave every morning because The Book said so. The Book says many things I don't pay attention to, but I like to shave. I hate these bristles on my face. I think I hate whiskers especially because Jib has them. He never learned to shave; he's as stupid as a gorilla. He has a long beard down to his belly, and it's always dirty and tangled with thorns. It stinks."

"Jib?" she said.

"Jib means *hyena* in Amharic," Ras said. "He lives with a band of gorillas up in the hills. Not with Nigus' band. With Menelik's. Jib is a white man, too. In fact, he's my brother. That's what Mariyam and Yusufu said. Mariyam said Jib has the brain of a gorilla because he made Igziyabher angry. She used to tell me that I'd be like Jib if I didn't do what Igziyabher wanted—until I pretended to be scared and cried, and then she quit. Besides, Yusufu told her that, if she didn't quit, he'd beat her silly."

Eeva looked puzzled and was thoughtful and silent for a while. But, by the time they launched the raft, she was in a good mood. She had coiled her long hair into what she called a "psyche knot," which she spelled out for him. He told her she looked much prettier, and this seemed to make her happier. She talked much, sometimes gaily. She told him about skiing in the mountains of Europe. Ras thought it would be great fun to hurtle down the slopes and fly off the hills. She pointed to the east, to a white-streaked mountain, and she described how snow felt in the hand and the face and between the toes. Ras knew the word, since Yusufu had told him what the white was on the mountains.

"You are sniffing down the back track of my life like a fox after a hare," he said. "You seem so amazed at everything I tell you."

"I said before that you were a unique. I don't think there's ever been anyone like you."

Ras went as far back as memory would carry him. He could describe some things that happened not too long after he had learned to walk.

"Remarkable!" Eeva said. "Very few people can recall so many things so early in such detail. If only you could remember before then! Mariyam's face is the first thing you can see? Nothing, absolutely nothing, before?"

Ras wept a little when he thought of Mariyam. He would never see that dear little brown face again, never feel her hugs, her kisses, hear her scolding, berating, laughing, loving.

Eeva looked embarrassed, but she continued to question him.

"You couldn't have been born in this valley. At least, I don't think so. Certainly, the dwarfs that raised you

—they were dwarfs, stunted humans, not apes—didn't originate here. The things they told you—let slip, I should say—show they knew the outside world well. But why did they pose as apes? Why that cabin by the lake, the books, and all that stuff? And what about this other white boy, Jib? He really lives with the gorillas? But then you said that you and your parents did, too, for a while. But Jib couldn't talk? Perhaps he was mentally retarded? Or a deaf-mute?"

"He could hear better than I could," Ras said. "And he was able to repeat four or five words I taught him. Water. Eat. Hurt. Man. And my name. But that took a long time. I used to play with him, although Yusufu said I shouldn't. Yusufu didn't agree with Mariyam about why Jib wasn't able to talk. He said Jib couldn't talk because the gorillas couldn't talk. Yusufu never wanted to talk much about Jib. He always got angry, or sad, when I asked him about Jib."

Eeva took her letters from the pocket of her shirt and asked to see his. She read them over again and said, "They make a little more sense now, though not much more. There was a third baby, too. He must have been the first. God! What a monster!"

"The baby?"

"No, you simple . . . sorry! I became so angry, I . . . never mind. I mean the monster who did this to you and the other two. You all must have been kidnapped. The writer of this was a businessman in South Africa, but he came from North America. That's evident, anyway. Who is The Master he mentions? What is The Book?"

"I don't know," Ras said. He shoved hard against the pole and sent the raft ahead in a spurt that brought water sloshing over its edges. Her talk made him angry, as if someone were gouging holes in a statue he had carved or had made fun of one of his drawings.

The morning and the afternoon had been stimulating and enjoyable. Now, all the questions and her certainty that something was wrong with his world soured him. He was about to tell her of this when he heard the chop-chop of the Bird coming down the green walls of the trees on the banks of the river. Eeva gasped, stood frozen for a second, and then dived into the river. She swam ten or twelve strokes, stood up, and waded to the slope of the bank, where she ran into the jungle.

Ras decided against following her. He did not have to hide. The Bird had never tried to hurt him. In fact, it had helped him when it thought that he was in danger.

He had no reason to think that its attitude had changed. Despite this, he felt uneasy when it appeared, roaring and flashing sunshine, a few feet above the treetops to the north, and then swung toward him. There were two men in it. One was at the controls, as Eeva had called them. The other was behind the pilot and looking out over the barrels of his twin machine guns, which Eeva had also described and named. Both men—Eeva had said they were men—were dressed in brown clothes and wore white masks.

The Bird—the copter—passed over him so closely that the air struck him, frothed the waves, rocked the raft, and deafened him. It went on down the river for about twenty-five yards while Ras turned to watch it. Then it stopped, the body turned, and it came back. The man behind the machine gun was pointing at the tracks Eeva had left in the mud of the bank. The Bird swung around again so that the guns were facing the jungle. Fire spat out of them. He could hear them through the bellowing of the copter. Leaves and bushes jumped.

Ras cried out, "Stop! Stop!"

The copter suddenly lifted, and then, only a man's height above the treetops, disappeared. But it came into view again, because it was climbing straight up. It was perhaps a hundred yards, perhaps a hundred and fifty, in from the river. Something about the size of a man dropped from the belly of the copter; it was a gleaming, tear-shaped thing. There was a roar, a red leaping upward, smoke, the leaves and bushes going outward with the suddenly created wind. Then there was heat, and the leaves and bushes were going inward with the wind. He smelled a strange reek. The heat increased. The jungle became a wall of heat.

Ras poled the raft to a place fifty yards downward, jumped onto the bank, pulled the raft upon the mud so that the currrent would not carry it away, and thrust himself into the jungle. He plowed through the brush as swiftly as he could on a course parallel with the flames. A bird, screeching, its feathers on fire, slammed into a tree and fell to the ground. The smoke from the burning feathers made Ras cough.

The fire was a circle about a hundred yards across and a hundred feet high. It grew outward as it ate up the trees and bushes around it, then died out on the wet vegetation, soaked by the heavy rain of two nights before. It was many hours before Ras could approach it, and even then the ashes were too hot for his bare feet.

By dawn, it had cooled enough for him to walk through the desolation. The bushes were gone. The larger trees still stood, but they were leafless, branchless, and eaten away. The stumps were gnawed away by the teeth of the flames.

Near the edge of the dead land was a lump that might have been a monkey. Its hair was burned off, the tail, hands, feet, ears, and nose were gone, and blackened bone showed through the chars of the head. Ras was sick and scared. It did not seem possible that Eeva could have escaped. Although the people in the Bird might only be men, as Eeva claimed, they had the powers of a god.

His probing uncovered a few more lumps of cooked meat, also near the outer part of the fire. If Eeva had been anywhere near the center of the fire, she would have burned entirely away. Even the bones would be ashes.

At dawn, the Bird returned to ferret back and forth over the area. Ras hid until it flew away and he could no longer hear it. Numbly, he went back to the raft.

It was not there. For a moment, he felt joyful, because he thought that Eeva had escaped the flames and then taken the raft. There were, however, no prints in the mud except his. He had not dragged the raft far enough up the bank, and the river had pushed at it until it had swung one end around, dislodged it, and carried it off.

Ras crouched behind the bush for a long time. Even in his rage, he was conscious of his imagery. He knew that his thoughts were like the sun when it begins to sink below the horizon. The red ball was his anger; the blackness approaching because of the disappearance of the sun was the gloom threatening him. He felt that he was sinking into the night and drawing after him all the beautiful colors: the pink of the underside of a cloud, the deep blue of the sky just above the east horizon, the small, smokeless fire-blue of the heart of a cloud, a splash of pale frog-green and a band of parrot-beak-yellow wavering in the dust to both sides of the sun. If he sank down, the lovely bands of life would go with him. All would be as black as a jackal's eye, as black as a leopard's intent.

The death of Eeva Rantanen was the final push to send the sun into the abyss.

CHAPTER 12

THE MANY-LEGGED SWAMP

He had not loved the pale woman as he had loved Mariyam, Yusufu, and Wilida. But his fondness for her had been increasing, even if she had frustrated, angered, and puzzled him.

Now, his rage was like the cooling, but still red, sun, and he would not allow it to sink into chill, numbing gloom. That sun in the sky had to set; his inner sun did not *have* to set. He wanted revenge. He wanted to kill Bigagi for what he had done, and he wanted to kill Igziyabher, because He had sent the Bird to kill Eeva. So he would follow Bigagi now and get that duty over with as soon as possible, and then he would go on to the river's end and make Igziyabher pay, and then he would return to the lake and somehow get to the top of the pillar, and the Bird and the men in it would die.

The red ball on the horizon of his mind—he could see it clearly—rose. The colors on the inward vault became brighter. The sun within could go backward, from west to east, bringing day again and shedding night as a snake its skin. This was the difference between the inexorable world outside his skin and the world inside.

He returned to the bank. At least, he had not left the bag and the two Wantso axes on the raft. He took these from behind a bush, where he had tossed them when he had gotten off the raft. Searching for and then chopping down and trimming poles of the desired length and thickness took him well past noon. He bound the poles together with vines. There was more delay while he hunted. An arrow brought down a parrot, and plucking feathers and building a fire and cooking took another hour. By then it was too late to start out.

Despite which, a half hour later, he knew he was too impatient to put off the trip until morning. He pushed the raft away from the bank, and the river carried it gently around several bends for a mile. The channel narrowed; the current increased; the raft picked up speed. Suddenly, the banks veered away from each other. Neighbors for so long, they had come to a parting. There was no river any more. The swamp, the Many-Legged Swamp, spread before him, and the pole with which he pushed went only a few feet into the brown water before being sucked into the mud. He had to push gently to keep it from being swallowed.

The sun was down behind the mountains now. The sky, seen in patches through the leaves and branches, was still bright blue. Under the branches, a gloom thickened. Vines hung down everywhere, as if a city of snakes lived here and were hanging by their tails to sip the water. Clusters of broad, flat pads parted reluctantly before the raft. A large insect, its wings near enough to his cheek for him to feel the air of its passage, fluttered by. A black thought in a black place.

The water sloshed over the deck of his raft and spread warmly over his feet. Something thin and sticky fell on his face, and he crouched down and wiped it away. He looked up to see a spider as large as his head scuttling down its web toward the disturbance. It was black now, though he had seen enough of them in the daylight during his first trip here to know that it was purple, with tiny yellow crescents over its body, and its eight eyes were crimson.

The Wantso said that a bite from the yellow-lined mouth would make a man scream until he drowned himself to put an end to the agony. Although Ras was not sure that he could believe the tales he heard, he did not intend to test their truth. Certainly, the spiders looked venomous.

Something slipped by in the water near the raft, curving silver behind it. Ras yanked the pole up and brought its end down against the blacker blackness. The pole struck something solid. Something thrashed in the water. Ras pushed the raft onward while the old wound in his foot burned with the ghost of the adder's bite.

A few seconds later, something hard and cold brushed against his shoulder. He gave a low cry and threw himself flat on the raft. The raft moved on. Trembling, Ras lay face down for a while. When he got to his knees and began poling again, he hunched down and kept looking to right and left. A web enfolded his head. While brushing it off, he pulled some more of the sticky strands down. His hand closed on the dried, sucked-empty shell of a large butterfly, and he threw it into the water. Cross-shaped, it floated away, turning slowly.

The night was still warm, but his skin prickled. He felt as if water bugs from the cold depths of a mountain spring were crawling over him. The feeling was so vivid that he could not restrain from brushing his shoulder just to make sure. This was far worse than being in a jungle full of leopards. There was nothing of beauty here. The spiders and snakes were dyed in the black of night, dressed in silence and poison. The archways formed by the low, thick branches and the dark, squat trunks seemed one door after another to death. Webs caught at him with weak but insistent hands. He was being covered with the gray, sticky stuff, wrapped up, wrapped around, wound into a shell as if he were a big butterfly for the spiders. Even the upper end of the pole had become gray with webs now; it was like a long, thin ghost itself—like the ghost of a snake, he thought, and then wished that he could not think of snakes.

When would the moon rise? There would be light up there in the leaves and lianas, some of which would trickle down here. Then he could at least see the great spiders as spiders. He would not be taking a large knot on a trunk as a spider waiting to spring on him, or every vine as a reptile.

He started. A lump of darkness raced across the branch ahead of him. He hit at it with the pole but missed. The raft slowed down and bumped against a tree trunk. He could hear only his own breathing. Then . . . a scrape of something on wood.

He turned around but could see nothing except a glimmering, far off at the end of row upon row of ragged arches of branch and trunk. He sighed deeply. There was much in this place to cause fear, but why should he be afraid? Was it the tales of its terrors that Mariyam had filled him with ever since he was old enough to talk? Or was it his own near-death from the bite of the adder? Or was it something else, something as old as death itself?

The swamp stank. The flowers of the water plants were invisible now, but they gave off an odor as of a rat two days dead. Decaying, water-logged wood and the dead worms in it added an undercurrent of stench. The water moved slowly, but it nevertheless moved, and so it should not have the odor of stagnation. Nevertheless, it stank. Thick with mud, it moved as slowly as the blood of a dying man. It even had the odor of blood. It had the odor of many unpleasantnesses.

This is my nose thinking with wild, scared, odorous thoughts, he said softly to himself. The water does not stink like blood. I just think it does. The spiders are not waiting to drop on me. They are frightened of me. If one should drop on me, it would be an accident. And the snakes! They will come near only by accident. They won't attack me; they can't eat me, and they know it. But accidents can happen.

When he had entered the swamp the first time, six years before, he had gone only a few yards under the branches before he had been bitten. It had seemed at the time that the adder had been waiting for him. It had been sent there by Igziyabher to bar him from the swamp.

So now, if Igziyabher did not want him to cross the swamp, He would drop a giant spider on him.

"Drop it on me, then!" Ras said loudly. "I will crush it, and I will go on!"

Nothing happened. He poled onward. Finally, the moon, as if it had been reluctant to stain its glory with the evil of the swamp, arose. Beams danced on the leaves of the uppermost branches, fluttering in the slight breeze there. Below, the air was as still as a beast lying in wait for its prey. Some light snaked through the leaves and patched the water here and there with moonshed, or cast a hummock into gray-green, or spread a decaying green over a pad, and once showed him a long, thin, drooping stalk with a dead-yellow flower sticking out from a crevice in a tree trunk.

The moonlight touched webs as if they were harpstrings; the twang was noiseless, but heard by Ras. A round object with twelve long legs ran across a web, flashed dark purple, and was gone. The web itself was asymmetrical, lopsided, with strands clustering thickly in crazy diamond shapes in some areas and only a few, widely separated strands in others. The spider that had spun this web had been sick or insane, Ras thought.

What starved and diseased thoughts could possess a mad spider? Tiny, red things hobbling on absurdly crooked crutches across the black, spongy floor of the minute mind? Hobbling toward a mote of a glow, the cracked diamond in the heart of the fleck-sized brain, to worship there or to warm their claws before its crystalline blaze? Overhead, jagged fissures through which light fell from each eye, light filtered by the webs within the stalks which held the eyes?

Something splashed. Ras jumped and swore in Amharic. Then he laughed, as the head of a large frog appeared in a pool of light. A gurrook-gurronk started up nearby. Others joined it. The swamp at once became less menacing. Ras pushed the raft on. The frog was ahead of him, swimming toward its goal, whatever that was. Probably a female or a meal of some kind, Ras thought.

Abruptly, the frog went under water. It did not dive. It had reared up, its webbed paws clutching upward, and then had slid backward and under. Briefly, the black, flat tail of some animal showed, and then there were only ripples and one big bubble that took a long time bursting.

More webs spanned the archways ahead of him. Now that he could see them in the light, he broke them with his pole, wiped the pole off, and pushed the raft until he came to the next web. The spiders ran down toward the thing they thought was caught in the strands, then stopped when the web was destroyed. Ras reached up with the pole to knock the spiders off or poke them so they would retreat. Once, a spider fell on his raft and almost caused Ras to tip the raft over in his efforts to get away from it and at the same time smash it with the pole. It scuttled back and forth before it sprang at him. The pole caught it in midair and swept it out into the water and the darkness.

This went on all night. By dawn, the webs were few and scattered. The trees were not so close together. The water became more shallow, and finally the raft bogged down in the mud. He had to leave it and walk in water that came no higher than his ankles, or in mud. He supposed that there were waterways for the raft, since the Sharrikt and the Wantso crossed the entire swamp in boats when they raided. To find them would take too much time. It seemed best to go ahead on foot, although he squirmed inwardly at the idea. The vegetation coming up from the water was thick enough to hide snakes. He used the pole to prod the growth before him. This made for a slow and nervous progress.

The mud gripped him up to his ankles sometimes and other times up to his calves. His feet came out with a sucking noise as if the swamp were trying to mouth him down. The grass had a tough, saw-toothed edge that cut his legs raw. He was bitten once by a small insect. The pain caused him to jump up into the air with a cry. After a while the pain ceased, but the bite left a purple mark the size of his thumb-end on his leg.

After a mile of this, he was able now and then to cross on slightly higher ground. He went on even more cautiously, since it seemed to him that he might be getting near the end of the swamp. A snake about four feet long, its head a shiny black, its body a dull scarlet, tried to evade his pole. He broke its back, cut off its head, stripped its skin, gutted it, and ate it raw.

He had not quite finished eating when he heard shouts ahead of him. He threw the body away and crept as quietly as he could in the mud. A waterway lay before him, and the low hill—or islet—from which the noise came. The water came up as far as his waist before it began to shallow. The islet was covered with trees, and the brush was thick between the trunks. Here the trees were close enough to allow him to travel from one to the other on the branches, if he proceeded cautiously.

Up in a tree close to the edge of the islet, he looked across a flat stretch of black, sandy-looking land about twenty yards long. On the other side was another islet not quite as high as the one he was on. Although the trees were also thick there, they did stand far enough apart so that he could glimpse two men now and then. Both wore white robes. Both were thin men, over six and a half feet tall. They had dark-brown skins and long, skinny legs. They hopped about, shouting or grunting, while one jabbed with a spear and the other slashed with a sword.

The man with the sword was Gilluk, king of the Sharrikt.

CHAPTER 13

CAPTOR,

WHO'S THE CAPTIVE?

Three years before, one of Ras's periodic visits to the Wantso village had coincided with the third day after the capture of Gilluk. From his observation post on a tree across the river from the western gate, Ras had seen the cage in front of the Great House. The bamboo cage had been about seven feet high and four feet wide. It had hung by a rope from a horizontal bamboo log suspended at each end on three hardwood legs. Both the cage and the support had been specially built for the occasion, as Ras had learned when he had moved in closer to eavesdrop.

He had listened to the women weeding in the fields and to the guards on the northern gate. The whole village had been swinging between exultation and apprehension. The capture of the king of the Sharrikt would be talked about, sung of, for generations. The Wantso had captured other Sharrikt—the last one four years before— but never had they caught a king. He would be treated royally; his torture was to last a month, if not more, before he would be burned alive in the cage.

This had been the cause of the exultation. The apprehension had been caused by the possibility that the Sharrikt might come in force to rescue Gilluk. It had been necessary to keep additional guards on the village and also to send out scouts to check on the Sharrikt movements. This had worked a hardship, because the Wantso

149

could not afford to tie up so many men with such duties. The guards and scouts should have been hunting. The reduction in the meat supply had already caused complaints. Tibaso, the chief, had made a speech to the men in which he had urged them to be patient and enduring. They were to silence their wives if they complained. This was a time of grave crisis but also a time for great jubilation. Nothing so good occurred without a need for self-sacrifice, hard work, and unceasing devotion and unremitting vigilance.

The Wantso would keep a united front and would defeat any invasion force, as they had done in the past. The Wantso were a great people—in fact, The People, the meaning of the word Wantso—and they must, by the very nature of things, win out over the Sharrikt, a kind of two-legged, very depraved animal. And so forth.

There had been loud shouts of approval, a mass repeating of his most fiery phrases, and much clashing of spears and drinking of beer. The whole village, men, women, and children, including the guards, had got so drunk the first night that the Sharrikt could have walked in before dawn and taken their king out without disturbing anybody except the chickens and hogs. Ras had heard this from the women, who had been laughing about it and also passing back and forth some gossip about events that night.

Tibaso had reprimanded his people the next day and said that they must stay sober until they were sure the danger was past. While making his speech, he had drunk beer to wet his throat and kill his hangover.

Ras had had no difficulty in learning how Gilluk had come to be captured. The women, and the guards, had gone over the event many times in much detail. It seemed that the Sharrikt made one raid a year. This always took place during the seventh day after the seventh new moon of the year. And so two Wantso juveniles had been stationed on a platform on a tree near the place where the river suddenly became the Many-Legged Swamp. They had seen the war canoe containing the seven Sharrikt enter the river mouth just before dusk. The invaders had stopped to camp on the bank a mile up the river, and the Wantso boys had paddled by them in the dark an hour later.

The next day, as the Sharrikt had crept toward the village, they had been ambushed. A heavy piece of mahogany dropped from a tree had knocked the king out. The Wantso had come down out of the trees and from the bushes to struggle for the unconscious body of Gilluk. The Sharrikt, outnumbered, with three wounded in the first volley of arrows and spears, nevertheless had charged the Wantso around Gilluk. One Sharrikt had been killed, and two more wounded. They had fled then and escaped, although the Wantso could easily have overtaken them. The Wantso had not pursued, because they had won a glorious victory with no dead or wounded on their side, so why should they push their luck?

Although the Sharrikt had left Gilluk behind, they had rescued the *bibuda*, as the Wantso called it. Ras had recognized the weapon that the king had carried, because the women had described it. It was, in English, a *sword*. Apparently, it was the only one in existence, even among the Sharrikt, and the king alone was entitled to carry it. In fact, if the Wantso were to be believed, the sword was the true king of the Sharrikt. The man who earned the right to bear it was only the keeper of the sword, and he was called king by courtesy only.

Gilluk, the man in the cage, was as dark as the Wantso. He was very tall and slim, unlike his short, stocky captors. His hair looked very curly, not kinky, although Ras could not be sure at his distance. It was long and coiled into a beehive shape on top of his head. The face was long and narrow, and the forehead was high and smooth. His eyes were dark and large. His nose was as eaglish as that of Ras's mother. The cheekbones were prominent; the lips, thin; the chin, jutting. His clothing was, except for the short, leopardskin cape, unlike anything Ras had ever seen before. He had worn a long-sleeved robe that had covered his body and fallen to his knees. It had been of some sort of cloth, white, with red and black symbols, geometric figures, around the hem.

Gilluk had stood in his cage, gripping the bars, and stared at his captors. These had jeered at him and poked sharp sticks at him. He had refused to flinch, except when a stick threatened his eyes. Then he had turned his head.

Ras had known what the Wantso would do to him. When Ras had been with Wilida and the other children, he had listened to vivid descriptions of the torture of the last captive. The children had rolled their eyes and licked their lips or giggled or shivered in mock horror. Only Wilida seemed to be even a little sorry for the Sharrikt. This was one of the traits that had endeared her to Ras. However, he had not understood why he liked it because she felt some sympathy for the fellow. If the Sharrikt had stayed away from the Wantso, he would not have had to suffer so. Why hadn't he minded his own business and remained south of the swamp?

Probably he hadn't, Ras had told himself, for the same reason that he was now taking a chance by spying on the Wantso. It was exciting and daring. But if you were caught, you had to suffer the consequences.

Curiosity, and the boldness of the idea, not a desire to save Gilluk from torture, had made Ras decide to steal the king. There had also been his hurt at his rejection by the Wantso men, and a wish for vengeance. And there had been the deviltry of it. What an exciting deed and what fun it would be! He had shivered with anticipation.

He had known it wouldn't be easy. He had had to take his time. The first night, he had climbed the sacred tree to observe more closely. A fire was kept going by the cage, and one man sat on guard at all times. He was relieved at roughly two-hour periods, and the new guard and the man being relieved usually squatted by the fire and talked for a long while.

The cage had had one side that swung open and was tied shut by a rope of antelope-hide. There had been nothing except the guard's vigilance to keep Gilluk from untying it himself.

There had also been guards on the platforms inside the palisade, one for each of the four gates. Theoretically, these were supposed to keep watch on the area outside the village. However, they had kept looking inside at the prisoner.

The following day, the village had resumed a more or less normal routine except for the unusual number of guards. The women had gone into the fields, and two men and two juveniles had left to hunt or to scout. Tibaso had sat in his chair and stared at Gilluk while drinking beer. Wuwufa, the spirit-talker, wearing a tall, conical headpiece and a wooden mask, had danced around the cage while he whirled a bull-roarer. Its deep humming and the twang of a harp played by old Gubado had gone on all day.

At noon, most of the men had gone off in small groups, probably, Ras thought, to scout for Sharrikt. The Wantso did not paint their faces when hunting unless they were after some unusual leopard or crocodile, one that had gotten a reputation, hence, a name. And when they did this, they traveled in one large band.

The only adults left in the village had been Tibaso the chief, Wuwufa the spirit-talker, old man Gubado, and three women taking care of the younger children. The other women and the older children had been working in the fields. Two men had been left as guards, one on the platform above the gate of the wall across the neck of the peninsula, and another man on the platform of the western gate.

Ras had thought that if there was a Sharrikt war party watching from the jungle, it could easily rescue the king. But the Wantso had not really been careless. There had been little chance that the original war party would have tried anything. And it would have taken some days for the invaders to return to the land of the Sharrikt, organize a large party, and return to the area of the village.

Ras, watching the scouts leave, had had an idea so daring that he had had to resist it. Why not enter now, through the northern gate, and uncage the king? By the time the western gate guard got down off his platform—if he had the courage to face the ghost—Ras would have the cage door untied. He would hand the king a spear and a knife, and they would kill the guard if he dared attack. Fat Tibaso and old Wuwufa would be no obstacles. Ras and the king could take one of the dugouts beached on the mud outside the village to get across the river and into the jungle. Gilluk might not want to go north with Ras, whose white skin would shock him because of the ghostly implications, but expediency would doubtless override this. If it didn't then Gilluk was stupid and probably not worth the effort by Ras.

On the other hand, Ras had liked the idea of stealing in at night, overcoming the guard, and whisking the king out. The biggest difficulty with this had been that entrance and exit would have to be via the branch over the spirit-talker's hut and the hut itself. If there was much noise, if anyone gave the alarm too soon, the entire population would be popping out of the huts. And while Ras trusted his speed and agility in getting away, he was uncertain of the king's. And if the first attempt failed, a second would have little chance. The guards around the king would be increased. Moreover, the gate guards were sure to see Ras as soon as he ventured out into the light of the fire by the cage.

"I'll do it now!" Ras had told himself. He had not known why he had decided that this was the time; he had just known that it was.

He had climbed down the tree and dodged behind other trees and bushes until he had stood outside the northern gate. It had been closed but not secured by the big timber bolt on the inside. It had squealed as he had swung it wide enough to slip between it and the wall sidewise. The bull-roarer, the harp, and Wuwufa's chanting had drowned the noise of the wooden hinges. Past the gate, he had run to Wuwufa's hut, under which he had crouched for a moment. There had been no outcry. Chufiya, the western gate guard, had had his back turned at the moment. Sazangu, the boy on guard on the wall at the eastern edge of the fields, had been drinking from a gourd.

Ras's heart had thudded like a Wantso stomping the hard earth during a dance. He had shaken, but he had taken a firm grip on his spear, breathed deeply, stepped out from under the house, and walked into the center of the village in the midafternoon sun as if he had lived there all his life. He had been twenty yards from the cage before anyone saw him.

Wuwufa had stopped twirling and chanting. The wooden bull-roarer at the end of the string had gone on whirling over his head, because the one arm holding the string had been rigid. The bull-roarer had slowed down; the noise of the air rushing through the holes in it had died to a whistling. The children had screamed and fled in all directions except toward Ras. Tibaso had heaved himself up from his chair, dropping his wooden cup and splashing beer onto the dust. He had yelled and then tried to get under his chair. Chufiya, the western gate guard, had howled. Wide-eyed, Gilluk had gripped the bars of his cage and shaken.

Wuwufa had come out of his rigidity to fall to the ground, where he had begun to roll back and forth, yipping like a wounded jackal. Ras had strode by him but had not been able to resist stopping long enough to give Tibaso's huge rump a little kick. Tibaso, his head stuck under the chair, had squalled and tried to crawl even farther under.

Ras had laughed and gone to the cage, where he had slashed at the antelope-hide rope with his knife. In Wantso, he had said, "Come on out, Gilluk! We have to get away fast!"

If Gilluk had understood him, he had given no indication of doing so. He had been gray beneath the deep-brown pigment, and his teeth had chattered. He had not resisted when Ras had taken him by the hand and pulled him from the cage. He had acted as if he were being taken away by Death Himself.

"I am not a ghost. I am the son of God," Ras had

said. Gilluk had groaned and continued to act as if his soul had left him.

"Do you understand Wantso?" Ras had said, and then, "Never mind."

He had decided not to give Gilluk a weapon. When Gilluk came out of his shock, he might attack his rescuer.

Ras, pushing Gilluk ahead of him, had walked toward the western gate. Chufiya, the chief's half-wit son, his eyes shut, had been standing on the platform and jabbing his spear in all directions while mumbling something. Ras and Gilluk had passed through the gate under him, and still he had blindly jabbed the spear.

There had been no pursuit. Gilluk had sat in the front of the dugout while Ras had paddled. By then, Ras had decided that he would go up the river for several miles before taking to the jungle, instead of crossing the river and plunging immediately into the cover of the green. It would be some time before the scouting party returned, and no one now in the village was going to try to track them down.

As they had left the dugout and walked toward the place where the king was to be kept, Ras had laughed. He had been happy. The whole event had seemed so delicious, now that the danger was over. He had felt like rolling on the ground and laughing for hours. He had danced a few steps. The Sharrikt king had flinched and quivered every time Ras had come near.

And so Ras had brought the king to his prison for the next six months. It had been a bamboo cage that Ras had originally built as a leopard trap. It had been in the forest near the edge of the cliffs below which the country of the Wantso began. Gilluk had crawled into it at Ras's gesture, and Ras had secured the door. Gilluk, being a man, would have been able to unlock himself in a few minutes, but Ras had arranged a device that would have shot an arrow into Gilluk if he had lifted the door. Moreover, if Gilluk had lain down to avoid the arrow, he would have had to push the heavy door out at an angle that would have required the muscles of a very strong man. At the same time, while the door was being opened, a mechanism would lower another, which had been fitted with sharpened bamboo stakes on its lower edges. These would come down on the man lying on the floor as he lifted the outer gate. When the outer gate reached a 45-degree angle, the arrow, which had been very close, would be released, and the mechanism would release the inner gate so that it would fall upon the man. Ras had been proud of the device and had had moments when he had wished that Gilluk would try to escape, so that he could see how well the mechanism worked.

He had explained to Gilluk what would happen. Gilluk had not seemed to understand at first, but the second time around, he had nodded his head and said something in Wantso. It certainly had not been quite the Wantso Ras knew, which difference was explained when the king later told him that he spoke only a little of the language, which he had learned from the slaves of the Sharrikt. The slaves had been descended from Wantso captives taken many generations before, and these slaves spoke a language that deviated from that used by the villagers Ras knew.

Ras had cooked some monkey meat, very rare, and offered it to Gilluk, who had refused it. Ras had not known whether monkey meat was tabu or if Gilluk had been afraid to eat a ghost's food. He had shrugged and left it to Gilluk to decide when—if ever—he would eat.

In the morning, Ras had started to learn the Sharrikt language. Gilluk had refused to talk until Ras told him that he would be released if he co-operated but would die if he did not. The king had decided to start talking at once. By noon, he had been eating. Ras let him out of the cage, at spearpoint, so that he would not continue to foul it with excrement.

The next evening, Ras had returned to the village. He had wanted to find out what kind of storm his passage through had left behind. He had climbed to a perch on the branch above Wuwufa's hut and, lying on it, had watched and listened. The entire adult male population, except for the guards, had been around a big fire in front of the chief's chair.

Bigagi, spear in hand, had been making a speech.

"This ghost is no ghost!"

"Ahh!" the men had said. "This ghost is no ghost?"

"This ghost is no ghost," Bigagi had said. "He comes from the Land of the Ghosts."

"He comes from the Land of the Ghosts?"

Bigagi had said, "He comes from the Land of the Ghosts. But this ghost is no ghost!"

"This ghost is no ghost!"

Bigagi had strode back and forth and brandished his spear at the darkness outside the walls.

"This ghost is no ghost. He is no ghost. He is the son of a female ape and of a tall spirit."

"He is the son of a female ape and of a tall spirit?" the crowd had chanted.

"He is the son of a female ape and of a tall spirit!" Bigagi had said. "The ghost himself told me so!"

"The ghost himself told you so?"

"The ghost who is no ghost told me so himself. That was when I was young, before I became a man. Wilida and Sutino and Fuwitha and Pathapi and I played with the ghost when he was a child. We played with him in the bushes on the bank of the river!"

"Ahh!" the men had breathed.

"Now Sutino is dead and is a ghost. You cannot ask him unless Wuwufa asks for us. But if you do not believe me, ask Wilida or those still alive."

"Ask Wilida or those still alive?" the men had said.

"They will tell you that I do not lie!"

"This ghost is named Lazazi Taigaidi!"

"The ghost is named Lazazi Taigaidi!"

"This ghost is no ghost!"

"This ghost is no ghost!"

"This ghost bleeds!"

"Ahh! This ghost bleeds!"

"I have seen him bleed! His blood is red!"

"His blood is red! Ahh!"

"Ghost blood is white! Ghost blood is white!"

"Ghost blood is white!"

"The ghost bleeds red blood!"

"This ghost bleeds red blood!"

"This ghost is no ghost! This ghost is the son of a female ape and of a tall spirit!"

Before the men could repeat, Tibaso, the chief, had interrupted. "Is not the son of a tall spirit a ghost?"

Bigagi had shouted, "This ghost can die! Thus, he is not a ghost!"

"This ghost can die?"

"Ahh!" Tibaso had said. "But this ghost lives in the Land of the Ghosts. Would a living man dare live in the Land of the Ghosts?"

Bigagi had shouted, "Shabagu, our great ancestor, led us into this land!"

"Shabagu, our great ancestor, led us into this land!"

"Shabagu was the son of a tall spirit," Bigagi had said. "His mother was Zudufa, a Wantso woman."

"Shabagu was the son of a tall spirit. His mother was Zudufa, a Wantso woman!"

Bigagi had yelled, "Shabagu died!"

"Ahh! Shabagu died! He did indeed die!"

"Lazazi Taigaidi is the son of a tall spirit! Shabagu was the son of a tall spirit! Shabagu died! Lazazi Taigaidi can die!"

"Ahh! He can die! He can die!"

The men had clashed their spears and shouted, over and over, "He can die!"

Wuwufa had sprung up from his squat and begun to dance. He had shaken a rod on the end of which were three gourds containing pebbles.

"He can die!" he had groaned. "He can die! The Ghost-Boy can die!"

The others had stood up and begun to dance while they had chanted, "He can die!"

Tibaso had heaved himself up from his chair and banged the end of his wand on the earth platform. The men had stopped dancing.

"Who, then, will kill the ghost?"

Bigagi had said, "This ghost is no ghost! I will kill the son of a female ape and of a tall spirit! I, Bigagi, with my father's spear!"

The spear thrown by Ras had thudded a few seconds later into the earth before Bigagi. Its shaft had quivered. The men had fallen silent; they had looked at each other and around them, and their eyes had rolled. At that moment, Ras had given the shrill, ululating cry that Yusufu had taught him. The men had looked up and, by the light of the fire, had seen Ras's white figure on the branch above Wuwufa's hut.

They had shouted and screamed and knocked each other over in their bolt for their houses. Only Wuwufa had remained outside. The old man had lain on the ground, his eyes wide open, his mouth working, saliva spewing from his lips, his body jerking.

Ras had given the cry again and left.

On the next visit, he had found that Bigagi had appropriated his spear. Bigagi had now claimed that Lazazi Taigaidi could be killed with his own spear and that he, Bigagi, would do it.

Ras had gone into the village late that night and taken the spear from Bigagi's side. As he had circled in back of the outer circle of houses to return to the sacred tree, he had stopped. Why not go into Wilida's house instead?

The more he had thought of it, the more excited he had become. He had walked back to her house, which had been in the inner circle, in front of the house closest to the western gate. As he had done at Bigagi's, he had gently pulled out one side of the bamboo matting let down at night to form a door. It had been tied with cords at the bottom ends to two small posts. He had slipped sidewise between the end of the matting and the doorframe into the hut. He had waited there until his eyes had adjusted to the lesser light within. The hut had been split into two rooms by a bamboo wall not quite six feet high. Wilida's father and mother had slept in the inner room. Wilida and her brother, seven years old, had been sleeping on mats against opposite walls of the front room.

Ras had lain down beside her and whispered her name in her ear. On hearing her moan softly, he had put his hand over her mouth. She had become fully awake then and had tried to get up, but he had pushed her head back down and whispered savagely to her. She had quit struggling, although she had been quivering. His other hand, on her breast, had felt her heart violently squeezing out the juice of terror.

"I will not harm you, Wilida," he had said. "If you will not cry out, I will take my hand off."

She had nodded, and he had removed his hand. She had said, softly, "O Ras, what do you want?"

"I want you, Wilida! I have ached for you for a long time. Haven't you ached for me?"

She had kissed him, but, before he could kiss her back, she had said, "Wait!"

She had risen and gone across the room, where she had fiddled around some pots, the clinking of which had made him nervous. She had returned, saying, "I have taken the potion that will keep me from conceiving."

"Why not bear my child?" he had said.

"Because they would know that it was the ghost's child, and they would throw it to the crocodiles and throw me into the fire."

An hour later, Wilida's brother had sat up and begun to cry. It was no wonder, Ras had thought, what with all the noise they had been making.

Wilida's mother had called out, and Wilida had answered, saying that she would comfort the child, who must have had a bad dream. Ras had rolled over to be hidden by her body. When she had left his side to go to her brother, she had exposed him, but he had lain still, hoping that Thizabi would not notice the white lump on the floor in the darkness.

Wilida had soothed her brother, and presently he had been sleeping again. She had urged Ras to leave then because it had been too dangerous for both of them. She had promised that she would meet him again, but outside the village, the first chance she got.

Then she had said, "I have heard the women talk. They think that Seliza has been meeting you out in the bush! Is that true?"

Ras was skillful in lying, since he had found it more convenient to do so when he wished to escape punishment from his parents.

"Ah, I would not touch Seliza if I ached so much that this thing were longer than my spear. I ache only for thee, Wilida!"

He had left the village an hour before dawn, just as a cry had risen from Bigagi's hut. The houses vomited people, who gathered around Bigagi. He had awakened, he had said, and had noticed at once that the Ghost-Boy's spear had been gone. Who had taken it?

Bigagi had no sooner asked the question than the spear had flown from the' darkness into the center of the village, near the earthen platform, and been followed by the ululating cry. Within ten seconds, everybody, including Bigagi, had been back in the houses.

Ras had gone down the tree and back to the place where Gilluk had been caged. Gilluk had begun to get over his fear. He had taught Ras his language, so Ras had been able to carry on a fluent conversation on a simple level within twenty days. Gilluk had taken advantage of his captor's knowledge of Sharrikt to complain about being cramped. Ras had built a larger cage.

A month later, Gilluk had complained again. Ras erected a cage that had really been a house, twenty feet by twenty feet by ten feet. It had had a thatched roof and mats that could be unrolled to form walls.

Gilluk had complained that his food was not cooked enough. Thereafter, Ras had served him his meat well done.

Gilluk had complained that he was suffering because he had no women. At home, he had three wives, each of whom he must nightly satisfy, except, of course, during the forbidden menstrual periods. Or else . . .

"Or else what?" Ras had said.

"Or else I will be thought failing, and a weakening king means a weakening kingdom. And so I would be fed to our god, the crocodile Baastmaast."

"There is nothing I can do about getting you women," Ras had said. "You will have to make love to your hand."

"A king does not do that," Gilluk had said. "Only little boys."

"Indeed?" Ras had said. "That may be true for the Sharrikt. But I have never seen why I should suffer, although my parents tell me I must. In some ways, you remind me of my parents. But tell me more of your curious customs."

One day, Ras had addressed him as king, and Gilluk had said, "I am no longer the king. The moment I lost Tookkaat, the divine sword, I ceased to be king. I could become king again, during the seventh new moon of the year, when the keeper of the sword, that is, the current king, must go alone into the Great Swamp and there defend himself for seven days against all comers."

Gilluk explained that anybody of royal blood who could kill the king during this time became king. Gilluk had slain all contenders in the Great Swamp for the past seven years. It seemed, though, that the sword had deserted him.

"If I let you loose, what would you do?" Ras had said.

"I would hide in the Great Swamp until the seventh new moon. Then I would kill whoever is king now and return to my village. But if I went back before then, the king would have me killed. He would be in his rights to do so, and he would be stupid if he didn't. There is no one of my people who is as great a warrior as I."

"How many men are there of royal blood?"

"All the Sharrikt are of royal blood."

"I am the son of God," Ras had said. "Would the Sharrikt accept me as king if I killed the man with the sword?"

Gilluk had taken so long answering that he must have been very surprised by the question, if not numbed. Finally, he had said, "How can a non-Sharrikt be king of the Sharrikt?"

"I can't see why not," Ras had said.

"It has never happened."

"Does that mean that it can't happen?"

"The hands of my mind cannot grasp the idea," Gilluk had said.

"What would happen if I killed the man with the sword and entered the Sharrikt village with the sword?"

"I don't think that the Sharrikt would know what to do. They would kill you, run away, or ignore you."

"I'm not easy to ignore," Ras had said.

A few weeks later, Gilluk had complained that he needed more space.

"But you have two rooms now," Ras had said. "You have as big a house as any Wantso—except for their chief, and he lives in the Great House, which is also a place of worship."

"My house in my land has many rooms," the king had said. "It has more rooms than I have fingers and toes. It is made of stone, and it is three stories high. And it has a wide, wooden veranda that runs completely around the second story. And a wide court in its center."

"You had that when you were a king because it was the king's house," Ras had said. "You are no longer a king."

"Yes, but my ways are still kingly."

For some reason, Ras had felt compelled to build at least another room. Gilluk had been a little happier, but he had not been completely satisfied. By then, Ras had been getting interested in the construction, and he had also been curious about how far Gilluk's requests would go. So he had built two more rooms.

Gilluk had said that it was a fine house, although it lacked a veranda on which he could take the outer air.

Ras had built the veranda. The king had watched him and now and then suggested improvements or ways to work more efficiently. When Ras had completed the veranda, he had had to construct a huge cage for the house. He could not allow Gilluk out on the veranda until he had some means of keeping him from walking away. He had had to construct it strongly, and then he had thatched a roof for the cage so that Gilluk could walk outside the house in the narrow yard during the rain.

While he was building, Ras had had to take time to hunt and cook for the king. He had also had to go home every few days to visit his parents. And he had gone down to the Wantso village to observe them, to make love to Wilida, or, if she could not get away, with Seliza and also with Fuwitha. One night he had confronted Thiliza, the chief's youngest wife, as she returned from the river with a pot of water. She had almost fainted, but he had talked quietly to her while he held a knife to her throat, and after a while told her what he wanted. She had been too frightened to say no, and, after that, she, too, had been making arrangements to meet him in the bush, since her terror had soon become enthusiasm. And there had been others as time went by.

Ras had told Gilluk about the women. Gilluk had taken delight in hearing the details, and he had seemed to think it was a good joke on the Wantso men. Then he had become depressed.

"I suppose you still want a Wantso woman?" Ras had said.

"Yes, unless you can get a Sharrikt woman for me," Gilluk had said. "After all, when I was king, I bedded three wives every night and also occasionally a good-looking slave woman or free woman during the day."

"If I brought you a woman, then I would have to keep her in this house, too. I couldn't ever let her go. She would bring the men back with her and they would capture you again."

"Don't let her go then," Gilluk had said, looking happier than Ras had ever seen him.

"Then the woman would be unhappy," Ras had said. "I don't hate the Wantso women. As a matter of fact, I love them. Why should I make one of them unhappy just to please you?"

The king had not answered. Ras had then said, "Two things puzzle me. One, why am I working so hard to keep you happy? Two, why haven't you tried to escape? I know that if I were in your position, I would have managed to get free a long time ago. And I think you could have, too."

Gilluk had said, "It will be six months until the seventh new moon of the new year. I have no place to go now. I don't want to live in the Great Swamp until then."

Ras had rolled his eyes and twisted his face and said, "So you will stay here in comfort and be fed, as if you were lolling in your stone palace."

"You are being rewarded for your efforts," Gilluk had said. "You are learning the language and customs of the Sharrikt. And you have the pleasure and profit of my company."

"But I could get all that with much less work," Ras had said.

"No. If I am not pleased, I won't talk to you."

"A little fire on your skinny buttocks would make you chatter like a monkey."

"No, it wouldn't. A Sharrikt does not succumb to torture. He laughs and sings and insults his enemy until his skin falls off and his flesh smokes off and his bones begin to burn. I would not do what you wish me."

Afterward, Gilluk had said that the house was beginning to be what it should be. But it was not furnished properly. Ras had groaned and asked him what he wanted in the way of furniture. Gilluk had described many things in detail.

"And how long did it take you to make these?" Ras had said.

"I? I didn't make anything. A king does not work with his hands to fashion objects. That is work for the artisans. A king rules his people; he shapes them; they are his work."

"You're not my king. But I'll make the furniture for you. Understand—I am doing this only because I like to make things, especially if they are to be carved from wood. I love to take the raw wood, the unshaped blocks, and reveal what is hidden in them."

"And I love to take raw people, the unshaped minds, and reveal what—if anything—is hidden in them."

"I, too, but not in the way you do," Ras had said. "I use words with people, not a knife as I do with wood, but I use words to help others reveal themselves to me and to themselves. You, however, if I understand you correctly, shape people to your idea of what they should be for your purposes. I have no purposes other than my curiosity and delight in knowing people."

"I shape them as they should be shaped for their own good and the good of the kingdom," Gilluk had said.

"I think that the best thing for the kingdom would be a people who shaped themselves in their true shape. Just as a block of wood has a true shape, which I expose with my knife. Now, this shape can be found only by me. A Wantso finds another when he carves wood. And a Sharrikt would find yet another. But you force all people to flow into one form—if I understand correctly what you told me of your work as king. This is not good. Every man should be his own sculptor."

"Then a kingdom would not be a kingdom. It would be like a pack of baboons."

"Baboons are the wrong example for you to pick," Ras had said. "Every pack is a kingdom, a kingdom such as you described to me."

"You are very ignorant," Gilluk had said.

"I agree," Ras had said. And he had set to work to build and carve the furniture for Gilluk.

The king had not been pleased when Ras had presented him with the first roomful of chairs, a table, a divan, two vases, and a statuette.

"The furniture and the vases started out to be Sharrikt. But they ended up something strange. The furniture in my great stone house is square and solid and heavy. It inspires confidence and security. But your works are curving and airy and light, and they go this way and that way and confuse me. They look something like chairs and a table and a divan and vases, but the resemblance has to be looked for."

"They look delightful to me," Ras had said. "And, yes, strange, but strange in a stimulating way. I had fun making them, and at the same time I was fashioning beauty. The furniture that you described to me seemed unutterably ugly."

"And that statuette?" Gilluk had said. "Now, really, do you think I look like that?"

"Not to the eye that sees the sun and the world it paints. But there is an eye behind the eyes above my nose. That sees you as this. If you don't like what I do for you, I shall take them away. You can make your own furniture."

"It's better than nothing, I suppose," Gilluk had said. "And I suppose I can get used to it. You are going to make me a bed, of course?"

"I'll do that next," Ras had said. "Only don't complain about it."

"What good is a bed without a woman in it?" Gilluk had said.

Ras had thrown his hands up and walked away from the enormous cage. It had seemed to him that if he kept on trying to please the king, he would end up with a house that would stretch from cliff to cliff and from the cataracts of the north to wherever the river disappeared in the southern mountains. He would have to chop down every tree in the world and carve them into furniture. And still the king would not be satisfied.

Ras had decided that he would soon free Gilluk. The seventh new moon of the new year had been only three weeks away. He would then finish the house for himself. It made a splendid place away from home, although it would have to be provided with several underground exits. Ras had not intended to be caught in it without more than one way out. Then he had begun thinking of how delighted his parents would be with it and how they would praise it. This had caused some conflict, because he had wanted a secret place all to himself, and yet he had wanted to share it with Mariyam and Yusufu. However, he had doubted that they would come this far to see it. They had never been south of the plateau—or so they had said.

He had been able to do neither. The day he had expected to release Gilluk, he had found that Gilluk had freed himself. Moreover, the house and the cage around it had been ashes.

For a while, he had been so angry that he had thought of tracking Gilluk down and killing him. But the anger and the hurt had lessened, and he had not been sure then that he would take vengeance even if he had the chance. Gilluk had not been able to help it, because he had been unable to appreciate beauty, and he had been under no debt to Ras to be grateful. He, Ras, had gotten more out of knowing Gilluk than Gilluk had out of knowing him. He had not had to build the house; he had done it because he had *wanted* to do it. Just as Gilluk had remained a prisoner only as long as he had wanted to be a prisoner.

CHAPTER 14

YOUR TURN NOW

There was silence for a moment, followed by more shouts. More silence. A thunking sound and a short, shrill cry. Silence again. Then chopping sounds. Ras came down out of the tree and slid down the steep, muddy bank. His legs sank into what had looked like solid ground. He pulled them out and began to slog through, hoping that the sucking sound would not be heard by those on the islet, although it did not seem likely. Before he was halfway across the level, he no longer cared whether he made noise or not. The semisolid stuff was up to his waist, and his feet found no support. He was sinking.

Panic almost made him thrash around. He remembered, however, what Yusufu had told him to do if he were caught in such a situation. Fighting against the impulse to struggle violently, he threw himself backward as hard as he could, his arms flung outward, his hands turned palms downward. He dropped the spear, which quickly sank. Although the upper part of his body began to sink, his legs came up. He rowed backward and managed to pull his legs loose and then to extend them straight out. His body continued to sink slowly. By presenting more surface per weight, he was decreasing the rate of speed of sinking.

However, his next move, to roll over quickly, was frustrated by the bow and quiver on his back. The quagmirish stuff was filling the quiver and adding so much weight that it had started to drag him down. His head was almost under by the time that he had freed himself of the bow

167

and quiver. The quiver disappeared almost at once. His sidewise position now made him lose his buoyancy, so he began to sink more swiftly. With a desperately swift roll, he succeeded in getting upon his back again and spreading out his legs and arms. His head was turned to one side, permitting him to see the depressions made by his body where he had just been. These were filling in rapidly.

The thin, sticky film of the quagmire covered his entire body and face. He could taste its grittiness and smell its stench. It smelled like death. Bodies at the bottom were sending up their rottenness.

Overhead, the sun shone fully upon him. From distant trees came the cries of birds and the chitterings of monkeys, all intent on their own business of feeding, excreting, mating, looking out for enemies, and quarreling among themselves. A large raven flew above him and cawed at him. Ras got a grim amusement out of the thought that this raven would not be able to eat him if the mire did get him.

However, he did not intend to die here.

The antelope-hide bag, attached to his belt, did not seem to drag on him. Although it contained the mirror, razor, and whetstone, it held enough air to give it support. As for the knife, it was heavy, but he meant to hang on to it until he had to choose between going down or getting rid of it.

He rolled over again, jerking his body at the same time to swing it around parallel with the bank. With one more effort, he would be in line to start his pattern of roll, lie flat, roll, lie flat, roll, until he reached the shallow part of the mire. The bag impeded his movements, but not seriously.

It was then that he heard his name called. He raised his head to see Gilluk on the land to his far right, just stepping onto a fallen tree that formed a bridge from islet to islet. In one hand, Gilluk was carrying his sword, bloodied almost to the hilt, and holding with the other to the hair of a severed head.

Ras attempted to increase the speed of his escape procedure. By the time he was able to stand up with a solidity of a sort under his feet, he found Gilluk standing on the bank above him.

Gilluk smiled and said, "Ras Tyger!"

Ras smiled and said, "Gilluk, king of the Sharrikt!"

"Not king until I kill all those who would be king," Gilluk said. "Of the four who came into the Great Swamp to kill me and take the divine sword from me, three are dead. Two heads are cached in a hollow tree. You see the head of the third here. One has not found me yet nor I him."

Ras was at a disadvantage. Up to his knees in the mire, he could not jump to one side or leap ahead. He could snatch out his knife and throw it, but the hilt was slippery and Gilluk would drop down on the ground at the first movement of his hand to the knife. If Ras then tried to come up the slick bank, he would be exposed to the sword. He could draw the knife and act as if he were going to throw it, then try to get up the bank before Gilluk would realize he was tricked. But he was sure that he could not move swiftly enough to do this.

"What do you intend to do?" Ras said.

Gilluk looked thoughtful. The head dangling by its long hair from his hand looked much like Gilluk. The skull was narrow; the face, lean and long. The eyebrows were bushy, and the eyelashes were so long and thick they looked like flower petals. The nose was thin and arched, the upper lip was long and broad, and the chin was cleft and pointed. The eyes were closed. Surprisingly, the mouth was also closed. The expression was that of downcast thought, as if the head were pondering this new state of death. A drop of blood fell from the jagged neck.

Gilluk finally said, "What am I to do with you?"

Ras thought that if Gilluk took long deciding, he would not have to make up his mind. Ras was sinking, and although his rate of descent was much slower than farther out in the mire, he would be completely under within a few minutes.

Gilluk must have realized this, yet he spoke slowly. "That mire has killed many animals and men. There is a very hideous and powerful god who lives at the bottom with his two wives. He seldom lets a victim get away. Yet you got away—to this point, anyway. You must be a favorite of the gods or else hard to kill. Or both. But then you said you were the son of the god you called . . . ?"

"Igziyabher," Ras said. "Not *a* god. *The* God."

"Of course there is one God," Gilluk said. "But He has many forms and many lives, all at once. Can you understand that? This sword is a god. I am a god, though I can die. However, I am not standing here to discuss religion with you."

"Why are you standing there?" Ras said.

"If I killed you and took your head back, the people would be amazed. And I would be regarded as a great king indeed. The minstrels would sing of me until the end of the world, when the sky will break into frozen pieces of blue stone and the great crocodile will lead all the devout Sharrikt past the ice and the fire to the land of plenty and of much war, where a man can fight all day and even be killed and yet arise at evening to eat all he wants and bed all the women he wants."

"That's interesting," Ras said.

"Not since the great king Tabkut has a king killed a demon," Gilluk said.

"The Wantso say that I am a ghost," Ras said.

"You can be killed, so you're a demon, not a ghost," Gilluk said.

"What's the difference between the two?" Ras said. "Also, how do you know that I can be killed? Have you ever seen me dead? Have I not been bitten by a green swamp adder and lived, fought a leopard with my bare hands and lived, been struck by lightning and lived? Why do you think I can be killed?"

He was talking to gain time, although he could not gain too much or he would just disappear from the conversation. He thought of trying to throw the knife, since it seemed the only thing to do. But, though he was now up to his knees, he did not want to force Gilluk to attack him. He would rather wait another minute.

Gilluk smiled and said, "I saw you cut yourself while you were building my house. Ghosts don't bleed, and demons have green blood that boils."

"My blood is red and doesn't boil."

"That was only an illusion to fool me. But you couldn't trick me enough to hide the fact that you do bleed."

Ras shrugged. Everybody he had known could think up reasons to justify his actions.

"Why are you here?" Gilluk said. "Are you running from the Wantso men because they would no longer tolerate your laying their women? Or do you still have that ridiculous idea of becoming king of the Sharrikt?"

"All the Wantso, except for one, are dead," Ras told him, and he described what had happened.

Gilluk was upset. "All dead?" he murmured. "That is unbelievable. And sad. On whom, then, will we make war? We have no enemies now—except you."

"I am no enemy," Ras replied. "Unless you insist that I am. But don't forget the Bird of God. It killed the Wantso because it thought they would kill me. Igziyabher, my Father, is looking out after me. If He saw that you Sharrikt had killed me, or even intended to do so, or even held me prisoner . . ."

Gilluk had seen the Bird a number of times during the past twenty years, although never close. To him, it was not the Bird of God. It was itself a god of the air —Faalthunh.

Ras noticed that the raven that had flown over him when he had been sinking in the mire had returned to settle down on a branch above Gilluk. Its hopes for Ras were renewed, and it probably lusted for the head dangling from Gilluk's hand. In fact, now that Ras thought about it, the raven would benefit no matter who won or lost here. Being a scavenger was not a hard life at all, unless a bigger carrion-eater came along.

"I can't believe," Gilluk said, "that the gods could care more for you than for any Sharrikt, and especially the king of the Sharrikt. Besides, I hold the divine sword, and surely it will protect me."

"It didn't protect the man you took it from or keep the Wantso from capturing you," Ras said. "How do you know it hasn't decided to give itself to me?"

Gilluk looked upset again. There was a long silence. Ras pulled his legs up one by one and moved to one side a little without objection from Gilluk. Now the mire was only up to his calves, but he was beginning to sink again. Gilluk said, as if the matter had been settled once and for all by indisputable logic, "You're not a Sharrikt. The divine sword wouldn't permit you to take it."

"Let me up on the bank, and we'll see about that," Ras said.

"No. It would be ridiculous," Gilluk said. "I think I'll . . ."

He jumped as the raven cawed loudly and flapped off the branch. Ras shouted, "Watch out behind you!"

Though he had seen no one, he knew that somebody —or something—had alarmed the raven.

Gilluk whirled. A man screamed something in Sharrikt. Gilluk ran out of Ras's view. Ras slogged out of the mire and crawled up the bank. Peeping cautiously over the edge, he saw Gilluk swinging with his sword at a Sharrikt who held a big club. The club had spikes of copper on the knobbed end and seemed to be of very hard wood. When the sword struck it, the sword bounced off and left only a dent in it. Its wielder was as tall as Gilluk, younger, and more powerfully built. His face had the same features as Gilluk's and the severed head's. The head was now lying on its back on the edge of the bank, where Gilluk had dropped it, and it was staring upward, the shock of falling having opened its lids.

Ras thought that, if he had been Gilluk, he would have thrown the head at the attacker instead of dropping it, and then rushed him as he dodged the head. Or he would have waited until he was close to the man and then hurled the head in his face.

Ras cleaned the mire from his hands and his knife and from his feet and then waited. The combat had a ritualistic form, or so it seemed to him. The contender would swing his club, and Gilluk would block it with his sword. The contender, instead of replying with a straight-in thrust of the spiked club at Gilluk, thus using it as a sword or spear while Gilluk's guard was down, would step back and wait. Gilluk would lift his sword, the contender would bring his club down against the raised sword, and so it went.

The two grunted at every impact of weapons. Their dark-brown skins gleamed, and their once-white robes were darkened with sweat. After a while, it became evident that Gilluk was tiring faster than his opponent. His previous battles must have taken much strength from him.

"Stab him!" Ras called. Gilluk paid no attention. "Use the point of your sword!" Ras added.

Gilluk was soon backed up against a tree. A few more blows from the club would knock the sword from his weakening hand. Then, Ras supposed, Gilluk would stand as steadily as the tree behind him to receive the death-blow. It was disgusting. A battle for your life was no time to subscribe to ritual or to any conventions. It was time for every trick you knew and any you might invent at the moment.

Gilluk's sword was torn from his grasp, and he *did* stand, erect, glaring, and unflinching. There was something to admire in this noble attitude, but not to imitate. Nor did Ras see why he should allow the execution to take place.

He picked up a heavy branch and walked toward the victor to knock him out. He was silent, but Gilluk's expression must have warned the other. Whirling, he lifted his club and charged. Ras dropped the stick, shifted the knife from his left to his right hand, and threw it. The Sharrikt screamed and fell on his side. Ras pushed him over to his back and removed the knife from the pit of the stomach.

"I would have reasoned with him if I'd had time," Ras said.

Gilluk did not reply. Ras supposed that it was because he did not know what to do next. He had never been in a situation like this. He did not make a move to pick up the sword and only murmured something unintelligible when Ras took the sword.

"Are there any more contenders?"

Gilluk nodded, the Sharrikt gesture for no.

"I asked you once what you intended to do."

Gilluk slid down with the tree trunk against his back. "You're not going to kill me?"

"Not unless you force me to."

"I can't go back as king. I can't go back at all. I lost the sword to another, and . . ."

"So here it is back in your hands," Ras said. He hefted the sword, admiring its length and heaviness and sharpness and hardness and the strange symbols on its guard and hilt. Then he threw it down so that its tip plunged into the earth and it remained upright.

"You're now king."

Gilluk said, "It isn't right."

"You croak like that raven," Ras said. He squatted down to be face to face with Gilluk. Tears made Gilluk's eyes shine like polished ebony in a dismal rain.

"Don't be so distressed," Ras said. "Look at it this way. The divine sword is a god, right? And it determines who becomes the king, right? So it has ended up in your hands, and the contenders are dead. So the sword has decided that you are still king."

"I am weeping, not because I don't know what to do, but because my young brother, Tannup, is dead."

Gilluk pointed at the head. "And because my cousin, Gappuk, is dead. And because the other two I killed are my nephews. I loved them all. And because, in a few years, my son Tinnup will be trying to kill me."

"If they loved you as much as you loved them, why did they try to kill you?" Ras said.

Moaning, Gilluk raised himself and pulled the sword from the earth.

"It is the custom for men of the Sharrikt to go into the Great Swamp and there try to kill the king. I killed my father, almost on this very spot, many years ago."

He raised the sword on high and brought its edge down upon the neck of Gappuk. The blade must have been dulled, or else Gilluk was weak from the fighting and from grief or both. It took two more strokes before

Gappuk's head rolled free. Gilluk picked up both heads by their long hair and, holding them with one hand and the sword with the other, strode away. They circled the quagmire, crossed the fallen log, and came to an open space. Two bodies lay side by side here. Gilluk, still weeping, took their heads from a hollow trunk, tied the hairs of each into a large knot, plaited the free ends of each together, and then slung all four over his shoulder. He walked off westward. Ras accompanied him on his left side. He was making sure that he was not within reach of the sword.

"Aren't you going to bury the bodies?" Ras said. "Or at least sink them in the quagmire?"

"I'll send slaves to bring them in. Then I'll conduct the funeral—I am the chief priest, also—after which the bodies will be given to Baastmaast."

"Oh, yes, the crocodile god."

"God *as* the crocodile," Gilluk said. "I believe I told you about him when I was your . . . guest."

He gave Ras such a peculiar look that Ras wondered what he was thinking.

Ras said, "I am placing myself under your protection."

"You may trust me to act as a king should," Gilluk said.

"You don't seem grateful that I saved your life," Ras said. "If I had known that it was going to make things so complicated for you and distress you, I wouldn't have interfered."

"It's just that there is no precedent. I'll work something out. However, don't you say anything about what happened. I won't lie to my people, even if it is for their own good. Not unless I'm forced to lie, that is. I'll just show them Gappuk's head and let them assume that I killed him."

After wading through a mile of swamp, they came to higher and drier land. Gilluk led the way on a winding path through thick woods. On emerging into more-open country, they were near the riverbanks. The river had re-formed at the edge of the swamp. The earth sloped gently down from that point.

Another stretch of dense trees and brush had to be crossed before they again came to the river, which had resumed its wandering. They climbed a high hill, from which Ras could see the country for several miles. The river abruptly widened to become a heart-shaped lake about a mile across, where it was widest. There were many boats with white-garbed fishermen on the blue waters, and, on the far side of the lake, a pink cloud. This, Ras knew, had to be a great flock of flamingos. There was a small island near the middle of the northern shore. On its humped back was a circular, open-roofed building of stone gleaming whitely in the sun.

"The House of Baastmaast," Gilluk said. "The bodies will be placed inside it, and Baastmaast will eat them and so conduct their souls in his belly to the underworld."

Near the lake shore was a steep hill, on top of which was a building, the largest Ras had ever seen. It was circular and of large, white-and-dark-stone blocks. Four tall and slender towers rose from the roof at the north, south, west, and east.

Between the lake shore and the east foot of the hill was a cluster of smaller buildings, which Gilluk said was the town, where the artisans, fishermen, and slaves lived. Cultivated areas ran out on three sides of the hill for several miles. Their green was crossed by brown paths and roads and a number of blue canals fed by the lake.

Ras was amazed. He had visualized a small, stockaded village and a field like the Wantso's. Gilluk had described many things about the Sharrikt while he was a prisoner, yet he had said little about this. Now that Ras thought about it, he knew why. Gilluk's descriptions had always been in answer to Ras's questions. These had been mainly about the language and customs and attitudes of the Sharrikt. He had asked very little about their dwellings or artifacts, except for the art works and musical instruments.

After having walked a quarter of a mile from the hill, they came to a watch post, where two men stood on top of a platform on a high framework of bamboo. These wore tall, conical hats of bright-orange river-hog hide and white robes. They carried large, round shields of hippo hide and long spears with copper heads. When they saw Gilluk, they clashed the spearheads together in salute. Thereafter, they gawked at Ras. Gilluk became impatient and asked them if they had lost their senses. Had they forgotten what they were to do when the victorious king came out of the Great Swamp?

The guards unfroze, and their eyes resumed their usual size. One began beating on a large drum. The other scrambled down the ladder and dipped one knee and his spearhead onto the earth. On arising, he looked more closely at Ras, and then he began to shake. It was some time before his teeth quit chattering.

Only when Gilluk gave a sharp command did the man

turn away to precede them on the triumphal march to the king's castle.

The guards looked as if they were half-Wantso and half-Sharrikt. They were taller than the Wantso but shorter than Gilluk, more sturdily built, and had thicker lips, flatter noses, and very tightly curled hair. Gilluk verified Ras's guess. The royal family, the administrative class, and the priestly class, were the only pureblood Sharrikt left, and the only ones classified as Sharrikt. The freemen were descended from Sharrikt masters and Wantso slaves. Gilluk seemed almost apologetic in his explanations. Originally, he said, when the Sharrikt came into this world, they had been pure. They had attacked the Wantso, who at that time lived where the Sharrikt now lived, had killed some, enslaved others, and driven the rest across the Great Swamp. From the beginning, death was the penalty for the Sharrikt who had children by a slave woman. Nevertheless, Wantso women bore children to their masters, and the penalty ceased to be applied within a few years after it had been decreed. A king who had had a dozen children by various slaves had changed the law. And, in time, so many were born to farmers and artisans that they had become freemen, through some development the history of which Gilluk did not know.

The pureblood aristocracy numbered about thirty-five. Thirty-one, now that four had died in the swamp. There were about eighty freeman farmers and artisans and about sixty slaves. A percentage of the freemen could bear arms as guards, defense soldiers, and policemen, but only the pureblood could go to war. This explained why Gilluk had been so upset on learning that the Wantso were all dead. There could be no more expeditions to test the courage and skill of the young Sharrikt and to entertain the older.

"The Wantso require that their young men kill an elephant, a buffalo, or a leopard before they become full-fledged warriors," Ras said.

"Oh, the Wantso!" Gilluk said contemptuously. "Among us, a youth has to kill a leopard as the first step to becoming a warrior. Then he must participate in a raid in which he kills or at least wounds a Wantso, before two witnesses. After that, he is entitled to contend for the kingship if he wishes.

"Oh, yes, take off that leopardskin loin-covering. Only Sharrikt are allowed to wear leopard. The people might become confused if they see leopard on you."

"If I do that," Ras said, laughing, "then every man in this kingdom will have to lock up his wife."

Gilluk looked grave and said, "You may be right. Very well. Keep it on—for now."

"I was only joking," Ras said.

They entered the farmland, where women and children ran up to the road to make obeisance to the king, and men followed to see what the excitement was about. Most of them stopped far short of the road when they saw Ras. Children hid behind their mothers' billowing skirts and peeped wide-eyed at him. Ras grinned, causing them to scream and cover their eyes.

"I see I'll have to educate my people," Gilluk said. "They must learn that you are only a bleached-out man, not a ghost."

"I hope so," Ras said. "I'm getting tired of scaring people."

"I think I can solve that problem," Gilluk said. Ras felt uneasy at this remark, one of many enigmatics uttered by the king since the battle in the swamp.

"Get behind me," Gilluk said. "No one is allowed to walk by my side, and only a herald, or a corpse in a funeral procession and its bearers, can precede me."

Ras stepped back a few paces. There were more people along the road now. The farms were closer together. There were many hogs, chickens, and goats, and a number of the buffalo domesticated by the Sharrikt. The fields were rich with yams, sweet potatoes, sorghum, millet, and other plants.

These people were more numerous and wealthier than the Wantso. It was evident that they could have sent an army to wipe out the Wantso if they had wished. And he had believed the Wantso when they had boasted of some day slaughtering the Sharrikt and ridding the earth of them!

Presently, as they neared the hill on which the king's house stood, ten freeman warriors, commanded by a cousin of the king (as Ras found out later), became their guard of honor. Gilluk's three wives, each standing under a parasol held by a slave-boy, greeted him. He kissed his fingers and touched the wet ends to their foreheads while they were on their knees before him. All three closely resembled Gilluk. Two were his cousins, and the chief wife was his sister.

The wives arose to walk behind the king. They had intended to crowd his heels, but Ras so frightened them that they dropped back twenty or more paces.

Gilluk's white-haired mother, carried in a chair by two strong Wantso slaves, came down the hill to greet them. She wept with joy because he was alive and with grief because her younger son was dead. A priest, wearing a white robe that trailed on the ground and a triple-tiered hat with a stuffed baby crocodile on its top, saluted Gilluk. While all stood in the sun, except for the wives and the mother, the priest gave a long speech.

Ras, hungry and impatient, interrupted the speech with several loud breakings of wind. The wives giggled. Gilluk turned around and glared, at which the three women became quiet. At last the priest finished, and the procession went up the hill on broad, stone steps. At the top, Gilluk led the parade through a wide and tall square entrance into the building, which was even larger than Ras had thought. Actually, what had seemed one building from a distance turned out to be two, with a high wall around them. In the space between the buildings, on a platform of wood, were several cages of bamboo.

Bigagi was in one.

Ras was startled. He opened his mouth to ask Gilluk how Bigagi had been caught and also why he had not said anything about this. Gilluk pointed at Ras and ordered the guards to put him in a cage. Since they surrounded Ras, the tips of their spears only a foot from him, he did not resist.

After he was encaged, Ras asked Gilluk why he had done this.

"It's a matter of justice," Gilluk said. "You kept me in a cage for six months, so . . ."

"And when the six months are up?"

"I don't know. You're a problem."

"Why am I?" Ras said. "Why can't I live with you Sharrikt as a Sharrikt? I mean you no harm."

"Well, I don't know what attitude to take toward you," Gilluk said. "You can't be treated as a divine Sharrikt. On the other hand, you're too dangerous to be a slave. You'd run off into the jungle and wage the same kind of war against us as you did against the Wantso. You can't be a freeman, since you'd never work a farm or take orders from us.

"Yet, you haven't harmed me or threatened the Sharrikt. And I do like you, in spite of your being a savage. So, I don't know at this moment what I'll do when the six months are up. Meantime, you must pay for having kept me a prisoner."

Gilluk smiled and said, "You'll be treated well, just as

you treated me well. That means, of course, you'll get no women. I asked you for women, you know, and you wouldn't get me any."

"Not wouldn't. Couldn't."

"Oh, you could have. You didn't want to."

Ras gestured at Bigagi.

"I have to kill him, since he killed my parents. What about him?"

"I'll think about him," Gilluk said. "He was caught the night before I went to the Great Swamp. He was trying to get a slave woman to run off with him, but she didn't want to. She had a husband she liked—the Wantso born here aren't circumcised, you know—and Bigagi had nothing except danger and starvation to offer her. She turned him in, and he killed the woman and a soldier before he was captured. He is a mad hyena. Normally, he would be tortured as a public example. Now, I don't know. It would be interesting to pit him against you. We sometimes match captured Wantso warriors against each other. They don't want to fight, but they do, because both would be killed if they didn't. In this case, however, each would like to kill the other, so it would actually be more gratifying to you than to us if you fought to the death."

Ras asked what the winner's fate would be.

"Well, if the Wantso knew that he would be tortured if he won, he might let you kill him to escape it. So, I'll promise him that he'll live if he wins, although he'll have to be blinded. If you kill him, you'll be tortured. It's only just. You will have cheated us out of torturing him."

Ras said that he did not see the logic. Gilluk replied that he could not be expected to do so, since he was only a bleached-out savage. However, he should not complain, because he would be given six months of easy living—except for the lack of a woman, of course.

"I may not have you fight the Wantso," Gilluk continued. "Who knows? I may allow you to live, even to go free."

"With my eyesight?"

"Who knows?" Gilluk's smile showed that he knew that this uncertainty was to be a six-months' torture.

"I don't want to do this," he said. "I do like you. But a king has to see justice done, no matter how it grieves him personally. Now, what can I do for you?"

"Bring me food," Ras said. "I'm hungry. And then go away, so that seeing you won't spoil my appetite."

CHAPTER 15

ONE DEAD, ONE DYING,

ONE ALIVE

"What is it you want now?" Gilluk said.

Ras could not tell him in one word, because Sharrikt had no "squirrel-cage." He described in detail what he wanted and how it could be built.

"I've already built you a larger cage with bars in it for you to exercise on," Gilluk said. "I've installed troughs and pipes and a water wheel and assigned slaves to work the wheel so you can drink and bathe any time you feel like it. That took much material and labor . . ."

"You found it interesting, didn't you?" Ras said. "It kept you from being bored, didn't it?"

Gilluk clucked, frowned, and said, "True. I've been thinking about building a water system for my quarters. But this rotating cage! Why do you want it?"

"I don't have enough space to exercise properly. I need to run and run fast, mile after mile. I can't do it in this narrow box unless I have a rotating cage. Of course, you could build me a cage a half mile long, then I'd have enough room."

Ras laughed. Gilluk said, "Why don't I just build a cage over the entire land? Would that satisfy you?"

"I'd still be in a cage," Ras said.

"All right," Gilluk said. "I'll do this for you, since you treated me fairly well when I was your prisoner. But don't ask for more. Don't ask for the moon."

"Could you get it?" Ras said. "I understand that one of your titles is Tamer of the Moon."

"As chief priest, I do have jurisdiction over it," Gilluk said. "Sometimes, I think you're poking fun at me. You don't seem to realize how serious your situation is. I may torture or kill you at any moment."

"You promised me six months. Is your word no better than a slave's?"

"Sometimes considerations of state force a king to go back on his word. The welfare of the people comes first."

He interrupted Ras's protest. "You haven't yet removed your leopardskin. I know I told you to keep it on, but I've changed my mind. My people are confused about this."

"Tell them that I am the son of God, hence, divine, and entitled to wear leopard."

"They wouldn't understand that, because you're a non-Sharrikt. And I reject that reasoning because it's not for the good of my people."

"Oh, then you admit that I could be the son of God?"

"Not in the sense that He was your immediate Father. Of course, all creatures are the sons of God in that He created them. And the Sharrikt are indeed His sons in the sense that He lay with the divine mother, Earth. But you, by your own admission, are the child of a female ape. This seems to indicate that you are a bleached-out Wantso, since they are descended from a hyena and a female chimpanzee."

"The Wantso don't—didn't—think so. They claimed to be the only true men. In fact, Wantso means 'Real Men.' "

"The jackal would like to be a leopard," Gilluk said. "Enough of this bindybandy. Are you going to give me your leopardskin?"

"If I don't?"

"I'll cut off your water and your food."

"I didn't deprive you of anything," Ras said. "Did I threaten you if you wouldn't take off your silly-looking white robe?"

"There was no reason for you to do so."

Ras hesitated. To give in seemed to be surrendering a principle. On the other hand, he did not care about the skin, and Gilluk was certainly stubborn enough to let him die of thirst. Yet, he would lose Gilluk's respect—and his own—if he agreed. But—he wanted to live so that he could escape.

Gilluk said, "Well?"

"You'll have to take it off me," Ras said. "Send in your men; let them try."

Gilluk smiled slightly. "You'd like to kill some, if you could? You probably would, too, before they subdued you. No. Hand the skin through the bars."

"Then you admit that I am superior to the Sharrikt warriors," Ras said. "If that is so, I must be divine, too, even more divine than you Sharrikt. Hence, I'm entitled to the leopardskin."

Gilluk scowled and said, "It's difficult to find flaws in your logic. However, I have an argument stronger than your logic. That is my power. I'll see how resistant or logical you are when your tongue swells in your throat and your body weeps dust because of its thirst."

Ras quivered with his struggle. He gritted his teeth and, after several minutes, said, "Here. You can have it."

He extended the skin through the bars and dropped it. Gilluk, smiling, gestured at a female slave to pick it up. Gilluk's three wives, standing a few paces behind him, giggled and whispered to each other. Gilluk quit smiling. Dark of face, he barked at them to leave.

Ras said, "I told you so." He gripped a bamboo bar in each hand and put his face between them.

"You may have my leopardskin. Yet, I am still wearing it."

Gilluk was startled. He said, "What do you mean?"

Ras tried to think of the Sharrikt word for "spiritual." Perhaps the Sharrikt had no such word. He said, "You have taken my material skin. Nevertheless, I am still wearing the idea of a leopardskin. A ghostly skin, as it were."

Although Gilluk snorted at this, he was intrigued. He asked Ras to explain.

"You can strip me of my leopardskin. You can kill me. But you can do nothing to strip me of the idea that I am worthy of wearing the leopardskin. Even if I am killed by you, I still have not agreed with you. And there is the idea, the idea that I am wearing the skin. It still exists, though I am dead."

"But . . ." Gilluk said. He stopped to frown. His eyes seemed to turn inward. "I'll have to think about that some more," he said. "You make my brain itch, and the more I scratch it, the more it itches. It was the same when you had me in your cage. Now, you are in my cage. Yet you are doing the same thing to me."

"The idea of my freedom still exists even when I am locked up," Ras said.

Gilluk, shaking his head, walked away. Ras was glad that he had not stayed to talk. He was not sure what he had meant. The "idea" had come to him like a ripened fruit falling off a tree.

Ideas were shadows. They appeared as suddenly as a shadow appeared when a man stepped out of his house into the sun.

Ras was excited. Were "ideas" beings with a life of their own? Were they like ghosts, or demons, that could possess a man, then move on when the man died or when the "ideas" were exorcised? If this was true, they must have a sense of discrimination, otherwise every man would have the same ideas. Why had this "idea about ideas," for instance, come to him but not to Gilluk?

The next day, the artisans arrived to get instructions from Ras on building the squirrel-cage wheel. Gilluk and two spearmen stood by to make sure that the artisans did not get close to Ras and that he talked only about the project. Later, when the artisans returned with bamboo and set to work, they were cautioned to keep their tools, the copper knives, saws, adzes, gougers, planes, drills, and axes well out of his reach. A small annex was built to the cage, and the wheel was installed in this. Artisans extended saws on the ends of long handles and cut through the bars of the big cage where they formed one side of the smaller cage. Ras was politely asked to throw the sawn wood out of the cage. He politely obeyed.

The construction took a week. During this time, Gilluk's mother and wives came often to watch the work. The wives spent more time observing Ras than they did the artisans, though they did this when Gilluk's back was turned. Gilluk would not allow them to talk to Ras, and he did not want his mother to do so. She paid no attention to his requests. Her life was painful and boring, and she was not going to miss this entertainment. For some years, she had suffered from swelling of the joints and a rigidity of the hands and feet. The conversation of her daughter and nieces was insufferable, and the trivialities of the conversation of the slave women irritated her. There was little of interest in the court life, and so she was delighted when Ras was captured. At first, she was content to sit on a cushion on a wooden chair and watch while two slaves fanned her and swatted the flies away. She listened to Gilluk and Ras talk. But after a while she began asking Ras questions.

He took a liking to the old woman, especially when he found that she had as keen a mind as her son's. She also had a sense of humor, when she wasn't being twisted with pain.

It was through her that he managed to get back his antelope-hide bag and most of its contents. Beginning with the second day of imprisonment, he had complained to Gilluk that he needed to shave. Gilluk had refused to give him the bag, saying that he would not permit him to have the razor or the mirror. The razor could be used to cut the rawhide rope that tied the door of the cage. As for the mirror, it was an evil thing. It would capture a man's spirit if the man looked into it long enough.

Ras said that he would return the razor each morning after he had shaved. And he needed the mirror to shave. What did Gilluk care if Ras's spirit were caught in the mirror? Gilluk continued to deny him. Ras's face itched as the stubble grew. He became irritable. Moreover, he planned to use the mirror for more than an aid in shaving.

Shikkut, Gilluk's mother, was fascinated by his beard and also repulsed. Ras explained to her how he could get rid of it and how uncomfortable it made him and how his parents had told him that daily shaving was a religious duty. The next day, Gilluk, looking sour, threw the bag through the bars. He left orders that Ras was to return the razor each morning as soon as he was through with it. He could keep everything else in the bag.

He walked away without answering Ras's question about why he had changed his mind. An hour later, Shikkut came down to tell him what had happened. She had pleaded with Gilluk to let Ras have the shaving equipment. When she had seen that gentle arguments were useless, she had given Gilluk a tongue-lashing. Her son always became uncomfortable, even distressed, when she did this. Finally, he had surrendered.

Ras thanked her and then continued talking with her. He learned much of the construction of the palace and the topography of Sharrikt land from her. Nobody else except Gilluk was given permission to talk to him except in the line of business.

Despite this, he talked to the two guards at night.

He had also tried to talk to Bigagi, but the Wantso would not speak to him, or to anybody. He squatted at one end of the cage and seldom moved.

One day, the Bird of God flew over the castle. Ras could not see it, because the top of his cage was roofed over. The Sharrikt, screaming, ran inside the building. Only the daytime guard and Gilluk stayed outside. The guard had been told he would die if he left his post for any reason. Gilluk, the defender of his people, had to demonstrate that he was ready to die for them. Waving his sword and shouting defiance, he stood in the sunshine outside the great square doorway. Soon, to everybody's relief, the Bird went on down the river. It came back about a half hour later, and the same scene was repeated.

Afterward, Gilluk said to Ras, "Do you think it was looking for you?"

"I don't know," Ras said. "I've never talked to it."

He knew that Gilluk was worried and that he was thinking of what the Bird had done to the Wantso.

Two days later, Gilluk announced that he was leading an expedition up-river. He wanted to examine the site of the Wantso village. Also, he hoped to capture or to kill Janhoy. Ras's description of the lion had intrigued him.

Ras said nothing. Gilluk said, "I've given instructions about you. Don't think you can escape."

Ras just grinned.

However, he found that he had no chance to try his plan. During the day he was surrounded by too many people, and at night three guards, not two, stood watch. He turned his attention again to Bigagi in an effort to rouse him. Bigagi sat like a gigantic ebony frog carved in the posture of just preparing to leap. His hunched shoulders and large mouth and seemingly unblinking eyes added to the frog image. The flies crawled over his face, across his nose and lips, and even across his eyelids. He rose only a few times each day to drink water, to eat, or to use the cucking jar. At nights he fell asleep while squatting. Four days had passed since the king had gone northward before Ras noticed that Bigagi was eating almost nothing. The fifth day, Ras saw him empty his bladder without getting up. It was not laziness or even indifference. Bigagi just did not know that he was relieving himself.

It was then that Ras saw that Bigagi was allowing himself to die. His people were dead, but he had made an effort to start the tribe again with the Wantso woman slave. Defeated, he had given up. Now, his life was evaporating from him as surely as a creek, cut off from the source of water, slowly disappears into the sun. His dying was a state into which the Wantso fell when they were bewitched or when exiled. Numb, pressed under heavy shadows, they let the soul slip out of them while the grip of mind and body grew weaker and weaker.

When he realized this, Ras became angry. He shouted taunts at Bigagi and threatened him with tortures. He reviled him and compared him to a snail, a jackal, a hyena, a stinkbug, a baboon. Bigagi gave no sign that he heard him.

"Your people died, yes!" Ras screamed. "But my people died, too! Yusufu and Mariyam, the only ones I ever loved besides Wilida! And she is dead, too! You worm, dweller in and eater of the anuses of dead vultures, why did you let them kill Wilida! Spineless, gutless, ball-less, prickless, why didn't you stand up and fight for her? And why did you kill my mother and father? They had never done anything to you! You did not have to kill them, my Yusufu and my Mariyam!"

Ras wept with grief and rage.

Gilluk's mother, sitting nearby under her parasol, called out. "Why do you do this? Can't you see that he is gone —or going—his ghost is halfway to the Land of Shades!"

"I do not want him to die yet," Ras said. "I want him to be fully alive and fighting to live when I kill him. I am being cheated!"

"I do not think that is why you are calling him back from the ghosts," Shikkut said. "I think that you still love him, or would like to love him, and so you do not want him to die."

Ras was so startled that he could not reply for a minute. He said, "Why should I love the man who killed my parents and allowed Wilida to be killed? I want to kill him!"

"You loved him once?"

"Very much," Ras said. "But he turned against me."

"Then you still love him, even though you also hate him."

Ras thought much about this remark in the following days. At no time could he see that she was telling the truth. He hated Bigagi; that stated everything.

Bigagi continued to thin out. The skin fell in between his ribs, and his skull pushed out toward the air. When he dirtied himself, he only moved away for his keepers to clean the cage when they shoved him over with a long pole. Silently and unflinchingly, he endured the bucketsful of water thrown on him. Then, for three days, he did not empty his bowels, perhaps because there was nothing to get rid of, but he did make some water. His eyes retreated deeper from the light into his head.

Gilluk's mother said, "My son will not be able to torture him. If he does not get back soon, he won't be able to feed him alive to Baastmaast."

"If he dies, he will stay in the cage to rot and stink until Gilluk returns?" Ras said.

Gilluk's mother shrugged. "I don't have the authority to do anything else, either. There was a time when women ruled the Sharrikt, and there were no priests, only priestesses. Then the great Tannus, who was at the time only the consort of the queen Fakkuk, killed the queen and became the ruler, with the backing of a small number of men. That was a long time ago, before the Sharrikt came through the hole in the mountains from the underworld to live here. The Sharrikt have been going to hell ever since."

This last phrase was, literally, "eaten by jackals," and could also be translated in English as "going to the dogs."

"That's interesting," Ras said. "But what can be done for Bigagi?"

"Nothing."

"I don't understand him. My loss and my grief are great also, but I won't just lie down and die."

"You are not a Wantso," Shikkut said. "Nor are you a Sharrikt. I think you'll get out of that cage, and when you do, woe to the Sharrikt. Especially to my son, Gilluk."

"That makes two of us," Ras said. "Tell me, do you love Gilluk?"

"I love him very much."

"I think you also hate him very much," Ras said. "He killed your husband, his father, and he also killed your younger son, his brother."

Shikkut was startled, but she recovered swiftly. She said, "You may be right. Nevertheless, he had to kill them. It is the custom. But, as I said, I think you will, somehow, get out of that cage. My son made a mistake when he didn't kill you at once."

Ras, grinning, said, "Would you help me to get out?"

She cackled and said, "Never! But I will take great interest in watching how you manage your escape. I say this because I am the descendant of queens and of priestesses. We have a knowledge beyond knowledge. We can see what hides behind the flesh of men and the shell of things."

Ras said nothing. He was thinking that she had delivered into his hands, over her son's resistance, a possible means of escape. Did she know this or did she perhaps just have a feeling that she was an instrument of events? A feeling that was rooted in wish more than foreknowledge? He doubted that she had known what she was doing when she had browbeaten her son into returning the mirror and the whetstone to him. Yet, she may have been aware, somewhere in her, that she was causing her son's ruin.

Eight days after Gilluk had left, he returned. His arrival was announced to Ras by far-off drums, harps, flutes, bagpipes, and marimbas. A few minutes later, a soldier dashed into the courtyard and shouted what everybody knew. The servants, slaves, the three wives, and Shikkut, carried on a chair, hurried down the hillside to greet the king. The only ones left in the palace were Bigagi, Ras, and two guards. One guard ran to the big doorway to look down the hill and call back to the other a description of the parade. The other did not move from his post. He did, however, turn his back on the prisoners to hear better.

Ras thought about using this moment to put the first step of his plan into action. After some hesitation, he decided that the situation was far from ripe. He closed his antelope-hide bag and went to the side of the cage nearest the entrance. After a while, the herald marched into view, followed by Gilluk, holding his sword upright with both hands, the hilt on a level with his face.

A head appeared behind Gilluk. It was huge and maned with brown-yellowish hair. Its eyes were as lifeless as green stone, and its red tongue hung out from its open jaws. Then the pole on which the head was transfixed became visible.

Ras cried out with grief and clutched the bars of his cage.

Behind the man staggering under the weight of Janhoy's head were the other young men of the expedition. Four carried a corpse among them, a man at each foot and arm. The two behind them carried the skin of the lion. The guard of honor trod on their heels. One of them held a rope the other end of which was around the neck of a prisoner. She was ragged and dirty and staggering with fatigue. Her face was splotched with the red marks of insect bites. Her eyes were ringed and baggy with black. The once-blond hair was a dirty brownish color.

Ras, seeing the woman he had thought burned alive, went numb.

Shikkut, borne in her chair, was next in line, and behind her were the three wives and Gilluk's uncles, aunts, cousins, nieces, and nephews. The band was close behind them with the freemen trailing them and a number of slaves behind them.

Gilluk stopped before Ras's cage. He said nothing until the courtyard was jammed, but his expression was triumphant.

"Your beast was huge and ferocious-looking," he said. "But when we came onto him, we found him sleeping on his back with his belly distended from hippo meat. He did not even wake up until we were a few feet from him. He got to his paws just in time to receive three spears. And I finished him off with the divine sword. That was the great cat that you said was king of the beasts."

Ras pointed at the corpse, now lying on the ground. "Janhoy didn't kill him?"

"No! She killed him!"

Gilluk pointed at Eeva Rantanen.

"Tattniss stumbled over her while we were looking around the Wantso village. She was hiding behind a bush. Tattniss tried to spear her, but he was in a panic. I've tried to convince my people that you aren't a ghost, but my mother is the only one who really believes me. Tattniss didn't have his heart in the attack, and so the woman managed to grab his spear. She threw herself backward and tore the spear out of his hand. Tattniss didn't get away fast enough. She speared him in the back. Then we had her surrounded, and though she obviously didn't understand us, she saw that I wanted to capture her, not kill her. So she surrendered."

"That makes good sense," Ras said. "For a woman."

"You didn't try to fight your way out," Gilluk said. He smiled maliciously.

"There were too many too close," Ras said. "However, if I had been in her position, I would have fought. But, as I said, she acted correctly—for her."

"It's better to live and take a chance that you can escape later; is that it? Forget it. You're going to be in this cage for six months. After that . . ."

Tattniss' body, accompanied by his wailing wife, mother, father, and brother, was carried off to the House of Baastmaast on the island. Eeva was put into an empty cage. Gilluk sat down on leopardskin cushions on a huge mahogany chair. He drank beer while the band played. The guard of honor drove the slaves and the freeman farmers out through the doorway, leaving only the Sharrikt and the artisans in the courtyard. When space had been cleared, the Sharrikt danced and the freemen and slaves clapped their hands in rhythm with the music.

Janhoy's head and skin were laid at Gilluk's feet, and

two slaves fanned away the flies attracted by the dried
blood and decaying flesh. After a while, the stench and
the flies got too much for Gilluk, and he ordered the
trophies taken away. Two tanners, who did not seem
happy to have to leave the festivities, carried the head
and hide down the hill. Ras watched the bobbing head on
the pole disappear below the curve of the hill.

"I suppose you plan to get revenge for the lion!" Gilluk
shouted at Ras above the noise.

"I will get it!" Ras shouted back.

Gilluk laughed and drank more beer from a goose-
necked gourd. He said something to his wives that caused
them to grin and look at each other and move their hips
forward and backward. Gilluk, seeing Ras take notice
of this, grinned at him. Ras scowled back.

Beer was brought up from the storeroom in one building and also from the town below the hill. After several
hours, the king's relatives quit dancing to sit on chairs and
drink beer. The freemen danced, breaking loose now and
then from the dance to dash over to the king and kiss his
knees. Gilluk's mother became tired and was carried up
to her quarters. Bigagi squatted motionless, his head
drooping. Eeva sat on the cage floor and tore meat from
ribs of pork and drank water from a jar. She looked at
Ras occasionally as if she would like to talk when she
could be heard.

The beer washed away the fear of the crowd for the
two whites. Some men came close to the cages of Bigagi
and Eeva and shouted insults and made sexual gestures.
Bigagi noticed them no more than he did the flies crawling
over him. A man made water on Bigagi while everybody
except the other two prisoners laughed. Another man
reached through the bars for Eeva. She bit his hand. All
except the man who was bitten laughed. Some men and
women tried to lay hands upon her. A woman shrieked as
Eeva twisted her hand. Gilluk rose up from his chair to
shout at them to get away. He was too late. A man had
backed into the bars of Ras's cage. Before he realized
where he was, he was seized from behind, his head banged
against the bars, whirled around, and brought forward
against the bars. Unconscious, nose bleeding and probably
broken, he was dragged away. After that, the crowd did
not need Gilluk's orders to stay away from the prisoners.

Ras felt better after that. The king did not seem angry.
The crowd, except for the injured, were in even a better
mood, since some blood had been spilled. The music
and dancing continued until the moon came up. By then,

Gilluk had had enough. Unsteadily, he arose, shouted at the band and the dancers to go home, and, supported by his wives, went upstairs to his bedroom. Ras was glad that the racket was ended, but he envied the king.

"Leave one down here for me!" he shouted, but the king did not hear him.

The moon rose to a dying-away noise of the castle and of the town settling down to sleep. Except for the distant howling of a jackal, silence lay thick in the courtyard. The guards, who had drunk some beer also, leaned waveringly upon their spears. Eeva was a black-and-silver figure in the cage. She was so quiet that Ras thought she had fallen asleep.

He said, "Eeva!"

She stirred, sat up, and said in a tired voice, "Yes?"

"I had thought you were dead."

"I came close to being killed," she said. "I thought you'd been killed. It seemed to me that that napalm bomb had caught you by accident. Or perhaps on purpose. I don't know what those people in the copter were trying to do."

She told him what had happened after she had fled into the jungle. To get as far away as possible from the machine-gun fire probing through the trees and brush, she had run, fallen, crawled, and then run again. Despite the heavy undergrowth, she had covered perhaps a hundred yards when the napalm was dropped. She had not been inside the area of explosion, but she had been close enough to be knocked onto her face by the blast. She had fallen on the other side of a ridge into mud, but the heat had seared her hair and made her clothes smoke. The backs of her arms and hands and her ears had been sore and red for several days afterward. Luckily, she had been breathing out at the first near-enfoldment by fire. Otherwise, her lungs might have been seared. She had held her breath long enough to run out of immediate danger, although she had wanted to scream. Possibly, she had been so far away that this precaution hadn't been necessary, but she had taken it anyway.

And she had dropped her gun sometime after the bomb had gone off.

A mile from the fire, she had come to a small brook. She had immersed herself to the neck and splashed the cold water on her face. She had done this to cut down the degree of whatever burns she might have had. At the time, she had not known whether or not she had been badly burned. She had not thought she had been, but there had been the possibility that she had been in shock and had not yet been able to feel the burns. Certainly, she had been in some kind of shock, although it had been her reaction to near-death and not to burns.

The copter had come over her hiding place several times. Once, a stream of bullets had fingered the bush a few yards from her. She had not moved, since she knew she could not have been seen. They had been firing blindly just on the chance that she could have been flushed into sight if she had escaped the bomb.

"I don't know why they're so bent on killing me," she said. "I'm no danger to them, and my chances for getting out of this valley are very small. It seems to me that they don't want me to be with you, for some reason. Why not?"

"Perhaps Igziyabher will tell us when we see Him," Ras said. Eeva snorted disgust or disbelief.

She had not returned to the place where she had left the raft until two days later. Although she had looked for her gun, she had not been able to find it. She had supposed that Ras had floated on down to the swamp or else the raft had floated away by itself.

Eeva had returned to the site of the Wantso village by the direct route, walking where there was land and swimming across the river whenever she had come to it. Several times she had detoured because of crocodiles. She had dug up some crocodile eggs and sucked out the yolk and later had killed a small python with a stick. The eggs and the raw snake meat had sustained her until she had reached the Wantso fields, where she had hoped to eat the vegetables in the fields. Monkeys, civets, hares, birds, and insects had gotten there first. The fields had been stripped.

While searching the jungle around the site, she had found a hare caught in a Wantso trap. Though the body had started to stink, she had eaten it. She had been sick for three days after that and had thought she was going to die. Then she had killed a young pig with a stick, only to be forced to climb a tree to get away from the enraged mother. Her hopes to eat the piglet after the herd left had disappeared when the herd ate it.

"It seemed as if I were the only one starving," she said. "Everywhere I looked, animals and birds were eating or about to eat. I was getting thinner and weaker, so weak that soon I would be eaten. Then I found a baby antelope with a broken leg. I had to drive off the mother—she was brave but a tiny thing—and also chase off two jackals. I put the poor little thing out of her misery and cooked her. I was so sick of raw, bloody meat that I didn't give a damn if anyone saw my fire or not. After that, I ate some fruit I saw some monkeys eating, and I caught a hare in the same trap in which I'd found that stinking animal.

"I went back to the Wantso site to look for spearheads and tools. I was going to arm myself, build a raft, and try to go across the swamp. I thought that you might be hanging around the Sharrikt country if you were still alive, and, in any event, I meant to look for an escape route at the end of the river. It didn't seem likely that I would succeed, but I was going to try. Then, the Sharrikt got me. And here I am."

She yawned and was asleep before Ras could ask any more questions. He said goodnight to the guards, who had been listening uneasily to the unintelligible conversation. He awoke at dawn and waited for breakfast, which was late because the slaves were as hung over as their masters. Eeeva, awakened by the flies, got up several hours later. She used the cucking jar in one end of the cage without the embarrassment she had shown when they had been alone in the jungle. She seemed pleased to get a full meal, and the black rings around her eyes paled a little.

Ras said, "Gilluk hadn't had a woman for some days when he found you. He's very horny, if what he says is true. Did he lie with you?"

"No. I don't understand Sharrikt, of course, but I got the impression he was discussing me with his men. I didn't think they'd bother me, because they were too scared of me. But I forestalled any ideas Gilluk might have by making sure he knew that I was menstruating. I couldn't be sure, of course, but it seemed probable that the Sharrikt, like most preliterates, had a menstruation tabu. I was right. It was evident that they all regarded me as unclean, which I was, because I was using part of my shirt as a pad. In fact, I got the impression that he put himself and the others through a cleansing ritual at the end of each day. And they all took pains to touch me as little as possible."

CHAPTER 16

THE DESCENT

The black pool under Bigagi had been small at first. It spread slowly while the soul dripped from his body, drop by drop, like water from the edge of a roof after a rain. The drops were eyeball-shaped, and black and soundless as a shadow falling. With every drop and stain, some of Bigagi's flesh turned to steam under the brown skin and jetted from the pores. The skull and skeleton burrowed their way outward, as if eager to bathe in the sun and to undarken. His eyes cowered back into the bone, crowding the brain. Each new sun spread a light that seemed weaker in its grasp on Bigagi.

"Bigagi!" Ras called. "Do not die! You will cheat me! I must kill you with my own hands, break your neck!"

Bigagi did not seem to hear. His mouth hung open while flies crawled in and out of it. A fly traveled over his eyeball, and he did not blink.

"What did you say?" Gilluk asked. Ras told him, and the king smiled. He said, "All right. You can kill him."

He clapped his hands and shouted orders. Spearmen formed a semicircle around the door to Ras's cage. A slave tried to untie the leather ropes binding the door to the cage. Impatient, Gilluk commanded him to step aside, and he cut through the ropes with his sword. After swinging the door out, Gilluk stepped back behind the spearmen.

Ras walked slowly out of the cage. He felt numbed; he could not quite grasp the idea that he was to be free to kill Bigagi.

Gilluk said, "You don't look happy, now that you can have your revenge."

"It's so unexpected," Ras said. "And Bigagi . . . he won't know! I mean, I thought he'd be fighting for his life and that he'd know he had to pay . . . but now . . ."

"Don't you want to kill him?"

"I should," Ras said.

Gilluk laughed loudly and rolled his eyes.

"It's not even like killing a leopard that has eaten your mother," Ras said. "You kill the leopard, but you don't hate it. It's an animal, and what it did, it did blamelessly. Now Bigagi isn't even an animal. He is nothing."

"Why didn't you tell me this before I ruined good leather ropes?" Gilluk said. "Why did you tell me how much you lusted for revenge?"

"It's like starting to walk down a steep, muddy bank," Ras said. "You might change your mind about going down, but by then, even if your legs quit moving, you continue to go on down."

Gilluk frowned and bit his lower lip. Then he smiled. He gestured for Ras to get back into the cage. Ras did so, and the door was secured with another rope. The bystanders, including Gilluk's mother and wives, looked disappointed. The king spoke through the bars to Ras.

"It's too late now to change your mind again, because I gave you your only chance. It seems to me that you should have killed him if only to satisfy the ghosts of your parents. You have let them down. But if you won't fulfill your duties, I'll do it for you."

Gilluk gave an order, and two men entered Bigagi's cage.

Ras said, "What are you going to do?"

"Baastmaast isn't hungry yet," Gilluk said. "It was only three days ago that he ate Tattniss. But if we wait too long, the Wantso will die."

"You're going to throw Bigagi into the pool?" Ras said.

"Tomorrow. Before the sun touches the western peaks. In the meantime, we have certain ceremonies to perform, and Bigagi must spend one night chained to the platform above the pool so that Baastmaast can see what we are giving him."

A chair carved out of lemonwood was brought in from a room off the yard. Four of the king's relatives carried it, two in front, two in back, each holding the end of a pole inserted through carved holes in the chair. The chair was covered with carved crocodiles.

Bigagi was set in the chair, in which he lolled, one arm hanging out, his head on one shoulder. Drums beat; bag-pipes shrilled; spears clashed. In a short time, a parade was formed. The king's herald led the march out the great door with the king twelve steps behind him and holding the sword with both hands straight up before his face.

Behind the king was Bigagi. When his chair was only a few paces from the doorway, he suddenly jerked his head up and then sat up. His shout was so loud that it startled the drummers and fluters and bagpipers, and the music slid off into silence. Gilluk spun around.

Bigagi's voice was weak after that great call. But Ras could hear him.

"Lazazi Taigaidi! Can you hear me?"

Bigagi's head was bent back now, its top against the high back of the chair. He stared straight upward into the sun.

"I hear you, Bigagi!" Ras shouted.

The voice of Bigagi was faint. It could be heard only because the Sharrikt were as silent as if they thought that a ghost was speaking.

"I did not kill your parents! No Wantso killed your parents! You have . . ."

"Who killed them?" Ras shouted. "Bigagi! Who killed them?"

There was no answer. Bigagi fell in on himself and sighed as if he were a collapsing bagpipe. The wail raised the eyelids of the Sharrikt and caused them to shudder. The men holding the chair-poles started, but they did not drop the chair.

Gilluk walked back to Ras and said, "He had no reason to lie."

"He must have lied," Ras said. "He had to."

Gilluk laughed and said, "You killed all the Wantso for something that they did not do."

Ras stared at him through the bars. Gilluk's face, and everything behind Gilluk, was as dark as if the sun had suddenly been eclipsed. There was a roaring in his head, and his chest was clenching.

"I will kill you for laughing," Ras said.

"Haven't you done enough killing?" Gilluk said. He laughed again and signaled for the parade to restart.

Only Gilluk's mother paid any attention to Ras. Her head was turned to look back over the chair at him un-til she disappeared down the hill.

There was silence then except for a distant roar from the town at the foot of the hill.

Eeva said, "What was that all about?"

Ras gestured for her to be still, since he wanted to think about what Bigagi had said. But she insisted that he tell her.

Eeva said, "Don't feel so bad! If you were tricked, you can't help it! You didn't know! What else could you think, with the evidence you had?"

"I killed them all," Ras said. "I killed even those that my hand did not kill."

He looked down at his feet for the black pool he expected to form there. There was nothing but the sunshine and the shadows of the bars. Nevertheless, he felt as if his soul had gushed out.

"Now Bigagi will die, too. Because of what I did."

He added, "Who did this? Who shot my mother with a Wantso arrow? Why?"

Eeva said, "Only one person could have done it, though I don't know why. It was the person who wrote those pages you call Letters from God. I think he did it because he wanted to deceive you into thinking that the Wantso had killed your mother, so that you would take revenge on them. But I don't know why."

"You mean Igziyabher did it?"

Eeva shook her head and said, "No, not God. A man. Whoever brought you here and caused you to be reared as a Tarsan."

"Tarsan?"

Eeva repeated the word carefully and this time voiced the *s.* "Tarzan. The hero of a series of novels about . . ."

"Hero? Novels?"

Eeva explained as best she could without wandering off to elucidate the background for "hero" and "novels."

"It's difficult to tell you anything at all about the outside world because you don't have a frame of reference. And I'm handicapped explaining this because I've never read a Tarzan book. I saw a movie when I was a child—my mother didn't know about it—but I understand there's very little relation between the book Tarzan and the movie Tarzan. Actually, I know little about Tarzan except for the movie and occasional references in newspapers and books. He was a white man who was brought up by some kind of gorilla-like apes in the African jungle. He's a sort of archetype of freedom from civilized inhibitions and irritations and tabus. A Noble Savage."

"What does all that mean?"

"It means that the writer of those pages, the man who is responsible for your being raised here, is psychotic.

That is, crazy, mad, deranged, insane. You were kidnapped as a baby and brought here to play the role of a Tarzan. Only events didn't work out the way they were intended."

Ras was silent for a long time. Even if he had not been numbed by Bigagi's revelation, he would have had difficulty understanding her. As she had said, he had no "frame of reference."

Suddenly, he howled, and he beat the bars with his fists. The guards shouted at him, but he paid no attention to them.

"I'll kill him!" Ras yelled. "I'll kill Igziyabher!"

"It wasn't God," Eeva said, "It was a man." ·

"I'll kill him!" Ras screamed, and he began to weep and sob.

Eeva waited until he was quiet. She said, "This man has to be on top of the pillar in the lake."

Ras gave a long, shuddering sigh and turned away from her. The guards, Tukkisht and Gammum, were side by side, their spears pointing at him, their knees and bodies bent, their eyes wide.

"If you have a plan to get out," Eeva said, "now is the time to use it. Everybody has gone to the island. At least, you told me they do when anybody is to be fed to Baastmaast."

Ras mumbled.

She said, "What?"

He replied, "I meant to do this some night when there was a storm and it would be dark and raining."

He opened the antelope-hide bag and removed the mirror and whetstone. He rapped the end of the whetstone against the center of the glass of the mirror, which cracked into seven triangular pieces. Since his fingernails could not separate the shards, he hammered one piece until it broke away. With a sliver from it, he pried loose an intact triangle. The others followed easily.

Gammum stepped closer to the cage and said, "What are you doing?"

Ras looked up, grinned, and said, "I'm making magic to let me loose."

Gammum's eyes rolled. He took one step backward but forced himself to come near again. "Stop it, or I'll kill you!"

"You can try to," Ras said. He used the whetstone to hone the edges of the glass shard. Then he began to saw on the leather rope securing the door to the cage.

Gammum jabbed his spear through the bars to force

Ras away. Expecting this, Ras seized the shaft of the spear just behind the head and threw himself backward. Gammum tried to hold on but was yanked so hard against the bars that his eyes crossed, his nose bled, and his knees loosened. The spear left his grip. Tukkisht yelled and ran up to the cage and thrust his spear through the bars. Ras had reversed his; he threw it between two bars. It drove into Tukkisht's arm. Tukkisht fell backward with the spear still in his flesh. He was up at once, jerked the spear loose, reversed it, and raised it to cast through the bars. Blood spurted over his arm and side.

Ras had picked up Tukkisht's spear, which he had dropped halfway into the cage. Gammum staggered back but not in time to escape entirely. Ras did not want to lose the spear, so he jabbed with it and stuck a half inch of copper into Gammum's thigh.

Gammum screamed and whirled and lurched across the courtyard toward the big doorway. His hands flapped, and he crowed.

Ras used the edge of the spearhead to saw through the leather rope. By the time it was severed, Gammum had disappeared down the hill.

Tukkisht called out to Gammum, but seeing that he was going to be deserted, advanced upon Ras. Ras kicked the cage door so that it swung outward, and he was out in a bound. Tukkisht was brave and a skilled spearman, but he was facing a man he believed to be a ghost, a man who had escaped in a few seconds from a seemingly escape-proof cage, and he was also bleeding heavily and weakening fast. Ras parried his few thrusts, drove him backward, and then knocked the spear to one side and sent his into Tukkisht's stomach. Tukkisht fell on his knees and doubled over while he clutched at his stomach. Ras knocked him out with the butt of his spear on his head and left him.

He ran out through the doorway. The seven-foot Gammum was lurching halfway down the hill like a sick stork. The town at the foot of the hill was deserted except for some small children playing in the street and a white-haired woman watching them. There were boats on the shore of the island and white-clad figures in a column the head of which had entered the tall, dark doorway of the building in the center of the island. The last boat was a few feet away from landing on the island. It was filled with slaves clad only in white skirts.

Ras caught Gammum in the back with the spear. Gammum slid down a few steps and did not move thereafter.

As Ras pulled the spear out, he heard a scream from below. The white-haired woman was looking up at him, her mouth open. Then she turned and ran down the street toward the lake shore. Some of the infants toddled after her. Some continued to play.

She was too far away for him to hope to catch her. Within a few minutes she would have rowed across the quarter mile of lake to the island and given the alarm. There was nothing else he could do except run back up the steps and to Eeva's cage. He slashed the rope on the door of her cage with a copper knife taken from Tukkisht.

"What do we do now?" she said. Her skin was pale beneath her tan, but her gray eyes were bright.

"I want my knife," he said. "And since Gilluk burned down the fine cage and house I built for him, his cage—and his building—will burn."

"We haven't got time!" she said. "If we left right now, we could get ahead of them and escape through the swamp!"

He shook his head, whirled, and ran to the nearest doorway.

The stairway was quartz-shot granite blocks, the edges of the risers worn down by generations of feet. It twisted up to a hallway between the rooms on the outside wall and those on the rooms overlooking the courtyard. The light in the hall was dim. Sunlight came through the open windows of the inner and outer rooms, but it was choked by the grass-and-bamboo curtains covering the entrances to the rooms. Unlit torches were stuck at 45-degree angles into holes bored into the granite walls. Ras removed several and told Eeva to get some for herself. Pushing aside a curtain, he entered a large room. There were several beds of carved mahogany frameworks, grass mattresses, and pelt coverings. Stone shelves rose against one wall from floor to beamed ceiling. These held at least three hundred skulls, Gilluk's ancestors, direct and collateral, and a number of broader, rounder, more prognathous skulls, Wantso victims of Sharrikt raids. There were also gorilla and leopard skulls.

Beside the great window was a tall-backed chair with arms and seat covered with crocodile-hide. A wooden rack held spears and war clubs and Ras's belt, sheath, and knife.

The only other furniture was a small copper brazier in the center of the room. It contained some hot coals of a heavy wood.

Ras strapped on the knife belt and applied the torches

to the coals in the brazier. Eeva lit torches from his torches. She said, "Why do you insist on wasting time?"

"Because Gilluk must realize that I am no ordinary prisoner. Because Gilluk must pay."

He told her what she should do. They tore down the curtains, set them in a pile by a huge, upright beam, and piled the wooden beds on top of the curtains. Ras set the curtains to blazing and then raked the skulls off the shelves with his spear. He threw the skulls on the fire and watched the flames curl around them.

After that, he and Eeva raced around the building, downstairs, and around the second and first floors, where they started other fires. Before he returned to the courtyard, he looked out a window toward the island. White-clad figures were streaming out of the temple toward the dugouts and bamboo boats on the island beach.

While Eeva stacked a few curtains and mats against the sides of the cages, Ras hammered with a large, three-legged copper brazier at the bars of his cage. The bamboo poles gave way, and he soon had an opening for the great exercise wheel.

"What are you doing now?" Eeva said. Her hair and face were black with smoke, and her gray eyes, wide with excitement, the whites reddened with strain and smoke, stared at him.

She recoiled at his savage expression and said, "Never mind! I give up! You're mad!"

He ignored her to run though the door of his cage, past the crackling flames, and into the annex that held the wheel. He lifted it off its support, although it had taken four men to carry it between them, lowered it, and rammed it through the open space he had made by knocking the poles out.

Smoke was beginning to fill the courtyard. It curled around them and made them cough. Ras rolled the wheel out through the great doorway, turned it a little, and halted it a few feet from the crest of the hill.

By then, three dugouts and one war canoe, Gilluk's, were drawn up on the mainland shore, with others coming in. The giant white figure of the king, the sun-glinting sword raised above his head, was running through the street. Behind him was his bodyguard, their spears flashing. Freemen armed with spears followed the king's relatives.

Ras turned the wheel once more and rolled it to a position near the northeast corner of the building. When smoke enveloped them, he and Eeva lay close to the ground and looked over the edge of the hill.

"I'd ask you what you're going to do," Eeva said, "but I'm afraid to."

"I moved the wheel over here so it wouldn't carry us into the houses," Ras said. "It'll get a straight roll down to the lake. And bring us near the dugouts."

Her nails sank into his biceps, and she said, "You mean . . . ?"

He grinned and said, "We'll get a good head start on them that way. They'll all be almost up the hill before we start down. We can get across the lake and up into the hills, and from there we'll get back to the swamp. We could take the boat up to the mouth of the river, but they could go faster on land and be at the river before we got there if they knew we were going that way. But in the hills, they won't find us. I'll make sure of that."

She almost wailed. "But we could have gone out the back way and been in the hills on that side, too, long ago."

"No. That way, there are three miles of flat land before we could get to the hills. I could outrun them, but you . . .",

He paused, then said, "Besides, I want to do it this way."

"All right."

She withdrew her nails from his arm, and she laughed. "*Jumala!* If my colleagues could see me now! They'd never believe it! Nobody will ever believe it!"

Through the smoke, Ras saw Gilluk striding up the steps, his guard and male relatives below him a few steps, and the freemen spreading out on both sides of the stone steps to form two lines across the face of the hill. Ten ran around the hill on one side and seven on the other, apparently to come up on opposite sides of the hill. And also to look out across the country on that side for him if he were escaping that way.

At the foot of the hill, just leaving the town to start up the steps, was a mob of slaves and artisans, some freeman farmers, and the Sharrikt women. The chair of Gilluk's mother was supported at an angle on the shoulders of slaves. She was holding her parasol herself as she bent her head back to look up.

"For God's sake, how long do we have to wait?" Eeva said.

Ras grinned again and stood up.

"Now."

The smoke was so thick that there were times when she could not see him although she was only several feet away. Coughing, she got down on her belly and crawled forward until her hand touched a wooden spoke. He was already inside and coughing violently.

"Hurry up!"

She slid through the opening between two spokes on the side of the cage. She gasped, "I can hardly see you!"

He was suspended in the cage, his hands around a spoke on either side and his feet braced against the spokes. Between coughs, he said, "It isn't going to work this way."

He lowered himself until his back was against the curved walk, after which he braced himself again.

"It'll be a hard ride," he said. "Whatever happens, don't let go."

Seeing that she was set, he eased himself up the walk so that his weight would roll the wheel forward. It moved a little, then stopped. Again, he climbed, his feet on spokes higher up. The wheel rotated slowly because Eeva's weight was holding it back.

Ras gave a shout that ended in a cough. He bent forward, his hands gripping spokes, his insteps hooked around spokes, and then he threw himself backward. The wheel rolled again, slowed, seemed to stop, and suddenly went over the edge.

Eeva shrieked. Ras continued to cough, even as he went down and then up and over in a forward motion. He gripped harder as his body sagged down and pressed against the walk. Shouts and screams came up the hill. Ras turned his head just in time to see Gilluk, about forty yards to one side, standing on a step, staring at him, the sword slowly sinking. Then Gilluk was upside down, the sun was below Ras, rightside up, upside down, and out of sight. A shrill squawk was slashed by the spinning spokes; a white-clad figure with a black face, white-rimmed eyes, and white teeth and black gullet flashed by. The wheel bumped as it hit a small mound, shot into the air a little way, and banged down, almost tearing Ras from his position on the upper part of the wheel.

The wheel tottered. Eeva screamed. The wheel regained balance and shot down the hill on a slightly different path, which was taking them toward town. Or so it seemed to Ras, who could get no accurate picture of their line of flight.

Abruptly, the stone walls and thatch roof of a house appeared hanging downward, sky below it, a frightened face in the window, spun over, was gone, another house, a cry from a doorway soaring out and away, the squawk of a chicken, a thump, a feather floating, a lurch, a splash of water, then the wheel so suddenly slowed it tore him free of his grasp, the lake covering him, uncovering him, and he was lying on the walk up to his neck in water and looking at Eeva, whose wet hairs hung like weeds over her face.

To get out, they had to hold their breaths while squeezing through the spokes under water. They waded to the shore, where the track of the wheel was the path of a monstrous snake. A small dugout with two paddles was on the muddy beach about thirty yards from them. Faces were at the windows of some houses on the edge of the town, and fingers jabbed at them.

Gilluk and the others were halfway down the hill, the king taking two stone steps at a time and holding his sword above his head with one hand. The others were strung out but converging; the common point would be Ras and Eeva.

"Get in the boat!" he said, and he ran toward the nearest hut while she croaked an unintelligible question behind him. As he neared the hut, he heard screams and then saw a woman and two children run from it. He entered the house and found two short spears, a hunting bow, and a quiver of arrows. Before he left, he kicked over a copper tripod containing a fire and threw some sleeping mats on it. He lit a torch and touched off the thatch roof. The houses were so close together that if one caught fire, many or all might, even if the breeze was from the west and this house was on the southeast corner of town.

Eeva was waiting for him in the dugout. She was on her knees, paddle poised, and looking over her shoulder. Her shirt and bra, already rotten and torn, had been ripped off during the descent or perhaps when she had squeezed out between the spokes. The skin on her breasts and stomach was red-raw from scraping against the spokes.

Ras hesitated, then said, "You go ahead; get a good start! I'll be along in another boat!"

He threw a spear into her boat and shoved it out into the lake. He threw the other spear into another dugout and put the strap of the quiver over his shoulder. Holding the bow in one hand, he began to shove the rest of the boats out onto the lake. They went easily enough, but he had to put down the bow and bend with all his strength and dig into the mud, to launch the two heavy war canoes. Fortunately for him, the Sharrikt had been in such a hurry they had not drawn the war canoes very far up onto the beach.

When all the boats were adrift, he ran back to the dugout. On the way, he glanced up the main street. Gilluk was halfway down it with about twenty close behind him and the others strung out. Ras shot at him, but the king saw him while he was fitting the arrow to the string, and he ran into the nearest hut. The arrow stuck quivering in a bamboo pole near the doorway. The other warriors scattered to duck behind the stone houses or to throw themselves onto the ground.

Ras took to the dugout and paddled furiously. Thirty yards out, he looked behind him. Gilluk was dancing on the shore and howling at his men, who were wading or swimming after the boats. The southeast-corner house was burning now, casting flames at its neighbor. A line of slaves and freemen were passing pots of water up from the lake to the fire fighters.

CHAPTER 17

THE EYE OF GOD

The island rose up from the lake as gently as the slope of shell of a half-submerged tortoise-god. Twenty yards inland, at the center of the island, was the House of Baastmaast. One hundred feet square, it was built of white limestone blocks. It was windowless and had one square doorway broad enough for two men to enter side by side. It shone in the sun, the only darkness about it being the shadows behind the doorway and a raven perched on one corner.

Ras told Eeva, who was waiting on the beach, to bring two paddles and the spears. He shoved one dugout out into the lake and lifted the other above his head. Carrying it, he walked along the side of the broad and deep canal that cut into the island and thrust through a square hole in the foundation of the temple.

At the doorway, Ras leaned the dugout against the wall and went inside. Eeva said, "Aren't you . . . ?" and closed her mouth.

Inside, the reason for the canal was evident. The water ran under the stone of the floor to feed a sunken pool in the center of the building. This was square and walled with blocks of limestone that rose a foot above the floor. A solid-stone tongue ran from one end of the pool about twenty feet into the water. Ringing the pool was an open flat space of hard-packed dirt ten feet in width. Entirely surrounding the pool, except for the aisle from the entrance, was a series of raised stone seats. These accommodated the spectators while—so Ras guessed—Gilluk and his assistants performed the rituals of sacrifice to Baast-maast. The victims would be thrown from the end of the stone tongue to the crocodile.

There was no roof; the building was open at the top. The sun would light up the interior of the building when it was directly overhead. Now, the sun had westered enough so that the lakeside walls cast a shadow to the edge of the pool. At its far end was a block of stone level with the water, and on this Baastmaast stretched.

Truly, the crocodile must have been as old as the Sharrikt claimed. It must have been dwelling in the pool when the Sharrikt came to the valley. The Dattum, in-habitants of this land before the Wantso came, builders of this temple and the castle on the hill and the houses of the town, had told the Wantso, who in turn had told the Sharrikt, that the crocodile had been living when they had entered this world. The Dattum had made the crocodile their chief god and built the temple around him, and he had been here ever since. The Wantso had fed him and made him a god, and then the Sharrikt had driven them out and possessed the temple and called the crocodile Baastmaast.

The crocodile had never stopped growing, according to Gilluk, who also said that snakes and crocodiles did not stop growing as long as they lived. And since Baastmaast was at least five hundred years old, according to Gilluk's chronology, he was almost twice as long as the largest crocodile Ras had ever seen. He was at least forty feet long.

"Ancient as stone, old as the first heartbeat," Ras mur-mured.

And then, "But stone wears away, and even the heart of a god must stop."

It was silent in the temple, so silent that Ras thought he could hear the cold, reptilian heart pulsing. The waters were dark, so dark that he could not see Bigagi's body anywhere in the pool. He walked around the pool, looking for the body but unable to keep from watching the enormous and awesome Baastmaast.

Eeva prowled around the place, and in a moment she gasped and then called him. She was standing in front of a pit at the foot of the far wall. It was deep and dark, but not so dark that they could not see Bigagi squatting at its bottom.

"I thought that the ceremony had been interrupted too soon for them to have given Bigagi to the crocodile," she said. "They must have lowered him into this until the time for his part in the proceedings."

The ends of ropes attached to Bigagi's waist and neck were tied to a small wooden post a few feet from the hole. Ras grabbed the ropes and hauled Bigagi out. Bigagi lay motionless; he did not seem to be even breathing, and he had no detectable heartbeat. If he was not dead, he was close to it.

"There is nothing you can do for, or to, him," Eeva said. "Forget about him. Think of us!"

She put both hands around his arm and looked up into his face. "Ras! Maybe you aren't scared of those people, but I am! They'll be here soon! Let's get off here, fast! Why are you waiting here?"

Ras pulled his arm away and said, "I must kill a god."

He walked to the far end of the pool and looked down. The crocodile's eye was open. The iris was a black lance on a yellow field. Or a leaf sprouting from the cold brain inside that armor. The eye had seen five centuries of this narrow world of the pool. Human flesh had fed it. And, during mating season, when it had bellowed with frenzy, it had had females brought it. The Sharrikt said that all the crocodiles in this world were his children. And so Eeva, when she had eaten the crocodile eggs, had fed upon divinity.

Ras fitted an arrow to the string and aimed. Baastmaast did not move; the lidless eye stared incuriously at him.

The arrow, driven through the eye and into the clot of brain beyond, would kill it. And five hundred years would die.

Eeva's voice was as sudden and startling as the twang of a released bow.

"Come on!"

Ras jumped. He had been standing with the arrow ready to go for a longer time than he had thought. Too long a time. He put the arrow back into the quiver. Why should he kill Baastmaast? To destroy the god of the Sharrikt would not destroy them. They would be shaken, but they would only make another crocodile their Baastmaast. This beast was a unique; it had lived so long that it would be a great evil to kill it. In a way, it was like Ras. Both were uniques; both had managed to survive much.

"We'll go now," he said. She ran ahead of him through the narrow, high aisle between the raised seats toward the doorway. Then she stopped so suddenly that he almost bumped into her. She had heard the faint, but unmistakable, chop-chop of the copter.

Ras gently pushed her to one side and went to the entrance, where he stuck his head around the corner. The closest boat, Gilluk's war canoe, was halfway across the channel, with the others several yards behind in a ragged semicircle. The copter was a mile away, flying about five hundred feet above the lake shore.

The eight paddlers on Gilluk's boat had stopped working. Along with the king, who was sitting on a little chair on a platform in the aft, they were watching the copter. The other boats were also slowing down, their paddlers motionless and staring.

"They saw the smoke," Eeva said behind him. She moved against his back and gripped his shoulders. He could feel her shaking. "They'll kill me."

Gilluk shouted something. His men unfroze and began to turn the boat around. The other boats followed, and all sped toward the lake shore. Ras wondered where they meant to hide, since the castle was burning, and four houses in town were now flaming, with the promise of more to catch fire.

Eeva dropped her hands from his shoulders and stood by his side.

"What can I do?" she said. "They'll see me for sure if I leave this building."

"Maybe they won't come here," he said. "Why should they?"

"They may have seen all the Sharrikt heading this way. They may wonder why they were coming here, when the castle and town were burning."

That seemed likely, but she wouldn't feel any better if he said so. He was silent as he watched the copter hover about twenty feet above the town. Its wings blew dust on the street and rolled flames out of the burning houses toward the others. There were two men in the transparent body, their profiles black against the sun.

The Sharrikt had run to the western end of town, where they were hiding from the copter.

The copter rose to a point to one side of the castle, circled it three times and went above it once. Then it headed straight toward the island. Ras and Eeva backed up inside the building until the noise indicated that the machine was going over the temple. They went back into the deep entrance while the copter hovered directly above the building. Baastmaast bellowed loudly enough to be heard above the copter.

Eeva pulled at Ras as the lower part of the copter came into their view, but he had already started to leave the doorway. While the wind and the roar blew through the opening, they pressed against the outside walls. Then the noise lessened as the copter rose, and they hid again inside the entrance.

Abruptly, the roar became louder. The copter was coming down for a landing just outside the building. Eeva mouthed something and ran inside. Ras followed her.

"There isn't any other way out!" she yelled. "We're trapped!"

Ras squeezed her shoulder and then pulled her close to him.

"They'll have to kill me first! I don't think they want to do that! I don't think so!"

He led her across the floor and pulled her up the aisle/ramp until they came to the highest level of seats. Beyond this was earth and the wall, the top of which was ten feet above his head.

Ras said, "I'll lift you up. They can't see you going over unless they come into the building or fly up again right now."

The roaring became a putter-putter, a whishing, a silence.

He faced her to the wall, bent his knees, gripped her buttocks, and straightened up. She shot from his hands and caught the edge of the wall. He gripped her ankles and pushed her, stiff-legged, up higher. After she had pulled herself up onto the wall, she turned and reached down to take the spear he held out.

"Get down on the outside and hug the wall," he said.

"I'll break my legs," she said, and then, seeing his expression, she said, "All right! I'll do it!"

He wheeled and ran down the aisle and across the curved strip of earth between the front row of seats and the pool. He did not dare to look around the corner of the doorway, because the men outside would see him. He could not allow them to know that anyone was inside, because then they could get back into the copter and fly overhead and drive them out.

The man entering the building walked slowly but not silently. The end of his shadow fell through the entrance but stopped and did not move for at least a minute. Ras wondered if both men were just outside the entrance, though it seemed logical that one would hang back to cover the other.

The shadow moved on in. Ras, knife in hand, was pressed against the wall. He would never have entered such an easy place for ambush, but then he did not have the arrogance-breeding weapons of these men. Or perhaps the man did not believe that anybody was hiding here, since he had seen the building from inside and outside.

The rifle barrel extended from the entrance and swung back and forth as if it were a snake scenting for danger. Ras reached out and pulled it and the man on through and around. The explosions deafened him; something sang by; stone chips struck him. Then the knife was in the belly and in the white throat, and Ras had a weapon he did not know how to use.

There was a shout from outside in English.

"Al! What happened?"

Ras took the pistol from the dead man's holster and the rifle, and ran across the floor and up the ramp. He threw the two weapons on top of the wall. Another shout came as the man heard the clatter. Ras leaped up, gripped the edge, and pulled himself up and over. Eeva was crouching against the foot of the outside wall. She looked up and made a gesture to indicate that she was all right.

"I killed one!" Ras said. "Here!"

He dropped the pistol, which she caught by letting the spear fall and grabbing out for the pistol. The spear made a clinking noise, which he hoped would not be loud enough to be heard on the other side of the building. He let the rifle fall horizontally, and she seized it with both hands. At that moment, the copter coughed and there was a whining sound.

"Shoot it down before it gets away!" Ras called.

Eeva sprinted around the building, doing something to the rifle as she ran. Ras let himself back down into the building and ran back to the doorway, beside which he had left the bow and arrows. He picked up the bow and an arrow and stepped outside just as the copter was ten feet off the ground and angling upward across the channel. The explosions from Eeva's gun made him jump even though he was expecting them.

Holes appeared in the transparent covering of the fore part of the copter. The man in it—he was white—jerked. Nevertheless, the machine continued to ascend and presently was heading toward the swamp. Eeva ceased firing.

"Damn! Damn! Damn!" she screamed, and then she wept.

"I think you hit him!" Ras said.

She put the rifle in the crook of her arm and put her face against his chest. Her shoulders shook while tears ran down his chest.

"If only I could have gotten him before he was in the copter!" she said. "I can fly one! I can fly one! We could have gotten out of here!"

"You're still alive, and we have guns now," he said. "And if you hadn't wounded him, he might have come back and dropped a fire-bomb. You'll have to teach me how to shoot. But later. We have to get away now. That man will tell the others that you're alive, and they'll be looking for you. And maybe they'll be after me, too."

He pointed across the channel. "The Sharrikt are coming out of the houses."

Eight houses were on fire. The townspeople formed three lines between the burning houses and the lake. Gilluk and his relatives were conferring near the shore. They looked often at the island and gestured toward it.

Eeva said, "This rifle has a scope. I can kill Gilluk from here."

Ras knew that the bullets could go a long way. Yet he was amazed. He felt that there was something unfair about such a weapon. Monstrous might be a better description for it.

"No," he said. "It'll be some time before Gilluk gets courage enough to come after us."

Eeva sighted through the barrel on top of the rifle, made some adjustments, and said, "I could get at least five before they got inside a house."

Ras told her that he wanted to break the rifle against the wall.

"Why are you so disgusted?" she said. "You practically wiped out the Wantso warriors!"

"I did it myself. I didn't use a machine!"

"Your bow is a machine! So is your spear! And your knife!"

"There's a difference," he said. He went into the building, she following. She looked through the dead man's pockets and found three clips of 7.5-millimeter bullets— so Eeva called them—and she took these for the rifle. There were also twenty .32 cartridges in his pocket for the revolver. Eeva also put on the belt with sheath and knife.

Her search found a pack of cigarettes, a lighter, and an envelope. Ras examined it and then removed a letter. It was in handwritten English. Ruth Bevans, a woman in Liverpool, England, had written a love letter to Al Lister, who now lay dead in the temple of Baastmaast and would soon go to feed a five-hundred-year-old crocodile. Ruth longed for the day when her lover would return, al-

though she hoped that he would not be as jealous and
angry as the last time he came home. He could trust her;
she loved only him and would not even think of looking
at another man.

The letter disturbed him because, for the first time, he
felt that a world could be outside the cliffs, somewhere
in the blue. There *had* to be another world.

Eeva said, "The letter was mailed from England a
month ago and delivered at Addis Ababa, Ethiopia. It
must have been picked up there."

She snapped the lighter, causing Ras to jump when the
flame leaped up. She lit the cigarette and drew in deeply
with an ecstatic look, which she quickly lost when she
coughed. Grimacing, she threw the cigarette down. "It
tastes terrible! Just as well, because when I'd smoked them
all up, I'd have had to go through the same withdrawal
symptoms again."

She tossed the package of cigarettes away and said,
"The pilot must have radioed in, and I'm sure that our
unknown enemy must have more than one copter left.
He wouldn't want to chance being marooned on that pillar. We have to get out now."

Ras dumped the body into the pool. It went under with
a splash and disappeared into the darkness. The great
crocodile was now under the surface. Ras examined Bigagi
again. He was convinced that Bigagi was dead or was so
close to death that he would soon be dead. He carried
him to the edge of the pool and said, "Forgive me, Bigagi! I truly thought that you had killed my mother and
father. I will kill the man responsible for this; I will kill
him even if he is not a man but a god!"

He raised the limp body above his head and cast it into
the waters. Bigagi went under immediately but rose again,
floating face upward, as if he wanted to take another look
at Ras. Then he sank. A few seconds later, Baastmaast
emerged at the other end of the pool, flicked his tail to
drive him a few feet forward, and sank.

Outside the temple, Ras picked up the dugout to carry
it to the east shore of the island. Eeva carried the rifle
and the revolver. The two paddles were in the dugout. Gilluk was aware of their departure, but he only stood and
stared at them. They went around to the other side of
the building, picked up the spears, and soon were paddling across the lake to the east shore. Here Ras carried
the dugout inland for a half mile before hiding it in a
ravine. They pushed on through the extremely thick
growth until they reached a tall hill. Eeva gathered fire-

wood while Ras hunted. He came back an hour later with a
pangolin. Eeva asked him if he had seen the copter. He
said that he had not seen it, but he had heard it. It must
have been searching around the island and lake shore
for them.

Eeva lay down and snored while he butchered the anteater, dressed it, and then, using the lighter, set fire to the
pile she had prepared. He was delighted with the lighter
but stopped after igniting it a few times. The fire smoked
somewhat, but he did not care. He cooked the meat and
then put the fire out and wakened Eeva. They ate. Afterward, she took the first watch, and he slept.

Darkness fell. The stars were out, but the moon would
not rise for several hours. They ate some more, and one
slept while the other did guard duty. The night animals
had taken up the strain that the day animals had slackened
with dusk. They returned to the dugout, which he carried
to the shore. There was no sign of fire across the lake.
Either all the houses had burned themselves out or the
fires had been put out.

Most of the passage across the lake to the river mouth
was by starlight. The sky was pale in the east, betraying
the stealthy climb of the moon near the horizon. Ahead,
the trees at the northern edge of the lake clumped to
form an unbroken, uprearing blackness. In its middle was
a gap that Ras sensed but could not as yet see. This gap
was his first goal, the widening and treelessness of the river
flowing from the roots of the swamp a few miles northward.

He sat in the front of the dugout. His paddle strokes
were slow but powerful. The wind from the west had
almost died out. He felt—or thought he felt—a fish brush
against his paddle. Something scaly, gape-mouthed, gog-
gle-eyed, had touched his paddle and whisked itself away.
Down there, cold and dark reigned. But no tears rained.
It was too cold and wet for tears. When you lived in the
midst of tears, breathed tears, moved in tears, you did
not weep.

Eeva, whose gasps had been getting louder, said, "Stop
a minute so I can rest! I can't lift my arms any more,
and my back is crystallized; it's going to shatter in a
moment!"

Ras could have kept on paddling while she rested, but
he took advantage of the chance to sit still and listen. The
boat slowed, stopped, and then began to creep backward,
pushed by the current, and its nose began to turn as if it
were sniffing for the scent of eastward. Ras listened. Loud-

est was the breathing of the woman. Between that and the lake shore was a zone of silence, and on the shore was the subdued kul-kul-gurruking of a bird. Faintly, far off, a crocodile bellowed. And, almost as indistinguishable under the bellow as a print in the mud below a just-lifted foot, was an almost familiar noise. Before it could be identified, it was gone. Its memory left him with an unease that quickly went away.

He leaned over, carefully so he would not tip the unstable dugout, and got his ear as closely as possible to the water. He could hear only the gentle slap-slap of the little waves against the wood of the boat. The wind carried no sound to him now. It carried only the odor of moldy wood, of mud that was partly flesh returned to mud, stench of rotting fruit, a green odor of some unidentifiable night bloom, and a tendril, quickly lost, as of a crocodile egg that had held a dead fetus until the shell was broken open by expanding gases.

He returned to his sitting position. Eeva said she could resume paddling—for a while. Again, the dugout slid ahead, and soon the shield of darkness parted to reveal a paler darkness between two masses. The boat resisted his urgings with the paddle more strongly now. It was close to the river's mouth. When they were about forty feet from the gap, two things happened at once. The moon pushed its shiny, gray-yellow arc above the top of the cliff, and its light ricocheted from a metal object rising into the air. The shining object was the head of a spear, and the arc it was describing would end in the water, in the wood of the dugout, or in his flesh or Eeva's. He yelled at the same time the ambushers yelled. The spear knocked off splinters from the dugout nose, and the shaft, deflected sidewise, banged against the side of the boat, and then the spear had slid into a gulp of water.

Five dugouts and a big war canoe poked out from the shadows of the trees on both sides of the river mouth. The moonlight was strong enough now for him to make out four figures in each dugout and nine in the canoe. Twenty-eight paddles were rising and lowering as if the arms that held them were on a string jerked by the king. Gilluk stood up on a little platform aft while he balanced another spear above his shoulder. He was probably reprimanding himself for not waiting until Ras had gotten closer. But the sudden emerging of the moon had made him fear that Ras would see the Sharrikt.

Eeva said, "Turn the boat broadside! Broadside!"

Metal snicked behind him. She was getting ready to

use the weapon against the Sharrikt. Gilluk yelled and at the same time hurled the spear. And immediately afterward, the sound that Ras had thought he had heard earlier became evident. Then the rifle erupted in his ear. He could hear nothing but it, and he felt heat from the belled muzzle. Long white lines appeared in the air from behind him, ghosts of the little greeters of death in the weapon's belly.

Eeva had called them tracers.

The moon sparked on the head of the spear, which did not come as close as the first. The spear made its own target in the water, created its bull's eye and concentric silvery circles out from the center.

The sound he had heard before became a chuttering, and then it ate up the voices of the men and was the only noise to be heard, since Eeva had quit firing the rifle. A light appeared at the same time. It was a great eye casting a beam of light as bright as the wrath of God. It flew about twenty feet above the surface of the river and came from around the bend of the river. It illumined the trees on both banks; it swung back and forth on the branches and trunks, and then on the green-brown river itself. The eye shot down the avenue formed by the trees on both sides of the river and then was out of the river's mouth and over the lake and the Sharrikt in their boats.

The eye suddenly halted, still twenty feet high, and it brightly fingered the area below it. It touched the dugouts and showed the bodies sprawled in them, the black-brown bottoms of dugouts that had been overturned when men had fallen dead into the water or had stood up and leaped out, and the floating bodies of the dead and the splashing of the living.

"Down!" Eeva shrilled. "I'm going to shoot! Down!"

Ras bent forward. Once again, so close that it was louder than the roar of the Bird's wings, the rifle bellowed in his ears. Fire flew over him; streaks of white painted the face of night; the streaks climbed up and up and swung, as they climbed, toward the right. Toward the Bird, the copter.

Suddenly, the eye winked into blackness and did not wink back into light again. A chattering was just barely audible below the chuttering. From the black body of the copter, fire streaked out; slashes of white raced across the surface of the lake, poofing silver in the moonlight, toward Eeva and Ras.

The streaks from the lake and the streaks from the air crossed. Immediately thereafter, like an evil thought too long held in, fire globed outward. The wind of the explosion chopped off other sounds, even his own cry. The glare blinded him for just a second. By the time he came out of the water, into which he had leaped without thought, he could see again. The copter was under the water, but its blood burned brightly in a pool only a few yards away.

The Sharrikt—those who still lived—had had enough. Most of them had jumped into the water. Gilluk's boat was the only one to still hold men; of these, all were dead or wounded except Gilluk. He stood on the little platform and stared out over the fire toward Ras. Abruptly, he ceased to be stone, jumped down from the platform, and seized a paddle. He dug the paddle into the water, but he was unable to turn the boat swiftly.

Eeva was beside Ras. She panted as she spoke in her native language, and then, when she spoke in English, she confirmed his guess. She had been swearing.

"I lost the rifle! Oh, damn, damn, damn!"

Their dugout was bottom up.

Gilluk's war canoe, heavied by the dead, was approaching as slowly as an elephant over unfamiliar mud. Gilluk was working frantically as he thrust the paddle in on one side and then on the other side to make the boat steer straight. He saw that he was coming too close to the fire, and he bent down and stabbed the water to get away from the blaze. Ras saw a paddle drifting before him, shoved it toward Eeva, told her to hang on to it, and swam to another. This he also sent to Eeva before uprighting the dugout again. Gilluk yelled once at them when he saw this and was thereafter silent.

Ras pulled himself into the dugout, took the paddles from Eeva and then got her in without flopping the boat over again. By then, the fire had spread out as if it were a wound, and the lake was bleeding. There was still no wind, so the smoke gathered over the fire, plumed up a little, and spread out. Gilluk was hidden. Ras sat for a minute to catch his breath and his thoughts. He could steer to the right and escape to the shore of the lake and thence up the mouth of the river. He could go to the left and confront Gilluk, perhaps surprise him as he came out of the smoke and so get to him before Gilluk could use his spear. Or he could circle the fire to the right and so try to come up on Gilluk from behind.

He turned around and told her what he might do. She said, "There might be another copter along very soon to find out what happened to the first. I think we had better get out of the lake and hide some place. As soon as possible. Why worry about Gilluk?"

The blaze, pushed by the current of the nearby river, was drifting toward them. Its heat was drying the water off their bodies and making them turn their faces away from it. A forerunner of the main cloud of smoke caused them to cough. Ras tried to pierce the smoke and the flame with his eyes to see Gilluk on the other side, but he had to turn his face away once more.

"More than anything, I want to kill the man or the god or whoever it was that killed my mother and caused me to kill the Wantso," he said. "But Gilluk killed Janhoy, and he has tried to kill me, and if I let him live now, he will be after me and will always be a danger behind me. He is near at hand now. I would be foolish if I let him get away. We will surprise him by attacking him directly. We will come out of the smoke and the fire and be on him before he knows what is going on."

Eeva groaned and said, "You're stubborn, stubborn, you ass!"

Ras was puzzled by the epithet. It had only one meaning for him and he could not imagine why she called him that now. But now was not the time to ask questions. He pushed the paddle against the water and drove the dugout along the expanding front of the fire. In a few seconds, he was forced to steer away from it to keep from being burned, but he did try to cling as closely as possible to its brush of fire and smoke for concealment. Gilluk should be coming around its corner soon. The last thing he would expect would be his enemy advancing against him.

Or would he? He had had enough to do with Ras by now to know that Ras would try for the unexpected. Could Gilluk be waiting for him around the corner?

Or perhaps he might have come around the other way to take Ras from behind?

Ras was too busy thrusting the paddle to shrug his shoulders, but he did so mentally. The future was the present come into being out of many possible beings. The future lay hidden in smoke like this smoke that was unrolling out across the lake, obscuring the moon, making him want to cough. Then he would be in the smoke and he would see. He would see . . .

CHAPTER 18

THE CROCODILE'S HEART

Blackness rolled back to reveal light and pain.

His head hurt. His back hurt where something sharp thrust into it. His mouth was dry, and the back of his throat was clogged. He coughed and sat up or tried to sit up, and his head pained him worse. The stuff in his throat came up and gagged him. He spat it out while he leaned on his left elbow. He was on mud and under a low bush. Above the bush and around him were tall trees interconnected with vines.

Eeva said, "Lie back down."

He did so, groaning, and then said, "Well?"

His legs were in damp mud, and his back and arms were on rough, tooth-edged grass. When he put his hand just behind the right temple, he touched dried blood on the hairs and a shallow trough of skin. He also touched off lightning of pain.

He groaned and again said, "Well?"

"A spear hit you in the head," she said. "It came flying out of the smoke—I don't know how Gilluk saw you, maybe he didn't, maybe he just threw it and was lucky, though it doesn't seem likely he'd waste a spear."

"He must have seen me," Ras said. "I didn't see him. I didn't see the spear, either."

"If it had hit you straight, it would have gone through the bone into the brain," Eeva said. "But it came in at an angle and bounced off your head. It almost got me; it went over my shoulder by an inch. It fell into the water. I couldn't get it."

"Where are we now?" he said.

After he had been knocked unconscious and was bleeding heavily—there was blood all over him and the front part of the dugout—she had turned the dugout and gone south. The fire was spreading; she did not know when Gilluk might come through the fire, and she would have been almost helpless against him. So, with many backward glances, she had fled as swiftly as she could. But Gilluk had never appeared. Under the bright moon she had paddled as far as she had been able, past the island opposite the town of the Sharrikt and to a point about two miles south. They were out of the lake and on the left bank of the river, in far enough to be hidden from the sight of anybody on the river or in the air.

Groaning, he lay back down. He was weak. But despite the pain in his head he felt a little hungry.

She slapped at his head to drive a buzzing fly away.

"Where's the dugout?" he said.

"Under a tree just over there. I had a hard time dragging you here and then getting the boat there. And I had to smooth out the tracks. It was hard work, and I was scared, too. I heard a leopard coughing somewhere near."

She was telling him this, he knew, because she wanted to be told what a good job she had done. He told her so, and she smiled and took his hand.

"I'm awfully discouraged," she said. "And I'm so tired! And I was so worried about you. If you had died . . ."

There was no need for her to finish the sentence. She was weeping now, anyway.

Ras waited until she was through and squeezed her hand and then said, "As soon as I can get some food in me, I'll be strong enough to paddle. And we can go north again."

There was a chuttering sound then, faint at first and later so loud that it seemed directly above them. They lay on their backs under a bush and looked upward through the green at the blue. The copter never came into their sight, but they knew it had to be close. After a minute the roar became less, and presently it faded away to the south.

Ras said, "We'll have to wait until night before we try for the swamp. But we can hunt in here; the jungle's so thick it will hide us."

She did not seem to be encouraged by this. She was pale and thin and shivering with nervousness and the cold of the night, which still had not been thawed by the rising sun.

Eeva's manner and expression told him that she did not want him to leave her, but she said nothing. She knew they had to have food and that he was the one who had the best chance of getting any. Even in his condition, he could function far better in this world—his world.

Ras set her to looking under rocks and fallen trees for insects and rodents and small snakes, for anything that could be eaten. She was to keep herself busy while he was gone, and she was not to regard her work as mere time-serving. She might have more for them to eat than he would by the time he returned. She shuddered and said that, being an anthropologist, she had eaten some repulsive food, but she had not liked it. However, she was almost hungry enough—almost—to relish beetles and worms, uncooked and living. She stood beneath a tree and watched him as he walked away. His one glance behind took in the tangled hair, yellow and dirty, the smudged face with the eyes that seemed larger because of the fatigue-stained bows beneath them, the almost naked, raw-skinned torso, the torn pants through which some white skin, some sunburned skin, and some dirt-covered skin showed, and the aura of loneliness and dependence.

Then he brushed at the flies trying to land on his gashed head, and he was into the green maze. But not for long. It struck him after a few minutes that he was not going to catch anything here except through sheer luck. He did not have the strength or patience now to look for a long time and, having found, to wait, to creep up slowly, to hurl himself, or his knife, at the last moment. He did try to entice a few curious monkeys close enough to him to throw his knife, but they refused to be attracted, even though he went through all sorts of antics to draw them near.

He went back through the jungle toward the river and once stopped to listen to a strange sound. Then he realized that it was Eeva moving about in the brush near the point where he had left her. He went on and presently was squatting behind a bush and peering out at the mud of the gently sloping riverbank. If the season had not already ended, he would have gone out to look for buried crocodile eggs.

The only life in sight was a kingfisher on a branch projecting from a tree near the water on the opposite bank. Ras called out softly, "*O mamago, mamago, mamago!*" This was the Wantso word for crocodile, which Ras hoped would go out over the waters and to the flesh-buried ears of a crocodile and so bring him to the caller. But when, after a half hour, no saurian appeared, he began to use the Sharrikt word. This was Sharrikt territory, and it was to be presumed that crocodiles would respond better to a familiar language.

"*Tishshush! Tishshush! Tishshush!*" he said softly. After a while, he left his hiding place and went down to the water. He dipped his hand in the water and cupped it up and poured it over the wound on his head. When the blood was leaking again, he bent his head into the water and let some of the blood flow out into the river. It was dissolved swiftly, but he knew that it was being carried downstream, and that even this dilution would not be weak enough to sieve unnoticed through the nostrils of a crocodile within half a mile or perhaps more. After a few minutes he raised his head from the river and let the sun dry out the hair and the wound. Flies buzzed around his head as if he were dead or dying, and when they found that he did not swat at them, they settled down on the wound as if he were dead. He lay on his front with his head turned so he could see downstream, and his right hand held the knife by his right thigh. When the stinging of the flies in the raw flesh seemed unendurable, and he was considering giving up, he saw the water at the bend of the river bulge brownly, divide, and slide off in two directions. The nostrils, like emptied eyes, and the knobs, like nostrils containing the eyes, were briefly broadside, and then he could see only the blunt, almost square, snout thrusting through the water straight toward him.

He watched it through half-closed eyes and, knowing crocodiles, was not surprised when it was suddenly gone, as if dissolved into the water. If intelligence was a firmament, and a man's skull housed many stars, the skull of a crocodile was a dark, dull arch containing only a few tiny, coldly flaming stars. But there were enough to shed some light, and the crocodile was not dumb enough to charge straight at the seeming corpse on the bank. It would approach stealthily, under water, suddenly emerge at a point so close that the human, even if playing dead, would be surprised and would, soon enough, be not playing. Or so it seemed to Ras.

He shifted enough so that he could see the crocodile when it would come up out of the water, knowing that, if he could not see it in the brownish waters, it could not see him while he was moving. So it was that he did not start when the water a few feet from him boiled and then reared up and hurtled in two parts down the head and back of the crocodile. He did not move until the long snout and many teeth were only three feet away from him. They moved swiftly; old Mamago looked slow as butter on a cold winter morning, but he was not slow when he was warm, and the sun was hot at this moment. He came up out of the water as if the river were suddenly rejecting a diseased portion of itself, as if it were vomiting the loathsomeness. Through his half-closed eyes, Ras saw the darker brown of the crocodile hump out of the lighter brown. Then the bellow followed, and, immediately thereafter, a shadow fell on him. Hot on the tail of the shadow was the bulk of the reptile. Water cast by the beast splashed and fell coolly on his arm and head. The jaws, which had been a few inches above him, lowered as the beast drove them into the mud with the intent of digging them in and under so it could catch Ras's arm or shoulder between the two jaws.

Ras moved then. He rolled away just a little; the jaws slammed shut with a clinking almost like that of metal. The left eye was even with his head; its lidless, slit-pupiled fishbelly-fleshed eye slid by. He rolled back then toward the crocodile, because he did not intend to let the tail break his bones. The five-toed paw hissed as it went by his nose and slammed into the mud, spraying mud on his chin. The crocodile bellowed again as it began to turn away from him and then at once turned toward him. Its snaky motion may have been designed to act as a brake. Whatever its reason for writhing, it continued on in the mud, digging a main trough with its body and four smaller ones, two on each side, with its paws.

As the foreleg went by, Ras continued his roll and brought his right arm, the knife in the right hand, up and over the back of the animal. He clamped down on it and then was dragged forward. His other arm came up and squeezed down on the juncture of leg and body. This grip enabled him to pull himself up to the point where he could throw his right leg up over the body. By then, the crocodile had managed to halt its forward motion.

It was possible that the animal did not know where the dead-meat-suddenly-come-to-life had gone. Ras did not think so. Though the hide on the upper part of a crocodile looks as dead and unfeeling as any armor, it must be sensitive to pressures. But it was possible that the beast did not feel Ras on it because it did not think of such a possibility.

Whatever the reason for its immobility, it remained still for perhaps thirty seconds. Ras waited like a fly that has settled down on a fresh wound but expects the swatting hand. He expected anything, including an effort to roll over on its back and so crush him. And what might have happened then was up to chance or to the behavior the beast had established, although that might not have governed it, since it was in a situation new to it.

New to Ras, too, who knew that he wanted to get the beast on its back so he could stick the knife into the relatively soft underpart, but at this moment did not know how he was going to do it.

Ras could hear his own breathing, a faint rasp, and the loud grumble of the crocodile and the yayaya of the kingfisher, now a blur of dark blue against light blue and ascending upward and at a tangent, a stone from the sling of terror. Then he heard the chuttering, which he would have heard long before this if the crocodile and kingfisher had not been so noisy.

The copter came around the bend with a flashing of sun and a roar. The crocodile bellowed, rose up on its legs, its decision made for it, turned, and ran toward the water. Ras clung to it for reasons that he was able to analyze only later. He could have fallen off and then jumped up and run for the shrubbery, but the men in the copter would surely have seen him. If he stayed on the back of the beast, he might not be seen. Or, if seen, not believed. The men in the machine would surely think they were mistaken, that the sun had played tricks on their eyes. What would a man be doing riding the back of a crocodile?

Stronger than this was the stubbornness and hunger of Ras. If he let the crocodile get away from him now, it would not be back. And he and Eeva had to eat.

The crocodile went into the water with a lurch and splash that almost unseated him with its force. It went under the surface and dived deeply at once, but, just before the waters collapsed over his head, Ras saw the machine dropping toward him. Then he was hanging on most comradely to the reptile, with one arm around its neck. This situation lasted for perhaps ten seconds, after which he slid around and under the body and began to drive his knife into the belly. It was not easy, because the water softened the blows; he had to overcome the resistance of liquid and armor-plate hide. But the knife did go in, and now the beast rolled over and over in an effort to throw him off. Presently, it had succeeded; despite all his frenzy, Ras could not hang on and was lost in water that was black with absence of sun and with blood from a dying reptile.

He did not believe the Wantso story that the crocodile could smell its prey under water, but it must be able to hear through water. For this reason, he stroked slowly, not away from the beast, though he had no way to know which direction was which, but toward where he hoped the beast would be. A little fright was near him but not touching him, and panic was even more distant. He was angry because he had lost his food, and he did not intend to let it go. Nevertheless, he felt as if the beast were moving toward him from his rear or coming up from the blackness below or perhaps even from the blackness above. He had to restrain himself from turning around and around, one arm extended as a feeler to detect the crocodile or perhaps the movement of water pushed ahead by its body. Six strokes, and he touched with the fingertips of his left hand the knobbled hide. He broke the sweep of his hand to bring it back into touch, but it went unopposed. The beast had gone to left or right, up or down. A sweep around and a slant down or up (he did not know which) touched only more water.

By then, he had to have air. After a few strokes, his ears hurt; he turned and went in what he hoped was the opposite direction. If he were going at only a slight slant, and not directly at right angles to the river bottom, he would soon drown.

It seemed that he would have to breathe and so die, when he saw the black become brown. A few more strokes and kicks brought him through brown to yellow and then to the white of the sun, bright blue of sky, harsh green of trees on the brownish-yellow mud. And a reddish-brown cloud drifting to the surface from that black world below. The copter was out of sight around the bend, its chutter becoming fainter. The kingfisher was on a branch about thirty yards upstream and braying indignantly. The river smelled fishy and reptilian and clayey, and faintly of dead wood and soaked leaves. There was also a very weak scent, ghost of a puff of stink, of reptile blood, and of bird crap in the water. Ras had always thought—no one had told him—that birds and reptiles were somehow linked closely. The monstrous, heavy-armored crocodile and the light, beautiful-feathered kingfisher were cousins and could claim as grandfather some squat cold-blood living in the days just after Creation. Now he knew it even more strongly. The bird crap was assuredly not only that of a bird; it was

the crocodile's as much as the blood was the crocodile's.
But it was also a bird's.

Presently, as Ras trod water, floating downstream, and
regained his breath for a second dive, he saw the blood
boiling a few feet upstream become even darker. Then
whiteness showed in the heart of the black, and the belly,
pale as the eyeball of a man, lifted water and blood
aside as it heaved up from under. The four legs stuck
a little in the air, as if the crocodile were indicating that
it had given up—do with me what you will.

Ras had to work hard to row the beast into the bank
and harder to drag the two hundred and fifty or so pounds
up onto the mud and then into the bush. He was weakened
by the blow on the head the night before, by lack of food,
and the excitement and stress of the fight with the beast.
While he was heaving and hauling and puffing, he heard
several bellows from down-river. They became stronger as
the reptiles followed the liquid winds of blood.

Always, every moment, he had to make a choice. Deciding which way to go, which thing to take, actually
created time. Without the necessity of picking this or that
course of action above others, he would not know time.
He would be suspended in forever.

Now he either had to drag the crocodile with much
labor through the jungle to higher land, where he could
butcher and cook it in relative comfort and safety, or
he could prepare it here, where leopard, crocodile, or
scavenger could approach him in any direction and where,
if he built a fire, the smoke might bring the Sharrikt,
who were only a few miles away, or might attract the
copter.

He wanted to eat a big meal now and smoke enough
meat to keep them going for several days. The large
animals, crocodiles, buffaloes, elephants, hippos, and leopards were not as easy to kill as they were to find. And
they were not easy to find.

The bellows and rumbles became closer, and soon the
brown-gray snout of a bull crocodile appeared, and then
the long, tapering bulk suspended on the four short legs
moved slowly into view from the brush. Ras did not expect any of the great reptiles to attack him, but it was
possible that one might lose its fear when the odor of
blood from the butchering became too much for it. He
shrugged and began the task of hoisting the body onto his
shoulder, preparatory to walking off with it. Once on his
shoulder, it sagged before and after him, the snout digging into the mud before him and the tail dragging in the

mud behind him. He had to lift it so he could get the snout clear, and this required an effort that he knew he could not keep up for long. Moreover, branches of trees, vines, and bushes seemed to want the carcass even more than he did. After a few yards of stopping to tear the body loose and twice almost falling down with the heavy body on top of him, he eased it to the ground. Thereafter he dragged it by the tail.

Eeva was sitting on a decaying, punky tree trunk and weeping. At her feet was a mass of white worms and grubs, still squirming, half-squashed beetles with kicking legs, a pale-green-and-bright-red-spotted tree frog whose bulging eyes looked as if she had choked it to death, and a brownish lizard on its back, its legs sticking up, its belly whitish. It looked like a miniature and short-snouted version of the beast Ras was dragging into the little clearing.

"I'm crying because I feel sorry for myself," she said. "To be in such a pitiable state that this disgusting mess almost looks appetizing. To eat this . . . this!"

Her shoulders shook with her sobs.

Ras said, "You ought to be crying with joy because you were lucky enough to get all this. I'm happy. If I'd come back without this, we would have had to eat your catch and we would've been glad to have it."

He let the tail fall with a flop on the wet earth. Eeva quit weeping and asked him what had happened. Although she could see the bloody wounds on its belly, she seemed to think that he had found it dead on the riverbank and that it might be in the last stages of decay. She said that she had heard the copter, of course, and had been terrified that he might be seen. But when it had kept on its course without hesitation, she had known that he was safe.

"Safe!" Ras said. "I rode that crocodile into the river and went to the bottom with him, and then he dislodged me, and Igziyabher only knows what would have happened after that if I had not been lucky! I kill a crocodile with a knife in dark and deep waters, and you say that I was safe! All this meat, good meat, and you think nothing of it!"

"I'm really sorry," she said, but she did not sound as if she meant it. "I know that it must have been a heroic feat, and any other time I'd want to hear all about it. But I'm so tired and hungry that nothing but food excites me."

"Then you ought to be coming with joy," he said.

"There's enough meat here to ground a flock of vultures for weeks."

He had changed his mind about dragging the beast up to the foot of the hills and there butchering it. He would cut out as many steaks as both could carry, wrap them in the leaves, and then walk to the hills. While he cut and sawed with his knife, she staggered off to collect the leaves. From time to time, he sliced a thick piece of the dark meat from a steak and ate it raw and bloody. By the time he was finished, he was stronger than when he had started.

Eeva, to his surprise, did not refuse to eat the raw meat he offered her. She had some trouble chewing it to her satisfaction and made several faces, but when she had downed the first piece, she asked for more.

Ras put the tree frog and lizard in leaves, and they started off toward the hills. By noon they were at the foot of the hills, and a half hour later they were on a ledge of rock halfway up a cliff. Pieces of fur and excrement and the chewed and cracked bones of small animals, plus a hangover of stink, told Ras that baboons used this place at night. The thrust of rock overhead made a shelter that could be leopard-proof if the baboon sentries were brave enough, and they usually were.

Eeva, hearing this, became worried, but he told her that the place could just as well be defended by two humans against baboons, and that they wouldn't be likely to try anything anyway, especially with a fire going. Besides, baboons did not make bad eating.

Ras had hesitated about building a fire, because the Sharrikt might be searching for him. But it seemed to him that it was unlikely that Gilluk and the others would be out in force after him. He did not think that they had enough men left after the battle near the river's mouth. What their casualties had been he did not know, but they must have been relatively devastating. The machine-gun fire from the copter had hit every boat, or almost every one. The total number of male Sharrikt, the divine ones, the aristocracy, was about twenty, and he had killed two before he escaped from the castle. Surely, at least half of the eighteen had been killed or wounded. The survivors would think of vengeance, of course, but they would be in no position to do much about it at this time. The burning of the castle and the town, and the deaths of so many Sharrikt males, would present problems demanding all of Gilluk's energies for some time. He was the king, the keeper of his people, and as such he had to take care of them.

Besides, even if there was a chance that they would be in this neighborhood and looking for the refugees, Ras wanted to build a fire and cook the meat. He just did not feel like putting in another cold and shivery night, and he seemed to have lost his taste for raw flesh.

Eeva had been sitting with her back against the stone, her head drooping forward. She looked up now and then through the dirty yellow hair fallen over her face. He thought she was dozing off from time to time, but when he got closer to her while he was building the fire, he saw that her eyes were wide open and tears running down her cheeks. They were washing away the dirt in stripes and leaving pink stripes beside the black ones. The coloring of the clean stripes resembled that of the crocodile's heart, which lay on the broad, flat rock beside the other chunks of meat and her catch of lizard, mouse, and insects. The heart was long and arrowhead-shaped and pulsed slowly and irregularly.

Ras got down on his knees and put his arm around her shoulders. She placed her head against his chest and warm tears trickled over his chest, ran down his belly, and wet his pubic hairs. She must have opened her eyes then, because she stiffened and tore herself loose from his arm. She crawled away before turning to face him.

"Is that all you think about?" she said. "Can't I even touch you without your . . . ?"

She struggled for speech, made some gargling sounds, and then spat many unintelligible words, which he supposed were Finnish.

Ras said, "It's been a long time." He left her to climb back down the cliff. After a few minutes, he came back with an armful of wood. Using the lighter, which she had carried in her pants pocket, he soon had a fire going. Eeva had said nothing during this, but she seemed to feel reassured by his deflation and moved closer to him and the fire. The world below the cliffs fell into darkness, and within a few minutes the sky darkened enough for a few stars to appear. Ras held a skinned leg on a hardwood stick over the fire until the juices began to drip in the flames and a black crust formed over the red flesh. Eeva sniffed deeply and came closer. Ras put the leg down and split it into even shares. The meat was so hot that she dropped it, giving a low cry at the same time. But she picked it up and ate without even trying to brush off the dirt.

Ras held his piece of leg with one hand while he held the liver over the fire at the end of the stick. When they had finished the leg, he offered her part of the liver. By now, the blood ran down her mouth and neck and stained some of the yellow hair. She did not seem to mind the blood now but licked it off hungrily and even wiped some of it off her breast and licked it off her hand.

The crocodile heart, lying near enough to the fire to absorb its heat, was still pumping, although not as vigorously. Ras wondered how long it would continue to live if he swallowed it whole. He could not do this, of course, because it would choke him, but he could feel it swelling and shrinking within him. The thought of its beating next to his heart was exciting, and the thought had its effect.

Eeva, looking down, suddenly stopped chewing. Then she swallowed loudly, and she said, "Don't!"

"Why not?" Ras said, even though he did not care to argue.

"Let's not even talk about it," she said. She started to rise.

"You won't have me," Ras growled. "You are dead, no better than a ghost, you white-skinned, yelllow-haired, ghost-woman!"

"You mustn't," she said. She was standing up now and beginning to inch away backward. The fire laid pale hands upon her so that the skin showed whitely where the tears had washed, redly upon the bloodied lips and chin and neck and stained hair, and grayly and whitely from the wide eyes.

Ras stood up, reaching out to pick up the heart with his left hand as he did so.

He hefted it, looked down at it, laid it upon the stone, and sliced it in half with the knife. Then he put the knife into its sheath and picked up one of the halves. The half on the stone and that in his left hand continued to beat.

"You don't want me?" he said. "Take this then!"

And he leaped outward, catching her outflung left arm with his right hand. He pulled her to him and forced her to her knees by twisting her arm, so that she had her back to him, after which he dropped the heart and used both hands to make her lie upon her back. She fought, but he tore the rotten clothing of her pants away until she was naked.

Silently, her face contorted, eyes wide, mouth working, she squirmed and writhed. But he held her down with one hand between her breasts while he picked up the half of the crocodile's heart with the other. Although he said nothing, his grin and the manner in which he waved the

flesh must have told her what he was going to do. Her
efforts to keep her legs together were useless. He pinned
one leg down with the weight of his body and pushed
the other outward with the back of the hand gripping
the heart. Then he took his hand away and, before she
could bring her leg back, he had thrust the end of the
crocodile heart into her.

The piece of meat was solid but only semistiff, and she
was dry. Nevertheless, he shoved it all the way in and
then rolled over on top of her so that she could not
move.

They were eye to eye. Her heart beat so hard it felt
as if it were trying to fly through her skin and into his.

She still said nothing. He kept grinning at her. After
a while, he said, "How does it feel?"

She closed her eyes. Her mouth was a little open. Ras
did not repeat his question. She began to shudder a
little, as if she were responding to the swelling and shrinking within her, as if she trembled each time it beat
against the walls of her flesh.

She shuddered, relaxed, shuddered, relaxed.

Suddenly, tears ran again, and she sobbed a few times,
and then the tears quit flowing.

Ras said, "Whenever you want it out, say so."

"And then you . . . ?"

"Of course. Unless you want both of us in at the same
time."

Eeva groaned and said, *"Jumala!"* It was the only Finnish word he had learned. It meant God.

"What kind of world do you come from?" he said.
There was no need to clarify his question. Eeva knew
what he meant.

She said, "Neither," in answer to his previous statement.

Then she whispered, "Please take it out. And leave me
alone."

"I won't," he said.

She opened her eyes, stared at him, and closed them
again.

She moaned again and said, faintly, "Oh, I wish I could
die! I want to be dead!"

"You are dead," he growled. "You haven't begun to
live. That dead heart is more alive than you are. Just now,
anyhow."

He felt between her legs, and he smiled. She had become so greasy that he had trouble getting hold of the
heart to pull it out. It was still flexing and unflexing, as

if the warmth and moisture and darkness had made it think that it was back in the crocodile's body. But, as soon as it was outside, it slowed down, and within a few seconds was dying swiftly. It gave a final quiver, after which he threw it onto the flat stone near the fire, which was now only red embers. The shock of the fall started the heart again. It beat three times and then died finally.

"It's no good," she said. "I'm no good. I'm cold, colder than that piece of meat, cold as . . ."

Her voice trailed off. She turned over slowly as if she could not believe that he was going to free her. Shaking as if the heart were still in her and beating against her, she got to her hands and knees. For a moment, she remained in that position, shaking her head back and forth and moaning. Ras touched the inside of her leg, where the lubrication was still running down.

"You want me below. You don't, above," he said wonderingly. He shook his head. "Very well. Say yes. And also say no. I will talk only to that part which says yes."

She stopped shaking her head and began crawling away. Before she had moved her knees and hands twice, she was down on the dirt and rocks with Ras pressing her from above. She gasped as she felt him drive into her from behind and under.

Ras cried out almost immediately and shook as she had when the heart was within her. It had been so long a time. He had burst with his burden.

He did not withdraw, and soon he told her to turn over. She did so without saying anything or without enthusiasm, as if she did not want to do so but knew that he would force her if she refused. Nevertheless, she was beginning to breathe heavily, and then she began moaning and rolling her head from side to side and after a while she clawed his back and kissed his lips and then bit them and was crying out in Finnish.

They fell asleep shortly before dawn, but not until Ras had rebuilt the fire and cooked some more meat. He took especial delight in cooking the heart and offering her a part. She hesitated a moment and then bit into it. She ate it all and then lay down to sleep, but she kissed him and muttered something that sounded like an endearment.

CHAPTER 19

THE WISDOM OF THE DEAD

When the sun was three hands wide above the cliffs, they were awakened by the stinging of the flies. She cursed him for what he had done. It she were pregnant, she said, she would killl him.

Ras grinned at her, although his expression was more of disgust than amusement. She was dirty, her ribs were like big teeth behind thin lips, her skin was bruised and bumpy from his maulings and from sleeping on the stone and splotchy from a hundred insect bites and scratches; her face was haggard, and she had big blue bags under her eyes.

She looked, and was, miserable. A moment later, she was struck with diarrhea. She continued to have attacks during the day. She became so weak that she could not walk, and so they stayed there the rest of the day and night. She was not so drained that she could not, however, curse him from time to time. He paid no attention to her words. He was busy cleaning up after her, fetching water for her, and making her comfortable. When he had ripped her clothes off, he had ruined them for any use except as rags, which he used to keep her clean.

He also scouted around the area for Sharrikt and hunted for some herbs that Mariyam had used for dysentery. He found some and prepared a tea, which she drank and which seemed to be responsible for the beginning of a recovery. Ras supported her while they walked to the river and carried her part of the way. At the river, he helped her bathe and washed out her hair, and then cleansed himself. She asked him if she had to go naked now and also added that she would freeze to death at nights if she didn't get some covering.

"You won't need it during the day," he said, "and at night I'll keep you warm. Don't worry about it. The end of the river can't be more than several days' journey away. I don't want to hang around here for a week while I hunt to get food to fatten you up and to get skins for you. It takes time and work to tan skins. We'll wait another day or so, and then we'll push on. You can take it easy; I'll do most of the work. Once we get there and find out from Wizozu how to get to Igziyabher's place, we'll worry about clothing you."

The evening of the night before they were to start again down the river, he sat behind her and combed her hair with the tortoise-shell comb his mother had given him. Eeva had said that he did not have to do this, but he insisted. She leaned forward as if to get as far away from him as possible, and she trembled. He talked softly to her for a while as he gently pulled the comb through her long hair. Then he dropped the comb and slid his arms around her and onto her breasts, and though she said, "No!" she shivered and did not struggle.

Later, she told him that she had only been able—up to now—to have an orgasm three times in her life. Once when she was drunk on wine (but she had refused to drink wine any more), once after she had smoked marijuana (but a second time with marijuana six months later had done nothing for her), and the night that she thought she and her husband would separate forever.

Until now, she said. But she did not love Ras because of what he gave her. She hated him. And she did not want to get pregnant. But she could do nothing about stopping him. Could she?

Ras said that she could run away or kill him.

She did not talk about her feelings thereafter, nor did she seem to object at all when he put his hands on her. His back became covered with bloody wounds, which had to be covered with mud during the day to keep off the flies.

Shortly before noon of the third day, the banks narrowed to a sixty-foot width. Where they had previously sloped gently upward from the water, they now began to rise toward the vertical. Moreover, the banks became taller, so that soon the surface of the river was twenty feet below their edges. The increase in speed was not alarming, but Ras wondered if he shouldn't put into shore and go ahead by land for some distance to see what lay ahead. By the time he had decided that he should, he found that he was too late. The banks were so steep that there was no place on which to beach the dugout.

Then they rounded a bend, and the twenty-foot-high walls became hundred-foot-high walls; the mud had given way to rock; the channel narrowed even more; the boat traveled more swiftly; the water began to get choppy.

Eeva said, "I should have recognized this, but it's been some time, and I saw it from the air. It looks different down here."

The canyon, curving slightly, finally straightened out. The walls became several hundred feet higher and over-hanging. The rock was black and lumpy. There were now no places where Ras and Eeva could take refuge even by abandoning the dugout.

"There's an island ahead," Eeva said. She was standing close to him as if she wanted some protection from the gloomy rocks. She was talking louder as if she had to be heard over a loud noise. The river, however, was still only growling; it had not yet begun to roar.

About a hundred and fifty yards away, the river split. It raced through two narrow channels on the sides of a low pile of stone approximately eighty feet across at its widest. At this edge—Ras could not see the other—the island was shaped like a spearhead, with the point directed into the stream. It rose from the water rather gradually, so that from the side it probably would look like the back of a turtle.

Beyond it, about three hundred yards, were the cliffs, and at their base a hole a hundred feet wide and fifty feet high. It held the end of the river, of the world that Ras had once believed was the only world and blackness like the end of the world.

On the top of the island was a large hut with a thatch roof. On all sides of it were many wooden, and some stone, statues.

Ras felt a chill, but he was too busy paddling the dugout toward the island. It came in exactly where he wanted it, its front end sliding upward on a shelf of rock betrayed by a white toss of water. The stop was so sudden that he and Eeva were hurled onto their faces, but they were not tossed off. They leaped up and off the boat and into the water. They had to work hard to get most of it onto the rock, because the river clutched it, but they managed.

When Eeva had quit panting, she said, "Who in the world would want to live here?"

"The ancient magician the Wantso call Wizozu and the Sharrikt call Vishshush," Ras said. "I've told you that. The Wantso say that he lived here before the Thatumu—the people the Sharrikt called the Dattum—came through the hole from the underworld."

Eeva smiled knowingly and said, "I doubt that that hut would have lasted that long. Or that anybody came through here. How could they have made their way up against the river?"

"Gilluk said that there was once a path through the caves in the mountain and that it went alongside the river and up above it. Also, at that time, the river was smaller."

"Perhaps," Eeva said. "Anyway, there is no Wise Old Magician here."

"Then I don't know who Wuwufa and Gilluk talked to when they came here as young men to get power and wisdom," Ras said.

"Oh, yes? And how did *they* get back up the river against that current?" she said.

"I do not know. But there is a way. Wizozu told Wuwufa and Gilluk how to get back safely, but he also made them promise to tell no one else."

Eeva tossed her head impatiently and said, "All this talk will settle nothing. Let's see what's in the hut."

"You stay here until I say you can come on up," he said. "Wizozu does not like women. They drain him of his power and his wisdom. He kills them as soon as he smells them."

Eeva rolled her eyes with disgust, but she sat down on a relatively smooth rock. He walked up the slope toward the hut. The canyon was quiet except for the rush of waters. There were no birds on the island or in the air and no plants whatsoever on the island. The sun, almost directly overhead, filled the canyon with light, but he had the impression of darkness brimming up from the waters.

The statues, carved from tree trunks, were twice as tall as he. Some had the bodies of frogs or crocodiles or leopards or unknown beasts. Most of the heads were half man, half animal. There were some carved heads mounted on tops of poles.

The hut beyond them was round and about twenty feet in diameter. Now that he was closer, he could see that most of the walls on this side were of thin slats of wood. The doorway was large and covered by a thin cloth of some material he could not identify at this distance. But he could see that something huge and black was on the other side of the curtain.

Gilluk had said that the ancient magician sat on the other side of the curtain and talked to him with a voice like the bellow of Baastmaast.

Gilluk had also said that his uncle had come here to gain extra power and wisdom so that he could slay Gilluk's father, but that the uncle had never returned. And when Gilluk had gone to the island, he had found his uncle's bones—which he recognized by their association with his uncle's war club—lying outside the hut. Vishshush had told him to throw his uncle's bones into the water and also to throw the other bones away. Vishshush had not told him why he had killed the uncle, and Gilluk did not feel like asking him.

If Gilluk's story was true, he had left the island bare of bones. Yet there was now a skeleton lying on the path about twenty feet from the hut. The skull and the bones looked as if they were Wantso. There were no weapons in sight.

Ras passed by the first statue, which was polished mahogany and represented a frog with a gorilla-like head. It must have weighed at least a ton, and this caused Ras to think of the power that Wizozu must possess to have been able to bring this heavy statue onto this island.

He went past the statue. The closer he got to the hut and the curtain behind which Wizozu bulked so blackly, the more nervous he became. He stopped once to glance back at Eeva, to make sure that she was obeying him but also to draw some comfort and courage from the fact that another human was in this place.

He turned away from her and took a step, and then stopped again. He felt even colder, and the hairs on his neck became stiffer, if that were possible. The gorilla-faced frog statue had been looking down toward the end of the island when he had passed it. Now it was facing him.

The body had not moved, but the head had swiveled.

He stood for a minute without moving, and then walked on toward the hut. He had expected strange and wonderful and frightening phenomena, so why should he hesitate?

But he heard Eeva calling him and turned around. She was running to him and shouting something. He angrily waved her back, but she kept on coming. When she was twenty feet from him, she said, "That statue's head turned, Ras! It turned!"

"I know it!" he shouted. "I know it! Go back before Wizozu kills you!"

"But you don't understand! It . . ."

The voice that roared from the hut was as he had imagined Igziyabher's would be. It bellowed louder than Baastmaast; it carried up the canyon and was bounced off a rock wall and came back at him. It seized him with terror; it numbed him.

It spoke in a tongue that he did not recognize for a minute. It was as different from Eeva's English and his, as his was from hers.

"Ras Tyger! Kill the woman! I, Wizozu, command you to kill her!"

Ras came out of his numbness as if he had just left the cold waters of the lake. He turned toward the hut and the huge, dark presence within it. He shouted, "Wizozu! Why should I kill the woman who has saved my life and whom I love?"

The voice was silent for a moment. Eeva said, "Ras! This whole thing . . ."

The voice carried her words away as if they were chips of wood on a cataract.

"Ras Tyger! Do you want to see your foster parents again, your Mariyam and Yusufu? I, Wizozu, can bring up their ghosts and you can see and talk to them again!"

Eeva screamed, "Ras! It's all a trick! Look up at the top of the cliff up there! You can see the television tower up there! The statue must have a TV camera in its head, and there must be other cameras! And that voice is coming over a loud-speaker! Ras!"

He did not know what she meant by *television* or *TV* or *loud-speaker*. But, looking at the edge of the cliff at which she was pointing, he could see a tall, branchless tree with long, stiff arms poking out of the top.

The voice bellowed, "Do not delay, Ras! Kill her at once! She is not the woman for you! Another woman is to be your true mate, a beautiful virgin! She has been prepared for you; she is worthy of you! Kill this slut, this vessel of impurity! Kill her at once!"

Ras shouted back, "What do you mean, Great Wizozu, when you say that another woman is to be my true mate, that she has been prepared for me? And what do you mean when you say that this woman, Eeva, is a vessel of impurity? She isn't diseased. I know, because I have lain with her. When she's had a bath and gotten some food in her belly and some sleep, she is sweet indeed! Although a crocodile's heart in her helps a lot!"

Wizozu roared angrily, "Do not talk such obscenities, Ras! Or I will kill you, too! Do as I say! I know what is best for you! Do not argue! I know! Kill that woman!"

"And if I do not kill her?" Ras yelled.

"Then I, Wizozu, may kill you! I will punish you in some way, you may be sure of that! For instance, if you do not kill her, I will not let you see and talk to the ghosts of your foster parents!"

"What do you mean, you won't let me talk to their ghosts?"

Even in the shock from Wizozu's statement, he noticed that Wizozu had called both Mariyam and Yusufu his foster parents. Was Mariyam, then, not his true mother? If she was not, who was?

"Can you really summon the dead from the underworld?"

"I do not talk idly!" the voice boomed.

"Show me. And then I will kill Eeva, if you can do what you say!"

Out of the corner of his eye, he saw Eeva, breast-deep in the water, hanging on to the rocks along the island's edge. She put a finger to her lips, and she waded slowly on by him. Apparently, she was going to try to attack Wizozu from the rear with her bare hands. Her courage was admirable, certainly, but her common sense was lacking.

Ras said, "O Wizozu! Let me see Mariyam and Yusufu and Wilida, and then I will say whether or not I will kill Eeva! I must make sure that you can do what you promise!"

Wizozu was silent for a long time. His shadowy bulk did not move behind the curtains. Eeva was out of sight now. He wished that he could tell her to return to the dugout. He would take care of Wizozu—one way or another.

He sweated in the sun while he waited for Wizozu to answer. The white rocks of the island and the nearby black walls of the canyon seemed to intensify the midday heat. A slight wind was at his back, but it did not cool him. The silence became difficult to bear, and finally he opened his mouth to speak. He had to say something. However, before he could get a word out, he was stopped by Wizozu's roaring.

"Very well! It doesn't matter whether she dies now and by your hand, or later! You shall see your beloved dead!

And then you shall know that I tell you the truth, and that I am so powerful that no one can oppose me!"

"Not even Igziyabher?"

Wizozu paused a few seconds and then said, "Igziyabher has given me power to do as I wish! I am His representative here!"

"I want to see Him!" Ras said. "I have many questions!"

"Ask the dead!" bellowed the voice. "Look, Ras!"

"Look where?"

"To your left! At the big boulder!"

Ras turned toward the nearest boulder, thirty feet away. It was of granite and about eight feet high and ten feet wide. It had appeared to be solid, but now a vertical seam split it in half, and then the two parts swung outward until they fully exposed the hollow interior. This contained a smaller boulder, on top of which was a granite cup carved in the form of a bird. Behind the boulder was a tall, curved, gray spout, still dripping. The spout sank back and slid downward and disappeared behind the small boulder.

"Drink from the stone bird, Ras!" Wizozu said. "Drink, and in a short time you will see your beloved dead!"

Ras did not hesitate. He walked to the boulder and picked up the stone bird by its outstretched stone wings. Its hollowed back contained water. Ras lifted the cup so that the water ran out of the hollow down a channel carved on top of the neck of the bird. The water shot down the channel and into a hole in the back of the head and poured out through the open beak and into Ras's mouth.

He had expected some strange taste, but the liquid seemed to be only water. He drank the bird dry, set it down on the flat top of the boulder, and then, as directed by Wizozu, stepped back. The two parts of the greater boulder swung toward each other until the boulder seemed a solid rock again.

Ras waited. He felt nothing except some apprehension and, after a few minutes, disappointment. Wizozu, however, thundered at him to be patient. Meanwhile, he should think about the ghosts of those he wished to see, and soon enough they would come.

He waited while the sun began to slide downward toward its black bed. Soon, he saw a patch of yellow to his right, beyond Wizozu's hut, on the edge of the back of the island, where it suddenly curved off. The yellow rose, and it was followed by Eeva's forehead, eyes, and nose.

Ras wanted to wave her back but did not dare. He was in an agony because he was sure that Wizozu would soon see her and then all would be over for her. The heads of several of the statues had been moving, but now they centered their gaze on Eeva.

Suddenly, the barrel of a machine gun stuck out of an opening on the side of the hut toward Eeva. Ras could see its extreme end as it lowered.

He shouted at Eeva and ran forward.

Wizozu boomed, "Back, Ras! You are forbidden to come any nearer!"

Ras continued to charge. Sections of the bamboo wall on both sides of the doorway fell back, and a machine-gun barrel poked out of each opening. The great, dark bulk of Wizozu did not move behind the curtains, but the voice became even louder and its tones were more urgent.

"Back, Ras! I don't want to kill you! You don't know what you're doing!"

Then the machine guns on the side nearest Eeva—he could see two sticking out now—exploded, and fire leaped from them. Dust and chips walked across rocks toward Eeva's head as if an invisible giant with iron-hard bird-feet were striding across the island.

Eeva withdrew her head. Ras kept on running, although he expected the guns pointed at him to start firing. He cast his knife, and it went through the narrow opening between the curtains, and plunged into the great body of Wizozu, seated upon a huge metal chair. He was close enough now to see the head of the sorcerer. It was four times as large as his, black, eared with wings, benosed with a forked horn, eyed with purple glass, mouthed with knives. ,

Ras wrenched his knife out of the soft, cloth body, and jumped into the center of the hut. The machine guns were no longer a danger; they had turned inward as far as they could go and now looked cross-eyed at each other. They had not fired once.

Wizozu bellowed so loudly that Ras's ears hurt. "Get out! Get out! I'll kill you! Aren't you afraid of anything?"

The voice came, not from Wizozu's mouth but from a big, metal horn-thing attached to a curved metal bar above the doorway.

The unknown controller, whoever he was, wherever he was, was powerless to hurt Ras now. Ras could not hurt him yet, but he was determined to destroy the trickery of the man who had deceived him into thinking that the Wantso had killed his parents.

He examined the hut, understood little of what he saw, but found a chest containing some devices he did understand. These were a large sledge hammer and a crowbar. With these he first wrecked the machine guns still firing at Eeva or at where she had been. He tore down the other machine guns—two on each side of the hut, and he smashed in the blind, glassy eyes on all the metal boxes inside the hut. The first one exploded, spraying glass all over the hut, but he was standing to one side when he smashed it and so was not touched. Thereafter he took care not to be in front of the one-eyeds. Eeva, entering the hut then, stopped him when he was going to cut a cable with a pair of bolt cutters.

"There is lightning in that cable," she said. "It kills as surely as lightning in the sky."

She searched until she found a trap door, and went down into it. Ras watched her, saw her light up the cellar with a flick of a button, saw the big, metal whirring things, smelled an unpleasant odor that she said was petrol, then watched the whirring metal things die as she pulled down on a thing that shot sparks when it came loose from another thing of metal.

They finished the wreckage by toppling over Wizozu and ripping off the soft padding over the wooden frame beneath and smashing that and the machinery inside.

Ras stepped outside to attack the statues, but he never reached them. A sound as of a giant tree breaking startled him. He looked up to see that the sky had become fire-red. The sun was a black ball against the fire. A head, larger than the full moon, thrust up above the top of the cliffs. It was the head of a white-haired, old white man with a long, white beard. It was Igziyabher as described by Mariyam.

Ras cried out because he was sure that Igziyabher was coming after him. His boasting and his sureness melted from him. What could he do against anything so monstrous?

The sky-filling head glared at him with eyes as pale and malevolent as a crocodile's. A hand that seemed as large as a quarter moon came up from behind the cliffs and seized the edge of the sky and yanked it down as if it were a curtain pulled from a window in Mariyam's house. The sky behind the blue sky was so many swirling colors that Ras could see only a chaos of glory. Then the hand opened, and the fire-red sky snapped back up to cover the many-colored, swirling sky.

Ras knew that he was shaking with awe, but he seemed

not to be entirely connected with his body, so that the awe was only a shadow of awe.

The island, which was shaped like the back of a giant turtle, became, for a moment, flesh. It arched, and he rose up with it, and then it slumped back and became rock and dirt again.

But lumps formed here and there in the earth; the lumps grew upward and shaped themselves into the figures of men and women and animals and birds. Foremost were Mariyam and Yusufu and Wilida. Behind them were the other little black people he had known when he was a child. And behind them were Bigagi and all the Wantso. And the Sharrikt he had killed. And the leopards, the monkeys, the river hogs, and crocodiles, the deer, antelope, and civets. Behind and above them were the birds he had killed. These flew about as if tied by strings from their bellies to the earth. Strings of earth did attach them to the world; they could fly only in circles.

Soon Janhoy pushed through the animals and the Wantso and walked majestically to Yusufu and crouched down beside him. His green eyes shone.

Ras wept with joy and ran toward them, but they moved away from him. Their feet did not walk on the earth; their feet were buried ankle-deep; their legs seemed to sprout from the earth; rather, to be sunk into the earth, and they seemed to have to fight to keep from sinking entirely back into the earth. They looked as if they were riding waves of dirt, and some sank as far as their necks before they began to rise again.

"Stay away, son!" Mariyam said. Her little, dark face was twisted with agony. "We cannot touch you, although we long to hold you and kiss you. We are dead. You are alive."

"If I can see you, why can't I touch you?" Ras said.

"Because the distance between the living and the dead is farther than that between sun and stars," Mariyam said. "It is the greatest distance in the world."

"Wilida!" Ras cried, hoping that she might not say the same thing. But Wilida moved away from him.

"Forget about her, son," Mariyam said. "She is dead, and you have a live woman to love. Forget about all of us."

"But I can't!" he said. "I grieve for you night and day."

"Don't do that, son," Yusufu said. "Or you will soon be with us, or might just as well be."

"What can you tell me?" Ras said. "If you can't touch

me, you can talk to me. Tell me something I want—
need—to know. You are dead; you have now seen the
truths behind the walls of the world. You know the answers to my questions. Tell me!"

Yusufu grinned with the ghost of his living grin. He
looked, at that moment, evil. Wilida, who had been staring
at the ground, raised her head and looked at him as if she
hated him.

Mariyam said, "The dead have nothing to tell you that
they didn't tell you when they lived."

"And that is all they have to tell you," Yusufu said.

Ras heard Eeva calling him from a long way off. He
looked around but could not see her. When he turned
toward the ghosts, he saw them all sinking back into the
earth. Mariyam was up to her neck, Yusufu was up to his
chest, and Wilida was waist-deep. They struggled soundlessly but desperately. Janhoy tried to rise to his paws,
but his body continued to descend, and soon only his
maned and noiselessly roaring head was visible.

Ras rushed forward to pull them back out, but the
earth seemed to spin them away faster than he could run.
And when, suddenly, he found that he was making progress, he reached empty ground. They were gone under. He
fell on his face and dug into the earth with his fingers and
felt the coarse thick hair on the top of Mariyam's head,
and then it was gone. He wept and moaned and called on
them to come back, and after a while he seemed to have
gone asleep.

Blackness succeeded blackness.

CHAPTER 20

THE HUNT

He was in a place so quiet that he could hear only the hum of no sound. He was standing on stone and in water not quite ankle-deep. His outsweeping hands felt nothing.

He moaned, wondering if he were dead, too, and if the ghosts had taken him with them.

A click made him jump, and the tiny flame that followed made him gasp. By the light, he saw a hand holding the cigarette lighter and the pale, anxious face of Eeva. Beyond were rough stone walls, a boulder in the shadows ahead, and more darkness. The water was a shallow stream about two feet across.

Eeva snapped the flame off. He felt her move against him. She spoke softly, as if the darkness and quietness subdued her. "Are you all right now, Ras?"

"I don't know. Where are we? How did we get here? What . . . ?"

"First, you tell me what happened to you," she said. "You ran out the door, and the next I knew you were acting crazy; you were talking to yourself and groveling on the ground."

Ras told her what had happened. She still did not understand how it could have come about until he mentioned drinking the water from the stone bird within the opening boulder.

Eeva said, "That drink must have contained LSD, or some kind of psychedelic drug. That's the only explanation I have for your hallucinations and your blacking out afterward. That also explains what happened to the Wantso and Sharrikt who dared face that thing so they could get religious revelations and power.

"This man that set all those statues and equipment on that island . . . I don't know why he did it. Unless he had something in mind for you eventually. Or maybe he wanted to play God with the natives and also wanted to keep anybody from trying to get out of the valley by the river, although anybody who tried that would have to be out of his mind.

"Anyway, he gave it to you so you would be in a suggestible state, easily handled. People that take LSD are often fantastically suggestible, you know. No, you wouldn't know. Anyway, he intended to tell you to kill me after you'd come under the influence of the drug. He suggested the ghosts to you, so you saw them. They all existed in your mind, Ras. But you fooled him by attacking before you were affected by the drug.

"I knew that this—this man—must be watching us through TV cameras . . . he's probably on the stone pillar in the lake . . . and he'd undoubtedly send a copter after me as soon as he knew we were on the island. He had us trapped, or so he thought.

"After you passed out—withdrew, I mean, because you could walk and would do what I asked you to—I got you into the boat. But you wouldn't co-operate very long; you'd paddle for a minute and then stop, and I couldn't paddle the boat back up the river against the current by myself. In fact, even if you'd tried your best, I don't think we could have gotten back up.

"It didn't matter, because I heard the copter coming. There was only one thing to do. I didn't want to do it, but at least that way we just *might* get out alive. If we stayed on the island, I'd get killed for sure, and I didn't know what the men in that copter had in mind for you. Maybe they had different orders now.

"So I just let the current carry the boat, and I shoved hard to help it along. I steered it into the cave just as the copter came around the bend. The men in it must have seen us, because it came straight after us. It didn't come into the cave—the entrance was big enough to let it in but not big enough so they'd have a margin of safety— but it shone a searchlight on us. It was terrible. The river rushed and boiled, because the channel suddenly got narrower. Then we went around a bend and almost capsized when we hit the side. The boat began to toss more than ever, and I couldn't see a thing. We were almost washed off by the waves.

"I prayed—even though I don't believe in God and still don't—and then the boat hit something and we were rolled right off it into water. But the water was shallow, and I got us up on higher ground, a rock reef, that is. I used my lighter, it was in your bag, luckily, and I saw that we were at the entrance to a side tunnel, a big one. It must be the bed for another river, dry now. The boat was gone, carried off. I didn't care about it, because I didn't intend to get back on it. We got lucky; at least, I'll think so until something bad happens. We can follow this old river bed on up to . . . who knows?"

Her voice trembled as she ended, and suddenly she was crying and hugging him. He held her for a while and then said that they should go on. He felt as if he had been weakened, but he was still strong enough to go for a long way.

"Tell me if you start to see or hear or feel anything unusual," she said. "Sometimes a psychedelic drug has a recurring effect."

He still felt somewhat dislocated, but any man who had seen what he had seen could expect this for a while.

His arm went around her shoulders, and they set off into the darkness. She could not stop shivering, she said, because she was so cold, cold not only from the cold of the wet stone but from fear. Every once in a while, she snapped on the light so that she could reassure herself there were no pits ahead, or to identify some obstacle that usually turned out to be a large boulder that the violence of the now-dead river had carried along its bed.

They walked for a time, the length of which they could not estimate, and occasionally drank from the little stream, which seemed to be pure. Ras said that their situation could be worse. At least, they did not have to worry about dying of thirst. Eeva did not laugh.

The time came when she insisted that she had to sleep. Despite the cold and the hunger pangs, she was so exhausted that she could no longer stay awake. They lay down on a rough, hard shelf of stone that seemed drier than the rock near the stream, and, though both awoke frequently, they did sleep. When neither was able to go back to sleep, they untwined from each other, rose stiffly, and began their tiresomely slow progress. However, they were able to proceed more swiftly than if there was no stream. As long as they were walking in water, Ras said, they did not have to worry about falling into abysses. Their feet were numbed by the water and their legs ached with the cold, but it was the safest road to travel. Moreover, the water was moving slightly, hence was flowing downhill, and the fact that they were going uphill encouraged them. They had no logical reason to believe so, but they did believe that the uphill direction would end in their coming out above the ground. And they had only one route to follow.

To himself, he said that they couldn't *get* lost, yes, but they could *be* lost. If the source of the stream turned out to be a small hole in the stone wall, and they could go no farther . . . well, he would wait until this happened. He did not really believe that it would happen.

They shuffled on until Eeva said that she had to rest again. She stopped and snapped on the lighter again for a quick look around before much of the almost-expended fuel was gone. She gave a cry and shrank back into Ras's arm. A few feet away, on top of a boulder, looking at first like a giant skeleton hand, were the bones of a bat.

Ras whooped with joy, and, shouting to her to keep the light on, ran ahead and around the corner. As he did so, he heard the distant roar he had hoped for. He called to her, and they walked for perhaps a hundred yards more. The roar increased, a faint light appeared ahead and grew larger and brighter, the air became so damp it was a cloud, and soon they were on the edge of a hole about forty feet wide and thirty feet high. The source of the stream was a number of trickles down the wall that converged to form a pool just inside the entrance. They were in the midst of a deafening roar and almost in solid water.

Ras put his mouth close to her ear and shouted, "I've been here before! This cave is behind one of the falls! I found it when I was a child! I explored this far, where the dead bat is! We're almost home! We've circled!"

Seven days later, at noon, they lay behind a bush on the edge of a high hill. The steep and rocky slope was sparsely grown with bushes and small trees. At its foot was a comparatively open space about two hundred feet wide and three hundred yards long. Beyond, the forest was a tangled denseness. Shouts and an infrequent rifle shot weakly climbed up the hill to them from somewhere in the forest.

Both Ras and Eeva had gained some weight, and their eyes were less black and hollowed. They wore antelope-skin clothes, and in their cave high up on the cliffs, their night retreat, were more antelope, monkey, and leopard skins to keep them warm. Both had bows and arrows that Ras had taken from the tree house, along with other items they needed. Eeva had been afraid for him to go near it, because she feared that the man on top of the pillar had set a watch there or perhaps had hidden TV cameras around it. Both had cautiously approached the two houses and prowled around for four hours before they decided that no men or cameras had been planted there. But they did not talk while they were taking what they needed, because Eeva had said that listening devices were so easily hidden or disguised.

The first four days had been busy with finding a warm, safe, well-hidden base, coverings, and food. Ras had hunted well, and they had more food than they could eat. The last three days they had spent observing the many flights of two copters from the pillars and some of the search parties in the forest and hills.

Eeva said that something had stirred them up; they acted as if they were under pressure or had a time limit. One copter spent all day over this area, and the other evidently was exploring south of the plateau. There was also a third, much larger copter that came once a day from over the top of the cliffs, and this, she said, must be bringing in fuel and supplies and also, to judge from the number on foot, more men. She doubted that there would have been any reason to have kept that many on top of the pillar all this time; it would have crowded them and also made a supply problem.

There were ten newcomers. Five were Negroes, like the Wantso, but much taller. Three had equally dark skins, but their noses were hawkish and their hair was straight. Two were white men, one much darker than the other, who was as tall as Ras and had bright red hair and pale blue eyes and a big scar down his right cheek. The dark white man led one party; the red-hair, another. These started out each day at distances from each other and worked toward each other.

Each party also had two animals that he recognized as "dogs" because he had seen them illustrated in several of the books that had been in the lakeside cabin before it burned down. Eeva said two were German shepherds and two were Doberman pinschers.

Ras could not understand why they were searching the forest. They should think that the river in the cave had gobbled them up.

Eeva said, "If he thinks you're dead, he might as well go back to wherever he came from—South Africa, I would think. But maybe he can't because evidence of what he's done still exists. Rather, somebody who knows what he's done is still alive."

"Who could that be?" Ras said.

Eeva shrugged and said, "I don't know. Maybe somebody got disgusted and tried to quit, or maybe some prisoner got loose. From what you've told me about hints dropped by your parents and from what that dummy, that Wizozu, said, you were supposed to be provided with a woman. Maybe that woman was brought in, but escaped, and they're looking for her. Maybe other explorers flew in and the same thing happened to them that happened to Mika and me. We haven't seen any wrecked planes, but that means nothing. The plane could easily be hidden anywhere in the forest on the plateau or could have fallen into the lake."

Much of the big animal life in the area had fled the noisy intruders and gone to other parts of the plateau or up into the hills. So far, the two parties had killed a leopard and three gorillas, apparently for no other reason than to kill, because a leopard wasn't going to attack so many men unless it was cornered, and the gorillas wouldn't attack except under circumstances that were not likely to occur with such noisy hunters.

Eeva thought that this was significant. This unnecessary killing would not be permitted unless there was no longer a need to conserve the animals in the valley.

"If he is interested only in killing whoever he's chasing, not in capturing him, he'll send in a copter as soon as the person is spotted and drop a napalm bomb."

Now, he and Eeva were up on the hill and trying to glimpse the hunters and the hunted. The shouts became louder, and the barking of dogs also louder and more frequent. From the noises, Ras thought that the two parties were closing in on somebody between them.

Then a figure burst out of the green into the sunshine of the clearing. Ras gasped and said, "Jib!"

Jib was shorter than Ras by a head, and he was emaciated and naked. His black, gray-threaded beard reached to his knees, and his hair fell over his face and also fell to the back of his knees. He sprinted across the clearing and then started up the hill and was lost from view for a moment by the jagged, wildly tilted boulders that covered the hillside.

Ras got to his feet to wave at Jib with the hopes of directing him to where he was hidden. He was not sure that he would not spook Jib as much as the men after him. Though he had played with Jib many times when he was young, he had always had to re-establish a new relationship after every long absence from him. Jib was as shy and frightened as the gorillas he lived with.

Ras forgot about Jib. Another figure had bounded from the solid green wall and was racing across the clearing on pathetically short and bowed legs. He was black and wore a shirt that had once been white, and had a long, gray beard.

Ras screamed, "Yusufu! Yusufu!"

His first feeling was almost insane joy. The next was almost insane fear for him.

He stooped over and picked up his spear. Eeva said, "What do you think you're doing?"

"I'm going to help him!"

"It's too late! You can't do anything now, and if they see you, they'll never stop until they find out if I'm alive or not!"

He jerked his head to follow the line of her shaking finger. Two dogs had run out of the forest, but they were being held on leashes by men. Other men were running after Yusufu, and three long-legged Negroes were only a few paces behind him. Yusufu turned then, and something that flashed in the sun flew out from his hand, and the legs of the foremost Negro failed him, his arms flew outward, and he slid on his face. Then Yusufu was running again, but the second Negro was on him and over him, and the two were rolling in the tall grasses. The third Negro rapped Yusufu on the head with the butt of a revolver, and the two Negroes carried him off between them. The rest of the party came on up the hill after Jib.

Jib reappeared from behind a slanting boulder. He bounded upward with many desperate glances behind him. His squalling became audible. Ras said, "Save your breath!" and he started toward him, then stopped. He did not love Jib; he did love Yusufu. If he put himself into danger for Jib's sake now, he might not be able to help Yusufu afterward. If he let Jib go on by with the two parties at his heels, the two men guarding Yusufu would be left behind. And he could deal with them.

Eeva pointed at one of the men, who was carrying a big, black, shiny object on his back and speaking into something he carried in his hand.

"He's calling in the copter. It'll be here in a few minutes!"

"Follow me," he said, and he began to work his way down the side of the hill away from the pursued and the pursuers. When they had reached the forest, he told her to wait for him. She said that she did not want to, that the two men left with Yusufu were armed and that she was skillful with a bow. He did not argue.

They were behind a tree on the edge of the clear space and only twenty yards from Yusufu and the two Negroes, when they heard the copter. They could not see it, and the foliage thinned its sound, but they knew that it must be coming from the pillar.

Eeva cursed. Ras said, "I'll shoot the man on the right. You take the one on the left. Then we run out, and I'll get Yusufu and you get the rifles. The copter people won't be expecting us. We can catch them by surprise and you can shoot them again, blow them up, as you did on the lake."

They stood up and aimed very carefully while the noise from the copter increased. Ras gave the signal, and both released their strings and then picked up another arrow stuck upright into the ground. Ras's arrow went halfway through the thigh of his target, and the man dropped, screaming, onto the ground. Eeva's arrow hit' her target but glanced off against the ribs and went up into the air. Her man was staggered for a moment; then he dropped to one knee and picked up a rifle. Eeva's second arrow drove into his forehead. Ras's second arrow again went too low; this time it ended quivering in the earth a few feet before the man with the arrow in his thigh.

The man sat up, screaming, and then he became silent and fell onto his side and started to work his way, on his left side, toward something in the grass—presumably a rifle. Ras yelled and dropped his bow and picked up his spear and charged out of the forest. At that moment the copter's shadow fell on Ras; the roaring beat at his ears. He paid it no attention and kept on charging. The wounded man was sitting up now and had the rifle to his shoulder, and then a pair of little black feet rose from the grass by his side and kicked so hard against his shoulder that he dropped the rifle and fell over on his side.

Yusufu, his hands bound behind him, was up on his feet, and had leaped through the air. The Negro sat up again just in time to receive the impact of two iron-callused feet against the chin. He fell down again and did not get up.

Ras looked up at the copter now. It was across the clearing by now and was rising at a slant. Ras at once understood that the men in the copter had not looked down at the scene below them; they were intent on getting Jib first.

He cut the ropes around Yusufu's wrists and then, smiling, tears blinding him, pushed Yusufu away and said, "Later, father! We got to get away!"

Eeva picked up the rifles. Ras carried the belts of ammunition the two men had been wearing. Yusufu took their knives and the items he looted from their pockets. The man with the arrow in his thigh was dead or close to death from loss of blood and shock; the wonder was that he had been able to recover enough to go after his weapon.

Abruptly, Ras gave his burden to Yusufu and Eeva and ran across the clearing to the man whom Yusufu had felled with his knife while being chased. He pulled the knife from the corpse's solar plexus. He got back to the forest without anybody on the hillside seeing him, as far as he knew. Once in the protective shade and green, he dropped his burden and took Yusufu into his arms. They cried and kissed and tried to tell each other at the same time what had happened. But they had barely started when they released each other and fell silent as they stared out at the top of the hill.

The hill looked as if it were spouting fires from its top. Flames climbed upward; smoke as black and thick as a thundercloud poured upward. The copter was off to one side, circling out of reach of the heat. The men on the ground were behind boulders.

Yusufu said, "They wanted me alive for some reason. Perhaps because Boygur wanted to talk to me to find out what was going on or maybe to torture me. But he didn't have any use for Jib; he just wanted to destroy Jib so nobody would get his fingerprints."

"What are you talking about?" Ras said.

Yusufu said, "I have much to talk about, but we don't have time. That copter, and those men, will be back, and as soon as they find those dead men, they'll be after me. You, too, because they won't think I could carry the rifles alone."

Eeva said, "Does he know how to shoot?"

She spoke in English, but Yusufu did not understand her way of speaking it. Ras translated into their type of English for the little man.

Yusufu replied that he had once been a trick shooter, but that he had not had a gun in his hands since just before Ras was born. Eeva showed him how to operate one of the rifles, which she said was an M-15. Ras watched interestedly and said that he would like to try shooting one. Eeva was firm in refusing to let Ras handle one. She said that a man used to guns could shoot one of these without too much practice. But he knew nothing of guns, and they had neither the time nor ammunition for practice.

By then the copter was hovering above the bodies, and the seven men and four dogs were coming down the hill. Eeva spoke to Yusufu, who still did not understand her. Ras translated for her. Yusufu seemed dubious. He thought they should get away as swiftly as possible before another napalm bomb was dropped. Then he said that perhaps she was right. They had to fight back some time, and they might never again be in such a good position for ambush. If only the chopper would come closer!

It did. The men in it apparently did not want to wait until the men on foot got down from the hill. About twenty feet above the corpse nearest the forest, the copter was turning around on a vertical axis while the man at the machine gun looked into the forest—or tried to do so. Then the copter settled down, and the roar lessened and the whirling blades above it became visible.

Eeva said that the pilot had undoubtedly informed the pillar of what was happening. And if another copter were available, it would soon be here to join the hunt.

The grasses were tall enough to hide them, now that the copter was down on the ground. Eeva went to one side and Yusufu to another. Ras stayed in the forest in a tree and sat on a branch while he fixed an arrow to his bow. From his vantage point he could see both of them moving in. Then Eeva got up on one knee and started firing, and Yusufu began to shoot a few seconds later. His fire was not as accurate as hers; his stream of bullets climbed into the air and expended itself on nothing. But he stopped firing and began over again and this time he hit where he was aiming.

The pilot, a white man with a heavy brown beard, fell at the first few shots from Eeva. The machine gunner, a skinny white man with long orange hair, raced for the copter and his weapon, but he did not make it. The machine went up with a great bang and a sheet of flame and spiraling smoke. The fire sprayed outward and caught two men who were also running toward it. Yusufu's second attempt downed two men. The three survivors began to fire back. By then, Eeva and Yusufu had crawled off elsewhere. Yusufu was between the three and the hillside, and Eeva went on her hands and knees back to the forest. Ras called to her, and soon she was beside him on the branch. She was smiling and weeping at the same time, but her aim did not seem to be shaken too much.

She could see the three men now, and with six shots she stretched all three in the grass. Then she and Ras got down from the tree and cautiously approached the bodies. Yusufu joined them. They found three men still living and one of the dogs alive. Yusufu killed all four with two bursts from his rifle.

Eeva was crying because the copter was burning. "We could have flown out of here!" she said. "We could have gotten away! Now we're still stranded here!"

Yusufu said, "The other copter is coming."

Ras could just hear it. He told Eeva, who said that they must get out of this area at once. Ras had thought so, too, at first, but now he said that he had another plan. It would be very dangerous, especially for him in the first stages. But if the others would agree, they might capture this copter. Or, at least, get rid of another. But there was no time for careful and detailed planning; they would have to improvise now, and if they did not care to do what he suggested, they would not be blamed by him. They were in the forest by then. Yusufu was carrying the walkie-talkie taken from a corpse.

Eeva and Yusufu listened, and then Yusufu said that it seemed like an excellent plan to him. Risky, but likely to succeed. After all, Boygur and his people must think that Ras was dead—Ras had told him about the river and the cave—and seeing him here would startle them. So far, they had made no effort to kill Ras; they had always made sure that he was not around when they had tried to kill Eeva, if what Ras said was true.

Ras had no time to talk. He ran out into the clearing and lay down about twenty yards from the edge of the forest. He lay on his face, head toward the forest as if he had been running toward it when something had happened to him.

He heard the copter overhead and felt the chill of its shadow for a moment. It went around and around him as its occupants apparently studied the situation. They must have been shocked by what had happened to their own men and shaken by discovering him. They would be talking to the man on top of the pillar—Boygur, Yusufu had called him—describing the situation and asking for orders.

Yusufu had said he could listen in on them, so he must have some idea of what they intended to do.

After a few minutes, the copter landed near enough so that the grasses by him bent away from the blast of air, and he could feel the air cooling off his sweating back.

Its noise almost drowned out the sounds of rifles shooting. On hearing this, Ras rolled over. One of the men who had been in the copter was about ten feet away. He was lying on his back, a shiny object near his open hand. It was small and barrel-shaped and transparent and had a needle end.

The pilot of the copter had remained at the controls. Now he took it up and away, but he suddenly slumped, and the machine turned over on its side and struck the earth. It did not catch on fire, but its blades were crumpled and its nose was shattered. The pilot made no effort to get out. Ras ran to him and found that he was dead. Eeva wept some more because the machine was wrecked. Yusufu did not seem to think things were so bad. He was alive and free, whereas ten minutes ago he had been a prisoner and expected torture and death. Also, his beloved Ras, whom he had thought he would never see again, was with him and well.

Besides, all they had to do was stay alive long enough, and they would be able to get out of this valley forever. An Ethiopian military plane had buzzed this valley ten days before—when Ras and Eeva had been in the old river bed underground—and it had been caught by machine-gun fire when it approached too closely to the pillar. It had crashed into the lake, but Yusufu was sure that other planes would be looking for it. That explained why Boygur, who believed Ras to be dead anyway, was frantically getting ready to desert the valley and his project. But, first, he had to destroy Jib, so that his fingerprints could not be traced, and he had to find and kill Yusufu, so that his mouth would be forever shut.

"There are so many things I don't understand," Ras said. He felt as if the world were a big trap door that had suddenly opened and he were falling through darkness.

"There will be time to explain later," Yusufu said. "There is much I don't know, also. Let us go to my camp, which is far closer than yours, and we will weep for Mariyam and talk of how we will get revenge upon this Boygur."

On the way, Ras asked what the man with the hypodermic syringe—Eeva had explained this to him—had intended to do.

Yusufu said, "I listened in on them. They did not know what had happened, but they were frightened and also angry with the anger that fear brings. They saw you stretched out face down on the grass. Boygur could not believe that you were there; he thought you had died in the cave. Then he became joyous and said that you were indeed a true hero, that you could not be killed. Now, instead of leaving the valley, he would stay and carry out his plans. He was sure that the Ethiopian authorities could be satisfied if he spread a great deal of money where it would be most effective. And he may be right. Anyway, he told the copter to land, and the gunner was to see if you were alive. Boygur had some second thoughts then; it occurred to him that just because you were there did not mean that you were alive.

"The gunner—Johann—was to examine you. If you were wounded, he was to fix up the wounds if they were slight. If they were serious, he was to bring you in for treatment on top of the pillar. If you were unharmed but unconscious, he was to knock you out with the hypodermic, and then they were to fly back to the pillar, pick up the girl—the girl who was supposed to be your jane— and bring her back here. They were to give her a chance to escape and then to pretend to look around for her, and then were to come back here. The girl would find you, and everything would go as expected. Boygur said it was none too soon. The girl was still on a hunger strike and would die soon if she didn't eat. He hoped that you would be what she needed.

"Rudi said that the situation looked menacing to him; surely you didn't do all that killing and destroying by yourself. He didn't want to land, but Boygur said he'd kill him if he didn't carry out orders."

Yusufu was silent for a while; then he said, "Boygur must have known a long time ago that things weren't working out the way he wanted them to and that they never would. But he wouldn't admit it to himself. The man is mad!"

"And now," Ras said quietly, "will you tell me everything—from the beginning?"

CHAPTER 21

GOD CAUGHT IN A NOOSE

The following day they spent hidden in the forest near the shore, where they watched the stone pillar in the middle of the lake. The thousand-foot thrust of shiny, black rock had always seemed sinister to Ras after Mariyam's explanation of its origin—an explanation he now knew to be false and indeed had never really believed—but now that he knew the truth, it seemed twice as menacing. Its blackness had become even darker.

Nothing happened. They could see no sign of life except for two fish-eagles soaring around it. Yusufu pointed out the place where Boygur often stood to look through the telescope at the scene below, most often at Ras himself. Ras strained, but he could see nothing.

Yusufu said, "He will have radioed for help; you can be sure of that. Tomorrow, or the day after, another helicopter will come. Perhaps it will be the great copter that brings fuel and supplies. Then the hunt will begin again. Boygur will never quit. I know that demon."

"Tell me more of that place," Ras said. "Tell me all about it, all that is needed for a man who would go there to kill."

Yusufu was startled. He said, "What? Surely you joke, son?" But he obeyed.

Ras listened, and asked many questions, and then told what he had in mind. He had to listen to loud and powerful and even hysterical protests and arguments from Yusufu and Eeva. Finally, Yusufu said to Eeva, "Do not waste your breath and wear away your spirit any more. I know that look. He is determined to go. Nothing except Death will stop him."

The rest of the day was used in getting ready. This involved a journey to the cave in the cliffs. Ras slept an hour in the evening, and then, at dusk, he entered the dugout with Eeva and Yusufu. They paddled in the moonless black until they were at the base of the dark pillar. Here Ras kissed both Eeva and Yusufu, quieted their tears and their final protests, and, armed with only his knife, leaped from the dugout.

Blindly, he gripped the projections he had gripped many times before, found more handholds, and began his slow, blind climbing. For the first time, he did not slip, perhaps because he was on fire and burned into the rock and so made his own clinging, or so it seemed to him. Painful and creeping as his progress was, it took him away from sight of the shadowy dugout too quickly. It was below him, a few yards away from the base, while Eeva and Yusufu waited to make sure that he did not fall. They would be there until shortly before dawn, unless he fell in before then and they pulled him living into the boat or dragged his dead body in.

Soon the moon rose, and he could now see the boat and the tiny figures in it. He waved at them, but they did not wave back because he was invisible to them. Or perhaps he was so high that he could not make out their hands.

He could see the silvered lake, the dark walls of the forest, and the white feather of one cataract. The moon rose higher, and he with it, though much less swiftly and less certainly. After a while, his fingers got cold. He was dressed in buckskin moccasins, trousers, and shirt, but the wind, coming over the cliffs and then down, as if weighted by icy particles, was chilling.

He continued to go up, handhold by handhold, foothold by foothold, grip by grip. At times, he had to angle across, and other times he had to go down before he was able to work his way back up again. Twice, he found himself a quarter of the way around the pillar and then had to find some holds to get back to the side that would take him to his goal.

The time came when he felt that he could not haul himself upward for another second; yet he could not stop, and he refused to return. He had climbed without the aid of picks or pitons or ropes; he had used his fingers and toes, and often had had to cling with only his fingers supporting his weight while the knobs or heads of rock seemed to be giving way. Though his hands and fingers were calloused, they were bleeding, and this made for slipperiness. He wiped his hands on his shirt until the sides of the shirt were a solid red. Finally, he decided that he had to put on the gloves that Yusufu and Eeva had made for him. They would dim the sensitivity of his fingertips in testing the strength of the rock projections, but he could not put up with more pain, more loss of blood, and the resulting lack of friction between hands and rocks.

For a long while he felt very heavy. Then he began to feel light and airy, as if the wind had plunged into him and made a balloon of him. He realized that it was fatigue and hunger and cold that were causing this dangerous sensation, but he could do nothing about it. He continued to climb. Shortly before dawn, while the sky was paling in announcement of the sun's approach, his upstretched hand felt a hollow and a ledge of stone that was too regular and smooth to be natural. He had found the window that Yusufu had described. And just in time. He had to summon all the strength in him to pull himself up and over the sill, and when he had done so he sat bent over with knees against his chest for a long time in the window as if it were a womb and he a baby waiting to be born. He certainly felt as weak as an about-to-be-born.

It was while he was squinting against the sun that panic seized him for a second. The notch in the top of the cliff to the east seemed to be moving, and he felt that the world was sliding away from him. Then he realized that the notch was not moving back and forth. He was moving. Rather, as Yusufu had told him years before, the pillar of stone was moving, swaying, pushed by the wind as far as it could be pushed, perhaps a foot, and then springing slowly back to its original position, only to be pushed northward again. It was incredible that such an enormous and solid mass could respond to the weak and invisible air. But it was. It had been doing so since it first became a thousand-foot-high column, and would continue swaying until the movement cracked it somewhere and the upper part fell off.

He let himself into the room, stretched, bent, and then began to explore. Yusufu had said that this room had been chiseled out of the rock a year before Ras had been born. It was a general storeroom. He tried the big door, which was made of thick wood, and found it locked. He would have to wait until someone unlocked it. According to Yusufu, a cook would open it shortly after dawn to get food for breakfast.

There were many things piled here, all labeled. He

wanted some ointment for his fingers and then some food.
He found the ointment after a few minutes' search, opened
a jar, and smeared it on. He had to pry open a box with a
small crowbar to get a can of meat. After puzzling over
the directions printed on the label, he pulled the little key
from the bottom of the can, and inserted the tab in the
slot of the key. The process was so novel and delightful
that he had to restrain the impulse to open all the cans.
The meat tasted cold, greasy, and too spicy, but he ate
all of it, and he felt much better when his belly was on the
way to being full.

After eating a can of peaches, which he had to open
with a can opener and therefore took more time to puzzle
it out, he examined the armory. There were boxes of
ammunition of all sorts, cases of revolvers and auto-
matic pistols, several sub-machine guns, and a variety of
rifles in racks. Ras took an M-15, which was the same type
that Eeva had shown him how to handle after they had
gone to Yusufu's hiding place. He inspected it for clean-
liness, loaded it, and got a canister of clips to take with
him. Then he sat down near the door and waited.

The sun's rays entered the window at a steeper angle
and brightened a machine that had been a dim, many-
angled bulk. The machine was taller than he and three
times as long as its height and had many toothed wheels
and a huge cylinder on which white rope was wound and a
long, metal neck on which were little wheels and more
ropes. The entire machine was on a platform with wheels
and could be pushed to the window, where the neck would
stick out for about six feet. The rope around the spool
was attached at one end to a big coil of rope on the floor,
and this coil to another, and so on until twenty great coils
formed a connected series.

This was the machine Yusufu had described, the "donkey," which was run by petrol and which could let down
a thousand feet of rope from the window to the surface of
the lake. Boygur had prepared this for the day when he
might be stranded on top of the pillar without helicopters.
Near the donkey were several fish-gray metal boats attached to frames and hooks, which would support the
boats while they were being lowered to the water.

Without leaving his post, Ras looked at the machine to
pass the time. Then he forgot about it to think of other
things, past and present and future. A fish-eagle slashed
the air outside the window with two screams. There was
no sound after that until, so suddenly that his heart
lurched, he heard a key in the lock. He ran to a large pile

of wooden boxes and hid behind it. A short, fat Negro wearing a brown shirt and shorts and a clean, white apron entered. He locked the door behind him and put the key in his pocket and went on by the pile of boxes. He stopped before a waist-high stack of boxes and leaned over it and came up with a bottle half full of some dark liquid. It was tilted to his lips when Ras hooked an arm around his neck from behind. The bottle fell on the boxes and was still gushing out the stinking amber liquid when the man's neck cracked. Ras dragged the body behind the boxes and threw the bottle onto the body.

He wiped the ointment from his fingers, because he would need friction if he had to handle his knife. After unlocking the door with the key from the man's pocket, he passed through it, locked it again, and stuck the key in his shirt pocket. Before him were ten steps cut from the rock. He went up them and found himself in a hallway the ceiling of which was only a few inches above his head. The hallway ended abruptly a few feet on his right; he had to go to the left. A few steps down the hall and to his right was a doorway flush with the floor, and about twelve steps farther on was another door to his right. Both were locked, and his key fitted the locks of neither. At the end of the hallway was a stairway of stone to his right, and on his left, just opposite the stairway, was a thick, wooden door with a small window in it.

Ras looked through it and saw a window with three bars of iron at the other end. Inside the small room was a stand with a metal washbowl, a pitcher, and a cup, and a white pot with a lid in one corner, and a wooden bed with some blankets and pillows. A woman lay on her side on the bed. She was dressed in brown clothes similar to those Eeva had worn when he had first seen her. The woman was thin, her yellow hair was tangled, and her face, as much as he could see, was gaunt. This woman would be his jane, the woman brought here against her will and now starving herself.

While he was standing outside her door and wondering what—if anything—he should do about her, he heard the faint, far-off chuttering coming down the stairway to the outside. So many times, like the beats of the wings of a demon, it had excited and frightened him. Now he knew it only heralded the approach of a dead thing, a machine, and some—but not all—of the mystery and terror was absent. Hearing this one, he felt eagerness more than anything. If it was the big copter that carried fuel and supplies, it could be used to bring consternation, panic, and death to his enemies.

He decided to let the woman stay in the room undisturbed. She would be safe where she was, and she could not accidentally betray him or get in his way. He left the cell door and stood by the wall just outside the entrance to the hall at the bottom of the staircase. He could hear men talking near the entrance at the top of the steps and others shouting at a distance. Then he heard the rattle of metal against metal. Somebody was coming down the steps. He ran down the hallway and hid in the stairway leading to the storeroom, but, a few seconds later, he stuck his head out far enough to see with one eye. A short, thin, white man dressed in brown clothes was just straightening up from a tray of dishes and pots on the floor. He unsnapped a key from a ring around his belt and inserted it in the lock to the cell door.

The man was intent on looking through the window in the door, so he did not see Ras, who walked silently and almost leisurely down the hall, until he was within knife-throwing range. The man whirled then, and his hand went to his belt, but he had no weapon and he could not have gotten it out in time if he had. The knife drove almost to the hilt into the solar plexus. The man staggered back and slumped against the wall and started to slide down. Ras leaped to him and dragged him back down the hall out of view of the man standing at the top of the stairway. The man held a rifle, but he was looking into the sky at the moment—perhaps at the copter—and he did not see Ras or the dead man.

Ras laid the body down and pulled the knife out and wiped it on the corpse's shirt. Then Ras heard the guard calling down in an English that he could only half understand. The guard had seen that the man with the tray was not there and the door was unopened. Perhaps he thought that the man was inside the cell and doing something to the woman. Or perhaps he knew that he had not looked away long enough for the man to open the door and go inside. Whatever his reason, he was alarmed. His boot heels clattered, and he leaped out into the hall and started to turn to face down the hall.

Ras threw the knife again; it went straight into the man's throat. He fell backward, his rifle clanking against the floor. Ras pulled him out of view of anybody passing by the stairway entrance, and then he looked into the cell. The woman had not moved, and her color was as gray-blue as a corpse's.

The roaring became louder outside, and then it lessened, and the blades chopped the air weakly and collapsed. Ras could hear the voices of men clearly now, though they seemed to be at a distance. He checked his rifle again and went up the steps and looked around the corner of the entrance. It was walled around and roofed —to keep out the rain, he supposed. There was a small, dome-shaped house on his right. Four wires attached to the central part rayed out to metal hooks imbedded in the stone. These, he had been told by Yusufu, were to keep the "quonset" huts from being blown off the top of the pillar by the big winds. There were several more at irregular intervals and close to the rim of the top. The rim was walled to a height of four feet with mortared slabs of stone cut from the pillar. Several stone enclosures, like the one in which he stood, were visible. These must be above entrances to other rooms carved out of the stone. At the far end, less than a quarter mile away, was a wide space partly occupied by a huge copter with a bellying body. Around it were hoses and pipes, and devices he supposed were pumps. Four men were attaching hoses to the copter, and two men inside the copter were handing boxes and sacks through an open wall to two outside.

A tiny thing, glittering in the sun, was another copter approaching.

Ras looked the area over as fully as he could without exposing more than his head. He did not see anyone fitting Yusufu's description of Boygur. The men working around or in the big machine were either whites or the dark but straight-haired and eagle-nosed men Yusufu called Ethiopians. Before the doorway of a "quonset" house with several poles and many crossarms projecting from its roof, halfway between Ras and the far end, stood a short, light-skinned man with a bald head. He was smoking a cigarette, but when one of the men near the machine gestured at him, he ground the cigarette out under a shoe. The man started to turn toward Ras, who withdrew behind the wall of the enclosure.

He had no way of knowing where Boygur was or how many more men were here or where they were. He would have to make his move and then act accordingly.

When he looked around the corner again, he saw a fat-bellied, red-faced white man leaving a large, domed building about thirty yards away. The man had a tall white cap and a white apron. He was probably on his way to find out what had delayed the first man.

Ras grabbed him as he came around the corner, choked him with an arm around his neck, and dragged him down the steps. He backed him against the wall and held the edge of the knife against his throat. The man was gray under the pinkish skin; his eyes were huge; he shivered.

"Where is Boygur?" Ras said in English.

The man chattered in a language Ras did not recognize as English until he made him repeat his words slowly. The language was still only half-intelligible, but Ras could understand enough of the stammering. Boygur was in the radio shack, the building outside which the bald, light-skinned man, the radio operator, had been smoking.

"How did you get up here, Ras Tyger?" the man said.

"I climbed up," Ras said.

He whirled the man around to face the wall and cut his jugular vein open and then stepped back to avoid the jet of blood. Whatever doubt he had had that the others were as guilty as Boygur was gone. This man had known his name and presumably all about him and also must have known about Mariyam's murder.

He dragged the corpse a little way down the hall to the other bodies and returned to the top of the stairway. The hoses still linked the big copter and the pumps and several raised iron discs, which must be the caps over the fuel tanks, which were placed in pits in the stone. The crew of the copter was in sight now. One was a tall, black-mustached white man, another was a shorter, brown-haired white man, and a third was a stocky black man. All three were walking toward the radio shack.

The other copter, a much smaller one, was nearer and apparently was going to pass over the big copter and land close to the radio shack.

Ras checked his rifle again and stepped out of the enclosure. He carried the gun in one hand and walked leisurely toward the shack. The black-mustached man slowed and turned his head to say something to the others, who were a few paces behind him, but none showed any alarm. Ras continued walking until he was almost to the door of the shack. He stopped, and for a moment was caught. The music swelling from out of the shack was like nothing he had ever heard before. It came from many unknown instruments the individual sounds of which thrilled him, and it had a complexity and a magnificence that shot him through with ecstasy. It spoke of the greater glories in the world beyond the sky, and it made him wonder what kind of men could create such music.

Then he shook himself and brushed his hand across his

face as if he were removing spider webs. The smaller copter was settling down; its transparent body revealed a pilot and another man.

Ras brought the rifle up and triggered off the spray of bullets. The weapon barked, and chips of stone and stone dust danced along and caught the three men near the shack. They had stopped, their faces pale, their mouths black holes, and then they were knocked down and back, and he brought the rifle barrel up and played the stream across the transparent body of the small copter. The pilot had taken the machine up and away as the three men died, and the other man was behind the twin machine-gun barrels and swinging them toward Ras. But the pilot jerked at the impact of bullets, and the copter slid sideways and downward. It struck the rim of the pillar, tore out some of the slabs on top of the wall, and rolled over and disappeared.

Ras continued to shoot, hoping that the rifle would not jam, as Eeva had warned might happen. The men tending the machinery near the big copter and the four men unloading the copter were crouched as if bewilderment pressed them down with a big hand. Then some threw themselves on the stone. One fell as bullets caught him running.

Ras fired at the hoses carrying the fuel and then at the copter itself, attempting to place the bullets, each tenth of which was an incendiary, near the places where the hoses connected to the body of the copter.

Suddenly, arrows of flame shot out, swelled, came together, became one, grew, and raced toward him. Smoke formed as if blown out of a giant mouth. The blast was like a crocodile's tail striking him. He was hurled against the side of the radio shack so violently that he dropped his rifle and, for a moment, did not know who he was, where he was, or what was happening.

Heat and smoke spread over him. He coughed. He was blind and deaf, but his senses returned quickly enough, and though he still could not see, he was beginning to hear the roar of the burning fuel. He rolled over to look under the smoke but could see nothing. Then a vagary of wind curled away a cloud for a second, and he saw a charred body. The smoke coiled back in. A door slammed. He saw shoes appearing out of the smoke, descending and touching the stone and disappearing again into the smoke. The owner of the shoes was coughing. The shoes raced by him a few yards away. The ankles were those of a skinny white man. The man coughed again, and then he was gone.

Another pair of feet appeared, disappeared, appeared, going in the same direction as the first. Ras found his rifle, fitted it with a fresh clip, and crawled in the direction the feet had taken. He bumped into the enclosure out of which he had first come. He lay down and stifled his coughing and listened. He heard nothing. The two men could be waiting down there for him or they could have taken refuge elsewhere. Or they might have gone down there to the storeroom to run the rope out the window with the machine and climb down it to the lake surface. Or perhaps neither might be aware of him. They might believe that the explosion was an accident. No, they could not think that, because even if they had not seen him, they had heard the rifle. The descending copter was noisy but surely not loud enough to drown out the sound of the rifle.

The wind blew more smoke down the stairway, so he could see no more than several feet down it. He quelled another coughing fit and crawled down the steps. At the bottom, he crouched and listened. The cell door was barely visible. Its little window was open, but no face looked out through it. He peered around the corner. The smoke was getting so thick now that he could not see its end. The two bodies were almost hidden in the clouds. He could see, however, that the rifle and pistol and ammunition belt of the guard were gone.

He grinned. Whoever had come down here had either gone on down the corridor to one of the rooms along it or to the storeroom, or else was hiding in the cell. Unless he—or they—had a key, however, they could not get into the cell, since he had taken the key from the guard.

One man could have gone on to one of the rooms behind the three doors down the hall and left the other man in the cell so that they could catch Ras between them.

At that moment, a face appeared in the cell-door window. It was one Ras had not expected, because he had thought that the woman was too weak to stand up. Nevertheless, her gaunt face was there, and her eyes, sucked empty of feeling, were looking at him. Her head lolled to the right, and her whole bearing indicated that she was being forced to stand at the window and perhaps even being held up by someone.

This feeling was enough warning. He had his rifle up and his finger pressing on the trigger when a face appeared behind the woman's and a rifle barrel slid over her shoulder and out through the window.

There was nothing else he could do except to shoot. He could not help it that the woman was in the way. And so she fell backward with her forehead broken open and spouting blood, and the face behind her also jerked away. The rifle roared flame once, chips of stone hit Ras in the face as the bullet caromed off the wall beside his head, and then the rifle uptilted and slid back through the window.

Ras emptied the clip at the door, aiming low so that the bullets—if they penetrated the wood with enough force—would hit the man on the floor. After reloading, he waited several minutes. The only sound was the muffled roar of the burning fuel. The wind must have shifted again, because the smoke had disappeared from the entrance to the stairway. In a short time, the smoke in the corridor had dissipated. Ras, looking around the corner of the stairway, saw no one. He rose and then leaped across the corridor to the cell door. Again, he waited. No head appeared at any of the entrances along the hall, and no sound came through the cell-door window.

He looked through the window. Neither the man nor the woman could be living with that much of their heads and necks carried away. The man could be the radio operator who had been smoking outside the shack.

Ras regretted that he had had to kill the woman. Even when Boygur was at the end of his life, he had managed to cause Ras to kill another innocent.

After making sure that a third party was not in the cell, Ras cautiously approached the entrance and then went down the stairway to the storeroom. He placed his ear against the door. Faintly, through the thick wood, he heard a rumbling, a hissing, and a clanking. What caused the sounds, he could not know, but he guessed that the machine with the rope coiled around the cylinder was responsible. He looked through the keyhole but found that it was blocked. Boygur—if it was Boygur in the room—had left his key in the lock. If the key were to be pushed out, its fall would warn Boygur. No doubt he was keeping an eye on it.

Ras returned to the surface. He still could see very little, and the smoke set him to coughing again. He groped through it until he had reached the stone wall along the edge. By hanging over the wall, he got away from much of the smoke and could also see all the way down to the lake. The tiny dugout with the tiny figures of

Yusufu and Eeva bobbed up and down. They were waiting; they must be quivering with uncertainty, wondering
what had happened after the smoke rose from the pillar.
There was too much smoke coiling around for him to be
visible to them, but he waved at them.

Still bending out over the edge of the wall, he worked
his way to a point directly above the storeroom window
through which he had entered after climbing the pillar.
The metal neck of the machine was sticking out the window, and the white rope was running out over wheels at
the end of the neck. The rope was halfway down the black
sides of the pillar. Its end was tied to a cradle, which held
one of the small, metal boats Ras had seen in the storeroom. In the boat were three long bundles, two paddles,
and a rifle. The sides of the cradle and the boat bumped
now and then into projecting rock, but the descent was
very slow at those times. The operator of the machine
was taking no chances of damaging the boat. His white-
haired head was stuck out the window as he observed the
boat. Ras watched him for a few seconds and then withdrew when the head started to turn to one side. He did
not want to be seen if the man should glance upward.

Ras hoped that he had enough time to locate a suitable
rope before the boat would reach the surface and Boygur
would have gone too far down the rope. He began looking
at once, but the search took him longer than he cared. He
went through the buildings at one side of the pillar. The
other buildings had either been flattened or destroyed by
the explosion or were too close to the heat for him to think
of getting into them. One building, which had to be Boygur's, would have held him enthralled at another time.
Just as he was about to give up and run back to the wall
on the edge, he found the rope he was looking for. It was
coiled on a wall in a room in Boygur's house. He recognized it at once as a rope that he had made and used
several years before. Then it had disappeared mysteriously.
He had suspected that a chimpanzee or a monkey had run
off with it, but here it was, on a wall with many large
photographs of himself and others and the mounted heads
of some animals and some Wantso and Sharrikt weapons
and the first spear that he had ever made.

He ran back through the smoke to the wall on the edge.
The metal boat was swaying back and forth but not quite
hitting the side of the pillar. It was apparently close
enough to the surface for Boygur, because he was crawling
out on top of the neck of the machine. He went very
slowly and with frequent stops. He was now wearing a

pair of brown pants and gloves to avoid rope burn when he let himself down the thousand-foot length. A holster on his belt held a revolver.

Among the weapons and tools that Ras had practiced with for over twelve years was the lasso. He dropped its noose over the white-haired old man's shoulders just as he looked upward. Boygur—it had to be Boygur from Yusufu's description—squalled. He threw his head back to look up; his eyes were wide; his beard stuck straight out as if stiffened with terror.

Ras pulled upward to tighten the noose. Boygur screamed and tightened his knees and hooked his feet around the metal frame. Ras could not use anything except his arms to haul Boygur up, but, nevertheless, Boygur, after a few seconds of desperate gripping, was broken loose. He twirled around slowly and swung back and forth under the push of the wind.

And so Ras hauled Boygur up as a man would haul up God caught in a noose, as the creature would haul up the Creator to ask Him why He had done such and such. Certainly, this old man, scratched, torn, bleeding, smoke-begrimed, was not Igziyabher. He was glaring like Igziyabher; his pale blue eyes seemed as angry and dreadful and mindless as the lightning of God. Yet he was only a man, though a man like none other. And if he was not the being who had created Ras, he was the being responsible for the shaping of Ras and the being responsible for many evils.

CHAPTER 22

QUESTIONS AND ANSWERS

By late afternoon, the fires had burned themselves out. The blackened skeleton of the great copter sat at the edge of dark ruin. The buildings nearest the fire were burned up or flattened or scattered. Smoke lay over everything outside the building. Ras, looking into the mirror on the other side of the room, saw a face black with smoke.

They were in a large room containing many shelves of books, a leather sofa, a large desk, and a revolvable chair on wheels. On one shelf above the desk was a row of books bound in gorilla skin, set between two gold-plated busts. The books, so Boygur said, were all original English-language editions of the Tarzan series, by Edgar Rice Burroughs. Each one had been personally autographed by Burroughs; Boygur had flown to California to get them signed by the author. Ras wondered why he spoke of this. Boygur seemed so proud and expected Ras to appreciate them, but the books and the pride were meaningless to Ras.

One of the busts serving as book ends was Tarzan and had been created for Boygur by a man called Gutzon Borglum. "It was made secretly," Boygur said. "Only Borglum and I knew of the deal, and it cost me plenty."

The other bust was of Ras and had been done by a sculptor who had studied photographs and films of Ras.

There were many paintings of Tarzan, most of them by St. John, whom Boygur said was the great illustrator of The Book and The Hero.

There were also five photographs of Ras taken at various

ages. Ras had been told about them by Yusufu, who had had to explain first what "photographs" were. One showed him as a baby in Mariyam's arms with Yusufu nearby and, in the distant background, five gorillas feeding or watching the human beings. A second was of Ras at about the age of five, a naked little boy with long, black hair playing with a baby gorilla while two females ate bamboo shoots nearby. A third showed him fishing from a dugout in the lake. A fourth had been taken inside the log cabin by the lake shore a year before it had burned down when hit by lightning. The angle was from his right, and he was sitting at the rough wooden desk and studying a big picture book, while two large candles burned before him. He realized now, because of what Yusufu had told him, that a hidden camera had taken that photograph.

The fifth photograph showed Ras, when he was sixteen, coming down a hill with the body of a leopard draped over his shoulders. The photograph also showed the dried blood smeared over his chest and shoulders and the claw marks. This was the time that Ras had been jumped by the gorilla-eater while Ras was hunting him. Ras had lost his knife in the first minute of fighting, but he had been able to tear himself loose, literally, and grab the leopard by the tail. The leopard had jumped into the air and at the same time had turned to get at him. Ras never knew later how he had done it, but he had whirled the big cat, which must have weighed at least two hundred and fifty pounds, around and around, gripping its tail with both hands and working a step at a time toward the nearest tree. The final step forward and the final whirl had slammed the head and shoulders of the leopard against the trunk of the tree. While the half-unconscious beast had tried to stagger to its feet, Ras had searched for and found the knife and got it into the throat of the leopard before he could recover. Later, Ras had been furious with Yusufu and Mariyam because neither had believed his story of how he had killed it.

Now he remembered that the copter had appeared while he had been coming down the hill with the carcass on his shoulders.

On a table was a huge, framed photograph of a much younger and beardless Boygur standing in some strange place with two men. The signatures beneath were of Edgar Rice Burroughs and Johnny Weissmuller.

Also on the table was a number of all-paper books that Boygur had referred to as magazines. The nearest was titled *The Burroughs Bulletin* and had an intriguing illustration on its cover. Under different circumstances he would have examined it in detail.

Of the many animal heads on the wall, one was a lion's. There was an ugly beast with two horns on its nose, an elephant head twice as large as that of the largest river elephant Ras had ever seen, and the head of a tiger, which he recognized because he remembered the pictures of tigers in the books in the cabin. This striped and awesome and beautiful cat was the beast after which he had been named. It was also, as Yusufu had explained, the name of his Norman ancestor, a great warrior who had crossed the Channel with William the Conqueror.

Ras had tried to visualize the Normans and the English Channel and Robert le Tigre and the other things Yusufu told of, but he could not do so, and the fact that Yusufu was vague about them did not help him. He did not see why he should be proud of being descended from English aristocracy when he had never seen an English aristocrat.

Neither had he seen nor known anything of this man Burroughs, whom Boygur called The Master.

Yusufu had said to him, the evening of the ascent of the pillar, "You must understand, my son, that this man Burroughs is not responsible for what Boygur believes or for the deeds of Boygur. The Tarzan books are only books that tell stories of this wild man of the jungle, who had been raised by great apes and has become a superman. Millions of people have read these stories—which are not true but are made up—and enjoyed them. And movies have been made of Tarzan—many movies—and people enjoyed them. In fact, I was an actor in a Tarzan movie years ago, before you were born. So were Mariyam and the others. We were in America then, and that is where I learned English.

"Many people, as I said, enjoy or even love these stories of Tarzan. To some, he *is* The Hero. But Boygur is insane, my son. He loved the stories too much. He became convinced that they were real, perhaps because he was small and skinny and weak of body and had to suffer much from larger, stronger people when he was a child and a young man. Perhaps he dreamed of becoming a giant who could defeat all other men and even great, dangerous beasts such as the lion with his bare hands or with only a knife. And he had to work hard, very hard, and suffered great poverty when he was young. He dreamed of a life of freedom and of ease from hard labor and contempt and unceasing demands. He dreamed of becoming this Tarzan. He was not mad enough to believe that he himself was this wild and free man of the jungle. But he was mad enough to think that he could live as a Tarzan through another person. And so, when he had made his fortune, when he had become what they call a multimillionaire, he determined to raise his own Tarzan.

"It was an evil thing he did, but Boygur does not know it. He is of this world—otherwise, he would not have been able to become so wealthy—but he is also not of this world."

The man now sitting with bound hands and feet on the leather sofa did not look as if he had possessed such great power and controlled so many people. Although small and thin, he would have been a handsome old man if his eyes had not been so baggy and ringed with black and his face so scratched and bloody and his beard so dirty and bloody. He had a full head of long, wavy, white hair, a broad and high forehead, thick, white eyebrows, a nose like the arc of a descending arrow, deep hollows under his cheeks, and thin lips. Even trussed up and bloodied and haggard, he had dignity, or would have had it if he had not wet his pants with terror when he had been pulled up by the rope.

"You do not understand, Ras," he said as he had said many times since being captured. "I made you what you are. If it were not for me, you would be nothing. You would only be a city-dweller, a businessman or teacher, a nonentity, a nothing. But you are Ras Tyger, and there is nobody in this world like you. You are indeed the Tarzan of this world."

This was something that Ras did not understand. He asked again for clarification, and Boygur told him again. He insisted that he was not crazy. He knew that no such being as Tarzan of the Apes, John Clayton, Lord Greystoke, existed on this particular Earth, in this particular universe. There were no language-using "great apes"; gorillas and monkeys and baboons did not talk; gorillas were not aggressive or rapers of human females; lions dwelt in savannahs or semideserts and did not infest the jungle; and there was no lost city with half-ape descendants of colonists from ancient Atlantis.

Not in this universe, anyway. But there were parallel universes, worlds that existed in the same space occupied by this world but at "right angles" to this world. And in one of these, perhaps in more than one, differing slightly each from each, there was such an Earth as Burroughs had described in his books. This Earth was similar to ours, except in those not very great differences. Burroughs knew about it, because he had a psychic key to it, and he had learned the story of Tarzan from The Hero himself. Sometimes the gates between the worlds opened, and Tarzan, and others, came through and told Burroughs their stories. And Burroughs, to make the stories appeal to Earth people, set the stories on this Earth and this universe. He said nothing, of course, of the existence of parallel universes. So Boygur had decided to create his own Hero, modeled after the Hero of the Master. Now Ras understood, didn't he?

Ras said, "No. I understand nothing—almost nothing—of what you say."

Yusufu had heard the same explanation from Boygur, and he had told Ras, but he had not succeeded in bringing any light.

"You will understand some day," Boygur said. "You are not educated yet, not in what the so-called civilized world calls education, anyway. But you will come into your inheritance, your birthright. You are an English lord, a viscount. Once the world knows about you, you'll get the title back from your cousin. It's unfortunate that your cousin sold the ancestral castle and estates to pay off taxes. If I'd known about it in time, I would have purchased them to keep for you. But you wouldn't want to live there, in England, anyway, would you? You'd prefer to live on a plantation in Africa, wouldn't you? Of course, Africa isn't what it used to be. There's little room for a white man any more. But you could carve out your own empire, perhaps stay in this valley, become king of the Sharrikt—they're a lost race and live in a lost city in an unknown valley—or . . ."

The old man babbled.

Ras thought of what Yusufu had told him. Somewhere in that cloudy country outside this valley, in a city called Pretoria, in a country called South Africa, a handsome man and a beautiful woman had lived. The man was the second son of a North-of-England lord, and he had come to South Africa to make a new life after a big war. His older brother had inherited the title after the father had died.

Ivor Montaux-Tyger Thorsbight had married the daughter of a Scottish baron, also an émigré, and they had had a son. And the baby, when a year old, had been kidnapped by Boygur because he met all of Boygur's specifications. He had been descended from English nobility, and he had been black-haired and gray-eyed.

The baby had been brought to this valley and given

into the care of a gorilla female who had lost her baby—because Boygur had killed it—but who had been conditioned to accept another infant and to nurse it. Six months later, after several illnesses, the baby had died of pneumonia.

The parents had grieved for a long time, even after the search for the stolen infant had been given up. A year and a half later, they had had another male baby, and this, too, had been stolen, despite the parents' intense watchfulness.

Ras, thinking of him, said, "My brother lived because you gave him all kinds of assistance. But he was raised among the gorillas, and these have no language, and so Jib got beyond the age at which he could learn a language."

"I didn't know about that until it was too late," Boygur said. "I found out when I couldn't do anything about it that infants have to learn a language of some sort at an early age or their brain or nervous system becomes inflexible as far as language learning is concerned."

"And so my brother became as dumb as a gorilla," Ras said. "And sickly and miserable. Better for him if he had died of pneumonia, too."

"I didn't do it on purpose, you know," Boygur said. "I had nothing but the best intentions."

"He could say three or four words," Ras said. "I taught him to say Wahss. My name. Wahss was as close as he could ever get."

He felt a lump in his throat and an ache in his chest. Suddenly, he was weeping.

Boygur said, "Nobody regretted more than I did that he was little better than an idiot. But a man has to learn by experience. Certainly, you are no idiot. Far from it. You are, literally, a superman."

Somewhere in that nebulous land outside the cliffs were two graves. In one was the mother who had died of grief after her third baby had been stolen. The parents had gone to England, because they supposed that the baby would be safer there. But, despite all their vigilance and safeguards, the baby had been taken away and they had never seen it again. A year after his wife's death, the husband had jumped off a boat in the Channel.

And so Boygur, knowing that a human baby could not be raised by apes and still be human, not in this world, anyway, had used the dwarfs as substitutes. They were a traveling acrobatic troupe accused of theft and murder in Addis Ababa, Ethiopia. Boygur had bribed the authorities and gotten them free, but they had had to promise to raise the baby in the river valley high in the Mendebo Mountains of Ethiopia. They were to pretend to be apes. The baby, of course, having no knowledge of what was or was not a true human being, would not know the difference. After Ras had become eighteen years old, they would be given their freedom.

Little Ras had been an affectionate and good-natured baby. But he was also unafraid and aggressive, and so Boygur had named him Ras Tyger—Ras because that was Amharic for Lord, and Tyger after that Norman ancestor who had founded the house of Bettrick.

Many things were explained now, but many more were not. He did know why Mariyam had become so confused and confusing with her reasons for this and that. Mariyam may even have been a little insane, but she had not been evil, and she had loved him. Ras had loved the Amharic dwarf even as he loved Yusufu, the half-Swahili, half-Arab dwarf.

The cabin on the lake shore was modeled after the cabin of Tarzan's father and mother in the first Tarzan book. Ras was to wonder about the two human skeletons and the infant gorilla skeleton, to find the hunting knife, to puzzle over the picture books, and to teach himself to read English, as Tarzan had supposedly done. But Ras had been more interested in using the paper and pencils to draw pictures like those in the books. Yusufu had been forced to teach him how to read, although he had done it out of sight or hearing of any of Boygur's spy devices. And, later, Yusufu had taught him to speak English, English with a Swahili accent, because Swahili was Yusufu's mother tongue. Yusufu had done it just to spite Boygur, although Boygur had never known about it. If he had learned of it, he would have killed Yusufu.

There was the golden locket with the woman's picture in it. Ras had found that in the cabin and had worn it around his neck. Six months afterward, it had disappeared, presumably stolen by a chimpanzee while Ras was swimming in the lake. The picture in the locket had been a portrait of his genuine mother.

There were many things in the cabin, but it had burned down, and everything in it had been destroyed.

"Things went their own way," Boygur muttered, as if he was thinking of the direction he had wanted reality to take and the direction that it had preferred to take.

"Why did you kill my mother?" Ras said. "Why did you

shoot her with a Wantso arrow so that I would think they had killed her?"

"Your mother?" Boygur said. He blinked. "Oh, you mean Mariyam! Why, son, it was necessary! The Hero's ape foster mother was shot through the heart by a savage black, and The Hero took vengeance on the killer and his tribe. There wasn't any chance of the Wantso ever getting close enough to Mariyam to do her any harm. I'd put the fear of the Ghost-Land into the Wantso before you were born so they'd stay out of that area.

"But I had to kill Mariyam so you'd revenge her death. Besides, the Wantso were corrupting, debasing, you. I knew you were laying the black women, and that was something that The Hero would never do. I wanted them dead, and I wanted you to fulfill your natural destiny by killing them. That part of The Book, at least, would come true."

Ras wanted to smash the old man against the wall. But he said, "Why did your men, those in the copter, kill *all* the Wantso? I had slain almost all their men by myself. They had me surrounded, but I would have killed the few men left. You did not have to kill the women and children."

Boygur said, angrily, "That was the fault of those two idiots! They thought you were about to be killed, and so they began shooting and couldn't stop, or at least that's what they said! They said they knew I hated all the Wantso, so they didn't see anything wrong with shooting them all, wiping them out. I reprimanded them for doing it without my orders, but the damage was done."

"And why did you try to kill Eeva Rantanen?"

"Because she wasn't supposed to be here! I didn't want her to spoil everything. I had just flown in the girl you were destined to meet, this Jane Potter, a beautiful blonde from Baltimore, a virgin, just right for you, very close to The Master's description of The Hero's mate. In a few days I would have arranged for her to seem to escape and to meet you. But she didn't have strength of character. Instead of trying to escape, she became hysterical, she went on a hunger strike, and she tried to kill herself."

"Where did you get her?"

"She was on a safari in Kenya with her father, who is, by the way, a professor. But he's not absent-minded or old. You can't have everything, however; you have to compromise. I was happy to get a girl who seemed to be very close to the specifications."

Ras did not know what he was talking about unless

he meant that the abducted girl was similar to the girl in The Book.

Boygur said, slowly, "So you climbed up the side of the rock? Who would have believed that it could be done? Yet, The Hero would have done it, so why not you? Really, I haven't failed, after all. You have done everything The Hero has done, or at least you could do it if you had to. I regret that you've never had a chance to fight a lion with just a knife or make friends with an elephant or killed a gorilla in hand-to-hand combat. But you're young . . ."

Ras got to his feet and said, "And you are old and have lived long beyond your time. You should have died at birth. You have killed, or caused to be killed, my oldest brother, and you have caused my other brother to become an idiot and to live sick and cold and wretched—oh, how wretched and lonely he must have been!—and then you killed him. You caused my true parents to die of grief. You killed my second mother, Mariyam, whom I loved dearly. You made me kill many innocent Wantso, and your men killed the rest. You robbed me of my true life with my true parents. You have made me into something modeled after a thing that never existed. You are as evil as a man can be."

Boygur shouted, "What are you talking about? I love you! I have always loved you! Believe me, I grieved because I couldn't take the place of Yusufu and personally direct you in every move, see you made no mistakes and became as heroic a man as the man The Master wrote about! I made you into a man like no other!"

"Yusufu was right," Ras said. "There is no use talking to you. You do think you are God."

He jerked Boygur to his feet and grabbed the ropes binding his feet. He dragged Boygur all the way to the rim while Boygur screamed, "No! No! No!"

Then Ras picked Boygur up and raised him above his head. Boygur stopped screaming and said, "You have to understand, Ras! My son, my son, let me explain!"

"You are no god, and I am not your son," Ras said. "I would like to make you pay for all you've done. But you can't make people pay for their evil. You can't do anything with evil people except stop their evil forever."

"I'm not evil!" Boygur screamed. "I'm not evil! You can't make a dream come true without some suffering, and . . ."

Ras growled and said, "Shut up! Would you foul the air even as you die!"

His muscles were tensed for the heave, but he waited. A fish-eagle, dark and claw-beaked and with eyes like arrow-points, was gliding downward toward a point directly below him. Ras waited, although he did not know why. He must have been unconsciously estimating the speed and angle of the fish-eagle's descent and the speed with which the old man would fall, because, suddenly, still not knowing why he had waited and now acted, he tossed the old man outward. Boygur screamed. The eagle screamed and banked away, but it was too late. The old man, trailing a shriek as if it were fire streaming from him, fell onto the eagle and at the same time seized it. His hands were tied together before him, and when he had put his arms out, he had slipped the rope over the head of the eagle and pulled it into his breast as if he were making love to it. The eagle fought with beak and claws; its wings flapped as if it would carry itself and Boygur across the lake to the shore and safety. But both fell swiftly, feathers flew, the shrill scream of Boygur and the harsh scream of the eagle mingled and became fainter. The two bodies became one, and then the one was a spout of water and widening circles afterward.

CHAPTER 23

THE PASSPORT

The plane bumped as its pontoons struck waves, and then the bumps were gone and the lake was dropping away.

Ras was in a seat next to the window. The wing, just ahead of him, bisected the waters below and cast a shadow ahead of it on the glittering waters. The plane turned, and the sunbeams spun off the whirling tip of the propeller like a jackal shaking off water after a swim.

Below, getting smaller with each second, were five planes, three with pontoons and two amphibians. By the beach, half-hidden now by the big trees, were the tents of those who had come in on the airplanes. On the beach was a helicopter, and down the valley a flash of white revealed another airplane.

The people had invaded his world as if the sky had been uptilted and poured them in. There were anthropologists, zoologists, military and civil service men from Ethiopia, policemen from Ethiopia and South Africa, reporters from many lands, publishers' agents, movie people from the United States, England, and Italy, and others whose business was unstated and may have been nothing but curiosity.

It had happened so swiftly, and so many men and women, all talking at once, had arrived. He was confused. However, he enjoyed it, and he did not let them hurry or push him. He knew, even when he did not really understand their reasons for being here, that most of them regarded him as a block of wood to be carved into an image that would give them access to some power or spirit they desired. Or perhaps they wanted to ride him to goals of their own, as he had ridden that crocodile into the river. If they *were* thinking this, they would find their knives turned in peculiar ways by the block of wood, and the riders would find that the crocodile had become a python coiling around them.

Others did not regard him so much as an inanimate object or wild beast as a man of whom they were jealous. His body, his face, his ease of manner, seemed to make some of the men envious. However, many of the women did not conceal their admiration of him. One, a beautiful young redhead, had given him a look that he had at once recognized, and he had returned the look in kind. Eeva had seen this exchange and had, for the first time, shown jealousy. Perhaps it was this that had caused her to tell Ras that they should get married as quickly as possible. She did love him now, and that was reason enough to get married. She was older, but that would be advantageous for them, since he needed an experienced woman to guide him in that bewilderingly complex world outside.

She was his agent and personal manager now, and she would protect his interests better if she were his wife. The legal reasons were, like everything else outside, difficult to understand, and she could explain only a few at this time. But he could trust her.

Ras had nothing definite to back his feeling that she was also protecting her own interests by marrying him. He did not care. If she wanted to marry, they would marry.

Eeva had a contract to write a book about her adventures in the valley and another to write Ras's "life." She also was "dickering" with some producers' agents about a film based on his life, with him playing the lead.

She had told him that the books and the movie would pay enough to enable them to live more than comfortably for a long, long time, perhaps for the rest of their lives. Even after "the government" took its lion's share of the money. She explained about taxes, and he felt for the first time a rage against "civilization." She tried to cool him off and said that if they hired some good, that is, expensive, that is, learned, that is, tricky, lawyers, they could get some of the share back from the lion.

"If you have to pay 'the government' an increasingly larger share the more you make," Ras said, "why not just make enough money to get what you need to enjoy life?"

"That's good common sense, and many people have

talked about doing just that," Eeva said. "But hardly anybody ever does this. Almost everybody works hard to make as much as they can even if they know they'll only get a small part of it."

She added, "It's the custom," and Ras became happy again on hearing these magic words. Other people had to obey their customs; he would work within them when he had reason to do so and outside them when he wished.

Now the plane was wheeling again. They were above the dark fish-eagles and the white-flashing pelicans and the pink smoke of the flamingos on the shore. They rose above the top of the rock pillar, and he could see the skeleton of the great helicopter and the blackened and smashed quonsets and the white rope still dangling from the window, like a worm crawling from a corpse. Or like white blood from the wound of a black ghost.

The body of Boygur had gone under the blue surface and never appeared. The fish-eagle had floated in to shore and Ras had buried its body beside the grave of Mariyam without knowing why he did so.

Eeva had come to him after that and told him that they could have waited a few days and by then Boygur would have been arrested. He had evaded exposure for years, but he had done too much to get away with it any longer. His sons had found out about the enormous sums taken from his personal fund and the holdings. Helicopters were toys that only a billionaire or a nation could afford to buy in quantities. Moreover, investigation by Boygur's sons and his ex-wife had disclosed the money being spent on the private army he used and the bribes he spent to ensure being left alone. Several governments had learned about some of his activities in the past. For instance, he had stocked the valley with gorillas and chimpanzees, which were not naturally found in Ethiopia, and with zebras and other animals that the valley had lacked. He had also imported leopards, because the Wantso and Sharrikt had killed off almost all the native leopards. He had taught the foreign leopards to be man-eaters and had overstocked the valley with them.

His activities over the years and his recent efforts to keep others out of the valley, especially the disappearance of the Rantanens, had been the final blow to fell his empire. Thus, Ras, Eeva, and Yusufu could have hidden for a few days, and the world, pouring into the valley, would have taken care of Boygur.

Ras was glad that he had not waited.

He looked out the window to the south. The green

forest and the green-brown plains ran between the black cliffs for some miles. The river writhed bluely, its head white with spume and smoke where it looped over the edge of the plateau.

Beyond and below was the land where the Wantso lived—had lived. And then the valley and the river curved together around the black cliffs, and he could not see as far as the Many-Legged Swamp.

On the other side of the swamp, Gilluk, the Sharrikt king, was being visited, inspected, explored, and pried into by several of the newcomers who called themselves "anthropologists." One had already declared that the divine sword of the Sharrikt was a Crusader's and that it had somehow fallen into the hands of the Sharrikt before they had come into the valley, but another man disputed this. Zoologists were prowling the land. One said that the crocodiles were a new *species,* perhaps a representative of a new *genus,* whatever those words meant. The valley had harbored many kinds of animals that had died out elsewhere or perhaps existed only here.

The man who had said this had also said that Ras was the only living member of the species *Homo Tarzanus.*

He shifted in his seat and sighed and thought of the ashes of Wilida, and the grave of Mariyam, and Bigagi in Baastmaast's belly, and Janhoy's head on a pole.

Then the plane rose above the tops of the cliffs. He gasped and squeezed Eeva's arm so tightly that she cried out. It was true! The sky was not blue stone that bounded the valley.

Something happened. He heard it plainly. It was the breaking of the strand of flesh that tied him to the valley. Or it was the sky unrolling like a scroll to show him the vastness and glory of the world beyond the cliffs. Mariyam had described the sky unrolling and described a scroll, and now he saw what she meant.

His eyes drifted in tears. A sob swelled his chest.

Eeva patted his hand.

Yusufu, in the seat across the aisle, called in Amharic, "This is only the beginning, O son! You will see many marvels, and perhaps the most wondrous of all will be that great city at the end of our journey—Los Angeles."

Yusufu was dressed in the clothes of an English child. The clothes had been flown in from Nairobi with those Ras now wore.

The pilot's voice came over the loud-speaker. They could unfasten their seat belts and smoke if they wished. The passengers began crowding around his seat to discuss what they wanted him to do. Eeva sent them away by saying that he was beginning to feel sick from the "shots." He felt nothing as yet of the deep sickness which might result from the many "shots" and the "smallpox vaccine" the doctor had given him shortly before they had left. But he allowed Eeva to speak for him. He needed time to be alone to think.

The airplane droned on, and soon the jagged mountains were behind them and they were over dry, brown land, and then they were over jungle. Eeva said that it would be some hours before they were out of Ethiopia. They didn't expect to have trouble in the next country. The movie people had "greased" the right palms.

The flight that morning had been planned the previous night. The Ethiopian military and police had been talking about taking Yusufu to Addis Ababa. He was still wanted for the twenty-two-year-old theft and murder. Yusufu said that he was innocent, but he did not want to stand trial, because he could not prove his innocence. Ras was also in trouble, because he was in the country illegally and also would have to stand trial because he had killed so many Wantso and Sharrikt, citizens of Ethiopia, even if they had not known it. Also, he had killed Boygur and his Ethiopian employees, and he might be tried for these deaths.

Eeva and Yusufu agreed that Ras might go free after a trial, but that he would probably die from disease while in an Ethiopian jail. Early that morning, Ras and Yusufu had led the Ethiopian pilot and officials into the hills to search for Jib's body. Ras and Yusufu had then sneaked away from the party and returned to the lake, where a plane-load of fellow conspirators waited for them. Ras had taken the shots and the vaccination, and the plane had carried them all off.

Mr. Brentwood, a movie producer, said that "accounts would be squared" with the Ethiopians later—apparently with more "palm-greasing"—and then the movie would be filmed in the valley, which would probably be leased by the company. All this would be very expensive, Mr. Brentwood said, but this picture was a natural to make millions.

So now they were high above the Ethiopia-Kenya border, and Marilyn Provo, the publishing-house executive, was standing by the seat and talking to Eeva and flicking long-lashed glances at him. By then he was beginning to feel sick. Before they landed to refuel, he became feverish and also nauseated, and finally fell asleep. The last thing he remembered was Eeva telling Marilyn that she was not worried about how he would get along. He was ignorant and innocent of the world, true. But he had an enduring courage, an adaptability, a true friendliness, great strength, charm, sensitivity, imagination, and quite a lot of artistic talent. He would do all right as long as someone who was both experienced and loved him was with him.

Later, after talking feverishly with Wilida and Mariyam and the other dead, he half awoke. The wailing sound came from the mouth of some device in the "ambulance." A "siren," Eeva, who was sitting by him, called it. And then he was being carried on a stretcher into an enormous white building. Lights burned steadily and flashed off and on and something roared and thrummed at a distance, and many brown and white faces were around him— Eeva and Marilyn among them—and then the light and faces wheeled and winged away like pelicans into the blackness.

A day later, he had recovered enough to sit up and to sniff in, with eyes, nose, ears, and touch, all the new that even this small and simply furnished room offered. He was downwind of the world and eager to start the chase, although he was not sure that this world was not a crafty, backtracking leopard.

To Eeva, that night, he said, "To be well in this world, in this 'civilization,' you have to get very sick first. Just as, to be fully alive, you must first die."

Eeva did not know what he was talking about. Contrary to her usual interest in his thinking out of things, she wanted to discuss nothing except "business." He humored her for a while and then said that he would like to go to bed with her. She was shocked. She couldn't. Not here. Somebody, a nurse, a doctor, or a visitor, would be sure to come in.

He did not plead. He kissed her and said that he would see her tomorrow.

A half hour later, after the nurses had made their rounds, Marilyn slipped into his room. She wasn't supposed to be here, she said, since visiting hours were over, but she knew that he would be glad of her company. He was, and, as he had guessed, she was less inhibited than Eeva. She had her own crocodile heart.

He went pleasantly to sleep but awoke in the middle of the night to find a nurse, Mariamu, fussing over him. She was a young and well-shaped girl, even under her

loose, white uniform, and she had a beautifully shaped
head and face that he knew he would have to sculp-
ture. He told her so, and although she seemed shy and
even a little afraid of him, she did not leave. She talked
longer than she should have, so, presently, the floor supervisor had to run her out. But she promised Ras that he
could do her head, and she gave him her address. The
supervisor, a big woman of about forty, but handsome,
did not leave the room. She seemed to be fascinated
by what she had heard about him and listened to his
story while her eyes grew bigger and she came closer
and closer. After a while, he had pulled her down to
him, and she did just the opposite of struggle.

Ras went to sleep again thinking that this world outside must have its many dangers, of course, but it also
had its compensating pleasures, if you knew how to get
them.